W9-CLH-534

WITHDRAWN

Hummingbird Lane

**Center Point
Large Print**

Also by Carolyn Brown and available from
Center Point Large Print:

The Lullaby Sky
The Barefoot Summer
The Lilac Bouquet
The Strawberry Hearts Diner
The Sometimes Sisters
Small Town Rumors
The Magnolia Inn
The Perfect Dress
The Empty Nesters
The Family Journal
Miss Janie's Girls

**This Large Print Book carries the
Seal of Approval of N.A.V.H.**

Hummingbird Lane

CAROLYN BROWN

CENTER POINT LARGE PRINT
THORNDIKE, MAINE

To my Montlake editor, Alison Dasho,
for continuing to believe in me.

Hummingbird Lane

Chapter One

E mma frowned at her reflection in the spotlessly clean window. She didn't look all that
much different than she had in college. The glass
distorted the fine lines around her eyes, but if she
put on a little makeup, those would disappear.
Her mother, Victoria, fussed at her if she didn't
put on her face every day. She said it would make
Emma feel better.

She could smile and pretend to be happy. She
had said, "I'm fine," to her folks when she quit
college, to many psychiatrists and doctors, and
even to Nancy, the therapist here at the Oak
Lawn Wellness Center, but in truth she felt like
she was drowning and everyone around her was
still breathing. Sometimes it made her angry that
their lungs were taking in oxygen and hers were
filling with dirty, muddy water. Other times, she
just felt a numb darkness draping itself around
her, and she didn't even have the energy to get
mad at those folks who had "happy times to hang
on to."

Nancy's words, not hers. Her therapist kept
telling her to find a happy time, use it for a
foundation, and build on it. But the only happy

times she had left in her memories were from before she was twelve years old. After that it was all downhill.

A bright-red cardinal and his less colorful mate landed on the windowsill. They sang like they were happy, but then, birds didn't get depressed. When a baby bird flew out of the nest, like she had when she went off to one of the most prestigious art colleges in Texas, it didn't come home wounded and unable to utter a word about its horrible experience. Birds just found a mate of their own species, laid eggs, and raised babies to fly away to live their own lives. A perpetual circle of life with no pills to try to cure a weeping soul. Emma wished she was a bird. Maybe then she could find a happy place again. Maybe in some realm of the universe, she could go back to that time when Sophie had come to the house a couple of times a week with Rebel and she'd had a true friend.

A soft knock took Emma's attention from the window, where she was looking out over a lovely flower garden. Her chest tightened and her palms went clammy until she saw that it was Nancy. The sign on her door said FEMALES ONLY, but sometimes a male orderly ignored it and came in to clean the room. Her last panic attack had almost sent her into intensive care, but then the guy who'd caused it was as big as—well—a linebacker on a football team.

"Good morning," Nancy said. "How are you feeling today?"

"I'm fine," Emma answered. "How are you today?"

Nancy sat down on the love seat and opened her computer. "I'm doing very well. Can you tell me your name?"

"Emma Darlene Merrill. I'm past thirty years old, and I'm fine," Emma said.

"Let's talk about what *fine* means. Does it mean that you didn't have a bad dream last night?" Nancy had dark hair that had begun to go gray. She always wore muted light-green scrubs. Emma thought the color was horrible on her, but then, that color was supposed to be soothing.

"*Fine* means that I'm all right. I've been here for weeks, and I'm ready to go home now." Where was the anger when she needed it? Why couldn't it come boiling up from her insides and rush out of her body like molten lava, like it sometimes did when she was alone? That kind of emotion or display of tears would make Nancy happy, but Emma just didn't have the energy to do either one that day.

"Have you thought of happy times, like I asked you to yesterday?" Nancy asked. "If we could dwell on those times today, it might make you really feel fine. Let's talk about your parents. Did you think about a vacation with them, or maybe a birthday party they threw you when you were a little girl?"

Emma shook her head. "Happy means Sophia."

Nancy sat up a little straighter. Emma knew that action meant that she was thinking they might be having what other counselors called a breakthrough. "Who's Sophia? She hasn't come up here or in the reports from the other therapists."

"Mother doesn't like for me to talk about her." Emma shook her head slowly. "But she has nothing to do with what happened in college."

"How do you know that?" Nancy asked.

"Because Sophie wouldn't hurt me," Emma said.

Nancy lowered her voice. "*Someone* hurt you. How does that make you feel?"

"Like I'm drowning," Emma answered. "I can swim. Mother made sure I had swimming lessons, so . . ." She shrugged.

"Do you want to remember?" Nancy asked.

"No," Emma whispered.

"Why?"

"Mother wouldn't be happy. When she's not happy, she's . . ." Emma turned her head to look out the window.

"She's what?"

Why couldn't Nancy be content with that much? That was more than she'd admitted to the other therapists.

"Will you tell me more about Sophia?" Nancy shifted tactics.

"She was my friend in elementary school, back when I got to attend public school." Emma's intention today was to talk so that Nancy would sign the papers for her to be released. This wasn't her first rodeo or her first visit to a mental institution. She knew she had to give this woman something or she'd never get out of the place.

"You're sure she didn't hurt your feelings?" Nancy wrote something on her pad.

"I called her Sophie, and she called me Em. Mother hated for anyone to call me by a nickname, so we were careful when she was around. Sophie and her mama, Rebel, were my . . ."

"Your what?" Nancy looked up from her notepad.

"They were more like my family than Mother and Daddy," Emma answered.

"Let's talk about them, then," Nancy said.

"Sophie's mama, Rebel, was our cleaning lady, and sometimes she babysat me when Mother had an appointment. I always loved the name Rebel. It sounded so free to me, something I was never allowed to be. Those were my happy times." Emma turned her head and stared out the window again. The cardinals were flitting around on the redbud tree, flirting with each other among the purple blossoms. Spring had arrived—a time for new growth.

"Go on," Nancy murmured.

"Sophie and I were going to be artists. We colored in books together when we were little girls, and when we got a little older, we drew our own pictures in sketchbooks." Emma held her hands tightly in her lap. If Nancy saw her twisting them, she would never get out of this place. "Mother didn't allow me to play with Sophie except when her mama brought her to our house. We weren't even supposed to be friends at school, but we were."

"Why?" Nancy had a soothing voice, not at all like the therapist who had come to the house once a week. That woman's voice had a raspy tone, and she always smelled like the peppermint candy she used to cover up her cigarette breath.

"Rebel didn't have a husband. Mother said she was low class and Sophie would grow up to be just like her," Emma said.

Break-through. Breakthrough. Emma could almost feel the terms emanate from Nancy. She had seen that look—one of excitement—on other therapists' faces in other places she had been put these past years.

"Where is Sophie now?" Nancy asked.

"Everywhere," Emma said. "She's a famous artist. Funny, isn't it? She didn't have a daddy, and her mama worked as a maid, and she's famous. My mother is one of the richest women in Texas, and look where I am." Emma paused

14

and watched a sparrow fly up into the top of the redbud tree. "Do you ever wonder why God made the male species so pretty and the females so plain?"

"We were talking about Sophie," Nancy said. "What does she look like?"

"She was about my size the last time I saw her, but when we were kids, I grew faster than she did. Mother gave her my outgrown clothes, but not after she fired Rebel. Sophie has blonde hair and big blue eyes. You told me to think of happy times, so I did," Emma answered.

"Tell me more about that." Nancy seemed to be all ears. "Describe one of those happy days for me."

"Sophie and I were lying on a quilt in the backyard under the weeping willow limbs. We were working with sketch pads and glitter pens. It was a hot summer day, and we had to be careful that the sweat on our hands didn't ruin our pictures. I sketched a calico kitten and made it look as realistic as possible. Sophie drew a lizard and colored it purple and yellow and red. I told her that lizards weren't that color, and she said that artists could make their pictures any way they wanted them. Rebel didn't come to work for us anymore after that day. Sophie and I stayed in touch when we could, but . . ." Emma shrugged. "That was my last happy time, so I thought about that lizard today."

"How did it make you feel?" Nancy asked.

"Like I was in a cage without a key," Emma said.

"Why?" Nancy whispered.

"Because my mother fired Sophie's mother and hired tutors for me to be homeschooled. She said that she didn't want me around the riffraff that went to public or even private schools, and nothing was ever the same after that." Emma shrugged again.

"Why was it never the same?" Nancy asked.

"Because Sophie was gone, and I was lonely, and I couldn't make Mother happy no matter how hard I tried." Emma sighed. "I begged Mother to let Sophie come to the house and be tutored with me. She said no, and when Victoria Merrill says no, we do not argue with her. I loved my art teacher, but I hated not getting to go to school with other kids, especially Sophie. We talked a few times on the phone, but Mother caught us talking once, and she got very angry. She changed the phone numbers and fired all my tutors. The next week I had different ones. We didn't make Mother angry in our house. I didn't see Sophie until we went to college, when we reconnected a few times even though we went to different colleges."

"How did you reconnect if you went to different colleges?" Nancy asked.

"I saw Rebel at a bakery, and of course, I asked

about Sophie. Rebel gave me her phone number, and I called her. That next Sunday, when we got together for ice cream, it was like old times, and we talked about everything." Emma almost smiled at the memory.

"What happened then? Did your mother—"

Emma held up a palm. "No, the Christmas holiday happened. I went home and . . ." Emma felt the world closing in on her. Her chest tightened, and she began to wring her hands.

"You went home for the holiday and never went back to school, right?" Nancy asked.

Emma nodded.

Nancy looked up from her notepad. "What happened right before that? Did someone hurt you? Did Sophie upset you?"

Emma crossed her arms over her chest. "You asked me that before, and I already answered it. Sophie would never hurt me."

"Did someone else? If so, did you tell Sophie about it?"

How could she answer that when she couldn't remember what had happened just before Christmas? "I didn't talk to Sophie anymore when I went home. Mama wouldn't let me. She said that Sophie was the cause of my problems."

"How did you feel about that?" Nancy asked.

Why did they always ask how she felt about something? Did they really expect her to explain how she had been so sheltered at home that when she was thrown out into the real world, she felt like she'd been tossed overboard from her daddy's boat without a life jacket? Her chest tightened more, and she felt a panic attack coming on.

Think about lizards. Think about lizards. She repeated the phrase over and over in her head until her breathing returned to normal.

She inhaled to her toes and let it out slowly. "College was tough. I wanted friends, but I hated to socialize. Mother made me promise not to touch liquor or drugs, so parties made me nervous. If I didn't drink, then I was a nerd. If I did, I knew I'd feel guilty," she answered.

"So, how did you handle it?" Nancy asked.

"Mother would have disowned me for doing what they were doing, so I was basically ignored." Emma stopped and stared out the window.

That was enough for one day.

"Let's talk some more about Sophie," Nancy pushed.

Emma didn't want to talk anymore, but she forced herself to say, "She had to work her way through college. No way could she afford to attend the place my folks sent me to. She went to the University of North Texas in Denton. That's where I wanted to go, but oh, no, I had to attend the most prestigious art school in the whole state of Texas." Emma yawned. "I'm tired now, but I'm fine, really, I am. Are you going to tell Mother what I said?"

"You can tell me anything, Emma, and I'm bound by confidentiality laws to not tell anyone without your written permission. Is there something else you want to talk about?" Nancy asked.

"When Mother made me sign the papers to check me into this place, she knew stuff that I only told the therapists. She knew I had trouble sleeping at night, that I hate the feel of satin, and that I get nauseated when I see a white fur rug. She answered all the questions on the admission forms and even told them that men should stay out of my room. How did she know that if someone didn't tell her?" Emma asked.

"I won't tell Victoria anything that you tell me. I feel like we're making progress, Emma. I'm glad Sophie and Rebel were in your life. Do you feel that they were the only ones who ever loved you?"

Emma almost smiled again. "That isn't a feeling. That's the truth. Thank you for not telling Mother we talked about them. She told me that if I ever mentioned Sophie's name again, she would put me in a place like this and never let me come home."

"Why would you want to go home?" Nancy asked.

"Once a week," Emma whispered.

"What's once a week?" Nancy's pen made a scratching noise as she wrote.

"This . . . ," Emma answered. "I only have to talk to a therapist once a week at home. Mother knows what I tell her"—she lowered her voice—"because there's cameras in my room."

"Which is worse?" Nancy appeared to shudder. "Talking to me every day or no privacy at all?"

"I want neither. I want to live in a tiny house by myself, take walks through a park, and watch the birds. That's what I want," Emma answered.

Nancy checked her watch. "One more thing before I go. How did your father feel about your mother taking Sophie away from you?"

"Daddy does whatever Mother says. She says she didn't get what she wanted in a husband or a child—that both of us are spineless and have the personality of milk toast." Emma put her hands over her eyes for a moment.

"I think we've done a lot of good today. You get some rest now, and before I come in tomorrow, will you try to remember what it is that you have buried in your memories? Until you face that problem, you won't ever be able to get over it or live in a tiny house all by yourself." Nancy took her notebook and eased the door closed behind her as she left.

Why doesn't anyone ever slam a door in this place? Emma wondered. She could almost hear the scratch of Nancy's pen again and could imagine what she was writing on the other side of the door: *We had a major breakthrough today. Maybe tomorrow we will get to the root of this problem and she'll talk about her repressed memories.*

"Think about the good times," Emma said as she forgot about a nap and turned her attention back to the redbud tree outside her window. "I wish I had colored the cat black with red eyes. An artist can do whatever they want. Sophie said so."

Sophie slammed a pillow over the ringing telephone. Whoever was on the other end had better hope they were a hundred miles away from her if they didn't hang up soon. The noise stopped and she went back to sleep, but five minutes later, it started up again. She rolled over in bed, threw the pillow against the far wall of her loft apartment in downtown Dallas, and, without even opening her eyes, answered the phone.

"Sophie, darlin', did I wake you?"

Her eyes popped wide-open at the sound of her mother's voice. "Yes, but is everything all right?"

"Everything is fine here," Rebel said. "I just came home from my water aerobics class at the YMCA. I've got two houses to clean today, but I had a few minutes to call you. I'm sorry I woke you."

"No problem, and like I've told you a gazillion times, you don't have to clean houses anymore. I'm putting enough money in your checking account each month that you can retire." Sophie covered a yawn with the back of her hand. She'd been up until dawn, putting the finishing touches on a landscape painting with the Dallas skyline in the background.

"Honey, you might need that money someday," Rebel said. "And like I've told *you* a gazillion times, I would go bat-crap crazy if I didn't work. Now that we've beat that dead horse some more, do you remember Emma Merrill?"

"Of course I do. Please don't tell me something horrible has happened to her." An icy-cold chill chased down Sophie's spine. She hadn't talked to Emma in years—not since that first semester of college. Then she had heard that Emma had decided not to go back to college. When Sophie tried to call her, she got Victoria instead, and the woman had given her a tongue lashing.

"Depends on what you mean by 'happened to her,'" Rebel said. "I go to my aerobics class with the lady who cleans for her mother these days. She said that Emma is in Oak Lawn Wellness Center somewhere over around Fort Worth. Anyway, my friend Annie said that she overheard Victoria talking on the phone and saying that they were going to put her in a permanent-care facility. I guess she's been in and out of places like that since she came home from college after the first semester."

"What in the world? Why would they do that?" Sophie shoved back the covers and slung her legs over the edge of her bed. Something horrible must have happened for Emma to give up on her artist dream. Hoping that Emma might be the one to answer the phone, Sophie had tried to call her one more time after Victoria's outburst. That time she got a recording saying that the number was no longer in use or had been changed.

"Seems she can't shake this depression she's been in since she quit college," Rebel said. "I thought you might want to go visit her before you leave to go down to south Texas. I loved that little girl and felt like we had deserted her. If Victoria's not there, y'all might get to spend a little time together."

"You shouldn't feel that way." Sophie opened her packed suitcase and threw in a few more items. "Victoria fired you. If anyone deserted her, I did. I gave up trying to get in touch with her when I should have marched up to that house and demanded that they let me talk to her."

"Victoria would have never let that happen, and honey"—Rebel paused—"I would have said no if Emma had talked Victoria into paying your tuition back in the day so that you could have been tutored with her."

"I had no idea that Emma tried that," Sophie said.

"Me either, until Annie told me a few weeks ago. It was water under the bridge, so I didn't mention it to you before now. Victoria was ranting about the fact that if Emma had never known you, she wouldn't be in the shape she's in now," Rebel said.

Tears welled up in Sophie's eyes. "What did I do that would put her in a mental institution?"

"Victoria says that Emma depended on you for everything and that when you deserted her, she was never the same," Rebel answered. "We both know that's a crock of bull crap. We were kicked out of Emma's life. We damn sure didn't leave her because we wanted to, but there's no telling what Victoria told her."

"Emma never mentioned anything like that when we met those few times that first semester of college, but, Mama, I'm glad I went to public school," Sophie said. "I'm just sorry that Emma couldn't have been there with me. The few times she called me after we couldn't go to her house anymore, she told me that she hated not getting to go to school. I'll go see her this morning and give you a call afterward."

"Better let me call you this evening. You know how these rich folks are about their maids talking on their time." Rebel laughed.

"Yes, ma'am, I surely do," Sophie agreed. "Love you. Don't work too hard."

"Never happen," Rebel said. "Love you, too."

Sophie laid the phone on the end table and checked the time. Straight up twelve o'clock noon. She wasn't one to work on a schedule. If she really got into painting, she might get up at dawn and work until noon. If she decided to paint a night scene, she might not go to bed until sunrise, which was the reason she had slept until noon that day.

As she got dressed, she did the simple math. If she spent thirty minutes with Emma, she could still be moving into her place near Big Bend National Park before dark. She loved that area and for the past several years had rented a little two-bedroom trailer in the Hummingbird Trailer Park, aptly named because it was located on Hummingbird Lane.

"I'm going to tell her that there's no way I deserted her, no matter what Victoria says," Sophie said as she closed her suitcase, threw a few more items into a tote bag that held her toiletries, and took one last look at the loft. Bed made. Dishes all done and put away. The last three pictures she had painted were covered with canvas. The rest of the past year's work— all thirty paintings—had already been shipped to London. They would travel from there to Paris and then to Rome for her gallery tour. Her boyfriend, Teddy, was over in Europe now, taking care of all the details, but he would be home in a few weeks.

She locked the door behind her, picked up her bags, and carried them across the hall to the service elevator. The thing moaned and groaned so badly every time she got into it that she held her breath and hoped that it didn't crash and burn with her. When it reached bottom, she went out through the back door of the old building to her SUV and loaded her things. She checked her collection of canvases of every size, brushes, paints, and equipment one more time before she closed the back hatch and got behind the wheel.

With noonday traffic, the twenty-minute drive from her place to the wellness center took over an hour. Now she wouldn't arrive at the trailer park until suppertime, and that was if she didn't stop for a snack in the middle of the afternoon. She parked in front of the fancy facility with its fancy sign and its perfectly manicured lawns and flower beds and wondered how much money Victoria had shelled out to get her daughter into the place. Before she got out of her vehicle, she sent Josh, the trailer park owner, a text asking him to turn on the air-conditioning in her place sometime around six that evening. Then she used the rearview mirror to reapply lipstick, shook her long blonde hair out of its ponytail, and took a deep breath before she swung the driver's side door open.

"I shouldn't have let so many years go by," she muttered to herself as she walked across the parking lot and entered a place that didn't look a helluva lot different than the house where Emma had grown up. Why was her childhood friend in a place like this?

Victoria would drive Jesus and the angels out of her house. This is probably a vacation for Emma. Sophie took a deep breath and pushed the button beside the spotlessly clean glass door.

"May I help you?" a slightly raspy voice asked.

"I'm here to see Emma Merrill," she said. Lord have mercy! Emma was locked inside the place. Emma, who would rather be outside than in her fancy suite of rooms on the second floor of Victoria's mansion, couldn't even step outside for a breath of fresh air. This just wasn't right.

"Come in and stop at the front desk," the voice said.

The lock on the door clicked. Sophie stepped inside a sterile-looking lobby, took two steps, and said, "Could you tell me which room Emma Merrill is in?"

"Are you family?" the woman asked.

"Of course." Sophie beamed as she lied through her teeth. "Can't you tell by looking? I'm her cousin."

"Visits have to be scheduled. We can't have

27

people just dropping by any old time. She's making real progress here, not like at the other places she's been. She'll probably be going home in a few days, so maybe you could wait and see her when she's settled back home." The woman eyed her carefully.

"Can't you make an exception this one time? I'm leaving town and won't get to see her again for weeks and weeks," Sophie begged.

"Sorry." The woman shook her head. "Rules are rules."

A woman with a notepad came up to the desk and eyed Sophie carefully. "I'm Dr. Nancy Davidson. And you are?"

"This woman wants to see Emma Merrill, and she hasn't made an appointment," the lady said.

"Sophie Mason." She stuck out her hand, and Nancy jumped as if she wasn't sure she'd heard right.

"I think we can make an exception to the rules this time and let Sophie talk to Emma," Nancy said.

"Thank you so much." Sophie flashed her brightest smile.

"Sign the visitors' log right there." The woman whipped a guest book around and pointed to a page with empty lines. "Room one-thirteen, just down that hall," she said and went back to typing something into the computer.

Sophie marched down the hall. When she

found the right room, she frowned at the sign on the door—FEMALES ONLY. What in the devil was going on with her old friend? She eased the door open and peeked inside to find the starkest room she'd ever seen. She had always envied Emma her bedroom when they were kids. All done up in pink satin and white lace with Disney princess posters on the wall, the suite had had a sitting room, a bedroom, a walk-in closet, and a beautiful private bathroom. This poor room had only a dresser and closet built into the wall. There was no television or phone, and the twin bed was covered with a light-green bedspread. The only inviting things in the whole room were a dark-green recliner and matching love seat.

From the appearance of the outside of the center and knowing how rich the Merrill family was, Sophie had expected to see a fully furnished room like the one Emma had at home. Why would Victoria ever put her daughter away in a sorry place like this? If she wasn't sad when she arrived, she damn sure would be before she left.

She opened the door wider and saw a dark-haired woman standing at a window. Slumped shoulders, arms hanging limply by her sides—everything about her said defeat.

"Em?" she whispered.

Emma turned away from the window and threw a hand over her mouth. "Sophie, is that really you?"

"It's really me." Sophie stepped inside the room and closed the door behind her.

Emma met her halfway across the room and grabbed her in a fierce hug. "I was talking about you this morning. I'm so glad to see you. I still don't think lizards are that color."

Sophie wrapped Emma up in her arms and held her tight. "An artist can make lizards any color that they want," she said and stepped back. That was the sort of banter that would have made her laugh, but now her childhood friend looked like death warmed over. Her skin was ashen, and her big brown eyes were lifeless. "How long has it been since you were outside?"

Emma shrugged. "Mother says I can't go outside—that I don't do well except inside. I had a panic attack at the mall, so she doesn't let me go to big places. I wanted to build myself one of those new tiny houses, but she threw a fit."

"How long has it been since you painted or even colored?" Sophie took her by the cold, bony hand and led her toward the love seat.

Emma began to twist her hands once Sophie released her. "I can't paint or color. The people here tried to get me to draw, but my hands shake every time I pick up a brush or even a crayon," she said. "I'm not doing so well, Sophie. They want me to remember things, and I can't. Sometimes I want to make up something just so they'll stop wanting me to talk to them."

30

"Well, hell's bells," Sophie said. "You were a better artist than me. What happened?"

Another shrug.

Anger boiled up from somewhere down in the depths of Sophie's heart. Who or what had caused her childhood friend to not even care about her art? Something catastrophic had to have happened to make her turn her back on her dream. Some friend she'd been all these years.

Sophie had never done anything on impulse, not even when the candy bars and magazines right by the checkout counters reached out to her. But right then, Sophie decided to change that. She couldn't undo the past, but she could fix the future. She couldn't let Emma stay in this dismal room one more day—or, for that matter, one more hour.

"Who checked you into this place?" she asked.

"I did," Emma answered, "but Mother brought me here and told me to sign the papers. She is still the boss about everything."

"So, you can check yourself out, right?" Sophie asked.

"When the therapist and Mother decide it's for the best. I can sign myself out at any time, but you know Mother. She'll be angry with me if I do." Emma's tone was flat, as if she'd given up hope.

"I never have lived by Victoria's rules. Let's get your things packed up and ready to go. You're going to check yourself out and come with me," Sophie said.

Emma almost smiled. "Mother will have a fit. She says if I even talk to you, she'll put me in one of these places permanently."

"Well—" Sophie opened the closet door, found a small suitcase, and set it on the twin bed. She returned to the closet to find a pair of jeans, a shirt, sandals, and a makeup kit. Hanging on the rack inside were several sets of scrubs, all pure white like the ones Emma was wearing. "Then I guess you'll just have to live with me from now on, and, honey, I would never put you in a place like this."

"It's not as bad as some of the others," Emma said.

"Is this all you brought with you?" Sophie stared at the suitcase.

"That's what I wore when I checked into this place." Emma glanced down at the white outfit she was wearing and flicked a piece of dust away from the top. "The last center I was in had pink scrubs. I liked them better than these."

Sophie threw the clothing out of the closet. "Put these on and toss what you are wearing on the bed."

"Where are we going? Shouldn't I call Mother?" Emma asked.

"Every summer I spend a while down near Big Bend National Park in southern Texas. I want to do a couple of landscapes down there for my next showing, and you're coming with me." Sophie hoped that she hadn't left room for arguments. "And no, don't call Victoria. You are over thirty years old, for God's sake. You can make up your own mind and color lizards purple or orange or even red if you want to."

Emma pulled the top over her head and tossed it on the bed. "Sophie, we'll have to go by my house. I don't have anything else to wear."

They couldn't go by Victoria's huge mansion of a house or Sophie would never get out of town with Emma. "We're about the same size. You can wear my things, or else we'll buy you something on the way or order you some new things online. I lived in your hand-me-downs when we were kids, so I'll be glad to share my things with you now. Have courage, Emma. Believe me when I say we have to leave this place, and we can't go get anything from Victoria's house. You need to go with me, so your job is to check yourself out. We can talk about the next step on the way to south Texas. If you want to go home after a couple of days, I'll bring you back, I promise."

Is this the right thing to do? You need to get a lot of work done in the next few weeks for the European showing. Do you have time to worry with Emma? the annoying voice in her head asked.

She was my best friend, and I should have been here for her before now, Sophie argued.

"I'm a mess, Sophie. This isn't the first place like this I've been since I saw you last. Are you sure about this?" Emma asked.

Like when they were kids, it seemed like Emma could always read her mind. "I'm very sure. I've been renting a trailer in a small park in south Texas for the past three years at this time of year. The snowbirds have all gone home, and it's peaceful and quiet." Sophie handed her the shirt. "Put this on now."

"Snowbirds?" Emma pulled the shirt over her head and then removed the scrub bottoms.

"People who don't like the snow and cold in the northern states, so they come south for the winter." Sophie handed her the jeans.

Emma jerked them up over her slim hips. They hung on her like a tow sack on a broom handle. There was a time when she had been a size bigger than Sophie. That's why Victoria had given all Emma's outgrown things to Rebel.

"I hate snow and cold weather," Emma said.

"That's a good sign, because where we're going, it's hot and dry." Sophie put the suitcase back into the closet. She took Emma's purse from the shelf and handed it to her. She noticed that it was a Chanel—but then, Victoria would be embarrassed if she or her daughter had anything but the best.

This is getting real. What if you make her worse? The voice in her head increased in volume.

Nothing could be worse than this, Sophie answered.

"Let's go," Sophie said. "Do you have a cell phone in your purse?"

"No, it's in the nightstand," Emma answered. "Mother calls every night at nine o'clock. There's no cameras in here"—Emma scanned the bare room—"or at least I hope there's not any, so she doesn't know what's going on. I tell her that I'm feeling so much better when she calls."

Sophie took the phone and the charger from the drawer, turned the phone off, and put it in Emma's purse.

"You can't do that—turn off the phone. Mother wouldn't like it, and you know how she gets when she's angry," Emma whispered.

"I promise we'll turn it back on as soon as we get to our destination, and that will be before nine o'clock tonight," Sophie said.

"All right then." Emma nodded.

She didn't expect to get all the way to Hummingbird Trailer Park before the center called Victoria and told her that Emma had checked out, but they had no idea where she was going, so that would buy her some time.

Emma's hands shook so badly when they stepped up to the front desk, but she crammed

35

them down into her pockets and said in a fairly steady voice, "I'm checking myself out."

The lady behind the computer looked up and asked, "What's your name?"

"Emma Merrill," she answered.

"For God's sake, she's been here all these weeks and you don't even know her name?" Sophie said impatiently. She had to get Emma out of this place in a hurry. If Victoria walked through the doors or by chance happened to call, all hell would break loose.

"Don't remember ever seeing her out of her room," the woman shot back as she hit a few keys. "You only have one week left in the program. Are you sure you want to leave? There will be no reimbursement of funds."

Nancy came from a room, noticed Emma, and ran all the way up the hallway. "Emma, what are you doing? I have strict orders to call your mother if you decide to check yourself out," she said between bouts of catching her breath.

"Nancy, I'd like to introduce you to Sophie," Emma said in a very formal tone. "This is my friend, and I'm leaving with her. We plan to spend a few weeks in southern Texas. Do you think I might see a purple lizard?"

Nancy gave a brief nod toward Sophie. "We met earlier."

"Does she need to sign something?" Sophie asked.

"Just one paper," Nancy answered. She nodded to the lady behind the computer and said, "Print it out." Then she turned back to Emma. "And I'm very busy right now, so it might be a couple of hours before I have time to call your mother. I hope you find many happy places where you are going, Emma."

"Yes, ma'am." Emma nodded and signed the paper that the receptionist put in front of her.

"Take good care of her," Nancy whispered to Sophie. "If anyone can help her, it just might be you."

"Yes, ma'am," Sophie said. "Will you get in trouble for this?"

"Not at all. Emma checked herself into our facility. She has always been free to check herself right back out. She's an adult." Nancy smiled.

"Thank you," Sophie told her.

Emma turned around. She wasn't smiling yet, but her eyes looked a little less dead when she said, "I'm ready, Sophie. Let's go find that crazy hippie lizard."

Chapter Two

I 'm sorry I haven't been here for you," Sophie said when they were underway. "I tried to call, but Victoria told me in no uncertain terms that I was never talking to you. The second time I tried, the phone number had been changed."

"Mother is *the boss*. And I wasn't there for you, either. I haven't been to one of your shows . . ." Emma looked out the side window. "But I don't do well in crowds or around men. Are there guys where we are going?"

"Ye-es." Sophie heard the anxiety in her friend's voice and wondered if maybe she had made a big mistake in taking her away from people who were trying to help her. She reached across the console and laid a hand on Emma's shoulder. "Arty is past seventy and does metal art. He used to make the big stuff out of junked cars, but now that he's older, he works on smaller projects."

"Is he a big man?" Emma wrung her hands. "Maybe you better take me back to the center. I don't want to be a bother."

I will not give up, not after what Nancy said as we were leaving. I might be Emma's last hope of getting well, Sophie thought.

"Arty isn't much taller than me, if that. He's a short, round guy who wears bibbed overalls. He's bald headed and reminds me of Ralph, the old gardener at your folks' place when we were kids," she said.

"I liked Ralph." Emma stopped twisting her hands.

"Me too," Sophie said as she drove south and caught Highway 20 going west. "And then there's Josh."

The hand-wringing started again. "Is he a big guy?"

Evidently just thinking about those kinds of guys made Emma very nervous. No wonder there was that sign on her door. Something had happened to her that involved a big man. That much Sophie was sure of. Thank God Josh and Arty were not imposing guys.

"Remember Marty Stephens from elementary school?" Sophie asked.

Emma drew her brows down in a frown and finally nodded. "He wasn't even as tall as we were, and he had trouble learning."

"Josh is kind of like that, maybe five feet three inches tall, only he's brilliant. He'll be our landlord—he owns the park. Arty told me he has the IQ of a genius, but he's really shy and kind of keeps to himself. Don't let that fool you, though—he's so kind. He's an artist, too. He works with pencil and ink instead of paints, though, and sells his stuff at the gift shops in that area. He's never made it big, but he doesn't care, because he hates crowds. I wanted to set him up with a gallery showing, but he told me that money wasn't all that important to him, either. He's got family money, so he doesn't depend on his art for his income."

"Marty was awkward, too. I felt sorry for him," Emma said. "The kids picked on him something awful."

"Until I knocked a couple of them on their butts." Sophie laughed.

Emma didn't laugh with her, but at least her hands went still. Sophie remembered that Emma had been so excited about her art classes and her freedom that first semester of college. Those were the days when she was still hoping to be a famous artist someday, and Sophie had had no doubt that she would be. She had the money from her parents to back her until she got a start, whereas Sophie had had to work anywhere from two to four jobs to support herself until she finally sold a couple of paintings.

"I was so focused on getting you out of that place that I didn't think to ask if you are on medicine that we needed to pick up at the desk or get refilled," Sophie said.

"The whole reason for me going to the center was so I could get off my pills and only take supplements. Mother is on a healthy kick these days. No sugar, no carbs, lots of exercise and vitamins," Emma said. "I won't be missing anything but more of those therapy sessions when they try to get me to remember something that I have locked away in my brain, and a sleeping pill at night that never works anyway."

"Why do you need sleeping pills?" Sophie asked.

"So that I don't have nightmares and wake up in a cold sweat. I didn't tell Nancy that the pills weren't working. I've never told anyone."

"Why not?" Sophie shrugged. "Maybe they could prescribe a better pill."

Emma shook her head. "I don't want any of that stuff, or any of the therapy sessions, either. I'm not sure I want to remember what it is I've got locked away. The only thing I'm sure about is that the only good times I've had were when you and Rebel were in my life. I want that feeling back. If Nancy knew I was having bad dreams, she would tell Mother, and I wouldn't ever get out of there."

"Where is home now? Do you have a house, an apartment?" Sophie asked.

"I still have my suite upstairs in my folks' house," Emma said.

"Pink satin and white lace?" Sophie asked.

Emma almost smiled again. "You remembered."

Sophie reached across the console again and laid a hand on Emma's shoulder. "Of course I did. I always thought it was a beautiful room, and to tell the truth, I wanted one just like it."

"You can have it. I hate it." Emma's tone could have put frost on the windshield.

"What kind of room would you want if you could change it?" Sophie asked.

"I've wanted a tiny house of my own for years, and I want it decorated in neutral shades with some orange and yellow accents to brighten it up," Emma answered. "But Mother says that will make my problems even worse. You remember she always said bright colors are bohemian."

Sophie laughed and gave Emma's bony shoulder a gentle squeeze. "Stick with me, and you can have a tiny house—and it'll even have orange countertops."

"I think I'll like that just fine." Emma really smiled that time.

Josh Corlen took the time to turn on the air conditioner for Sophie and then went to his own small one-bedroom trailer house. He stripped out of his work clothing, tossed it all in the washing machine in the hallway, and took a shower. Filly and Arty would have supper on the picnic table out under the live oak tree at seven, and he didn't want to be late. Filly's chocolate cake was his favorite dessert, and Arty had made an amazing pot of clam chowder.

He dressed in khaki shorts, an orange T-shirt,

and matching Crocs and got to the table just as Arty was setting the pot down. Arty had always reminded Josh of his grandfather—short, balding, bright-blue eyes, and slightly cocky. If Grandpa had been alive, he and Arty would have even been about the same age.

Filly was setting disposable bowls and a loaf of her homemade bread on the table. She wasn't any taller than Arty, and from the day Josh had bought the trailer park, she'd been his surrogate grandmother, friend, mother, and favorite aunt all rolled into one person. She had braided her hair into two long plaits that hung over her shoulders and wore her usual flowing skirt and T-shirt—from her part-hippie heritage, she said. Her given name was Ophelia, but no one called her that, not even Leo, the buyer from the local gift store who came by once a month and picked up Arty's metal pieces, Filly's jewelry, and Josh's drawings. She was Filly to everyone, and Josh loved her.

The chocolate sheet cake on the other end of the wooden picnic table was still warm enough that a little steam floated above it. Josh took a deep breath, drawing in all the mixed aromas.

"This sure looks good. Thank y'all for cooking for us every evening," Josh said.

"We all got to eat, and it's hard to cook for one," Arty said. "Besides, Filly would starve plumb to death if I didn't cook."

"No, I wouldn't. I might die of a sugar over-load, but I wouldn't starve," Filly argued. "I love to bake, but cookin' ain't for me."

"Together, y'all make a great team." Josh smiled.

"*We all* make a great team." Arty dished up the chowder. "I made plenty in case Sophie hasn't eaten when she gets here."

"So, what did you work on today?" Filly asked after Arty said a simple prayer over their meal.

"I finished up that old oil derrick." Arty pinched up a thick slice of bread and dunked it into his chowder. "This one is three feet tall. I'm going to make one about a third that size next, and then before our buyer arrives, I've got a mind to make a lizard."

"Big or little?" Josh asked.

"Maybe a foot long. I saw a lady on the tele-vision last night that had a chameleon brooch about that size on her sweater. Dang thing looked like it was crawlin' right up to her shoulder. Hers had all kinds of fancy jewels on it, but it set me to thinkin' about makin' one. If women are usin' them for jewelry, they might buy one to set on their coffee table, too," Arty answered.

"Hell's bells, Arthur." Filly shook her finger at him. "Ain't you realized yet that folks buy your art to put behind glass doors in them fancy cabinets and treat it like an investment? They pay enough money for those pieces that they aren't going to put them on a coffee table to get dusty. Most of them brag to their friends that they own a signed Art Crawford metal piece."

"Ophelia!" he shot back at her. "Don't call me Arthur."

"If you call me by my birth name again, you'll go without dessert for a week. You know I hate that." She shook her spoon at him.

"Not as bad as I hate Arthur."

"Shh . . ." Josh put a finger to his lips. "I hear a vehicle."

"Maybe it's Sophie," Filly said.

"One can only hope." Arty glared at Filly. "I'm ready for a fresh face around here. She won't be as hateful as you are."

"Now, honey, you know I love your chowder even if I did call you Arthur." Filly giggled. "Besides, you called me Ophelia."

"You did it first," Arty said.

"I hope it's not someone who's just going to turn around and go back," Josh whispered. When Sophie was there, or when the other three trailers were filled with their winter snowbirds, things always went smoother at the supper table.

"Yay!" Filly clapped her hands. "I can see the license plate on the front of her car. Our Sophie has come home for the summer."

The silence between them was comfortable, but during the last hour of the trip, Sophie had

45

continued to question her decision to practically kidnap Emma and take her to an almost wilderness existence. What-ifs circled around in her mind like a hamster on an endless wheel. Emma had lived in the lap of luxury her whole life. What if she hated living with the bare essentials in a small two-bedroom trailer house? Victoria had dressed her in the best that fashion had to offer—what if she hated wearing Sophie's clothing? What if living in a world of cactus and wildflowers depressed Emma even more and she needed medicine?

Whoa! Hold your horses! Rebel's voice in her head was loud and clear. *You saw where Emma was living and what she was wearing. I'd say what's more important than physical things right now is that you are going to try to help her get her head on straight.*

"Yes, ma'am," Sophie whispered under her breath.

The sun had begun to drop below the mountains in the distance, leaving nothing but an orange glow over the tops of the six trailers arranged in a semicircle around a huge live oak tree that shaded a picnic table and benches. When Sophie parked in front of the first trailer on the right, Emma took a deep breath and let it out slowly.

"This is the most beautiful place I've ever seen. Is this your trailer?" Emma whispered.

"This is home for the next couple of months."

A heavy what-if load lifted from Sophie's shoulders. "The trailer is old, but Josh keeps it well maintained."

"It's perfect," Emma said. "It reminds me of a tiny house."

Sophie smiled. "It kind of does, doesn't it? Are you ready for supper?"

Emma dropped her chin to her chest and shifted her eyes from one to the other of the two people who'd left the table. "Would it be rude if I scrounged through the cabinets and maybe got a bowl of cereal or a peanut butter sandwich and met them all tomorrow?"

"Not one bit. *You* are in charge of what you want to do while you are here," Sophie answered. "That's Filly and Arty coming this way, and Josh is sitting at the table."

Filly was dressed as usual in a long, multi-colored, flowing skirt and a T-shirt that had been belted in with a hot-pink scarf. She was barefoot, and her braids flopped around as she ran toward the vehicle. A rim of gray hair circled Arty's bald head, and he wore his usual flip-flops, bibbed overalls, and faded T-shirt. Their smiles and open arms said they were as glad to see Sophie as she was to see them.

Emma's eyes darted around like those of a bunny who had been caught in a circle of coyotes, and she started wringing her hands again.

Sophie's chest tightened. Maybe she'd done

47

the wrong thing by breaking Emma out of prison. She inhaled deeply and shook off the doubts. She had to try to help her or she couldn't live with herself.

"You just sit tight for maybe five minutes, and then we'll go inside." Sophie laid her hands on Emma's. "It's going to be all right. I promise. Remember what I told you. *You* are in control here. *You* make your own decisions."

She got out of the SUV and hugged Filly and then Arty. "My friend Em is in the car, and she's going to be staying with me. She's pretty tired, so I think we'll go on inside and get unpacked."

"Sure thing," Filly said, "but she's welcome."

"Any friend of yours is a friend of ours," Arty told her.

"I'll just get her inside, and then I'll be out for supper," Sophie whispered in Filly's ear.

Before Filly and Arty could turn around, Emma stepped out of the SUV and nodded toward them. Her face had lost what little color it had, and her voice trembled. "Sophie told me about all of you. I'm very glad that she invited me to spend some time here."

"We're glad to have you. We got clam chowder for supper," Arty said.

"And chocolate cake," Filly added.

"That sounds delicious, but . . ." Emma looked longingly toward the trailer.

"Give me a few minutes, and then I'll come out

48

and get some for each of us," Sophie said. "Em and I both have phone calls to make. It's already past midnight where Teddy is, but I should send him a text at least. And Mama is expecting me to call as soon as we get here."

"Of course," Filly said. "I'm sure glad you're here. Arty's bein' a jackass."

"We just been spendin' too much time together, and, woman"—he shook his finger at Filly—"don't be a tattletale. Is Teddy going to come see us in a couple of weeks?"

"Yep, hopefully," Sophie said. "He's in Europe right now setting up things for my showing."

"I can't wait to see him," Filly said. "If I was twenty years younger, I'd take that man away from you."

"You'd have to be forty years younger and a helluva lot prettier." Arty snorted as they walked back toward the supper table.

Emma's eyes widened, so big that for a split second Sophie thought she might faint right there beside the SUV. Sophie looped her arm through Emma's and led her toward the trailer. "They banter like that all the time. They aren't serious, and they aren't fighting."

They walked up the porch steps, and Sophie threw the door open.

"I've never been around anyone like that," Emma said. "I'm sorry if I embarrassed you."

"You didn't embarrass me." Sophie gave her a

hug. "You're just used to folks who are so uptight that . . ."

Emma giggled. "As uptight as a bull's butt during fly season. That was one of Rebel's sayings, and I always thought it was funny. Mother would shiver all the way to her toenails if she saw me eating from red plastic bowls out of a communal pot of chowder. And was that a bumblebee flitting around on the chocolate cake?"

"Victoria isn't here, and what she thinks doesn't matter on Hummingbird Lane," Sophie told her. "I'm going out to get our things. Take a look around and acquaint yourself with everything. I'll be right back."

She found Josh standing at the bottom of the stairs when she went outside. "I hope it's all right that I brought a roommate with me."

"It's your trailer. You can do what you want while you are here. Need some help?" he asked.

"I never turn down help." Sophie smiled. "Just the suitcase and the tote bag tonight. I'll take care of the art supplies tomorrow. They're in the back seat. And thanks, Josh."

He kept his eyes on the ground. "Glad you're here."

"It's good to be back," Sophie said. "Just set them on the porch."

Emma was standing in the doorway, and Josh stole a sideways look at her. His body language and the fact that he averted his eyes said that he was as uncomfortable as Emma was. "I'll just set your things on the porch and then get on back to have dessert."

"Thank you so much." Sophie smiled again.

Emma took a step away from the open door when Josh set the bags down, and then he made a hasty retreat back to the picnic table. His orange Crocs caught her eye. She had always wanted a pair of those, but her mother said they were ugly. Any guy who wore orange shoes had to be all right.

Her mouth watered at the thought of having a piece of that cake. She couldn't remember the last time she had cake or sweets of any kind. Her mother said that fresh fruit was much better for her than sweets, and the center where she'd been for weeks served fruit for dessert.

"Oh!" Emma gasped as she crossed the small living room to look out the sliding glass doors at the mountains in the distance. *Look at that sunset. Sophie should paint that picture. It takes my breath away,* she thought as she pushed the doors open and inhaled the night air. "There's a porch and chairs."

"So, you like it?" Sophie startled her when she slipped an arm around Emma's shoulders. "I will be setting up my easel out here for the next few weeks, because I'm going to paint what you are looking at. I have three paintings planned. A night scene, one with a sunrise, and then the same at midday. I've already shipped the pictures for the showing in Europe, but hopefully if they want another showing next year, I'll have these for then. What do you think, Em? Think you could find your way back to painting on this porch?"

"Maybe . . . someday if I can . . ." She shook her head and stammered, "I don't know who I am anymore. I have . . . to know . . . what inspires me before I can pick up the brushes. I love your idea for all three of those paintings. Is there really nothing between here and those mountains? I mean, like, houses or more trailer parks?"

"Josh owns all the land from here to the mountains, and there's nothing but cactus, wild-flowers, and"—she smiled—"purple lizards. We've both got some phone calls to make."

"Can I sit on the porch while I'm making the phone call?" Emma had no doubts that her mother was going to be furious with her. Victoria had never hit Emma, but her words could cut through the heart like a machete through soft butter. Her mother would send out a search party for her if she didn't tell her where she was, and she would definitely get even with Sophie in some way.

"Rule number one is that you are the boss of you while you are here," Sophie answered. "You will need to turn your phone back on. I'm glad you let me turn it off. I was afraid that Victoria would talk you into going back to that place or else send someone to get you and arrest me for kidnapping."

"Thank you," Em sighed. "But you can't kidnap me. I'm not a kid anymore, and, Sophie, you're a good friend. She's going to be mad at me, you know, but I'm really glad I'm this far away when she starts whispering and telling me that I'm delicate and stupid, that I can't make decisions for myself. She'll say that I should remember what happened when I tried to live on my own in college."

"It won't be the first or the last time she's been mad about something, will it?" Sophie asked.

Emma dug deep into her memories and tried to remember the last time she had made her mother angry. "Probably not, but the last time she got really upset was when I refused to eat because she said you wouldn't be coming back to our house, and that I would be having tutors instead of going to school. I don't think she's been that mad at me since, but I learned to be careful and not get her all riled up."

"Really?" Sophie blinked a half dozen times in rapid succession. "Are you serious?"

"If I do what she wants, she's happy, and she's so mean when she's mad that Daddy and I just let her have her way," Emma told her.

"Well, we're going to change that. You are not delicate. You are a strong, talented woman, and we'll prove it right here on Hummingbird Lane in trailer number thirteen," Sophie said.

"I only counted six trailers," Em said.

"That's right. But back before Josh bought this place, there must have been more. Only four of them are occupied right now. Arty lives on the other side of the circle in seven. The two next to us are vacant until fall, and then there's Josh's place, and Filly lives between him and Arty." Sophie headed down the hallway. "I'm just going to take a bathroom break and then make a couple of phone calls. Then I'll get us some food. We usually eat together in the evenings, but it's not mandatory, so . . ."

"I'll try, but not tonight," Emma said.

"That's good enough for me. Like I said, everything is up to you." Sophie disappeared into the restroom.

"I'm not sure I can handle making my own decisions," Emma muttered as she got her phone out of her purse, turned it on, and called her mother.

"Where are you?" Victoria asked without even saying her usual proper "Merrill residence, Victoria speaking."

Emma went outside and sat down in one of the red plastic chairs. She sucked in a lungful of night air, but her chest still felt like an elephant was sitting on it, and the stars in the sky went all blurry for a few minutes. "I'm in south Texas somewhere close to Big Bend National Park. I'll be here for a while."

"No, you will not," Victoria declared. "I'll send Jeffrey to get you tomorrow morning. What is the address? You are not staying with Sophia more than tonight. The center called me an hour ago and told me that you'd checked yourself out. Have you lost what little mind you have left? You'll be dead in a week if you don't listen to me. I may have Sophia charged with kidnapping."

Emma giggled. "I knew you'd say that. If you do, I'll run away and live on the streets. I'm not going back to an institution, Mother."

"Jeffrey will be there tomorrow morning, and don't you ever use that tone when you talk to me." Victoria's voice had dropped to that place that scared Emma. "You will do what I say, when I say, and you will not argue with me. Jeffrey—"

"I will not come home, so spare Jeffrey the trip," Emma declared with as much courage as she could muster. "I am a grown woman, I'm past thirty, and this is my decision." She reflected that much of that was said for her own benefit.

"You are much too delicate to be away from home. Where are you living, anyway?" Victoria asked.

"In a trailer house with Sophie." Emma hoped that poor old Jeffrey didn't suffer the wrath of Victoria Merrill. He was close to seventy and had been the Merrills' driver and the pilot of their small plane for as long as Emma could remember.

"I'm not a bit surprised. I knew that girl would always be trailer trash," Victoria hissed.

"Goodbye, Mother," Emma said and quickly turned off her phone. The first time she'd skipped out on a therapist's visit and spent the afternoon in the park, her mother had installed a tracking device on her phone that let her know exactly where Emma was at all times.

"But only if the thing is turned on." Emma pulled her knees up to her chin and took a deep breath. Talking to her mother hadn't been nearly as difficult as she'd thought it would be, but then Victoria wasn't standing in front of her with her mouth clamped in a disapproving expression and her eyes boring holes into Emma.

She eyed the phone in her hands as if it were a rattlesnake. "I can use Sophie's phone when I want to make a call, and I see a landline over there on the kitchen counter. Mother will hate me . . ." She removed the back of her phone, took out the battery and the SIM card, and went inside the trailer and found a hammer in a drawer. She carried it outside and laid the phone down on the wooden porch floor.

"Sophie says I'm in charge of me. I don't want Mother to find me," she said as she drew back the hammer. With one well-placed hit, she crushed the battery and the SIM card, then drew back again and brought the hammer down on the face of the phone. Just to be sure, she hit it again until it was nothing but a pile of bits and pieces.

"That's step one," she said, but her hands were shaking when she laid the hammer on the porch railing and then swept all the pieces into a dustpan and took them into the trailer.

"What is all that?" Sophie asked.

"My phone," Emma said.

"Wow, what did that phone do to you?" Sophie asked.

"My mother's voice came through it," Emma answered.

"Then good job," Sophie said. "I'm going out to call Mama and Teddy and then get us some food. I'll be back in a few minutes."

"I'll be right outside," Emma said. And in that moment, sitting on a wooden porch in a red plastic chair, Emma felt more alive than she ever had in her entire life.

Sophie sat down on the top step of the porch, waved at the folks around the table, and pointed to her phone. Filly nodded, and Arty gave her a thumbs-up.

Rebel answered on the first ring. "I've been expecting your call for the last hour. How did things go?"

Sophie hesitated for a second too long.

"What happened?" Rebel asked. "Did you have car trouble, or did you and Teddy break up? I

57

wouldn't be a bit surprised if he told you to go find another boyfriend since you refuse to marry him."

"No and no, but I did go see Em in that place. Do you have any idea what happened to her to make her quit college?" Sophie asked. Rebel couldn't possibly understand that Sophie had her reasons for not wanting to get married.

"That poor, sweet child. All Annie has heard is that Victoria said Emma was too delicate to endure the pressure of college and had to come home. Victoria has always pounded it into that girl's head that she was fragile and never let her do anything for herself. I thought it was a bunch of bull crap, myself. A kid is as strong as you let her be," Rebel said.

"I couldn't stand to leave her in that dismal place, so I brought her with me," Sophie blurted out.

"Jesus, Mary, and Joseph," Rebel gasped. "Victoria is going to go up in flames. How did you manage such a foolhardy thing? And why did you? You've never been impulsive in your life, girl."

"Em is in a bad way. She has no self-confidence, and something horrible has happened to her that she doesn't want to remember. I wonder if it isn't something to do with Victoria. There was a sign on her door that said, 'Females Only.' That suggests to me that she's been hurt, and probably by a man. Knowing that Victoria was talking about putting her away forever, I just had to try to help her." Sophie finally stopped for a breath.

"Well, good luck," Rebel said. "And I do mean that. You've got work to do for your overseas showing, and you need to spend time with Teddy when he can get away, and"—Rebel stopped, and Sophie knew it was to collect her thoughts—"and a million other reasons that you already know. The last of which is that Victoria will send a hit man out to kill you for taking her delicate little orchid away from her. I've always wondered if she didn't treat Em the way she did so that everyone would think Em was crazy. I saw a show on television that had to do with Munchausen by proxy. That means that—"

"I know what it means, Mama," Sophie butted in, "but Victoria never did things to make Em sick just so that she would get attention for taking care of her."

"There's more than one sickness," Rebel said. "There's physical sickness and then there's mental. It could be the latter one, but no matter what, she'd best not send anyone to hurt my child."

"What would you do if she did?" Sophie giggled.

"I'd have to do what I've wanted to do for more than twenty years. I'd have a very good reason to march up to her house and stomp her fancy ass into the ground," Rebel answered.

Sophie's giggles turned into laughter. "Don't do it until I get home. I wouldn't miss that show for anything," she said when she could catch her breath again. "Don't worry about me and Em. She already likes it here."

"Honey, anyplace on earth would beat that cold mansion she's had to live in her whole life," Rebel said. "I've got to go. Annie and I are catching a late-night movie down at the theater."

"Good night. I'll holler at you on Sunday if not before," Sophie said.

"Lookin' forward to it," Rebel told her.

Sophie tried to call Teddy, but the call went straight to voice mail. As always, his deep voice on the outgoing message sent little shivers through her whole body. She hadn't been impressed with him the first time she saw him, but when he spoke, all that changed. There was something soothing and yet exciting about the deep southern Louisiana twang he had.

After the beep she said, "Hello, darlin'. I miss you. I love you. I'll call tomorrow morning, which will be in the afternoon for you. I've made it to the trailer park and am hoping to start painting tomorrow." She ended the message, tucked her phone into her pocket, and headed across the yard to the table.

"So, tell us about your friend," Filly said. "Is

she all right? She seemed like she was afraid of her own shadow when she got out of your vehicle. Her little hands were shaking, and she wouldn't make eye contact with us. What's happened to her?"

"It's a long story, but the best way I can describe her is that she's like Coco," Sophie said.

Josh nodded. "Go easy with her, right?"

As if she'd heard her name, a big calico cat jumped up on the bench beside Sophie and meowed. "I'm glad to be here, too, Coco girl." Sophie smiled. "Thank you for the warm welcome."

The cat had appeared in the trailer park during Sophie's first year there. She'd been a tiny kitten so wild that no one could touch her, but Josh had kept working with her until, by the end of summer, she would let him pet her. Sophie remembered him saying that he understood the cat, because he was leery of most people, too.

"Is Emma sick, or is she just wary of strangers like Coco was when she first adopted us?" Arty asked.

"Not either one, really," Sophie answered. "It's more like she was so sheltered and protected that the real world was too much for her."

A smile played at the corners of Josh's mouth. "I'll share Coco with her. That might help."

"I'm sure it will," Sophie agreed. "I should be taking some food back for our supper."

"Just take the pot," Arty said. "There's about enough for two people left in it."

"And the chocolate cake, too," Filly said. "We've all had our fill of it, and tomorrow, I want to make dumplings."

"I'll help you carry it," Josh offered.

"Thank you, again, for everything." Sophie stood and picked up the pot of chowder.

Josh cut off a piece of cake. "Something for my midnight snack," he said and then set the rest of the loaf of bread on the empty end of the cake pan. "I like chocolate cake and a glass of good cold milk before I go to bed."

"Me too," Sophie said. "Thank y'all for saving some supper for us."

Filly waved her away with a flick of the wrist. "We're family. We take care of our own."

"Have you and Em been friends for a long time?" Josh followed behind her with the cake and bread in his hands.

"We were inseparable until we were about twelve years old." Sophie stepped up onto the porch. "Then she had tutors that came to the house to educate her, and I stayed in public school. The first semester of college we saw each other some, but I hadn't actually seen her in more than a decade until today. She went to one college and I went to another, and they were only about fifty miles away from each other, but she went home after the first semester."

"I hope she finds peace here," Josh said.

Peace might be stretching her expectations for Emma. If she could just gain a little self-confidence and be like the little girl that Sophie had known all those years ago, that would be a great start.

"So do I." Sophie opened the door and went straight to the short bar separating the kitchen from the living area. "Supper has arrived, Em," she called out as she set the pot of chowder down. Josh handed the pan in his hands off to Sophie, bobbed his head in a quick goodbye, and was out the door before Emma made it to the kitchen.

"I haven't had chocolate cake in forever," Emma said. "Oh!" Her voice showed more emotion than it had all day. "A cat! Can I pet it?"

"Yes, you can pet her. She's very tame. Her name is Coco, and she loves attention," Sophie answered. "Did Victoria ever let you have a pet? I remember that you always said you wanted a cat when we were kids."

Emma dropped down on her knees and picked up the cat, hugged her to her chest, and kissed her on top of the head. "I love cats, but Mother says they shed all over everything, and she said that I'm probably allergic to them anyway."

"Well, we don't care if Coco sheds, and you aren't sneezing, so I don't think you've got an allergy," Sophie said. "Coco brings us all so much joy that we'll gladly brush the cat hair off the sofa or run the vacuum over the carpet. Out here in the boonies, you can enjoy her all you want. You want some chowder? It's been hours since you had lunch."

"We had a snack up near Odessa when you stopped for gas," Emma reminded her. "I'd rather have a piece of that cake right now."

Sophie cut off a big slab and plopped it down on a paper plate. "We don't have a table, so do you want to eat it on the bar or sitting right there on the floor?"

Emma's eyes showed a faint bit of light. "Right here on the floor, and after I eat it, maybe I will have some chowder."

"Remember that old saying about life being short?" Sophie got misty-eyed at the idea of Emma getting so excited over chocolate cake.

"Eat dessert first," Emma finished the old adage. "I should sketch those words in fancy lettering and make a plaque to hang on my wall if I ever get a tiny house."

"Sounds like a plan to me, but first you have to pick up some brushes or at least crayons," Sophie said.

Emma held her plate above the cat's head and took the first bite. "This is so danged good. When I was in college, I ate whole boxes of chocolate cupcakes, but they didn't taste like this. I remember when Rebel let us have a picnic on a quilt one time. We had peanut butter sandwiches, and Rebel had brought chocolate cupcakes that she'd made. They tasted like this, but I felt guilty later. You never came back to my house again. Mother said that Rebel left because she didn't like me. I asked her what I'd done so I could apologize, but she just gave me one of those looks and said that I drove her best housekeeper away. For weeks afterward, when she was interviewing women, she would tell me that it was all my fault that she had to take time to find another one. I was careful to never make friends with another housekeeper again."

"Oh, honey." Sophie tried to take in Emma's rambling that jumped from cupcakes to house-keepers, and just the idea that her friend wasn't thinking straight put tears in her eyes. "That's not the reason we left, and you did nothing wrong. Your mother thought your father was having an affair with my mother. Mama tried to tell her it wasn't true, that she would never do that, but Victoria wouldn't listen and told her to get out."

Emma's eyes filled with tears, too. "I'm sorry. I always thought Rebel was sent away because of me. Why would Mother do that?"

"You don't have to apologize. You and I did nothing." Another wave of guilt washed over Sophie for not trying harder to stay in touch with her friend. She was beginning to think maybe Rebel was right about Victoria driving Emma crazy so that she could have attention for taking care of a delicate child. That didn't sound like her, though. She didn't want to take care of anyone but herself. She would have an agenda, but what could she gain by treating Emma like she did? Why would a mother do that to her own child?

"Mother told me once that she had never wanted children. Maybe she was ashamed of me because I wasn't strong like her," Emma said.

"I wouldn't know about that, but you are going to get strong while you're here," Sophie said. "How'd your conversation with her go? I guess not well, since you murdered your phone."

"She said she was sending Jeffrey to bring me home. I told her that I was staying right here. I'll need to use the house phone or yours to call her each night. She gets really angry if I don't call, and she's horrible when she's mad," Emma said.

"You can use anything that's here anytime you want, but why did you destroy your phone?" Sophie brought her cake to the living room and sat down across from Emma.

"Because it has a tracker app on it so she can see where I am every minute. I skipped out on a therapist visit a long time ago and spent the day in the park," Emma explained between bites. "I just wanted some time to sit and think without her telling me what to do and when to do it. That was the last time I got to go off on my own. I'm ready to get well, or at least I think I am."

"You don't really have to call Victoria every night unless you want to," Sophie said.

Emma thought about that for a while and then shook her head. "I don't guess I do."

"That's up to you," Sophie said. "And you can use either of the phones anytime you want. I talked to my mother tonight, too, but I'll have to call Teddy tomorrow."

"Why?" Emma was still working around the idea of not talking to Victoria every evening.

"Because of the time difference. Over in France, it's about seven hours later than it is here," Sophie answered. "I'll call in the morning when it's just early afternoon there."

"Are you going to marry him?" Emma polished off the last of her cake. "We always said we would be married to our art, not a man."

"We were just kids back then," Sophie said, "and neither of us had much in the way of a positive outlook when it came to marriage, but Teddy and I might never get married. We don't need a marriage license to know that we are committed. We've been together for ten years. We love each other, and we're fine the way we are."

Besides, he deserves someone a whole lot better than I can ever be, Sophie thought.

Emma shivered. "I'm never getting married, but when I build my tiny house, I want a cat."

"Then you'll have one," Sophie said.

Chapter Three

Sophie awoke the next morning at dawn, made a hasty trip to the bathroom, and then pulled on a pair of denim shorts under her ragged nightshirt. She stopped in the kitchen long enough to put on a pot of coffee, peeked into Emma's bedroom door to find Coco curled up beside her, and then eased out the front door. No one was up and around yet, so she quickly unloaded all her painting supplies into the living room and then called Teddy.

"Hey, my gorgeous girl. I love you, and I miss you, too," he said.

"Hey, right back at you," Sophie said.

"I miss you so much, darlin'. I feel like half of my heart is in Texas with you, but we'll be together soon. Hey, I just got confirmation five minutes ago that everything is now in London and will be stored in a climate-controlled room until the showing."

"Thank God," Sophie said. "I always rest easier when I know the art has arrived."

"Don't worry, darlin'. It's all there, and nothing can go wrong now. In a few months everyone in Europe will be itching to buy your paintings. So, how are things in the desert?" he asked. "You always do your best work when you're in that area. We should retire there someday."

"I'd love that," she said.

"Got to go. The assistant is waving me in to talk to this gallery owner. Wish me luck," Teddy said.

"You don't need luck," Sophie said. "You're amazing."

"Hugs and kisses," Teddy said—always his choice instead of "goodbye."

"Hugs and kisses." She blew him a kiss and ended the call.

"Mornin'." Emma came out of the bedroom with Coco at her heels. "Do I smell coffee? Where did it come from?"

"Josh and Arty go for groceries every week for the group, and I sent him a list last week so he could stock the place before we arrived. There's junk cereal, breakfast toaster things in the cabinet, and sausage biscuits in the freezer. Help yourself," Sophie answered.

"Junk cereal?" Emma asked.

"If you don't like any of that, there's eggs to make an omelet and a waffle iron in the cabinet to make our favorite breakfast." Sophie chose a canvas and locked it down in her easel. "Remember when Mama made us waffles and let us put strawberries and whipped cream on top?"

"After Rebel left, I never got them again, but

this morning I want junk cereal." Emma headed to the cabinet and took down a box. "I especially like this one. I don't get this kind of stuff at home. Hazel usually makes me a smoothie with lots of kale."

"That sounds horrible." Sophie shuddered.

"It is, but Mama says it's good for my delicate condition," Emma said.

"Well, you don't have to drink that green garbage here." Sophie shook her head and changed the subject. "We've got a lot of catchin' up to do. Do you still like country music?"

Emma shrugged. "Don't know. Haven't heard anything but classical since I came home from college. Is George Strait still your favorite?"

"Probably, but now there's Blake Shelton, Alan Jackson, and a whole raft of others that I love just as much," Sophie said. "How long has it been since you heard Simon and Garfunkel— or Sam Cooke and Etta James? When we were in the sixth grade, you were the nerdy one who liked jazz."

"College." Emma answered in one word as she poured chocolate-flavored cereal into a bowl and added milk. "I listened to whatever I wanted in college and ate what I wanted, but that all changed when I went back home. Mother said that if I had to listen to music, it should be some-thing that calmed me . . ." She shrugged. "Like I said, we do what we must to keep her happy."

Sophie poured herself a bowl of cereal and headed out to the porch. "Why did you go home, anyway?"

"I don't know. I just remember that I couldn't stay in college, but let's don't talk about that today. Those were sad days. I just want to enjoy this beautiful day. I'm going to eat outside, then take a walk. Is that all right?" Emma carried her cereal outside and sat down in one of the chairs.

"How old are you, Em?" Sophie asked.

"You know the answer to that," Emma said. "Why are you asking?"

"Because you keep forgetting that you don't have to ask me for permission about anything. There's food in the cabinet and the fridge. We eat at night with the others, but you don't have to if it makes you uncomfortable. You can take walks, sit on the floor while you eat, sleep with Coco— everything is up to you. But if you're going for a walk, don't forget to take one of my hats with you. Your pale skin will burn pretty quickly," Sophie told her.

"Making my own decisions is hard for me to even imagine."

Sophie quickly swiped a tear away from her cheek with the back of her hand. After spending less than a day with Emma, she could never— not in a million years—tell Rebel how much she appreciated her upbringing.

• • •

Emma wondered if it could have been the choco-late cake that kept her from having the recurring nightmares the night before. Or was it the fact that she was so far away from that big mansion of a house and her overbearing mother, or even the many centers she'd been sent to for more than a decade? Whatever happened, it sure was nice to sleep all night without drugs and horrible dreams. If it was because she'd arrived at Hummingbird Lane, then Emma didn't ever want to leave the place.

She wondered about those things as she watched Sophie get her palette ready. Emma rubbed Coco's fur with her bare foot and enjoyed eating sugared-up cereal for breakfast. When her bowl was empty, she set it down on the porch so Coco could drink the milk. "I wonder how much land sells for out here." She dropped a hand and rubbed the cat from her head to the end of her tail. "I like this place, and I would only need a little bit of ground to build a tiny house on."

"I don't have any idea," Sophie answered. "Josh might be able to tell you what he spent on this place. I think I overheard Arty say that it's about two miles out to the mountains, and Josh owns all the land between here and there. Why do you want a tiny house?"

"Because I can see all around it, and no one can hurt me. I hate big houses, and I really hate satin sheets." Emma picked up the bowl, took it to the kitchen sink, and rinsed it before putting it into the dishwasher. "Is it really all right if I borrow a T-shirt?"

"Why do you think you hate big places and satin sheets? And of course you can use any of my things," Sophie answered. "There's also underwear in my dresser drawer, but I don't think you can wear my bras. We'll share what we can for the next couple of days until we can get an order for whatever you want sent here."

"Big fancy places, bigger than Mother's house, are where I am in the nightmares. I'm on a higher floor, and I'm really scared. I'm trying to find my way down to the lobby of the building, but my feet are like lead. They are hard to move," she answered. "I told my first therapists about the dream, but that evening Mother said it was a sign that I had too many problems to live alone. My apartment was on the third floor when I was in college."

"Do you think that's what it means?" Sophie asked.

Emma giggled. "You sound like my therapist. I've tried to figure out what it means, but the only thing I can come up with is that I felt like I was a prisoner no matter where I was. Mother had all the control, and I had nothing. I want to get away, but I can't because I'm too stupid to take care of myself."

"That ends here. You are not stupid, and you're going to take care of ordering yourself some new clothing right now." Sophie handed her phone to Emma. "We can get whatever we need by mail in only two days."

"Are you serious? The mailman comes this far out into the boonies?" Emma asked.

"Rain, hail, sleet, or snow—isn't that what we read about in elementary school?" Sophie grinned.

"That was the Pony Express. They don't ride horses out here, do they?" Emma thought about Jeffrey always bringing in the mail and putting it on the credenza in the foyer. Victoria took care of it when she came home each day. For a while, Emma made it a point to beat her mother to the foyer so she could see if she had something personal—like a letter or a note from Sophie or Rebel—but when nothing came, she even gave up on that.

"Strange as it may seem, we're only about five miles from a small post office. We do have to drive about forty-five minutes to get to a grocery store, though," Sophie answered. "But for now, let's do some shopping. Just thought of a question first, though. You had a phone. Why didn't you at least listen to music or else watch movies on it?"

"The cameras in my room had audio," Emma answered. "Mother said they were for my own protection since the therapist at the first center was concerned that I might be suicidal."

"Were you?" Sophie asked.

"Nope, but now that I'm away from there even for a day, I'm wondering why I wasn't." Emma pulled up a shopping site and sighed. "What do I order? I've never done this. Mother picks out everything for me."

"Start with underwear. You won't need a lot since we have a washer and dryer here in the trailer. Then move on to jeans, shorts, and whatever else takes your eye. Just put it in the cart and then we'll complete the order."

Emma sat back down in one of the chairs, typed "bras" into the search engine, and picked out a pretty lacy one, but she didn't know what size she wore. She laid the phone down and hurried inside, checked the one she'd worn the day before, and then went back out. "Crazy, isn't it? I have no idea what sizes I wear."

"What did you wear at home?" Sophie asked as she started to do a rough sketch of the mountains.

"Slacks, sweaters, shirts—unless I was going to the beauty shop, and then I had to be dressed up," Emma answered.

"What do you want to wear?" Sophie asked.

"Don't laugh at me, but I liked what Filly was wearing last night. Long flowing skirts and sandals. I think I might have been a fortune teller in another life," Emma replied.

"Then order whatever will make you feel good when you wear it," Sophie told her.

"What do you like to wear?" Emma asked as she scrolled through the site.

"I have two pair of bibbed overalls I've cut off to make shorts that I wear when I paint. I can wear one and wash one, so I only need a couple, and I can use the pockets for my brushes. I have the normal little black dresses for gallery showings, and seasonal things for when Teddy and I go out to eat. From now until then, that will be sundresses and Filly's jewelry. I always buy at least two or three of her pieces while I'm here." Sophie sketched as she talked.

Emma's chest tightened again when she thought of what her mother would say if she saw the virtual cart loaded with lacy bras and bikini underwear and the skirts and tank tops. Victoria would tell her that hookers dressed like that and that her daughter was a dignified woman. She almost deleted everything and went back to start all over with sensible bras and white underpants, but then she heard Sophie's words—loud and clear in her head—about making her own decisions.

A screen popped up asking for her shipping address.

"What's the address here?" Emma asked.

"That would be Hummingbird Trailer Park, Hummingbird Lane #13, Terlingua, Texas, 79852," Sophie answered.

Emma held her breath as she punched in her

credit card information next and let it out in a whoosh when she finished.

She pressed the "Submit" button. A screen immediately popped up that said her credit card was invalid. She couldn't remember the last thing she'd bought with it, so the card company was probably just being super careful. She laid the phone aside, went to her room, and got the actual card from her purse. Using the landline, she called the number on the back and found that her card had been closed as of that morning.

"Mother is really in control of my life," she groaned.

Sophie poked her head inside the open doors. "Did you say something to me?"

Emma slid down to the floor and put her head into her hands. "Mother has shut down my credit card and probably frozen my bank account."

"How can she do that?" Sophie asked.

"She insists on being on all my accounts. What money I have comes from what my grandmother left for me. I didn't get a job while I was at college. The interest goes into my checking account each month and Mother's name is on the account as well as mine since I'm . . ." Tears spilled down Emma's cheeks. Her newly found freedom had only been a pipe dream.

Sophie picked up her cell phone, poked a few buttons, and said, "There, I fixed it."

"How?" Emma asked without raising her head.

"I used my credit card." Sophie shrugged and went back to work.

"I can't let you do that," Emma said.

"The wrong time to tell someone that they can't do something is right after they've already done it." Sophie came into the living room and sat down beside Emma. "You gave me all those beautiful hand-me-downs when we were growing up. I'm just repaying the debt."

"B-but . . . ," Emma stammered as more tears flooded her cheeks.

Sophie slung an arm around Emma's shoulders. "There are no buts in friendship. Your things are ordered, and you will be beautiful when they arrive. And, honey, it's tough to shut off a grown-up's credit card, so we'll check into this."

"Sophie, you don't understand." Emma tried to suck it up, but it felt so damn good to cry that she gave up and sobbed like she hadn't done in years. "I have maybe a hundred dollars in my purse. I can't begin to pay . . ." She buried her head in her hands and wept.

"I guess you'll have to find a job or make something to sell." Sophie motioned toward all the art supplies stacked in the corner of the living room. "The buyer comes out here every few weeks to get Filly's, Arty's, and Josh's work. Produce something that will interest him, and you won't need to depend on Victoria for anything."

"I haven't touched brushes since . . ." A flashback of the last painting she had been working on came to Emma's mind.

"Since when?" Sophie pressured.

"I went to my apartment . . ." She frowned. "The night I went to my apartment and used a knife from the kitchen to slash my painting."

"Why did you do that?" Sophie asked.

"I have no idea. The vision just came to me in a flash. My therapists say I have repressed-memory syndrome. Something happened that I won't remember, but I just now remembered cutting that picture all to pieces," Emma answered.

"What was the picture? Landscape? Portrait?" Sophie pulled her closer to her side.

"White clouds that looked like the snow angels we made one winter when we were little girls. Sunshine behind them and wheat fields ready for harvest on the ground below them," Emma answered as she stared at the picture in her mind's eye. "I was so angry about something that I destroyed the picture."

"What did you do then?" Sophie asked.

"I don't remember much past that. The next thing that comes to mind is being in an institution. Nancy would call this a breakthrough," Emma said as she reached up over her head and picked up the phone from its base.

"Who are you calling?" Sophie asked.

Emma's hands shook, and her insides quivered. This was Friday. Jeffrey would be driving her mother to get her weekly massage and facial at this time, so Emma called her cell phone number.

"Hello, who is this?" Victoria asked.

"It's Emma." The acrid taste of chocolate cereal mixed with stomach acid stuck in her throat, threatening to come up at any second, but she swallowed it down. Another vision popped into her head. She was leaning over the side of a bed covered in satin sheets and throwing up all over a white fur rug. She didn't ever remember being in that room before. Was that the reason she hated the feel of satin?

"Are you ready to come home?" Victoria asked. "If not, we have nothing to talk about."

Was this tough love? Emma wondered as she punched the speaker button. Knowing that Sophie was close by and could hear gave her the courage to go on. "Why did you cancel my credit cards? Did you freeze my bank account, too? How am I supposed to live?" she blurted out.

"If you want to make your own decisions or depend on Sophia to make them for you, then you can figure that out on your own. I'll be damned if that gutter child gets a dime of my money," Victoria told her.

"But that money is from Grandmother," Emma said. "It's *my* money, not yours, and Sophie is a famous artist. She doesn't need my money."

"Don't sass me." Victoria raised her voice an octave. "When you came home from college in a mental mess, we thought it best to let me handle your affairs, including the money that *my* mother left you. You should have stayed in the wellness center until I could find you a nice place where you could get help the rest of your life."

"You were going to send me away forever?" Emma whispered. "Has this been your plan all along? To finally convince everyone that I had lost my mind and needed to be put away?"

"It was for your own good. You would have other people who had problems like yours to visit with in group therapy every day, and folks who could take care of you. Your father is retiring this summer, and I'm planning to sell the company. You would never be able to run a huge corporation, so why keep it? We sure can't leave you alone to fend for yourself, especially while we travel, and you're not in any shape to go with us," Victoria told her. "We would come and visit you often in your new assisted-care center, and we would bring you home for Christmas. When you wake up from this folly and return to us, we will take you to see the place. It's really quite pleasant."

"So, the bottom line is come home and get locked up somewhere for the rest of my life, or stay where I am with no money?" Emma asked.

"I don't like your tone," Victoria said, "and Jeffrey is parking now, so I should be going."

"You didn't answer my question." Emma was amazed that she hadn't thrown up.

"Why should I? You know the answer, but to make things perfectly clear, yes, Emma, that's the bottom line. Call me when you want Jeffrey to come and get you, or else be independent and make your own decisions with no money. But that's not your choice forever: you've only got a few weeks to make up your mind, and then I'll fix it so you can't come home again—ever. I suppose I can reach you at this number in case of a dire emergency?" Victoria asked.

"That's right." Emma felt her chin start to quiver and pursed her lips to make it stop.

From the sound of a car door opening and slamming and Jeffrey's voice saying something about returning in two hours, Victoria must have been going into the salon. "Like I just said, this is not an open-ended offer. Understand me when I say that you only have four weeks to come home, or else I will transfer all your money into my account."

"I think that's called theft," Sophie said.

"I expect that's Sophia. She's always been a thorn in my side. I wouldn't be surprised if she's not your half sister. Goodbye." Victoria ended the call.

Emma threw the phone across the room. "She's lost it, Sophie. She's crazy, and I'm the sane one. Looking back, I think she's planned this from the time I was twelve years old, or maybe from the day I was born. How could I not have seen this sooner? Even if Rebel and Daddy were having an affair, you were already born by then."

"My father is dead," Sophie assured her. "He was in the army when he and Mama met at a party. They had a wild two weeks, and he went back overseas, where he died without ever even knowing she was pregnant. Mama had no idea that my father was married when she had the fling with him. And she didn't start working for Victoria until I was four years old," Sophie said.

"I wish Rebel had been my mother," Emma said. "I don't know why Mother has to be so controlling, and I'm so sorry I can't repay you for all those things you ordered for me."

"Shake it off," Sophie said. "You don't need money right now. You just need to get stronger and be that girl who fought to get to stay in public school with me or for me to get to be tutored with you. Go get dressed and take that walk you talked about. This is a great place to think. Take my phone with you and write down the landline number in case you need me."

Emma wanted to shake her head to clear all those memories she had locked away and suddenly remember why she had cut up that painting. For the first time, she wanted—no, she *needed*— to face her fears, and yet all she had were flashes that popped into her head at the strangest times.

Like that memory of leaning over the bed with satin sheets and throwing up on a white rug. Victoria loved satin sheets and had them on most beds, but there had never been a white rug in the Merrill mansion, so where did that vision come from?

It's only been a day. It's been more than a decade since you buried whatever happened, so don't expect for it all to come flooding back in twenty-four hours, the voice in her head said.

"If I was as strong as Sophie, I wouldn't have repressed memories," she whispered as she put on the jeans she'd worn the day before and then opened Sophie's closet door and chose a T-shirt with paint stains on it. She found an old pair of Sophie's cowboy boots that looked like they'd fit and slipped her feet into them. When she made it to the living room, Sophie tossed a wide-brimmed hat toward her. "You'll need this to keep the sun from burning your face. You're white as the driven snow right now."

"Thanks." Emma caught it midair. "I haven't been out by myself since the day I went to the park. Which way do I go?"

Sophie laced her fingers in Emma's and led her out to the porch. She slipped her cell phone in one of Emma's back pockets along with a piece of paper with the house phone number on it and stuffed a bottle of water into the other one. "There's no wrong way to go. Enjoy the walk. If you get lost, I'll send Josh on his four-wheeler to rescue you. If you're not back by dinner this evening, I'll send out the National Guard."

Emma giggled. "Wish me luck." She gave Sophie a brief nod and took the first step off the porch. That's where her bravado ended. Her boots filled up with concrete, and she panicked. Her heart pounded so hard that it sounded like thunder in her ears.

You girls are going to be famous artists someday. You are both strong. I can see that from the way you use your imagination when you color. Rebel's voice came to mind. She couldn't disappoint Rebel, so she took a step and then another one, repeating to herself that she was a strong woman. In half an hour she allowed herself to look over her shoulder and was surprised to see that the trailer looked like a toy out there in the distance.

All kinds of cacti surrounded her, some with beautiful purple blooms, others with yellow and hot-pink blossoms. At home, the gardener kept the grass so thick that it was like walking on velvet, but here, sparse green stuff that resembled grass grew in clumps, interspersed with wildflowers. Maybe she shouldn't compare the two places, but she couldn't help it. There, she was stifled and agitated most of the time. Here, there was stark beauty and a modicum of peace.

She caught a movement from the corner of her eye and spun around in an instant adrenaline rush. She was about to tear off back to the trailer when she saw the little rabbit hopping toward a thicket of trees. No one was following her. She didn't have anything to worry about except getting a sunburn.

"I'm strong," she reminded herself.

Funny how just twenty-four hours at Hummingbird Lane had made her remember things that made no sense and also let go of a few fears. Why here, and why now?

She pulled the water bottle from her pocket and took a long drink and then plodded out toward the mountains. She'd gone a few hundred feet when a slight breeze out of the south kicked up and brought the haunting sound of music with it. She removed the hat and cocked her head to track where the noise came from.

She tucked her hair behind her ear and started walking to the west. As she drew nearer, she recognized the tune as "Red River Valley." One of the boys at her college used to sit on the lawn and play the harmonica, and he often played that song. She kept walking toward it until she saw Josh sitting on the ground with a sketch pad in front of him and a harmonica at his mouth.

Spots of brilliant color in the cactus blooms dotted the landscape all around him. Purple, red, yellow, and shades of pink looked like splashes of paint on a blank canvas. She studied the yellow bloom on a cow's tongue cactus closest to her and thought about how it would look on a small canvas. "I can't do that—not yet. I'm not ready," she muttered.

The sound of the music Josh made with that simple instrument sank down deep into her soul. Memories of being somewhat free that semester in college flooded over her, and right then, standing near a thicket of scrub oak trees with cacti all around her, she felt stronger than she had in years.

"I'm beginning to think that Mother really was trying to make me believe I couldn't survive on my own," she whispered. "I bet it was so that she could sell the company instead of passing it down to me like Grandmother said she was to do."

She stood as still as possible and listened to him play. Out there in the raw earth, where everything struggled for a place, Josh's music was the most beautiful she'd ever heard. He finally put the instrument back in his pocket, picked up his sketch pad, and began to draw. No matter how hard she squinted, she couldn't see what he was working on. She took a step forward, but that was as far as her newly found strength would allow her to go. Finally, she turned around and started back toward the tiny dots that were the trailers in the far distance.

When that antsy feeling that someone was close by came over Josh, he put his harmonica away and picked up his sketch pad. A coyote was probably hiding in the copse of young scrub oak trees about fifty yards behind him and trying to decide whether to have Josh for a midmorning snack since he couldn't find a rabbit. Every hair on Josh's neck stood up until he glanced up at the rearview mirror of his four-wheeler, which was parked close to him, and saw that it was a dark-haired woman. What would some stranger be doing out here on his land? He'd told at least a dozen developers that he wasn't interested in selling even one acre of what he owned. Dealing with those people made him nervous, but he could and would say no again.

He squinted until his eyes were nothing but slits before he finally figured out that it was Sophie's friend Emma. From what Sophie had said, she was an introvert like he was, but he didn't know much more than that. His mother, a psychologist, and his father, a physician, had had test after neuropsych test run on him from the time he was four years old. The final prognosis was that he was simply one of those smart people who did not adapt to society. His only niche in life seemed to be the pictures that he loved to draw.

That day he was working on a picture of a hawk coming in for a landing. Dark clouds hovered behind the bird with its widespread wings, but there in the pupils of his eyes were the reflections of a sunrise.

Do your homework. Drawing pictures is never going to get you anywhere. His father's big, booming voice was so loud that he dropped his pen in the dirt and covered his ears.

He was supposed to be their wonder child, but what they got was a kid who didn't talk until he was four years old, who hated school and wound up liking to spend time with his grandfather and his grandfather's old buddy Harry more than anything other than drawing pictures.

"Who would have thought that one day my grandfather's best friend would leave me a fortune? His will said that my dad didn't need his money since he and my mom were making their own millions. Dad was furious, but he couldn't do anything about it." Josh talked to himself as he picked up his pen and gathered up his supplies to push all the internal voices away. "Now I don't have to listen to my father yell at me." He got on the four-wheeler and started back to his trailer to make himself a sandwich for lunch. When he got closer, he could see Emma going up the stairs to the back porch of Sophie's trailer.

Sophie waved at Emma and then went inside to get two longneck bottles of beer. By the time she got back, Emma was sitting on the porch. She set one beer down on the wide porch rail next to Emma and took a long drink from the bottle in her hands.

"How was your walk?" Sophie asked.

"Amazing," Emma answered. "Did you ever watch *Big Bang Theory*?"

"Did you? I thought that Victoria . . ." Sophie paused to regroup.

"Sometimes when she was gone, Daddy and I would watch it together in his study. That was one room she didn't have control over," Emma said. "Have you seen it?"

"I have all twelve seasons of it on discs," Sophie said. "I brought those and *Castle* with me. We don't get many television stations out here. Why are you asking?"

"Leonard Hofstadter, a character in that show, reminds me of Josh." Emma slumped down in the chair and picked up the beer, turning it to look at the label. "I don't drink."

"Because you don't like it or because Victoria said you couldn't?" Sophie asked. "And why does Josh remind you of Leonard?"

"He's not tall and he's a little backward, like me. And he wears those black-rimmed glasses and has a square face," Emma answered. "I don't know why I don't drink. Mother insisted that I have a glass of champagne when we had guests one evening. The first sip put me into a panic attack, but maybe it was just something in the champagne that sets me off. Do you think it has something to do with the nightmares?" She stared hard at the bottle in her hand for a moment, then took a sip. "This is pretty good. It doesn't feel like it's going to make my chest go into spasms."

Spasms? Sophie wanted to ask a million questions, but patience was the key here. If Emma was ever going to truly get well, she needed space to figure out things on her own.

"Tell me more about your walk. Did you see anything to paint?" Sophie asked.

"Too many things to count, and it was wonderful to take a walk by myself," Emma answered. "I have to admit that a simple little bunny almost put me in flight mode, though. I thought for sure Mother had sent either Jeffrey or some medical people to drag me back to Dallas. Everything is different here than back there. I've always felt so cooped up there, like I'm being smothered or drowning in deep water. Here I feel free."

"I'm with you, sister." Sophie sat down in the other chair. "When I come here, it's like I'm coming home."

"I saw Josh and heard him playing a harmonica. The music was beautiful. I wanted to see what he was drawing, but I didn't want to disturb him," Emma said.

"Do you like this feeling of freedom? Is it going to help you figure out what happened to make you have these regressed memories?" Sophie asked.

"Repressed, not regressed," Emma said, "although I suppose they're both right. About these snowbirds, as you called them. Are Filly and Arty snowbirds? Do they ever leave?"

"No, they're the permanent residents," Sophie answered. "There's three retired couples from up in one of the northern states who come down here for the winter months. They usually arrive in late October and stay through March."

"Does Josh own all six trailers? If you've already told me this, I'm sorry." Emma took another sip of her beer.

"Yes, he does," Sophie replied. "His grandfather had a close friend who died a few years ago and left Josh a huge fortune. His parents weren't happy about Harry giving Josh a big inheritance, but Josh was a grown man and Harry had had no kids, so there was nothing they could do about it. He used part of the money to buy this place. I don't know a lot about his background, other than he's super shy and a terrific artist. You're right about him looking like Leonard and being kind of like that kid. He's got a kind heart and a sweet nature like the character in the show." She stood up and started into the house. "I'm going to make a plate of nachos for lunch. Want me to make enough for two?"

"Yes, what can I do to help?" Emma asked.

"It's a one-person job, so just sit here and enjoy the view." Sophie went inside but left the sliding glass door open so she could talk to Emma without yelling.

"Sophie, last night I dreamed about that angel picture again. I was wearing scrubs, gray ones, and I never wore that color in any of the centers that Mother put me in, not even once," Emma said.

"Did you figure out why you were so angry? Or if you ever even painted a picture like that?" Sophie raised her voice above the noise of opening a bag of tortilla chips.

"Not why I was so angry at the world, or even one person. Maybe it was Mother." She shrugged. "I just can't remember anything other than hurting . . ."

"Physical pain or mental?" Sophie asked.

Emma frowned as if she was trying to remember, and then she put a hand on her thigh and one on a breast. "It was real pain, not in my head. I felt like my chest was bruised, and my legs hurt so bad."

"Did Victoria finally snap and hit you?" Sophie asked.

"No." The frown got even deeper. "She rules with an iron hand, but it's through manipulation, not violence. I was so mad when I first got back to my apartment, and I did really paint that picture. In our art class we were supposed to do something with kind of a sci-fi theme for our final grade. I don't like that kind of thing, so I asked the professor if I could do a cloud like an angel. He must have agreed, because it was right there on the easel in my apartment. I had to have already showed it to him and gotten a grade on it, because that was the last thing I had to do before the semester ended," Emma said. "When I slashed it all to pieces, I cut my hand on the knife. I couldn't go back to the hospital or Mother would be angry with me. She was quick to send me away to one institution after another, but she never wanted to take me to the emergency room. If I got sick, she called a doctor to come to the house."

"You said *back* to the hospital," Sophie said. "Why were you at the hospital originally?"

Emma shook her head. "I don't know. I don't think I was injured, but I had a fear of going back, so I laid down on the floor and cried myself to sleep."

Sophie covered the bottom of a platter with chips, poured nacho cheese over them, and added sliced jalapeño peppers to the top. Then she popped the whole platter into the microwave to warm the cheese and thought about what Emma had told her. That had to have been the night that something terrible had happened. She carried the platter of nachos out to the porch and set it on the plastic table between the two chairs.

Emma picked up a chip and popped it into her mouth. "Why would I be wearing scrubs in the dream, and why was I crying? I don't think I hated the picture that much."

"Maybe you're mixing two different times into one memory or dream." Sophie sat down and reached for her first chip. A wave of worry washed over her. Was she about to hear something that meant Emma needed more help than Sophie could provide?

"I don't think so," Emma said. "I've worn blue and pink scrubs in centers, but never gray. When a person is a depressive, gray isn't a good color for them."

"You picked up a lot of stuff not to have gotten much help in those facilities," Sophie said.

"I guess I did. But until now"—Emma took a sip of her beer—"it's hard to explain, but somewhere down deep inside, I know something had happened right before I slashed the picture, and it wasn't right. The therapist who came to the house after I ran away that day told me that I had something like post-traumatic stress disorder and wanted to know if I'd been hurt or abused. Other than Mother's constant need to control me, I couldn't think of anything but those nightmares and the need to get away from a big house. I think that I'm afraid to remember because I know it's going to be painful. Not hurt like when I felt like my chest and legs hurt, but that mental stuff that might put me into a place I can't ever get out of. Right now, it's in a box and locked away."

"What changed your mind about wanting to get past all this and live an ordinary life?" Sophie didn't care if Emma's normal was more like Josh's, as long as she was happy.

"You did." Emma flashed a smile that reached her eyes. "You cared enough to march into that room and rescue me."

"Why do you think you were so mad at the angels in the clouds?" Sophie hoped like hell she wasn't pressing too much.

"Because painting was my salvation and my escape from Mother, and something took it away from me," Emma said between bites. "I don't know why she let me out on a leash rather than hiring more tutors for my college education, but it was wonderful to be free. And I even got to see you a few times. I wouldn't have done anything to jeopardize that, so something must have happened that I couldn't face."

"Were you dating someone?" Sophie asked. "Did y'all break up or something?"

"I didn't date in college," she replied. "I was never sure how to act around guys. After I was discharged from the first place Mother put me in, she made me go out with a guy that was a son or a nephew"—she frowned again—"of one of her friends. I can't remember the connection, but she said he was wealthy and rather nice-looking, and I needed to think about getting married and producing an heir for the business like she did."

"So, Victoria wanted you to have an 'heir' for the business, did she? That sounds so like her." Sophie air quoted the word *heir*.

"It seemed strange to me, too. She'd constantly told me that I was too shy to ever marry, and then there she was pushing me toward this guy . . ." Emma gasped.

"What?" Sophie asked.

"She just did that to prove that I wasn't capable of a relationship, didn't she?" Emma asked.

"What happened on the date?" Sophie wondered if Emma's state of mind had more to do with Victoria than anything else. Rebel had been right when she called it Munchausen by proxy, only instead of making her daughter sick, Victoria had done her best to drive Emma crazy. She must hate her daughter a lot to do that to her, or else she was just a manipulative bitch who didn't want Emma to have the company when Victoria either retired or died.

"He tried to kiss me good night, and I had a panic attack," Emma answered. "Then Mother told me that she knew I wouldn't be able to handle a date, and that I would be seeing the therapist twice a week from then on."

Sophie stood up, rounded the small table, and wrapped Emma up in her arms. "I wish you had run away and come to live with me and Mama."

"Me too," Emma said, "but Mother would have found me, and she would have been so mad."

Sophie went back to her chair and together they finished off the nachos in comfortable silence.

"You cooked lunch. I'll get dessert. I saw some Fudgsicles in the freezer." Emma picked up the empty plate and carried it inside with her. "Tell me more about your college stuff. Did you ever slash a picture into ribbons?"

"Nope, not one time." Sophie giggled. "But I have to admit I thought about it more than once when I couldn't get the effect I wanted."

Emma returned and handed Sophie an ice cream bar. She sat down and took a bite of hers. "Whatever happened is right there at the edge of my mind, but I can't grasp it. Maybe it wasn't meant for me to remember. Maybe I'm just supposed to find happiness without the memories."

"When it's time, it will come to you. Your mind is probably waiting until you are strong enough to face it," Sophie told her. "Did you have a car accident? Maybe that's why you were in gray scrubs. You had a bad wreck. They had to cut your clothes off at the hospital, and they sent you home in scrubs."

"My car was just fine. I drove it home, but Mother traded it in for a new one," Emma answered.

"Why would she do that?" Sophie asked.

"Jeffrey couldn't get the horrible smell out of

it. Mother thought maybe a field rat had gotten inside it and died. I always thought that my soul had bled to death in the back seat." Emma had been about to take a bite of the ice cream, but her hand stopped midair. "I *was* at the hospital. I *remember* a lady nurse helping me remove my clothes and telling me it wasn't my fault. That was the smell of blood in the car. The seats were black fabric, so it wouldn't have showed."

"What wasn't your fault?" Sophie asked.

Emma shook her head. "I don't know. I can get a flash of myself lying on a hospital bed with curtains around me, and even that much makes me jittery."

"Are you sure that you were not ever in an emergency room when you were a kid?" Sophie suggested.

Emma cut her eyes around at Sophie. "You know I was never allowed to do anything that might get me hurt. The only time I felt free was when Rebel watched us."

"Then that rules out the idea that you might be mixing up a trip to the hospital in your youth with the business of slashing the painting." Sophie blinked back tears and tried to swallow down a lump the size of a grapefruit. Emma's freedom— her ability to face whatever happened to her—was tied up with the feelings she had when they were together. Sophie sent up a silent prayer that she wouldn't make a mess of the responsibility.

Chapter Four

The warm shower water beat down on Sophie's back, easing the sore muscles in her shoulders from painting all day. A visual popped into her head of a tiny shower in the bathroom of her dorm back at the beginning of the second semester of her freshman year. That time, she had turned on the water and then slid down the back wall to sit with her knees pulled up against her chest. Her salty tears had blended with the warm water until she couldn't cry anymore.

Had Emma gotten pregnant that first semester of college, too? Coming from her background, she would have felt even more guilty than Sophie still did. Sophie had never told anyone about that time in her life, not even Rebel, and she couldn't imagine Emma having to tell Victoria such a thing.

Like mother, like daughter, the voice in her head taunted. *You were the product of an affair, and then you turned around and did the same thing as your mother.*

"Maybe so," Sophie agreed. "But neither of us knew those sorry bastards were married."

She didn't have to close her eyes to see the

dark-haired artist in her freshman class, or to feel the excitement when he flirted so blatantly with her. He had been brought in as a substitute professor for the six weeks that the regular teacher was on maternity leave. His name was Lucas Deville, and he was from Chicago. Sophie's affair with him lasted the last three weeks he was at the college, and then he was gone. When the teacher returned, she told them that Lucas had gone back to Illinois and had gotten there in time to be present as his wife gave birth to their third child. That was the first that Sophie had heard about the man being married. Standing there under the spray of the water that evening in the trailer, she felt the same guilt that she had felt that day.

She turned off the water and threw back the curtain. She wrapped a towel around her body and another around her hair. Unlike Emma, Sophie could remember every single memory of that time clearly. They were etched into her mind like they had been branded there. Lucas had courted her, seduced her, and then left without ever mentioning a wife or children. Not that she could lay all the blame on him. God only knew how flattered she had been when he paid so much attention to her. She could have said no that night he asked her to go to his apartment for a drink. He had been her teacher, after all.

At Christmastime, Sophie had gone home for

the month and thought she had the flu. Rebel fed her noodle soup and lots of hot tea. When it was time to go back to college, Sophie had kicked the rotten bug and could keep food on her stomach. A week after classes started, she realized that she'd missed a period. She bought a pregnancy test but refused to believe the results when it showed her the positive sign. She went back to the store and bought three more—all turned out positive.

She didn't want to be a single mother. She had a career ahead of her, and yet, she couldn't live with herself if she gave a child away. Her mother had kept her and sacrificed her pride by working for wealthy women who looked down on her and even accused her of affairs like Victoria had. Sophie had woken up every day worrying about what to do, and then, six weeks later, she lost the baby.

She had cried for three days after the trip to the emergency room. In her mind, she had killed her own baby with negative thoughts because she didn't want it to ruin her career. Now, she was thirty-five and her biological clock was ticking louder and louder. Teddy wanted children, but Sophie wasn't sure she deserved to be a mother again.

"Did Emma lose a baby, too?" she muttered as she padded down the hall and into her bedroom.

She dressed in a pair of shorts and an orange tank top, brushed her still-damp hair up into a ponytail and headed out to have supper with Josh, Arty, and Filly. When she reached the living room, she noticed the sliding doors to the back porch were open. Emma was sitting with her bare feet propped up on the railing, and Coco was curled up in her lap.

"Are you coming out for supper?" Sophie eyed Emma closely. Had she had a baby and given it away, then repressed all that pain?

"Is it all right if I stay right here?" Emma looked nervous, but her hands remained still.

"That's perfectly fine. I'll bring you a plate," Sophie told her. "Did you remember anything else today?"

"No, and I don't deserve food brought in for me. I should be strong enough to go out there and eat," Emma said. "I'll get myself a bowl of cereal."

Victoria wouldn't have let Emma have a child. She would have made her have an abortion, and that would have set Emma on an even bigger guilt trip.

"Nonsense," Sophie scolded. "We all understand. You've come a long way in only one day, and if you want to stay in, that's fine. You'll lose Coco in about ten minutes, though. When she hears Arty say grace, she comes running from wherever she is."

"Thank you," Emma said. "This has been the best time of my life, Sophie, and I mean that."

"Good. Maybe I can talk you into doing some paintings pretty soon." Sophie visualized days when she and Emma had lain under the shade trees in the backyard and colored in their books or sketched. Emma was always whistling or humming in those days. Sophie wanted Emma to have those kinds of moments in her life again.

Josh waved when Sophie stepped out onto the porch. "Arty made pot roast tonight, and Filly has apple dumplings with caramel sauce," he yelled across the courtyard.

"Sounds wonderful," Sophie said as she made her way over to the picnic table and took her usual place.

"Is Emma coming out tonight?" Filly asked.

"Not tonight. She's had a big day," Sophie answered. "She's been through a lot, and she's"— she struggled for the right word—"she's really, really shy right now."

Arty said his quick grace and handed a big spoon to Filly. "You can dip the food up."

"Do you think she'll ever feel like joining us?" Josh asked. "Is Coco helping her a little?"

"She's working her way through a lot of problems right now. Whatever they are, she's buried them down deep since she was eighteen years old, and it's real hard for them to surface, and, yes, Josh, I believe Coco is helping her a lot. I just hope that living here among all of us will also help her get over whatever it is that's holding her back from having a real life."

Somedays, Sophie wished that she could bury her own guilt over the relief she'd felt when she had lost her baby. The child would have been a teenager now. That was hard to even imagine.

"Earth to Sophie." Josh chuckled.

"I'm sorry." She shook her head. "I was woolgathering. What did you say?"

"It was me talking to you," Filly answered. "I asked if you'd pass your plate."

"Yes, ma'am." Sophie picked up the disposable plastic plate and handed it to her. "This all looks delicious. I'm starving."

"What do you think happened to Emma?" Arty asked.

"I don't know, but it had to be traumatic enough for her to just let her mother take over her entire life, and that is not a good thing," Sophie answered. "Victoria has controlled Emma her whole life. She was never allowed to make any decisions on her own—clothes, meals, extracurriculars, nothing. When Victoria was away from the house, and Mama and I were in the house, she could be more herself. All she ever got from her mother was criticism, and her dad just went along with whatever Victoria said. I feel so guilty that I didn't make a bigger effort to see her before now."

Josh nodded several times. "I can so relate to that. My parents are still disappointed in me. I was a genius, so I was supposed to force myself to use my brain for something other than drawing pictures with pen and ink."

Sophie thought of Rebel, who never told her that her dream of being an artist was stupid. "I'm finding out that I had the best mother in the world," she said and then tried to change the subject. "Arty, how have you outrun the women all these years? Any man that can cook like you do should have been dragged to the altar years ago."

"He can cook, but he's not got a romantic bone in his body," Filly answered.

"Well, neither do you," Arty snapped back at her. "If you couldn't bake, and I didn't have a sweet tooth, I would have strangled you years ago."

"Oh, hush," Filly shot across the table at him. "Now, back to Emma. Could she have been molested or maybe seen some horrendous crime that scared the bejesus right out of her?"

Sophie hoped that neither one of those things had happened. But Emma had mentioned going into a panic when her date tried to kiss her good night, so maybe Filly had hit on something important.

"You've been watching too many of them cop shows," Arty fussed at Filly.

She narrowed her eyes at him. "Probably so, but I know at least forty ways to kill you and bury you out there in the cactus field with no one the wiser, so maybe I've seen just enough of them to get away with a crime." She turned back to Sophie. "Whatever it might be, she needs our help. You should take her some good hot supper before it gets cold."

"Much as I hate to admit it, she's right. We'll do whatever it takes to help Emma." Arty dipped up a plate of food. "You'll need to carry that with both hands. I'll take the dumpling up to the door for you."

Sophie took the plate from him. "Thank you, and thank all of you for understanding."

Arty reached for the dessert, but Josh beat him to it.

"I'll take it." Josh stood up. "You're still eating, and I'm finished, except for dessert."

"Thanks." Arty nodded. "If this old woman wouldn't argue with me, I'd be done already."

"Humph." Filly almost snorted, but her eyes twinkled.

Sophie loved the easy banter between Arty and Filly. And, of course, she loved the communal meal every night—which reminded her, she needed to give Josh her share of the grocery bill as well as her personal grocery list by the next morning.

"Come on inside," she said as she and Josh reached the porch. "You and Arty will be going to the store tomorrow. I've got my list ready."

Josh followed her into the trailer and set the bowl on the counter, but he looked as nervous as the only one-legged rooster at a coyote convention. Just thinking about one of her mother's sayings put a smile on Sophie's face.

"Hey, Emma," she yelled out to the back porch. "Is there anything food-wise that you want for next week? Josh goes to the store for us on Saturday."

"Chocolate cookies," Emma said.

Sophie added that to her list and handed it to Josh, plus an envelope with cash in it. "Thanks again for doing this for us."

Josh cocked his head to one side and weighed the envelope of cash in his hand. "This feels a little heavy."

"There's two of us eating, so it should be," Sophie told him.

"That's not necessary," Josh said.

"Yep, it is. Now, get on out of here and go eat your dessert. I'll be back out there in a few minutes for mine." Sophie motioned toward the door.

"Yes, ma'am." He pushed his wire-rimmed glasses up on his nose and closed the door behind him.

"Supper is served," Sophie called out. "Might be easier to eat if you come inside and sit on a barstool. Coco will try to share it with you if you stay out there."

"I still don't feel like I deserve this," Emma said as she made her way to the bar and slid onto a stool. "Oh, but it does look good. Is that an apple dumpling? I haven't had one of those in years." She picked up the plastic fork and dug into it.

"I'm going back outside to have my dessert with the folks. Enjoy the dinner."

"Tell the cooks thank you for me. This is amazing," Emma muttered around the food in her mouth.

Chapter Five

Emma ate. She slept. She and Sophie talked about paintings, colors, and their childhood, but she didn't even venture beyond the chairs on the back porch. Just the thought of sitting down to supper with people still terrified her. As she was getting ready for bed on Friday evening, she noticed a framed quote above the light switch in her tiny bedroom. She stopped and read it, then went back and read it another time. The last two lines really appealed to her: *Surrender to the beauty of revealing yourself to yourself, and to the ones who saw you before you saw you.*

"Sophie says I'm strong, so I'm going to do my best to believe her and surrender to that," Emma whispered as she pulled back the covers and crawled into bed. "Can I really reveal myself to others? I feel antsy tonight, but I haven't had a sleeping pill since we got here. I don't need one now." She closed her eyes, but her mind kept replaying that dream about the satin sheets. Her mother always had satin sheets on her bed, so maybe she was thinking about something that happened when she was just a little girl. Had she walked in on them when they were making love?

No, that couldn't be right. Her mother and father had slept in separate rooms. Maybe her mother had yelled at her when she'd tried to crawl into bed with her during a storm.

She shook her head. Neither of those could be right. They locked their bedroom doors at night, and it was Viola, her nanny, who took care of her, right up until she was in the sixth grade. That was the year Victoria announced that Emma had outgrown the need for a babysitter. Emma had been glad to see Viola leave, because at the end of every day, the woman tattled to Victoria if Emma did one thing or ate anything that would upset her mother.

She finally slung back the sheet, turned on the bedside lamp, and got out of bed. She hadn't finished the apple dumpling that Sophie had brought her for supper, so she started to the kitchen for a midnight snack and noticed the framed piece on the wall again. She stopped and read the whole thing: *Love will put you face-to-face with endless obstacles. It will ask you to reveal the parts of yourself you tirelessly work at hiding. It will ask you to find compassion for yourself and receive what it is you are convinced you are not worthy of. Love will always demand more. Surrender to being seen and being loved. Surrender to the beauty of revealing yourself to yourself, and to the ones who saw you before you saw you.*

It was signed *Vienna Pharaon*. Emma made a mental note to look that person up on the internet. She either had gone through something traumatic herself or else she had an amazing understanding of folks like Emma.

Compassion. Worthy. Revealing. Those words kept going through Emma's mind as she got the rest of the dumpling out of the refrigerator and carried it out to the porch. The few times she'd tried to go outside by herself in the dark after she had come home from college, she had had a panic attack. That night she eased down into her chair, but her chest didn't tighten up and she had no trouble breathing. Out in the distance, a coyote howled, and another one farther out answered him. The mountain, more than a mile out there, was a black blob with a half-moon hanging above it. A single star left a million others behind, trailed by a long tail as it streaked across the sky.

Sophie had told her when they were children that you got a wish when you saw a star falling out of the sky. The only other time that Emma had seen one before that night was the evening before she went off to college. That night she wished for the hundredth time that she would someday be a famous artist.

She watched until the shooting star was completely gone and then shut her eyes and wished that she could remember those repressed memories. Not knowing was harder than facing the fears—or was it? She frowned at the thought. Maybe she wasn't as strong as Sophie thought she was, or even as that quote on her wall talked about—could she reveal parts of herself that she worked so hard at hiding? Would knowing what they were destroy her altogether?

"You couldn't sleep, either?" Josh's voice coming out of the dark startled her so badly that she almost jumped up and ran into the trailer.

He was standing at the end of the porch steps, and Coco chose that moment to jump up into her lap. She remembered what she had wished for and wondered if fate had sent Josh to help her.

"Yes. I mean, no. What I mean is that I couldn't sleep." She hoped that she didn't sound like a total idiot. "So, you have trouble sleeping, too?"

"Yep," he answered. "Sometimes a walk helps me calm down. I have trouble settling down at night. No, that's not right. I have the same trouble in the daytime, but my artwork helps me with that."

"ADHD?" she asked.

"They tested me for that and thought I might be in the higher-functioning range of the autism spectrum, but the tests were all in the normal range." He sat down on the bottom step. "My mother tried to diagnose me with her own psych tests and finally decided I'm socially challenged. Daddy said I was just lazy. Mother said I could overcome it with lots of therapy."

"Mother has always said that I'm antisocial and basically that I can't take care of myself," Emma blurted out and wished she could take the words back. She didn't talk to very many people, most especially to a man she didn't even know, and she surely didn't tell anyone personal things like that, but there was something about Josh that she kind of trusted.

Josh chuckled. "Well, I'm that, too. Probably the reason I'm uptight tonight is that Arty and I are going to the store tomorrow. I hate to leave the trailer park, but Arty is right. I need to face my fears at least once a week."

"I'm afraid of men." Emma's voice seemed to have a mind of its own.

"I'm uncomfortable around men *and* women," Josh admitted.

"Why?" Emma asked. This wasn't a contest between them.

"I'm afraid they'll make fun of me, like the kids did when I went to public school. My folks finally hired a tutor and I finished my schooling at home." He didn't look at her but at the porch floor.

"I had the exact same life, but Sophie is helping me to be strong. We probably both should tell folks to go to hell if they don't like us." A surge of protectiveness shot through her. She had always wished she had the courage to say those words to the kids who bullied her because she was so shy, or better yet, to her mother.

"Aw." Josh grinned. "I can't do that. It just ain't in me. Accepting who I am has been one of the good things about living out here in the boonies."

"I hope that I can do the same thing someday." Emma's tone sounded wistful even to her own ears. "I sure like it here. There's something eerily peaceful about this place, even at night."

"Does the dark bother you?" Josh asked.

"Maybe," she answered. "How about you?"

"I love the night. When I was a little boy, I used to crawl out on the porch roof and pretend that I was the only one in the whole world. Just me and the moon and the stars," Josh answered. "No one was ever mean to me in the night."

Emma couldn't agree with him there. Whatever had terrified her had happened at night. Even though Victoria scolded her for being a big baby, she still had to have a night-light or she couldn't sleep at all.

"I should be going. Nice visitin' with you." Josh stood up and waved over his shoulder as he disappeared into the darkness.

Whatever I don't want to remember happened at night, and it had to do with a man and satin sheets. She rubbed Coco's fur from her head to the end of her long, fluffy tail. *I know that much, but the rest is a mystery. Josh is a nice person. I'm not afraid of him, but maybe my fear of men has been because I was assaulted.*

115

The cat purred loudly, then jumped down off her lap and ran in the same direction that Josh had gone. Emma stood up, went back inside, put on her jeans with the borrowed nightshirt she was wearing for the second night, and shoved her feet down into the cowboy boots beside her bed. *Courage.* That's what the quote on the wall said. If she couldn't sleep, she'd see if Josh's remedy to take a walk in the night would help. She made it to the bottom step before she lost her courage and turned around to go back to her chair.

Then Josh appeared out of the darkness again. "I didn't go far, but I'm not ready to turn in just yet. Want to stretch your legs a little bit?"

"Maybe," she said. "I don't know. Probably not."

"How about just once around the trailer park? That might help and you won't be more than a stone's throw from your own place," he suggested. "I'll be glad to go with you."

You are strong. You can make your own decisions. Sophie's voice was clear even if it was just in her head. Josh seemed like a nice person, but the thought of leaving the safety of the porch made her chest tighten, but it was time. If she wasn't going to do anything but sit in a trailer, she might as well be back at the center.

"Okay." She took several deep breaths and stopped just short of leaving the porch steps.

"You haven't seen the back sides of the trailers

yet," Josh said. "They're not all just alike. Sophie's place here is a two bedroom, but that one"—he pointed—"is a three bedroom. The snowbirds that come in late October to winter and rent that trailer are the Howard couple. They make quilts while they're here. They each use a bedroom as a craft room."

Emma didn't even realize she was off the porch and on the ground until they had passed that trailer and he was pointing at the next one. "This one is a lot like your place, only the bedrooms are on either end of the trailer. The Johnston couple stay here. They're into making Christmas tree ornaments from wood, mostly scrub oak, that they find out there in the desert." He waved toward the land between the park and the mountains.

"Christmas tree ornaments?" She could hardly believe that she was walking beside a man and didn't feel like running away and hiding, or that she was enjoying the short trip around the trailers.

"Yep, they sell them online," he answered. "He's got a little scroll saw and she's pretty good at painting them."

"Who stays in Sophie's trailer in the winter?" she asked.

"The Bluestones from up north in one of the Dakotas. They collect bird feathers and make jewelry out of them," he answered.

There went any hope of Emma renting it on a permanent basis like Filly and Arty did. She was amazed that the thought even entered her head, but if she was going to be independent like Victoria said, she would need to find a place of her own and a job.

"This is my place. It's the smallest of all the trailers and only has one bedroom. I'm more comfortable in small places than big ones," Josh said.

"Did you grow up in a huge house?" Emma asked.

Josh nodded. "It overwhelmed me, so when I bought this place, I chose the smallest of the trailers, and I've never regretted it."

She could well understand what he was saying. She wouldn't regret living in a trailer the rest of her life, either. "I was raised in a huge house, too. I had my own suite of rooms on the second floor, and my nanny had her own rooms right next to mine. The house has always overpowered me . . . ," she said, "or maybe it overwhelmed me. Whatever the word is, I've always wanted something small.

"I wanted to build one of those tiny houses, but my mother said no," she continued. "You've got a table back here, too. Is this where you work?"

"Sometimes," he answered, "when I don't need to be by myself. On the other days, I take my equipment out toward the mountains and work out there."

They rounded the curve, and Josh whispered, "This is Filly's place. She and Arty live here permanently. I'm glad they do. They're like grandparents to me."

"Oh, my!" Emma gasped when she saw dozens of hummingbird feeders hanging across the back of the long trailer.

"That's where we get the name," Josh explained in a serious tone. "Hummingbird Trailer Park is located on Hummingbird Lane. In most places, that species shows up in the spring and then migrates in the winter, but we're just far enough south that we have them all year. We buy sugar in twenty-five-pound bags so we can keep them happy."

"What's with the long table and chairs?" Emma asked.

"That's where Filly works when the weather is nice. She loves company, so anytime you feel like it, just pop around here and watch her paint." Josh kept walking.

"And this last one is Arty's place. You can see that he has a workbench. He does metal art, and he has a welder to help with some of it. Things get pretty messy in our backyards, but it doesn't matter. We're all artists of one kind or another." He rounded the end of Arty's trailer. "And that's our supper table. Want to sit awhile?"

Emma covered a yawn with her hand. "Maybe another time. I'm really sleepy right now. Thank you for the tour."

"You are very welcome. I'll walk you to your porch, since you ain't too fond of the dark," he said.

"That's so sweet of you." She smiled.

When they reached the bottom of the steps, he backed off several feet and said, "Good night, Emma. Feel free to roam around anywhere you want. You are safe here."

"Thanks again." She nodded and opened the unlocked door.

"Hey, are you all right?" Sophie rubbed her eyes as she poured a glass of milk.

"I couldn't sleep, so Josh showed me around the trailer park, but I can hardly hold my eyes open now." Emma yawned again. "Did you have trouble sleeping, too? And why is the door unlocked?"

"We never bother locking doors out here," Sophie answered. "If you'll remember, we drove five miles on a county road to get to the trailer park, and Hummingbird Lane is a dead-end road. Teddy called. It's already breakfast time in France. He's done over there and is flying to New York today. Hopefully I'll get to see him in a couple of weeks."

If Emma ever did have a relationship with a guy, she wanted it to be just like what Sophie had. She wanted to have the same gleam in her eyes as Sophie had.

"Will I be in the way when he comes to see you?" Emma asked.

"No, honey, by then you should feel right at home here in the trailer. Teddy will pick me up and we'll go on a little mini vacation for a few days or maybe a week if he can be away that long. I'll leave the SUV for you in case you get stir-crazy and want to take a drive," Sophie said. "But that's only if he can take the time off."

"How do you manage a long-distance relationship like that?" Emma asked.

"It works for both of us. We love each other, but we're kind of married to our careers," Sophie answered. "Want a glass of milk before you try to get some sleep?"

"No, I'm good." Emma went to her room, kicked off the boots and her jeans, and got back into her bed. She closed her eyes and went right to sleep.

Chapter Six

Emma couldn't remember a time when Victoria had not preached—more like drilled into her—that the clothes make the woman.

"She is so right," she said to her reflection in the floor-length mirror hanging beside the living room door. "And this is the woman that's been hiding inside me for years."

"What was that?" Sophie asked as she came out of the bathroom with a towel around her body.

"The clothes do make the woman." Emma twirled around and checked her reflection from the back. "I love being able to order things and have them delivered right to the house."

"That orange tank top matches the gauze skirt just perfect. That bright color puts a tint of pink in your cheeks," Sophie told her. "Are you going to eat with us tonight—no pressure, but you look so pretty."

Emma took a deep breath and let it out very slowly. She wanted to go eat with Josh, but to do that, she would have to get over her fear of strangers. "I'm not afraid of Josh. I was comfortable with him when we took a walk the other night. Part of me says I can do this without knowing why I fell apart, but the other part wants to know the truth so that I won't be afraid to go eat with nice people."

"You ever think that hiding from the truth is what put you where you are right now?" Sophie asked.

"No, but you could be right." Emma nodded. "And I want to be stronger physically"—she took a step away from the mirror—"and mentally healthy."

Sophie turned around and started for her bedroom. "The first step in getting well is facing the problem head-on."

"You really sound like a therapist now, but I know you are right. To get through the present and into the future, I have to figure out the past. That's what has put me where I am. I wish I'd faced it when it happened." *Be careful what you wish for—you just might get it.* She remembered her father saying that when she was a teenager. She tried to think about why he had said it, but nothing came to mind.

She wondered if he was talking about the fact that he had married Victoria for money. Did he ever wish that he had never wanted to live in luxury, or feel that he'd paid too high a price for it? No answers fell out of the cloudless blue sky, but Emma thought that just maybe that's what he was talking about when he cautioned her about making wishes.

Sophie returned with her damp hair still hanging limp and went straight for a drawer in the kitchen. "Want a rubber band to pull your hair up in a ponytail?" Sophie laid a couple on the bar.

"Sure." Emma nodded.

"Mother has told me ever since I was twelve years old that grown women don't wear ponytails, braids, or pigtails." She combed her hair up on top of her head with her fingers and secured it with a band just like Sophie had done. When she finished, a couple of strands escaped to frame her delicate face. She glanced back in the mirror again. "I like it."

"Keeps it off our necks," Sophie said. "Are we ready?"

Emma fought the urge to twist her hands.

"If you get uncomfortable, just say so. This small crowd understands, believe me." Sophie looped her arm into Emma's and urged her toward the door.

"Glad to have you with us," Arty said when Emma sat down beside Sophie.

Filly and Josh sat across from her, and Arty had the place at the end of the table.

"Thank you," Emma said just barely above a whisper as her heart warmed toward these strangers.

"Tonight, we've got smoked brisket," Arty announced. "I started it this morning at five o'clock, so it's real tender. I made potato salad and baked beans to go with it."

"And I brought a relish tray and a blueberry cobbler," Filly added. "And, darlin', you look lovely this evening. You remind me of myself when I was your age, but, honey, if you're going to be a hippie, you need some jewelry. We'll fix you up with that after supper."

Before Emma could answer, Arty bowed his head and began to say grace. When the amen was said, she raised her head and, for the first time, noticed that Josh had a short brown ponytail at the nape of his neck. She could feel the chill of Victoria's disapproval from almost three hundred miles away. Perhaps it was the distance between them, but she shook off the icy feeling, and just that gesture gave her courage.

"It's good to see you smile," Sophie whispered.

"Didn't realize I was," Emma said out of the corner of her mouth. "I was thinking about how I didn't really care who disapproved of me tonight."

"Good for you," Sophie said. "Arty, as usual, you've outdone yourself."

"I get lots of planning for my projects done when I'm cooking. Today, I decided to make a windmill while I made the potato salad," he said as he passed the food around.

"What about you, Filly?" Emma asked, surprised that she could open her mouth at all. "Do you plan out jewelry while you bake?"

125

"No, when I bake, I sing. When I go to bed at night, I think about the jewelry I'm going to make the next day. Sometimes I even dream about it," Filly answered.

"Me too," Josh added. "But I get my best ideas when I'm taking a midnight walk. How about you, Sophie?"

"This year, I'm doing a series of landscapes from the back porch of the trailer, and I plan to go into the Big Bend park and sketch out a few places that I didn't get to last year. I've got an idea book that will keep me busy until I die," she answered.

Emma wanted to belong to this group in more ways than just eating supper with them. Filly made fancy jewelry. Josh did drawings, and Arty worked in metal. Sophie worked in oils. If Emma picked up her brushes, her work might be trash, but at least she would fit in with the rest of the trailer court family.

"You'll be painting when you're a hundred years old, won't you?" Emma ventured another question.

"I can't imagine life without my paintbrushes, and the smell of oils is like vitamin pills to my soul," Sophie answered. "When are you going to pick up the brushes again?"

Emma was glad she was chewing so she didn't have to answer right away. The thought of getting paint under her fingernails and inhaling brush cleaner was calling her name. "I've got this idea, but it's probably crazy." She held both her hands on her lap to keep from twisting them. Could she really tell this group of people the idea she'd kept buried ever since she saw the first tiny house in a magazine?

"Making jewelry from rocks or bits of wood and leather was called crazy at one time, but I'm making a pretty fine living at it," Filly told her. "Tell us your idea, and we'll be honest about what we think of it."

Emma focused on Sophie's face. Even as a child, whatever she was thinking was right there on her face, so she would know if her idea was bat-crap crazy by Sophie's expression.

"I hate big houses. They bewilder me. That's why I wanted to build myself a tiny house, and why I love the trailer we have right now. So . . ." She paused. Could she really put her idea out there in the universe? It was so much easier to keep it inside her heart. She glanced at Josh, who seemed to be hanging on her words, and suddenly got a burst of courage to go on. "I was thinking maybe I'd like to paint some small pictures to go in tiny houses. Those folks would like art, too, but big pictures wouldn't work in their homes, or in travel trailers or even small houses with limited wall space."

She shifted her eyes back to Sophie, expecting

to see disappointment, but her friend was smiling, and her blue eyes twinkled.

"That's a great idea." Sophie's tone spoke volumes of encouragement. "If you will get maybe twenty of those done while we're here, I'll put them in with my next gallery showing. It's something no one else has thought of in the art world. You could be famous on your debut."

"Are you serious?" Emma asked.

Sophie laughed out loud. "As serious as Victoria was that day Mama let us have chocolate cake for lunch instead of real food. Your mom got so mad!"

"When are you going to start on the first of these small pieces of art?" Filly asked.

"It was just an idea," Emma answered. "I hadn't thought about when and what, and I'm not even sure about a gallery showing. Maybe if the art buyer likes them, I could sell locally like all y'all do."

Filly took another slice of brisket and then passed the platter around the table a second time. "I think you should paint a hummingbird first. They're small and would make a perfect subject for a cheery picture. I'll share my table with you anytime you want to come watch them for inspiration."

"I just might do that." Emma could hardly believe that her idea had taken root and was already growing among these sweet folks. Just days ago, she'd had no future except more rounds of therapists and a sterile room in an institution, and now the world was open to her. Just thinking about it was exciting—and a whole lot scary.

Josh could see a little of the haunted look leave Emma's eyes. That made him think about how much Arty had helped him. He had been more than a little overwhelmed when Harry had passed away suddenly and left him a fortune. Josh had never liked living in the city or in a big house. He went straight to the lawyer who had been hired to help manage his newly found fortune about buying something small in the southern part of the state—away from his parents.

Had Harry not left him the means, he would never have been able to leave his parents' home, and he never would have met Arty and Filly. His folks didn't think he could live on his own out in the big, wide world, no matter how intelligent he was, but he'd wanted to be out of their house and on his own. He had even looked at a few apartments, but then he became rich, so he adjusted his thinking to buying rather than just renting. He had looked at a few houses, but when the real estate agent his lawyer was dealing with mentioned a trailer park and a lot of land, he asked to see it.

His folks thought he was crazy. His lawyer tried to talk him out of buying it. He had never lived in a trailer before, or managed a small park, either, but he proved them wrong.

He owed Arty for suggesting that Josh show his artwork to Leo, the art dealer. The night before the man came to the park to buy Filly's and Arty's work, Josh hadn't slept a wink. Now his work was known all over the United States, and people paid good money for a Josh Corlen original. Yep, he wouldn't have the confidence he had today without Arty's help and Harry's faith in his ability to take care of himself. Hopefully, Emma would look back someday and see that she had friends right there on Hummingbird Lane who helped her.

"I'm going to take a walk tomorrow to work on a picture of an eagle." Josh kept his eyes on his plate. "Every now and then he flies overhead and I get another detail or two by shooting a picture of him with my camera. If you want to go with me and maybe sketch some cactus blossoms, you are welcome, Em." He held his trembling hands in his lap and wished he hadn't said anything at all. What if she said yes out of pity because she didn't want to hurt his feelings? Or worse yet, what if she said no because she was afraid of him?

"Yes, I'd like that." Emma smiled.

"I'll be waiting on your back porch about ten o'clock, then. I usually see the eagle about ten thirty." His pulse stopped racing.

Emma gave a brief nod. "I'll be ready."

"So, you like to be called Em instead of Emma?" Arty asked.

"Yes." Emma nodded again. "It reminds me of happy times."

"Then Em it is," Filly said. "I don't like to be called Ophelia. It sounds so pompous and stilted. Filly says that I'm a free spirit. Em is kind of the same. Wearing that beautiful outfit, and with your hair all pulled up, I can see that you got a little bit of rebel blood in you, too."

"That's so sweet. Sophie's mama's name is Rebel, and I always wanted to grow up and be just like her," Emma said.

Arty pointed toward the southwest. "Looks like Mexico is sending a storm our way."

"Well, dammit!" Filly swore. "If it rains, we won't get much of a visit, and I was hoping to talk y'all into a game of gin rummy tonight. Maybe after your walk through the cactus fields, you can come over for coffee tomorrow, Em?"

"That would be nice." Emma nodded.

They had barely dipped up the cobbler when a dark cloud moved across what sun there was left, and a loud clap of thunder sent Coco running for the pet entrance in the front door of Josh's trailer.

"Time to go inside." Josh was disappointed, too. He liked card games and the banter that went on between Filly and Arty when they played. "I can smell the rain, and if you look out there, you can see it headed this way."

Arty put lids on the plastic containers of food, stacked them up, and started for his trailer. "Temperature is dropping, so we might even get some hail."

Filly re-covered the cobbler with foil, set the relish tray on top of it, and hurried off to her trailer. "Y'all hunker down until it's over. If it's rainin' tomorrow night, we'll have supper at Arty's place."

Josh jogged across the yard, but he didn't make it inside before enormous drops of rain began to fall, and the wind picked up. He hurried inside, took time to wipe the water from his glasses, and then opened the door to the back porch. He loved the smell of rain and the sound of it beating on the metal roof. For the first time, though, he wished it would only be a passing storm, not one that lasted through the night. He didn't mind walking in the rain or getting wet, but he wasn't brave enough to go out when there was lightning.

He sat down on the sofa in his living room and glanced over at the easel where he'd set his latest work. He refused to be nervous about the next day. He had to calm himself or else he would have insomnia. Only one thing ever got rid of the jitters, and that was work, so he moved from the sofa to the easel and began to put the tiny lines into the eagle's feathers that would give them life and movement.

"We're all afraid of something," he muttered. "Even someone as pretty as Em has fears. I'll have to take it easy with her if she's ever going to be my friend."

In Emma's mind the dream was real.

Emma couldn't move. She kept thinking that if only she had been the girl who wore a flouncy skirt, she would have the strength to fight that guy off. She'd gone willingly to his apartment. Dallas was one of her fellow art students, after all. He had said that Terrance had a painting he wanted her to critique. It was an unusual abstract painting, and Emma told both guys that she had no expertise in that kind of art. Then they had offered her a glass of champagne to celebrate Terrance winning the picture in an online auction. She told them she didn't drink, but they assured her that one or two sips of champagne wouldn't hurt, and it would be rude not to celebrate with them. She didn't want to be a nerd, so she'd drank maybe half of what was in the glass.

Dallas and Terrance were talking about something on the television in the living room, but they sounded as if they were in a tunnel. Everything appeared to be covered by a thick gray fog, and then Dallas took her by the arm and led her into a bedroom that opened off the living room.

"You should lie down and take a little nap," he said.

"Take. Me. Home." Words, even that much, came out slow and labored.

Suddenly, it was as if Emma left her body and was watching everything take place. She yelled at herself to get up and run. Climb out a window. Lock herself in the bathroom. Nothing worked. Her body was only semiconscious and couldn't move.

"I'm sorry, darlin'." Dallas kissed her on the neck and whispered, "But I owe him a lot of money that I don't have. He'll forgive every dime of it for a virgin."

Dallas laid her on the bed that had black satin sheets on it. She remembered a white fur–looking rug beside the bed and the thought had gone through her mind that everything wasn't black and white. Sometimes, things were a gray fog, like her mind was in that night. She raised her voice—or thought she did—and told him again to take her home. Then Terrance, the star football player for another college nearby, came into the room, patted Dallas on the back, and told him he'd done a good job. Dallas closed the door as he left the room. Then Terrance jerked her jeans down around her ankles. She fought and clawed at the six-foot, beefed-up guy. She yelled at him to stop, but she was helpless in her semidrugged state. The last thing she remembered before she passed out was excruciating pain and a heavy weight on her whole body.

Then she was back in her body, and it wasn't a dream. Her stomach lurched, and she leaned over the side of the bed and threw up on the white fur rug. Pain radiated through her female parts, and her legs ached where Terrance had forced them apart with his strong hands. There was blood on the sheets. When she pulled up her underpants and jeans, even more blood stained them. She was still wobbly when she eased the door open and pulled a small pistol from the side pocket of her purse. Terrance and Dallas were sprawled out on a nearby sofa, playing a video game, drinking beer and laughing, but the apartment went quiet after she put a bullet in the back of each of their heads. She staggered out into a long hallway and held on to the walls to get to the front door. When she made it outside, a hard, cold wind slapped her in the face, and that helped to steady her so that she could get into her car. She drove straight to the hospital.

"I've been raped, and I killed the both of them," she had told the nurse. "My mother can't know."

"How old are you?" the nurse asked.

"I'm eighteen," Emma answered.

"We don't have to call your parents if you don't want us to, but, honey, we should call the police," the woman said. "You take off all your clothes and put on these scrubs. I'll be back to

135

process you for evidence, and then we'll make some phone calls. And remember, none of this is your fault."

"No, no, no!" Emma yelled.

She was sitting up in her bed, eyes wide-open and seeing nothing, when Sophie switched on the lights. For a moment, she didn't know where she was or even if she was still dreaming. She wiped tears from her eyes with the sheet and begged Terrance to stop.

"Wake up. It's just a dream. Come on, Em, wake up." Sophie sat down on the edge of the bed and wrapped her arms around Emma.

Emma hugged Sophie tightly and sobbed into her shoulder. "It wasn't a dream. I know what happened. I saw it. I felt it."

"Talk to me, Em. Tell me about it. Maybe it was only a nightmare."

Emma shuddered and told her what had happened in the dream in full detail. "It was real, Sophie. I killed them both. I shot them in the back of the head. There was blood on them and blood on the bed and even in my underpants and jeans, and there was blood in my car. The reason my legs and chest hurt was because he was a big guy and he was heavy on my body. He forced my legs open and he"—her chin quivered—"raped me. That's what I couldn't remember all these years. I'm sure of it. It's all so clear now."

Sophie's blood ran cold, and she shivered right along with Emma as she continued to hold her tightly. "Are you sure you killed them?"

Emma's eyes popped wide-open, and her back stiffened. "I was raped, and I killed both of them in the dream. Dallas and Terrance were laughing about it, and I shot them in the back of the head. There was more blood on them than what was on me. I stumbled down the stairs to the lobby of the apartment building where Terrance lived. That's why I hate big houses, isn't it?"

"Did you dream that they both . . ." Sophie couldn't bear to even think that Emma had been gang-raped, much less say the words.

"Not Dallas, but he was guilty of tricking me into going to Terrance's apartment and then convincing me to drink the champagne. It had to have been drugged, but I only drank half of it." She jumped up and began to pace the floor. "It all makes sense now why I blocked it. Dallas gave me to Terrance because he owed him money. Terrance wanted a virgin. I remember being wobbly and my hand shaking when I pulled the trigger, but I didn't care. They both deserved to die after what they did to me. The gun was heavy in my hands, and . . ." She stopped and stared out the back doors. "Why would I figure out this much and all if it isn't true? I couldn't tell Mother, so . . ." The words trailed off to nothing.

Sophie didn't believe for one minute that her friend had killed someone. Emma couldn't swat a mosquito when they were kids without worrying if it had a family or children.

Emma's eyes had glazed over, and she stared off into space. "I went to the hospital, and the nurse told me to take off my clothes and put on gray scrubs. Then she said she was going to call the police and my parents. The police wouldn't do anything, not when Terrance was the big hot-shot star of the football team. And Mother . . ." She stopped and put her hand over her eyes.

"Sweet Jesus!" Sophie gasped. "Victoria would be awful if she knew that you had been raped or had killed someone."

"She would have locked me away forever, after she screamed at me that it was all my fault for being weak like my father, and that's pretty much what Mother did after all, even though she didn't know what happened." Emma's face was totally without color when she dropped her hand. "I thought if I left the hospital, that if I pretended it didn't happen, then no one would know, and Mother wouldn't be angry with me."

"Are you sure you killed them?" Sophie asked.

Emma shook her head. "Right now, I don't know for sure what's real and what's nightmare, but I know down deep in my heart that Terrance raped me. Can we look them up on the internet and see if they're still alive?"

Sophie took her by the hand and led her to the living room. She opened her laptop and nodded for Emma to research those two horrible guys. Sophie sat down beside her. "There's no way you killed anyone. There would have been dead bodies, and they would have found your DNA all over the bed. Look at me, Em. You did not shoot those two bastards, even though they deserved it."

"If I did and it's still an open case . . . ," Emma whispered, "there is no statute of limitations on murder."

But there is a statute of limitations for rape, and that's long past, Sophie thought. That meant *they* couldn't be brought up on charges. Not even if Emma was strong enough to face them in a courtroom, or if she had the evidence to back her accusations. A nightmare and years of treatment for depression sure wouldn't look good for her defense.

She watched Emma as she typed the fellow's name into the computer. Three different possibilities came up, but with only a few keystrokes, Emma found the Dallas who had gone to school at the same college that she did. His obituary said that he had died five years ago during a robbery in an illegal gambling establishment owned by one Terrance Farnsby. Just a little more research and they found out that Terrance had been sentenced to five years in prison and had died six months before his term was up.

"I hope they didn't do that to any other girls, but thank God I didn't kill anyone," Emma sighed. "But it was so real in the dream."

"Since that part isn't real, is there a possibility that the rest isn't?" Sophie asked.

"No, that's what happened," Emma answered. "I remember the details now—the satin sheets, the pain, and all of it. Now that I'm thinking rationally, Mother would have said I was stupid and irresponsible to get myself in that situation, and then she would have asked me if I'd been leading them on by wearing inappropriate clothes."

"Nothing could make me madder or sadder or . . ." Sophie's voice cracked. "Or make me want to shoot someone myself than thinking about what was done to you. You trusted your friend, and he betrayed you. The first time you went to a guy's apartment, he molests you. You don't trust your mother enough to tell her what happened. I'm so sorry this happened to you, but I'm most sorry that I wasn't there to help you through this." The waterworks turned loose, and Sophie sobbed. "No woman or girl should ever have to endure something so horrible. Please remember, none of this is your fault."

"My mind is reeling." Emma grabbed Sophie in a fierce hug. "All these years and now I find out that I'm really, really damaged goods. Even if I could ever be"—she wiped her eyes—"in a relationship, who would have me? Please don't tell the others. I couldn't bear the sympathy right now. I need to sit on this for a while before we tell anyone else, not even Rebel."

"Whatever you need, I'm here. We can talk. We can take walks. Whatever you want to get through all this. It won't be easy." Sophie hugged Emma again. "It's up to you when we tell other people, if we ever do."

"I blamed myself." Emma wiped her wet cheeks on her shirtsleeve and then buried her face in Sophie's shoulder. "Even in the hospital before I ran away, I knew I was at fault. I shouldn't have gone. I shouldn't have had any of the champagne. No one would ever have believed me if I had told. He was the big shot on the football team. So I made myself believe that it didn't happen. Do you think the nightmares will ever stop?"

Sophie hugged her even tighter. "Like I said before, and I'll say every day from now on, none of this is your fault. Remember that most of all. Hopefully, in time the dreams will stop."

"Do you really think that's even possible?" Emma's chin quivered.

"Yes, I do. You will find your strength, Em, right here away from everything and everyone in your past except me. I love you like a sister. And the other three folks here—well, they already care about you, so you're among friends. If you

141

want to throw stuff or scream or curl up in a ball and cry, I'm right here for you," Sophie said.

"Look at us." Emma tried to smile. "We look like we did that last day when we knew we wouldn't see each other again. We both cried, and after Rebel left with you, I curled up in a ball in my bed and wept until there were no more tears."

"Tears wash our souls," Sophie told her as she stood up and went to the kitchen.

"Tears on the outside fall to the ground and are slowly washed away. Tears on the inside fall on the soul and stay and stay and stay," Emma whispered. "I'm glad you are sharing this soul cleansing with me."

"Who said that?" Sophie opened the refrigerator and brought out a quart of strawberry yogurt.

"It was a framed quote on one of my many therapists' walls. I have no idea who said it." Emma took the last paper towel on the roll and wiped her swollen eyes. "I thought friends cured their emotional pain with ice cream."

"Not artists." Sophie handed Emma a spoon. "We color lizards purple and neon green, and we eat strawberry yogurt right out of the container when we hurt."

Chapter Seven

The sun was barely peeking over the horizon when Sophie's eyes popped open. "My poor Em," she sighed. "I'm not sure I'm smart enough to help her through this, but I'll do my best."

She went to the bathroom, washed her face in cold water, and then headed to the kitchen to put on a pot of coffee. While the coffee brewed, she went out to the porch and stared at the painting she'd been working on. No wonder Emma couldn't paint. She had related that last work she'd done with the horrible experience.

"Nothing smells better than coffee in the morning." Emma yawned as she made her way into the kitchen. "Do you still know how to French braid?"

"Of course, but I still can't braid my own hair. You want to do it for me?" Sophie stepped inside the trailer. "How are you holding up?"

"I was afraid to go to sleep last night," Emma answered. "I finally got up and went out on the porch. I told myself that those stars up there were the same ones that were shining the night all that happened, and they'd gone right on living, so I could, too. I'm not sure if knowing what happened is any better than not knowing. Then Coco showed up and followed me into the house. She curled up beside me, and then I slept like a baby."

"We should get a cat when we go back to Dallas," Sophie said.

"I'm not ready to go back, Sophie. This is where I'm figuring out things. I don't even know why, but I love it here—all of it. The trailer, the cat, the people, and maybe someday, if I stay long enough, I'll even love myself." Emma waved her arms to take in the trailer and everything that made up Hummingbird Lane. She crossed the living room and opened the refrigerator door. She took out the milk and made herself a bowl of cereal, shaking the box in Sophie's direction as if to offer.

How could Emma think about food at a time like this? Sophie's heart was breaking again for her friend, and yet she understood so well that comment about maybe someday even loving herself.

"I'm not hungry right now. I'll eat later. You want to talk some more about things?" Sophie asked.

"No, I want to put it away for a while. If I keep reliving it every hour of every day, I'll never be able to move on," Emma said.

"So, you want French braids this morning?" Sophie changed the subject.

"I'll do yours if you'll do mine. With all these layers, it's hard to keep it up and off my neck." She sat down on one of the two barstools.

Sophie brought rubber bands from the cabinet drawer and then pointed at the calendar. "We're celebrating Easter today. We celebrate everything here. Cinco de Mayo. July Fourth. We've been known to even celebrate things like National Ice Cream Day, and sometimes, like now, we don't celebrate it on the day that it really is."

Emma giggled and then stopped abruptly and looked at her reflection in the mirror. "That felt strange. I can't remember the last time I felt like laughing. But why are you celebrating Easter when it's already over with?"

"The folks here always wait until I'm here to celebrate Easter because they know how much I love it, and Filly likes to buy the little plastic eggs when they go on sale after the holiday. And when you laughed, it reminded me of when we were kids."

Emma pointed to the mirror. "I love the idea of not sticking to a strict schedule. It's so artisty. But look at me, Sophie. Do I look like I'm about to go to church services? Mama would stroke out if she could see me, especially when I wear my flower-child clothes."

Sophie shook her head slowly and then laughed out loud. "I should snap a picture of you when I get your hair braided and send it to her."

Emma dug into her chocolate-flavored cereal. "She would drop dead if she saw me like this, and I'd have to wear one of my long skirts to the funeral."

"Then she'd raise up out of that casket and give you a lecture," Sophie said.

"Yep, she would, but thinking of Easter Sunday, it seems fitting that I figured out things last night, doesn't it?" Emma shuddered at the picture of her mother in a casket.

"How's that?" Sophie was suddenly hungry, so she popped a sausage biscuit in the microwave.

"I feel a little like I've been resurrected from being dead after what happened to me. Like maybe someday I'll be all right." Emma yawned.

"Then happy Easter again." Sophie poured two cups of coffee. She handed one to Emma and raised her cup in a toast.

Emma touched her cup to Sophie's and then took a sip. "I don't expect an instant miracle. When I think about having to be in the presence of big men, I may always get jittery. I know I'll always hate satin. But knowing what the problem is and facing it is half the victory. At least that's what all the therapists have said. I know I said I wanted to put it out of my mind, Sophie, but everything keeps working its way right back around to the rape. The way I handled it has robbed me of so much."

"We can talk or not talk anytime you want," Sophie assured her.

"Do you think I'll ever be comfortable enough to have a relationship with a guy?" Emma sipped on her coffee.

"Give it time to fade away. After a while you will get to where you don't think about it every day," Sophie said.

So, when is the day coming when you don't think about the baby you lost? the aggravating voice in her head asked.

This isn't about me. It's about my best friend, Sophie argued.

"I wish I'd drunk all that champagne so I would have been knocked out altogether, but I was just groggy enough to know what was going on and not be able to fight back. I cried and begged him to stop, but I'm glad I didn't really kill them."

"Me too," Sophie said.

Emma swiped at a tear rolling down her cheek. "Thank you for that and for everything. You rescued me, Sophie. Maybe someday I can repay you, but with your strength, I don't think you'll ever need it."

Sophie laid a hand on Emma's shoulder. "Together we can conquer anything."

"I believe you." Emma nodded. "I remember what Rebel used to tell us."

"You are two smart little girls," Sophie said.

"You are two strong little girls who will go far in life," Emma quoted.

"Together you can do anything," they said in unison.

"So, let's just concentrate on one day at a time, and get each other's hair braided," Sophie said.

Emma nodded again. "This is Easter. I'm resurrected. Let's just rejoice in that and worry about tomorrow when the day gets here," she said. "Are we going to hunt eggs today?"

"Oh, yes, we are." Sophie brought out the rubber bands. "Will you do mine first?"

Emma headed down the hall to the bathroom to get a comb. "There's no kids here, so who's going to dye them? Or are all the eggs plastic?"

Sophie sat down on the floor in front of the sofa and laid the rubber bands on the coffee table. "Honey, artists never grow up. We're like Peter Pan. This afternoon, we'll all meet at the picnic table, and each of us will dye a few eggs. Then, after supper, we will have an egg hunt behind the two empty trailers. Arty hides them, and the four of us will go look for them."

"What about Arty? Doesn't he get to hunt them?" Emma sat down on the sofa and started working with Sophie's hair.

"He says that his joy is hiding them," Sophie answered, "and then he teases us about the ones that we can't find. There's even a prize egg. We take turns putting something special in that one. There's candy in the other plastic ones. I look forward to it every year."

"The last time I hunted eggs was that spring before Mother . . . well, you know," Emma said. "Rebel hid them for us, and then we hunted them even though it was the Friday before Easter. Wouldn't it be great if sometime she were here to help us dye them and maybe even enjoy hunting them with us?"

"She would love that." Sophie smiled. "Good Lord, girl, how tight are you braiding my hair?"

"The strands will loosen up in a little while." Emma chuckled. "If I do it right, the braid will last a couple of days."

"Not washing your hair for that long?" Sophie giggled. "You've turned into someone else entirely!"

"Yep, I have," Emma said. "And I love it. Maybe letting my inner soul come out and play will heal me."

"Does the inner you worry about what Victoria thinks?" Sophie asked.

"More than I like to admit, but then I can't expect to get over more than thirty years of Victoria conditioning in a few days or even weeks," she answered.

Friendship was a powerful thing, and the bond that she and Emma had shared when they were kids had just been lying dormant, like the trees in winter, waiting for them to get together again to bloom.

Josh was glad that not one single wispy cloud floated in the blue skies so he could draw that morning. His eagle was far enough along that he could finish it inside if it rained, but he felt like he did his best work outside. Butterflies flitted about the cactus blooms, and he had caught sight of an eagle floating through the air when he took his morning coffee out on the porch at daybreak. If things went right, he might be able to finish the project he had been working on all week. Leo would be coming by in a few days, and Josh would love to have the eagle done when he arrived.

He slipped his canvas into a waterproof sleeve and made sure he had enough ink and pens in his backpack for the morning. He added four bottles of water, a couple of protein bars, and another couple of candy bars and slipped his arms in the straps. His equipment was ready, but Josh was nervous about spending several hours with Emma. What if she got bored, or worse yet, what if she hated being with him? He did not carry on conversations well—not with anyone other than his trailer park people. Besides all that, he'd never spent that long with a woman—especially a beautiful one like Emma.

A memory of his grandfather flashed in his

mind. They were sitting at the edge of the pond on the estate where Josh's folks lived, and Harry was on the other side of him. The wind was blowing, and Harry had been holding his old floppy hat down with one hand.

"Grandpa, why am I like this?" he had asked.

"If God made everyone just alike, the world would be a boring place, now wouldn't it?" Grandpa had answered.

"Accept who you are and be good at what you do. Now, if you're going to finish the drawing of that duck, you'd better get busy," Harry had said with a chuckle.

When he came around the bend, he could see Sophie painting and Emma sitting on the porch steps with a backpack beside her. When he was only a few feet away, Sophie waved with a paintbrush in her hands. Emma looked up and nodded.

"Good morning, ladies," he said.

"Mornin'," Emma and Sophie both said at the same time.

"Want a cup of coffee?" Sophie asked.

"No, I already had too much caffeine this morning, but thank you," he said and then glanced over at Emma. "Are you ready?"

"I hope so," Emma said with a shy smile. "Sophie expects me to be productive today, but I haven't painted anything in years." Emma stood up and slipped her arms through the straps of her backpack, fastened the hook in the front, and gave him a brief nod. "I'm ready," she said.

"Not quite," Josh said. "You need a hat."

"He's right. Take this one. It's got a good wide brim." Sophie jerked her straw hat off her head and handed it to Emma. "I've got another one in the house."

"Thank you," Emma said.

"Y'all have a good morning," Sophie called out as they walked away.

Josh waved over his shoulder.

With her dark hair all done up in braids, Emma was a pretty woman, and when she smiled, her brown eyes sparkled. Josh had the urge to draw her in pen and ink with that twinkle in her eyes. If he could capture the sadness that surrounded her but still get the eyes just right, he would have a masterpiece for sure—one that he probably would never want to sell.

Neither of them said a word until they reached a copse of mesquite, where he removed his backpack. "I thought we'd set up right here. I'm almost finished with my project, but if I can see the eagles, it inspires me."

Emma unfastened her backpack and laid it on the ground. "This is a great place."

They brought out their folding stools with canvas seats and popped them open. Emma sat down, and her eyes darted from one flower to another as if she was trying to decide whether to really work that morning or just study the land-scape.

Josh assembled a portable easel and got out bottles of ink and several pens. "Need help with anything?" he asked.

"No, I'm good. It's just been years since I've had brushes in my hands. I don't know whether to sketch first or just start painting on a canvas." Her tone sounded downright bewildered.

"There's no wrong way to start. You are the artist. It's your work, and you can even toss it when you're done if you don't like it." Josh dipped his pen in the ink and made a few strokes on the eagle's wings.

Emma got a small stretched canvas from her backpack and then brought out a palette and several brushes. Her chest tightened up so badly that it ached. Visions of the cloud picture that she'd slashed chased through her mind. That moment had tangled together the fact that her mother was right about her being too weak to make her own decisions and the pain in her body from the rape.

Deep breaths, she reminded herself when she felt a panic attack approach.

"Are you all right?" Josh asked.

"I'm just trying"—she inhaled deeply—"to decide what to paint. Everything is so beauti-ful."

"When you decide, you'll dive right in." He smiled.

I'm not ready, she thought.

Today just touching them and thinking about painting would be enough. She sat on her small stool for several minutes, staring at a pink bloom on a cactus, memorizing every detail.

Tomorrow I'll paint, she promised herself. *Today I'll just study that flower.*

Tomorrow never comes, the voice in her head said.

With trembling hands, she picked up the small tube of red paint and squirted a tiny bit onto the disposable palette. A soft breeze stirred the scent and sent it straight to her nose. At one time that smell had been like vitamins to her, too. She had hummed and even whistled while she worked, but today all it did was bring back the taste of fear as she had a flashback of slinging open the door to her apartment and inhaling the pungent aroma of oils.

"I have to do this," she muttered. "I have to overcome all of it."

She held her breath as she squirted a dollop of white paint beside the red and used a knife to stir the two together to make the color of the cactus flower. She couldn't work without breathing, so she let the air out in a whoosh and forced herself to think about the flower.

"It's like riding a bicycle, I would imagine,"

Josh said. "It will all come back to you when you get started."

"What if I've lost my touch?" she asked.

"No one says everything we do has to be perfect. Sometimes we all make something that's pure crap. Just do whatever you want because it makes you happy," he answered.

"Paint the lizard purple," she muttered.

"What did you say?" Josh asked.

"Just thinking out loud," Emma said as she looked at the sky and picked up the tube of blue paint, and then the green and the burnt umber.

A butterfly lit on the cactus and seemed to be staring right at her. If she could ever have wings to fly, she had to put the past behind her and pick up the brush. With trembling hands, she chose the smallest brush, dipped it in the pink paint, and outlined the cactus on the small canvas.

"What did you finally decide to work on?" Josh asked after the first hour.

"See that pink cactus right here?" She pointed and then turned what little she had managed to do around for him to see. "There was a butterfly on it, but I want to give the buyers something special, so I intend to hide the word *hope* in every painting."

"That's pretty amazing," Josh said.

"I thought of it when that butterfly lit on the cactus. It was so delicate, and yet it has the strength to survive. Sophie rescued me, and y'all have taken me in. That gives me hope in humanity again, so I want to pay it forward in my art. Does that even make sense?" she asked.

"It's as clear as a summer sky to me," Josh said and continued working on his eagle picture.

His drawings and Harry's generosity had sure enough given him wings to fly, so he understood Emma's reasoning all too well. If a little butterfly could talk her into painting again, she might get to feeling better about herself.

"Thank you for understanding." She made eye contact with him and smiled.

"Takes an artist to know an artist," he said. "Those are Arty's words, not mine. When I first bought the trailer park, it wasn't with the thought of ever selling my drawings."

"What happened?" she asked.

"Arty saw one of my pieces when I was working on the back porch and talked me into letting Leo look at it." Josh shrugged. "And that was the beginning of my career. Are you going to let Leo see what you're doing?"

"I'll have to think about it," Emma said. "I've never sold anything before."

"First time for everything," Josh said. "I'm living proof of that."

The sun was straight up overhead when Josh brought two bottles of water out of his backpack and handed one to Emma. "We should take a break and have a snack."

She dug down into her backpack, found two apples, gave him one, and then twisted the top off her water and took a long drink. "Can I see what you've done?"

He turned around his drawing, and she gasped. "That's breathtaking. It's like that eagle is coming right at me and his eyes can see right into the depths of my soul."

Josh's chest puffed out a little at her praise. Sure, Arty and Filly told him all the time how talented he was, and Leo always brought news of how he was considered an up-and-coming pen-and-ink artist. His neighbors were both artists, but there was something special about hearing it from Emma.

"Thank you." He felt like kicking the dirt like a little boy who had just gotten a compliment. "There's a lot of feeling in that thing you're doing, too, Emma. You work those oils like magic."

"Hope overcomes darkness," she whispered as she bit into her apple.

"Amen," Josh said.

Sophie had just finished eating a peanut butter sandwich and had twisted the top off a beer at noon when her phone and the landline both rang at the same time. Worried that Emma might need her, she let the answering machine pick up the one and answered the other.

"Hey, darlin'," she said when Teddy's face popped up. "Where are you today?"

"I'm finishing up over here and flying home tomorrow. Things went better than we could have ever hoped for. We're booked for four shows. I should be picking you up the middle of next week. We'll be staying in Del Rio for a day before we fly to London. We've got a lot to talk about," he said.

"Do I need to make reservations in a hotel?" she asked.

"Nope, we're staying in a house this time," he said.

"Sounds wonderful to me," she told him. "What are we going to talk about, other than me saying that I love you a hundred times a day?"

"Lots of things," Teddy said. "Will Em be all right without you for a whole week?"

"I hope so. I'm leaving her in good hands, and I'll call her several times a day," Sophie answered. "I've missed you more this time than any other, and I'll be counting the days until you get home."

"I like that word, *home,*" Teddy said. "I'm so ready to wake up with you beside me every morning. I'll tell you one thing we're going to talk about is that I'm not taking any more of these trips alone. A month at a time away from you is too much."

"It sounds like you're ready to make a lot of changes." Sophie had thought their relationship had settled into a routine. A short burst of panic made her chest tighten. She didn't want things to change—what if he wanted to get married and start a family?

"Oh, honey, I am, and I think you're going to love what I've got in mind," Teddy said. "I'll be there with you as soon as I wrap up things here. Love you."

"Love you more," she said as he ended the call.

She carried her beer out to the porch, set it on the table, and picked up her palette, but she flat out couldn't make herself work. She had hated surprises since she got hit with that positive pregnancy test all those years ago, and Teddy was about to spring a huge one on her. She could feel it in her bones.

"Why do we have to change?" She put the palette aside and sat down. "Everything is fine the way it is."

She finished her beer and then paced up and down across the porch. Time stood still as she worried about whatever had Teddy so excited. Time was running out if they were going to have children. If they did, what would that do to her career, and what kind of mother would she be anyway? She'd felt relieved when she lost her baby. Was that a sign that she shouldn't be a mother? She went from thinking about that to worrying about Emma. She had just figured out that she had been raped. Would she really be all right if Sophie left her alone for a few days? Some friend she was—rescuing Emma and then not being there with her. "Filly will help me out and keep her company, and Josh and Arty are here. It's not like I'm leaving her totally without support."

But none of them know about the rape, the annoying voice in her head shouted. *You didn't think this through when you kidnapped her, did you?*

"Hush!" She put her hands over her ears and then caught a movement in her peripheral vision. Josh and Emma were almost back to the porch, and she hadn't gotten anything settled. She glanced down at her phone and could hardly believe that it was already four o'clock.

"Well? How did the day go?" she asked when they made it to the porch.

"I got my eagle's eyes done right," Josh answered and headed on down the path to his trailer.

"And I painted, too. It took every bit of my willpower to do it, but I got one tiny picture done today." Emma handed it to her. "Be truthful. What do you think?"

Sophie took it inside and laid it on the bar. "Do you even realize the emotion in this? The dark clouds and then that ray of sun on the butterfly

160

wings, and the tiny dewdrop on the cactus flower. It's like the hard times are behind you, and the tears have been shed, and wait a minute . . ." She held the picture up to get a better look. "Did you write *hope* in the butterfly wings? Nice touch. You should do that in all your pictures. It could be your brand."

"You're not just shooting me a line of bull to make me feel better?" Emma asked.

"I am not," Sophie said emphatically. "I'm telling you the truth. You haven't lost your touch. How did you feel when you were painting?"

"Here comes the therapist again." Emma went to the refrigerator, got out the milk, and poured a full glass, then brought out the chocolate cookies and sat down at the bar.

"Whoa!" Sophie grabbed up the painting and took it down the hall. "I'll just put this on the closet shelf in my room to dry. Coco doesn't need to leave paw prints on a masterpiece. When I get back, we need to talk."

"Yes, ma'am." Emma nodded. "But I'm not sure I can put into words just how I felt."

Sophie made sure the doors to the closet were closed tightly, and then she went back to the kitchen. She got herself a glass of milk and carried it to the sofa. "Bring the cookies over here so we can be comfortable while you tell me about your first painting in all these years."

As she dipped her cookies in the milk and ate

161

them, Emma told her about the emotions, the memories, and what had happened that morning. "Nancy would call it a breakthrough."

"That's exactly what it was. You overcame the fear and the memory. I wish I could overcome the fear of change." Sophie went on to tell her about Teddy's call. "I couldn't paint after he called. I'm afraid of commitment, and I'm scared that's what he's going to want—a wife and a family. What if this showing in Europe goes badly? What if . . ."

"That's tomorrow's worry." Emma laid her hand on Sophie's shoulder.

"I'll be gone for a week. You're not ready for me to leave you alone. I took you out of that place, and now I'm deserting you. Some friend I am. I thought I'd have more time but they moved the showing up."

"I'm not really alone. You've brought me to the park. I've got Filly and Arty and Josh. You need this trip, and . . ." Emma seemed to be searching for the right words. "It's scary, but you need to do this, and I would feel horrible if you didn't. I might fall apart, but if I do, I'll go see Filly. I promise."

"I'll call every day," Sophie said.

Emma gave her a sideways hug. "Just remember what Rebel said. We are strong, and just because there's an ocean between us doesn't mean we're not together in spirit. I want you to go."

"All right then, but I'll still worry." Sophie nodded.

"And I'll worry about you and the showings. I know how important this is for you," Emma said. "Now let's talk about something else."

"All right. How did things go with Josh? Were you comfortable with him out there?"

"I really was," Emma said. "He said that it takes an artist to know an artist, so we have a lot in common even though we work with different things. He's so good at what he does. His eagle drawing is just awesome. I wasn't afraid of him. To tell the truth, I was comfortable with him. That's saying a lot for me."

"Yes, it is, and Leo is going to love your picture," Sophie said. "But even if he doesn't, I think it's beautiful, and the fact that you are working again means more to me than what you are working on. It says that you're taking control of your life again."

"I hope so, but it means more to me that you like it," Emma said. "Tell me about Leo. Is he a big man? Is he going to intimidate me or remind me of Terrance?"

"You don't need to be afraid. He's a big guy, but he's sweet and has a kind heart," Sophie told her.

Emma held her hands tightly in her lap. "Maybe I can give you some money to help with expenses if he buys it."

"I told you"—Sophie shook her finger at Emma—"no money is needed. You could have a couple more paintings done by then. You should call your work the Hope Collection. By the end of the year, folks will be buying prints, and your originals will go for big bucks."

Emma sat down in one of the red chairs. "That's dreaming too big for me today, but painting again was liberating. Maybe tomorrow I will do another one, and maybe you can get past this fear of commitment and get something done tomorrow, too. That reminds me—Josh said that it's going to rain tomorrow. Maybe you should paint the rain and a lightning storm in addition to sunrise and night."

"That's a great idea," Sophie agreed. "Will you do something with rain, too?"

"Maybe a bird on the porch rail?" Emma said. "Or a lizard crawling up the porch post and blinking at the raindrops. You do remember that rain, dirt, and clouds are tough to paint, right?"

"Oh, yeah, but a challenge is good for the soul." Sophie finally felt a little peace settling the turmoil in her heart and soul. "Let's get cleaned up for supper. We'll eat at five tonight so we can have time to make our eggs and hunt them before dark."

"Where do we eat when it does rain?" Emma asked.

"Always at Arty's place, since he cooks the

main meal of the day. Filly brings the dessert then, too. His dining area is quite a bit bigger than any of ours," Sophie answered. "If you get antsy while I'm away, will you promise that you'll go talk to Filly? She's like a grandmother to me, and I know she'll be here for you."

Emma laid her hand on Sophie's arm. "I can't promise that I won't be lonely without you here every day, but I will promise that I'll talk to Filly if I think I'm having a panic attack."

"Let me show you who I always talk to when I get worried or antsy." Sophie brought out her phone, hit a few icons, and then handed it to Emma. "That's my Teddy. Those were taken just before he left."

"Oh. My!" Emma gasped. "He's not at all what I thought he would look like. I thought he would be six feet tall, dark, and . . . oh!" She slapped a hand over her mouth. "I didn't mean . . ."

"Mama had the same impression." Sophie laughed. "I dated the tall, dark, handsome, sexy, well-built guys in college. Teddy isn't much taller than me. He's a little pudgy around the middle and he wears wire-rimmed glasses, as you can see. He likes his ivy hats because his hair is getting thin on top. But, honey, he makes me feel like I'm a queen, and he makes me laugh." Sophie didn't tell Emma that one of those tall, dark, brooding guys had gotten her pregnant and failed to even mention that he was married.

"You mean like a *Great Gatsby* hat?" Emma asked.

"Exactly." Sophie grinned.

"Well, I'm glad he makes you happy," Emma said.

"Oh, he does, and I'm a lucky woman to have him in my life." Sophie kissed her forefinger and laid it on the picture.

Filly had boiled two dozen eggs to decorate after supper and had given five to each person in the group except for Arty, who only got four. Oil had always been Emma's choice of painting medium, but painting a little yellow chicken on an Easter egg with fast-drying acrylics was a lot of fun. She felt a lot like the little peep with its soft yellow down and wide eyes. Even with the obstacles ahead of her in overcoming the ordeal she'd gone through, she had made a start that day. She had popped out of the confinements of the egg and was now holding a paintbrush. She was making her own place in the little artist group—and that made her happy.

"Why do I get cheated?" Arty asked.

"Because you hate to paint," Filly told him, "but you do like to cook, and that ham tonight was delicious."

"So was the coconut cake," Sophie told Filly.

"Thank you," Arty and Filly said in unison.

166

"Now, do something spectacular on your four eggs," Filly fussed at him.

"You want to see artwork?" Arty smarted off. "When I get done with my eggs, you won't even want to peel them for deviling when we get done hunting them."

"Show, don't tell," Filly told him.

Arty dipped his first egg in warm wax and then picked up a small tool that Emma had only seen used for picking out nuts. He carved an intricate lizard on the egg and then dipped it in purple dye. "What do you think of this, Miz Em?" he asked.

"Oh. My. Gosh! Look, Sophie! He's made our purple lizard," Emma squealed.

"What's this about a purple lizard?" Arty asked. "I just did that to get a rise out of Filly."

"You old fart!" Filly slapped the air at him.

"Emma and I spent hours coloring in books when we were little girls," Sophie explained. "One day, she made a calico kitten that was perfectly right, and I colored a lizard purple."

"And I told her that lizards weren't that color," Emma butted in. "She told me that artists could do whatever they wanted."

"That's right." Filly glued colored stones on her pink egg. "Artists have the rule of the world. We can do whatever we want. If people like it, that's great. If they don't, that's their problem."

"Speaking of artists and their rights, Em painted

today. She did an amazing picture that y'all have got to see," Sophie said, and then glanced over at Emma. "Is it all right if I show them your painting?"

As usual when she was nervous, Emma's hands began to tremble. Living with her mother had taught her early in life to read people by their body language and expressions. She would know if Arty and Filly thought her work was crap, and she wasn't ready for that. If she was ever going to sell her work so that she could be independent, then she had to learn to accept criticism, constructive or otherwise. "Sure, but it's not dry yet," she finally said.

"No problem," Sophie said and jogged from the table to the trailer. In minutes she was back with the small painting in her hands. She laid it down, and everyone leaned in for a closer look.

Emma sat on her hands, determined not to start wringing them. Everyone stared at the small picture for what seemed like an eternity. She was sure that they were trying to figure out a way to tell her that it was childish—nothing more than a coloring book painting that any six-year-old could have done.

"That's about the most powerful picture I've ever seen," Filly said. "It tells a story of a lost soul coming out of the dark and into the light. That dewdrop is a nice touch, and the sunlight reflecting off the butterfly wings is breathtaking with all those dark clouds back behind it. You need to make more of these, Em."

The weight on Emma's heart crumbled into tiny pieces. If Nancy had asked her how she felt, she would have said, "Like the darkness is gone."

"Sneaking the word *hope* into the wings is the crowning glory," Arty said. "You should put that word into all your paintings to mark them as yours. Folks will go crazy to own a hope painting by MM."

"I didn't see it, but I do now. That makes it even more amazing." Filly kept staring at it.

"And the *MM,* for Em Merrill, is a great way to sign your work, but I'm wondering why you've been hiding such great talent all these years," Josh added.

Oh, Josh, I didn't hide it. It was stolen from me, but I'm finding it every day now, thanks to everyone here in this trailer park.

"When are you going to do another one? Leo comes Wednesday. Think you could have one more done by then?"

"I didn't even notice the *MM* down there in the spines of the cactus," Sophie said. "Nice touch, Em."

"Thank you," she whispered. "Y'all did miss one tiny detail, though. And I plan to put something like that in every painting I do to give it life."

"What is it?" Josh leaned closer to the painting. "I was right there with you . . ." He smiled. "I see it."

"What?" Sophie bumped Josh's forehead with her nose, trying to get a closer look.

"Right there." Emma pointed. "If you look close, I embedded a tiny cactus spine into the paint."

"Perfect!" Filly clapped her hands. "But what is that symbolic of? Buyers will want to know."

"That life has thorns, but there's hope in each new day." Emma had been through the briar patch for more than a decade, but now she was smelling the flowers. Hopefully, someday she would be able to forget all the pain of the thorns and wouldn't even remember the rape.

Filly nodded and smiled. "That's powerful. You do realize that this place is your muse, don't you? You should consider staying right here with us forever. If Josh won't let you rent a trailer permanently, you can live with me when Sophie leaves us."

"Thank you, and I can't think of anywhere I'd rather live than here," Emma said. "There's no telling where we'll all be in another few weeks, but right now, this minute, I would love to stay right here. My mother threatened to lock me up forever, but now that I'm thinking clearly, I know that it was just something she was using to control me. I'm an adult, and I had to sign myself into the last few places where she thought I could get treatment."

"Well, the offer has no time limit," Filly said. "Which reminds me . . ." She pulled something out of her pocket and handed it to Emma. "With this necklace, I christen you a bona fide flower child, just like me."

Emma slipped the necklace over her head. The soft leather with small feathers attached felt like silk, or even freedom, against her bare skin. The flat rock with a picture of a rose painted on it hung down between her breasts. She felt like she had just been given the Hope diamond.

"I love it," Emma whispered.

"I'm making matching earrings, but they aren't finished yet. Every real hippie needs dangling earrings," Filly told her.

"I'll wear both them and this necklace with pride." Emma smiled.

"Good," Filly said. "Now, let's finish up these eggs so Arty can hide them. What's your favorite memory of Easter, Em? Hunting eggs? Getting a new dress?"

"My folks are CEO Christians. That means Christmas and Easter only." Emma toyed with the necklace. "Mother picked out an outfit for me to wear to church on those occasions, and I never did like it, so getting a new dress wasn't a good memory."

"Why didn't you like it?" Filly asked.

"They were always so stiff and fit so tight, and the shoes hurt my feet," Emma answered. "I would rather have had something like I'm wearing now. New shoes nearly always made blisters on my heels, and I couldn't wait to get home and take them off. The only time I ever hunted eggs was when Sophie's mama let us decorate them with crayons and watercolors and then hid them for us. That would have to be my favorite memory."

Arty chuckled. "I love that about being a CEO. That's what most folks probably are. I grew up in a big family. Twelve kids in all, and I was the baby of the whole bunch. They're all gone now, but on Easter, my mama would boil dozens of eggs, and we'd color them. Daddy would hide them for us out in the pasture. But my favorite memory is the last year she was alive, when she let me help her make the family dinner. We had ham and baked beans, and she even showed me how to make her hot rolls. How about you two?" He nodded toward Josh and Sophie.

"Mine's the same as Em's." Sophie smiled.

"Easter was just another day before I moved here," Josh answered. "I do remember the year before he died, Grandpa and I went fishing. I always liked spending time with him, whether it was a holiday or not."

"We had broom-jumping weddings on Easter when I was a little girl," Filly said.

"I thought that had to do with the Black community," Emma said.

"It did and it does, but there's a dispute about just where it did originate. My folks liked to think it started in Romania at some point in my ancestors' ethnic community. The Romani didn't feel like the government should have any part or place in their marriages. They had rules, too. The feet of both parties had to be in the air, and later if the Romani elders condoned it, they could annul a marriage by jumping backward over the broom. In the carnie life, even though some of the folks weren't Rom, and even if some of them went to the courthouse and had the whole marriage license thing, we still had the ceremony to celebrate their union," Filly explained.

"Are you—" Sophie started to ask.

Filly butted in before she could finish. "My grandparents on my father's side were Romani. They came to America and started a carnival and hired some of their friends and relatives to help run it. My mother was not Rom. Even though she embraced their culture, my grandmother never really liked her very much. By blood, I'm half Romani. By heart, I'm all hippie."

"Did you ever jump the broom?" Emma asked.

Filly shook her head. "Never was good at getting both feet off the ground."

"Did it always involve a real broom?" Sophie asked.

"Sure." Filly nodded. "Each couple brought their own broom, and after the ceremony, it was given to them as a wedding gift. No preacher or justice of the peace asked them to promise to love, honor, and obey until death parted them— the couple just said their own vows to each other. Then the groom took the bride by the hand and, together, they jumped over the broom that was all decorated up pretty with bows and ribbon. The jump signified that they'd left their old single life behind. The joined hands said they were committed to be a couple. And the other side of the broom was their bright future."

"I like that," Emma said. "Makes more sense than a huge wedding."

The word *wedding* sparked a vision of the huge portrait hanging over the mantel in her folks' house. To her, the big smiles on their faces were all farce. She'd never seen them hug each other or even give a peck on the cheek. They shared a house, not a relationship, and if that's what a wedding meant, then Emma wanted nothing to do with it.

Chapter Eight

Excitement filled the whole little trailer park that evening as Sophie, Filly, Emma, and Josh all waited at the table for Arty to hide the eggs. Finally, after half an hour, Sophie heard the familiar sound of the bell.

"What's that?" Emma asked.

"That's our call to line up," Sophie explained. "Arty has hidden the eggs, and it's almost time for us to find them."

Filly passed out the four baskets she had decorated. "We'd better go get ready so Arty can fire his gun."

"A real gun?" Emma asked.

Sophie nodded. "A little .22 pistol he uses to shoot snakes, but he'll be firing blanks this evening."

"This really is a production." Emma took her pretty yellow basket and followed the other three to the back side of the trailers.

Sophie looped her arm in Emma's. "Yes, it is, and I'm glad you are here with me so we can do this together again."

Arty waited on Sophie's back porch, gun in hand and Coco in his lap. A piece of gold

Christmas tree tinsel lay stretched on the ground from the edge of the steps out about ten feet. "Toes on the gold," he said. "When I fire the gun, you can take off, but first study your path."

"Just shoot the dang gun and let us loose," Filly yelled.

"I can't believe that I'm doing this at my age," Emma said.

"Don't think about Victoria," Sophie told her. "Just enjoy the fun."

"She's always there in my head," Emma whispered, "telling me that I'm stupid and a big disappointment."

"Shut her out for the next hour," Sophie said. "Tell her to get lost."

Arty put Coco on the porch, stood up, and fired the gun into the air. Filly moved fast but left a lot of eggs hiding behind cacti, wildflowers, and even clumps of grass. Josh took his time, finding what she had overlooked. Emma moved around the outer edge of the area, filling her basket slowly. Sophie stopped several times and watched Emma gather eggs for her yellow basket. To see her come this far meant that Sophie hadn't done the wrong thing when she rescued her.

"Fun, ain't it?" Sophie bent down and picked up two eggs.

"Are you going to ask me how I feel?" Emma smiled.

"Hadn't thought about it, but now that you mention it." Sophie grinned back at her.

"The same excitement that I did when Rebel let us hunt out in the backyard. Mother would have thrown a fit, and she probably would now if she could see me," Emma answered.

"Why?" Sophie saw a bright-colored plastic egg in the grass, but she let Emma find it.

"She said eating eggs that had been boiled the day before would make me sick," Emma replied, "but they didn't. Why do we get the mothers that we do? I would have rather had Rebel."

"Don't know, but I'm glad I got her. Remind me to call her this evening and tell her happy Easter," Sophie said.

The sun had begun to sink below the western horizon when Filly shouted that she had found the prize egg. She carried the big, gold plastic egg apart from the others. When she got to the porch, she popped it open to find a hundred-dollar bill.

"Do we all donate toward that?" Emma whispered to Sophie.

"No, each year one person takes care of the prize egg. This year was my turn, and I had no idea what to put inside it, so I opted for money," Sophie answered.

"I'm going to buy a bottle of whiskey for us all to share, and a new skirt like the one Em is wearing," Filly declared. "Now, let's go peel the

177

eggs, and I'll devil them for our snack. This has been the best hunt ever. Not just because I found the prize, but because you girls are here with us."

Sophie loved her grandmother, and Filly reminded her so much of Granny Mason. She was past eighty and still a flower child who didn't give a tiny rat's butt about society's rules.

Emma laid all her beautiful eggs out on the picnic table and sighed. "They're too pretty to break open. We should figure out a way to preserve them."

"Oh, no." Arty shook his head as he cracked the first one open on the edge of the table. "I've been looking forward to our traditional snack all day. Filly makes wonderful deviled eggs, and she won't tell me her secret, so we only get them once a year."

"Besides, darlin' girl," Filly said, "this is a spiritual lesson on many levels. We have the beauty, and then we crack them open and remove the outer shell, which is just physical prettiness anyway, and then we see what's inside." Filly picked up the egg that Arty had designed and smashed it on the tabletop. "What's inside is the real prize, both in the real eggs and the plastic ones."

"Amen," Josh agreed. "Kind of like me buying this place. It didn't look like much when the

Realtor brought me out here to see it, but there's an inner beauty to it."

With another long sigh, Emma picked up the first egg and gently cracked the shell. Was this like figuring out the nightmare? Was the yolk symbolic of her heart, sitting close to the center of the egg and trying to break away from the cords that had bound it for so many years?

"I love the friendships I've made here." Sophie had already peeled four of her eggs. "And the fun that we all have together."

"We're a family, and we're adopting you into it just like we did Josh and Sophie," Arty said.

Emma didn't say a word, but she hoped like hell they weren't like her biological family. From her experience, family meant tension and control. She'd far rather that they all just be friends.

Maybe if you'd had a backbone, Victoria wouldn't have run over you like she did, the voice in her head said.

I'm getting one now, Emma shot back. *If push comes to shove, I will stand up to her.*

Sophie nudged her on the shoulder. "You look like you're ready to chew nails."

"More like railroad spikes," Emma said, "but I'm finding a heart inside this brittle shell, just like Filly said."

"That's great. Want to talk about it?" Sophie asked.

"Not now. Maybe later." Emma hoped the heart

that she had finally located would someday be soft enough to let other people inside, and not hard-boiled like the centers of the eggs.

Dark had settled on the trailer park when the party broke up. Emma and Sophie took half a dozen leftover deviled eggs with them. Coco followed them into the trailer and curled up on the sofa. Sophie's phone rang, and Emma could tell by the tone of her voice that Teddy was on the other end.

With a wave over her shoulder, Emma headed out onto the back porch to give Sophie some private time. "This is me," she muttered as she sat down, drew up her knees, and tucked her skirt around her legs. "I might be broken, but I'm living in a place that makes glue to put me back together. Sophie is here. So are Filly and Arty and Josh. With their help, I can be whole again. I might have cracks, but then, no one is perfect."

She heard a door open and close, so evidently Sophie had taken the phone to her bedroom. Emma went inside, took a quick shower, and wrapped a towel around her body and one around her wet hair. When she opened the bathroom door, she could hear Sophie talking to Coco, so evidently, she and Teddy had ended their call.

"Come on out. No one is here but us," Sophie said.

Emma didn't even parade around in the privacy of her own suite in a towel. If Victoria had popped in, she would have thrown a hissy fit. Bathrobes were made for that purpose. Towels were made to dry the body and to then be tossed into the hamper in the bathroom.

"Go away, Mother. You aren't welcome in my world anymore," Emma whispered. She went into the living room and sat down on the sofa. "Are you getting excited about spending time with Teddy?"

"Always," Sophie answered.

"Do you think you'll ever be able to be with him all the time?" she asked. "Like Etta James singing 'At Last,' when she says her love has come along."

"I don't know," Sophie answered. "That idea scares me. What if we couldn't survive in a world where we got to see each other every single day? I'd rather not have a permanent living arrangement if it ruined what we've got now."

"Have you told Teddy that?" Emma asked.

"No, I haven't, but surely he's figured out that I'm afraid of commitment. We've been together for years." Sophie opened the door so Coco could get out. "Smells like rain out there."

"I've done that." Emma got up and went to her bedroom. She pulled on a pair of underpants and a nightshirt and then returned to the living room.

"You've done what? Smelled the rain?" Sophie asked.

"I've changed the subject when a therapist

asked me a question about what I'm afraid of, especially when they wanted me to work harder at bringing the repressed memories out into the open," Emma answered. "I couldn't until recently, but you *know* what you're afraid of, so face your fears, like you told me to do."

Sophie bit the inside of her lip and smiled. "The student becomes the master. Did you ever think of studying to be a therapist?"

"Nope. I just want to paint my tiny pictures and never go back to Dallas, but that's a pipe dream. I hope, by the time we have to leave, that I've gained enough strength to take over my own life and tell my mother to go to hell," Emma answered. "Would it be running away from my problems if I stayed here? Josh said he would make arrangements for me if I wanted to, and that sweet Filly offered me a place in her home." She took a deep breath. "Or would it be running toward an amazing future if I didn't leave?"

"That's totally your decision." Sophie started down the hall and then turned around. "But until you make the choice, you've always got a home with me. You never have to go back to the way things were again."

"Thank you." Emma yawned. "It's been a big day. I'm off to bed. I'm looking forward to doing another painting tomorrow."

"Look how far you've come already. By the

time we go home, you'll be strong enough to lift an elephant."

"I sure hope so." Emma covered another yawn with her hand and went to her room. She stopped long enough to read the framed quote on the wall. "Love will put you face-to-face with endless obstacles"—she touched the picture frame—"and these days my mother is the biggest obstacle out there."

She had no trouble falling asleep, but at midnight, she awoke. She hurried to the bathroom, dropped down on her knees, and threw up until there was nothing left but dry heaving. Then she crawled over into the corner beside the tub, drew her knees up, and locked her arms around them.

"Are you all right?" Sophie poked her head in the door.

"I'm fine," Emma answered, but that wasn't the truth. Her eyes were burning, and she felt as if her world was falling apart again.

Sophie slid down beside her and draped an arm over her shoulders. "You are definitely not fine. Talk to me."

"I thought," Emma sobbed, "that it would be over when I dreamed that I killed them. I thought"—she wiped her wet cheeks on the back of her hand—"that meant they were dead to me, and I could move on, but the dream was there again tonight."

Sophie pulled off a wad of toilet paper and dried

Emma's tears, then tossed it in the trash can. "It took more than ten years for you to remember what happened to you. You can't expect it to be over in a few weeks."

"But the nightmares are so vivid." Emma shivered. "It's like I'm living it all over again, only this time I'm not drugged, and I woke up as I was stumbling down the stairs. Mother was waiting at the bottom of the steps, and she told me that she wished I'd never been born, that she never wanted kids and I'd been the biggest disappointment of her entire life."

Sophie gave her a gentle squeeze. "Was there anything new about this dream? Tell me the details."

"I bent over at the waist and threw up on her shoes. When I woke up, I barely made it to the bathroom before . . ."

"What would your therapist say?" Sophie asked.

"She would ask me how it made me feel." Emma's hands trembled, so she held them together so tightly that they began to ache. "I feel like I did when I was twelve years old."

"What happened then?" Sophie asked.

"I was pouting because I couldn't go to school with you." Emma's memory was so vivid that she felt the same knot in her stomach that she had had that day. "That was the first time she told me that she had never wanted kids. I was brazen enough then to ask her why she had me," Emma said.

"And?" Sophie pressured.

"She said that her mother had told her if she didn't have a child by the time she was thirty-five so it could take over the business . . ." Emma cocked her head to one side and drew her brows down so tightly that her head hurt. "Why am I remembering this now?"

"Keep talking," Sophie said.

"My grandmother said that if Mother didn't have a baby, she would leave everything to a charity when she died," Emma answered.

"So, Victoria got married and had you." Sophie removed her arm, stood up, and extended a hand toward Emma. "Let's go to the living room where it's more comfortable."

Emma was glad for the helping hand, because her knees still felt like jelly. Sophie led her to the living room, got her settled on the sofa, and then went to the kitchen. She poured two glasses of sweet tea and got a box of crackers from the cabinet.

"I'm not pregnant." Emma managed a weak smile.

"No, but after throwing up, this will settle your stomach without irritating it," Sophie told her. "Now tell me more about when you were twelve years old."

"Mother was so mad at me," Emma said. "She

never raised her voice, but she could cut steel with a whisper. She said that she tried to produce a decent heir for my grandmother, but that I was going to be like my worthless father."

"Why did she marry him if he was so worthless?" Sophie asked.

"Because having a child out of wedlock would have been a disgrace. My grandmother held the purse strings, so Mother found a husband and had me. My grandmother died when I was three. I never knew her, but she left a big chunk of money in a trust fund for me." She stopped and took a sip of tea. "You know what happened to that."

"And you're supposed to inherit the company?" Sophie asked.

"I'm not sure. Mother had me sign a whole raft of papers when I first came home from college. She was impatient and just kept flipping the pages and telling me to sign here and here. I didn't even have time to read them. I wouldn't be surprised if the company is off the table completely by now. Do you think maybe this was her plan all along? To declare me mentally incompetent to get back at my grandmother for making her have me?"

"Knowing Victoria, I wouldn't put it past her," Sophie answered. "And while we're talking about her, she can't just take your inheritance from you. If the company is set up to go from daughter to daughter, then it will be yours. And I'm going to talk to my lawyers about her freezing your accounts. That's just not right."

Emma didn't care about the company or the trust fund. In her life money had only brought about bad decisions and unhappiness. "Thank you, but I'm not sure I even want the company. At twelve, I just didn't want to have tutors and be homeschooled. Now I realize what a horrible life my father has lived, and why I never liked the idea of power and money."

"Why did he marry her?" Sophie asked.

"Mother found him in the mail room at the company. He never knew his birth family and was raised in foster homes," Emma answered. "Now that I'm not on meds, things are clearing up. He must have wanted a place in the world. She needed a husband to produce a child, and he was also a little way to get back at her mother for insisting that she get married."

"But there's that huge picture of them on their wedding day hanging over the mantel," Sophie said.

"Mother said that was Grandmother's idea. All the women in the family had their picture taken on their wedding day and hung it in the living room," Emma said. "I'd forgotten all this until now. Why would it come back to my mind tonight?"

"Because you dreamed that Victoria was in

the hallway when you left Terrance's apartment. You *are* like your dad. Neither of you ever felt wanted." Sophie opened up the sleeve of crackers and handed a couple to Emma.

"But I wanted Mother's approval, right? By letting myself get lured into Terrance's apartment, that made me pretty dumb in her eyes." Emma sighed. "I wish it could be over, Sophie."

"So do I, but it's a slow process. I bet that sounded like your therapists for sure, didn't it? Do you think she really would have blamed you? Rebel would have wanted to strangle those guys if that had happened to me. Hell's bells, she would still want to murder them for doing it to you," Sophie finished.

Emma nodded slowly. "I don't feel like I ever pleased her with anything, so yes, she would have that attitude if I'd told her about the rape. In the dream, I dropped to my knees and begged her to forgive me, but she just walked away and left me there. But we should be getting to bed. We're going to paint rain tomorrow."

"Hey, I can stay up all night, sleep until noon, and then paint if you want to talk," Sophie offered.

"I'm fine." Emma said the familiar words, but she couldn't believe them herself—not yet, anyway.

Chapter Nine

The sound of rain on a metal roof reminded Sophie of the trailer that she and her mother had lived in when she was a little girl. She'd especially loved the weekends, when she and Rebel would curl up under one of Granny Mason's handmade quilts and watch old movies. Sophie pulled the covers up to her chin and pretended she was back in that trailer.

If she had had a daughter, would they have been in the living room watching movies that morning? She tried to picture what a daughter would have looked like when she was seventeen. Would she have dark hair and dark eyes like her father, or would she have been a blonde with blue eyes like Sophie? Like Victoria, Sophie had not wanted a child, but unlike Victoria, she would have loved her baby.

Her phone rang and brought her out of the past and into the present. She knew it was Rebel by the ringtone and answered it with, "Good morning, Mama. Is it raining in your part of the state?"

"The sun is shining here. Happy late Easter. Annie threw a little party for our cleaning lady club. My phone was in my purse, and so I missed your call. Did you hunt eggs with your artist friends?" Rebel asked.

"Yes, I did," Sophie answered, "and Emma and I talked about the year when you let us color a dozen eggs and then hid them for us. We decided that was one of our favorite memories."

"How's she doing?" Rebel asked.

"I can't talk about it. She told me in confidence," Sophie said.

"Told what?" Emma peeked in the bedroom. "I'm going to make coffee. Want some eggs for breakfast today?"

"This is Rebel. She asked how you were doing, and I'm good with cereal," Sophie answered.

Emma gave her a nod. "You can tell Rebel. I'm okay with it."

"Mind if I put it on speaker?" Sophie asked.

"No, I don't want to talk just yet. Tell her that I love her, though." Emma turned around, and in a couple of minutes, Sophie could hear rattling dishes.

"She's had a couple of horrible nightmares," Sophie replied and then went on to tell Rebel the whole story.

"I'm so sorry that she had to endure that awful experience." Rebel's voice cracked. "I hope it doesn't damage her for life. She was so sheltered. No wonder she's been in and out of centers all this time."

"She painted a gorgeous picture yesterday. I think she's going to be the next big thing—only in small pictures." Sophie told her about Emma's love for tiny houses and how she wanted to do paintings to decorate them.

"At least she's got a dream now," Rebel said.

"Mama, did you ever wish that you hadn't gotten pregnant and had a child to support all on your own?" Sophie blurted out.

"No! Good Lord, Sophie, why would you ask that?"

Sophie sucked in a lungful of air and let it out slowly. "Victoria told Emma that she never wanted children. I just wondered if you felt like that, especially when you found out you were raising me with no help."

"No, I didn't." Rebel's tone was blunt. "I had help. My mother came and stayed with me for six months after you were born. Then I got a few jobs cleaning houses where they didn't mind me bringing you with me. Honey, you were my best friend, even as a baby and a toddler. Don't ever feel like you upset my dreams or my life. You've always been a blessing." Rebel chuckled. "Back that up. You were a little monster from the time you were about fifteen until you graduated, but I just figured I was payin' for my raisin'. Your grandmother Mason said I was the same way."

Sophie closed her eyes and smiled. "Thank you, Mama."

"No, darlin', thanks go to you for completing my life," Rebel said. "On that note, I've got to get ready for work. It's Monday, and today I've got two houses to clean. I'm sorry Emma grew up knowing that she wasn't really wanted. Give her a hug from me."

"Will do, and love you," Sophie said.

"Right back atcha, kid," Rebel said and ended the call.

Sophie stared at the ceiling for a long time. If she was given the chance at having another child, would she be a good mother? She could never be like Victoria and almost despise her child, but would she be a loving one like her own mother? No answers came floating down from the ceiling, so Sophie laid the phone aside, crawled out of bed, and followed her nose to the kitchen, where she smelled coffee brewing. Emma had already set up painting equipment on the bar and had roughly sketched in a cardinal sitting on the porch rail. Sophie stopped by the barstool where she was perched and gave her a brief hug.

"What's that for?" Emma asked.

"Surviving that horrible nightmare, and this one is from Mama. Thank you for letting me talk to her about it." She gave her another hug and headed for the coffeepot, poured herself a cup, and then topped off Emma's. "Looks like the weatherman was right and we'll be inside today."

"I loved Rebel's hugs, and I've always trusted

her." Emma smiled. "Daddy gave good hugs, but"—she frowned—"I don't remember Mother ever hugging me at all. Do you think that if I ever do come out on the other side of all this and become a mother, I'll be like her?"

"Of course not. If either one of us ever has kids, we're going to be like my mother." Sophie hoped with all her heart that she was telling the truth and that neither of them wound up acting like Victoria.

"I hope so." Emma didn't ever want to bring into the world a child who would feel the way she did. She had given up on ever thinking that she could alter herself so that her mother would love her like Rebel loved Sophie. Yet, somewhere deep in her heart, she wished that Victoria would change.

"I've changed my mind. I'm going to make a breakfast burrito," Sophie said. "Want me to make you one?"

"Love one." Emma started to move the paints.

"We can eat on the sofa and open the door a crack so we can smell the rain," Sophie told her.

Emma slid off the barstool and opened the glass door a little. "I love the sound and the smell of rain."

"Me too," Sophie said. "I wish we could paint the smell of a good rainstorm."

Emma carried her coffee to the living room and sat down on the sofa. "As real as your pictures are, I can feel the warmth of the sun coming off that one, so I bet I could smell rain if you work on one like that today."

"You give me way too much credit. I see you're doing a cardinal, but not a male one." Sophie tilted her head toward the small canvas on the bar.

"The female needs to be recognized," Emma said. "She lays the eggs, sits on them, takes care of the babies. She should be recognized, and besides, I found a tiny feather on the porch yesterday from the lady bird to work into my picture. It was an omen for sure. I'm painting it with a very faint rainbow in the background to show that we have to endure the rain if we want to have the rainbow."

Sophie handed her a paper towel and a burrito. "You are a walking example of that."

"Do you really think I'll ever get to see the rainbow?" Emma sighed and dabbed at the single tear finding its way down her cheek.

"Yes, you will." Sophie sat down on the end of the sofa. "You are going to have lots of rainbows in your future, and many pots of gold at the end of them."

"I don't even care about the gold. I just want the rainbow, because to me that will mean that all this rape stuff is finally over. But I don't want to talk about that today. What are you going to paint?" Emma asked.

"I've decided to do a long, thin picture today—

just a slice of the mountain and maybe a yucca plant in the foreground with rain falling on the bloom."

A rap on the door startled Emma so badly that she almost dropped her burrito. Then the door opened and Filly dashed in without an invitation. She had cut a hole in a black garbage bag for her head and one in each side for her arms. She carried a pan across the living room and set it on the cabinet, and then she removed the garbage bag and tossed it in the trash can.

"I brought cinnamon rolls for y'all's breakfast. I need some inspiration for my jewelry this morning. Nothing seems to appeal to me. What are y'all working on?" She poured herself a cup of coffee and carried it to the rocking chair that had been shoved back in the corner so Sophie could set her painting up to dry.

"Emma is going to paint a mama cardinal in the rain, and I'm thinking about doing one of the mountain that's in that picture"—she pointed to the one that was finished and drying—"but mine will have a big yucca in the foreground in this one, and where that one has the sun peeking over the mountain, this one will have rain."

"I knew I could find something to kick me in the butt and get me going if I came over here. I never thought of painting rain on my rocks. Maybe three rocks on one necklace," Filly said. "Dark clouds, rain, and then a rainbow."

"Sounds beautiful. Those cinnamon rolls smell wonderful," Emma said. "Have one with us."

"I plan on it," Filly said. "I've got a question for you, Em. What made you decide to be a flower child like me?"

"Remember what you said about cracking the eggs so we can get to the heart of things?" Emma asked.

Filly sipped her coffee and nodded.

"This has always been the real me." Emma shrugged. "I was closed up in a shell until Sophie rescued me, and now I'm coming out, kind of like that little yellow peep I painted on one of my eggs."

"Or like a caterpillar in a cocoon?" Filly asked.

"That's right. Now one for you. What made you a hippie child?" Sophie asked.

"I was born one," Filly answered. "Remember that I told you I grew up in a carnival?"

Emma nodded. "I always wondered what it would be like to grow up in one of those. Rebel's mama lived in one when she was growing up. She told us about it one time when she was at our house. I met her one time when she came to clean our house with Rebel. I thought she was beautiful, and I loved her name. Is a carnival kind of like a commune?"

"If you live in a commune, you pretty much stay in one place. A carnie is someone who travels with the fair. My mama was the fortune teller. Daddy was the lion tamer. I grew up on the move for nine months out of the year," Filly told her.

"That sounds so exciting." Emma couldn't even imagine such a lifestyle, not with her fears and social problems, but to grow up wild and free would be like living in heaven.

"It was life," Filly said. "We were kind of like a commune when we wintered down around Texas City for three months. That's when we repaired the equipment and got things ready to go again in the spring. That's also when I started gathering small rocks and making jewelry. Mama sold it for me in her fortune-telling wagon. She put all the money up for my college."

"Did you go to college?" Sophie asked.

"Hell, no! I took Mama's place as a fortune teller when she retired. When I got tired of doing that, I came here and kept on doing what I love, which is designing jewelry." Filly finished her coffee and went back to the kitchen, where she dished up cinnamon rolls for all three of them. "I've always been what you see right here, except that I could read your palm and tell your fortune."

"For real?" Emma's heart skipped a beat. "Could you do it right now?"

Sophie moved over to the bar and held out her hands. "Would you read mine right now, too?"

"Be glad to." Filly moved into the living room

and patted the sofa. "Come and sit right here beside me."

Sophie left the barstool and sat down beside Filly.

"All right, first thing is that you place your hands on this pillow"—Filly laid a throw pillow in Sophie's lap—"and relax. Then what I'm going to do is take your hands in mine and feel your skin, gently, like this." Filly held both of her hands and rubbed the tops and then the palms. "You have medium skin, probably coming from the higher aspect of your heart, and that's what makes you a good artist. Now I'm going to squeeze your hands from side to side. Your hand has bounce to it. That means you have energy."

"That's the truth," Emma said. "She even shares that energy with me when I'm low."

"She's a generous person for sure," Filly said. "Now I'm going to bend her fingers backward just a little, not so much as to hurt, but it will show me if she has flexibility of the mind, which she does. Now that I've determined her personality, I will look at the hand. Look at this beautiful padding on the top of her palm, which is the map of Jupiter, and now the padding at the side, which is the map of the moon."

Emma was totally mesmerized by what Filly was saying. She scooted over closer to her so she could see better.

"See how her pinkie stands off by itself? Sophie

doesn't do that on purpose. That's the Mercury arc type that means she's good in business and shows that she's her own person and likes to act very independent," Filly said.

"I thought you would just look at the lines and say Sophie would be blessed in love," Emma said.

"Honey, reading palms is an art," Filly said. "Now, Sophie has Jupiter for leadership, Saturn for hard work, and Mercury for independence; she's got the moon for dreaminess, intuition, and imagination. Most people have a flat Jupiter, but Sophie's is full, which means she is actually a late bloomer. That's kind of hard for teenagers to accept, but in the thirties, it means that the best is yet to come."

Emma looked at her own hand as Filly talked. She had pads at the top of her palm, too, so hopefully the best in her life was yet to come, too.

"See these little pads on her fingers?" Filly said. "That means she has wisdom and will keep blooming the older she gets."

"Me too!" Emma said.

"Hold your hand up beside Sophie's," Filly said. "I don't normally do two at once, but you are right. You have full Jupiter pads and good signs from the moon area, but your Mercury arc isn't as pronounced as Sophie's, so that means you aren't as good in business. It is fuller than normal, which means you are or will be independent."

"I'll take that much and be happy," Emma said.

Filly studied both hands. "You both have a very creative curve to your head line, which means you are alike in your love of art. You don't just want the facts, but you need time to think and to dream. In a relationship this means you need both togetherness and a little time apart for yourself. You are both seekers after wisdom, and you will get better and better every year of your lives."

Emma leaned in a little to look at the differences and the similarities in their hands.

"Now see this line?" Filly touched Sophie's palm with her own and then did the same with Emma. "This is the life line. It's pinker and deeper than most people's life lines, which means that each of you will have someone come into your life who will feel your influences, and your relationships will be energized by the whole complex range of emotions and love. You will both have many interesting things unfolding in your lives."

Filly sighed. "That's all, girls. You've had your palms really read, not just told that you will meet someone tall, dark, and handsome. You have wonderful opportunities ahead of you, but you have to be open to them."

Emma continued to stare at her hand. "Where were you to give me all this confidence years ago?"

"I wish I had been there for you," Filly said. "But let's have our cinnamon rolls and some more coffee and talk about something else now. You both have a bright future if you open up your minds, hearts, and souls, and that's what I see. Is that your newest work over there, Sophie? I feel like I could walk right into that painting and search for tiny flat rocks."

Me too, or live right here where I can see the mountains forever, Emma thought as she stared at the painting with the other two. But was it the place that made her feel safe, or was it being with Sophie? Or believing and trusting in what Filly had just said?

She didn't dread the time she'd spend alone but rather looked forward to it. She'd enjoyed her semester in college until that unfortunate evening.

Until you were raped. Own it and let it make you stronger. Rebel's voice showed up in her head.

"Yes, ma'am," she whispered ever so softly.

Loneliness was nothing new to Josh. That feeling had been with him most of his life. According to his mother, kids with a high intelligence like he had often didn't fit in with their peers. But that morning, the emptiness in his heart and soul was more acute than ever before.

He opened a bottle of ink and set up a new canvas on his tabletop easel. He had always had ideas and even a list of what he would produce next, but that rainy morning, Emma was stuck in his mind. He dipped a pen tip into the ink and began to draw.

At noon, Filly poked her head in the back door and yelled, "If you ain't dressed, you better run for the bedroom, because I'm comin' in."

"Come on in." When he glanced up from his work, he realized it had stopped raining. "Want a glass of tea or a root beer?"

"I'd love a root beer, but I can get it for myself. Have you seen the rainbow?" Filly kicked off her flip-flops just inside the door and set a plate on the bar separating the kitchen and living area. "I brought ham sandwiches from last night's leftovers."

"I didn't realize that it was so late." Josh's stomach growled. "And no, I haven't seen the rainbow." He set his pen aside, put the cap back on the ink, and crossed the room to the sliding glass doors that led out onto his deck. "It's gorgeous—thanks for lunch. Mind if I eat while we talk? I'm starving."

"Not at all, but that right there"—Filly got out a can of soda from the refrigerator, sat down on the sofa, and pointed at the picture—"that's prettier than any rainbow God ever slapped in the sky."

Josh could feel the heat coming from his neck to his cheeks, but there wasn't a thing he could do about it. "She was on my mind this morning, and since . . ."

Filly leaned back on the worn leather sofa and studied the portrait. "Are you selling it?"

Josh removed the plastic wrap from the plate and picked up a sandwich. "Nope. Someday I might give it to Emma, like on the day she and Sophie leave the park. I'm hoping that she doesn't ever leave us. She fits in so well with our little group, and"—he blushed—"she needs us."

"Are you attracted to her, Josh?"

Josh almost dropped his sandwich, suddenly tongue-tied. "I don't know," he finally managed to get out. "She's so pretty, but she deserves someone strong to put her back together again."

"Maybe so, but then again, she might just need someone to be there for her while she learns to put *herself* back together. I spent some time with the girls this morning, and I even read their palms," Filly said.

"And?" Josh asked.

"They've both got a bright future ahead of them," Filly answered.

"Does that mean Em is leaving?" Josh asked.

"Only if her future isn't here. If it is, then she will stay," Filly said.

"I hope she sticks around even after Sophie goes back to Dallas. I could sure use a friend like her. We're so much alike, and she's so easy . . ." He struggled for the right words.

"Easy for you to talk to, right?" Filly came to his rescue.

Josh nodded. "Yes, and she fits in with our little family here, too. She's not strong like Sophie, so maybe she needs us, too."

"Sophie isn't as strong as you think. She has her demons, too. She just covers it better than you and Em are able to do," Filly told him.

"Why?" Josh wondered out loud.

"Artists portray their feelings with their creations," Filly said. "I've known for a long time that Sophie has something difficult in her past. Her art tells me that."

"What does mine tell you?" Josh asked.

"That you live in a black-and-white world. You're afraid of color because you're afraid to get hurt if you let anyone into your life." Filly yawned. "It's about time for my game show, so I'd best get going. See you at supper. Arty is making fried chicken tonight." She stood up, and when she left, Coco dashed inside the door.

Josh pinched off a small piece of the ham and offered it to her. Evidently, she wasn't hungry, because she acted offended and curled up on the sofa. He sat down beside her and stared at the half-finished picture of Emma. What Filly said about color kept running through his mind. What if he made her eyes light brown in the picture? That would add a subtle touch—kind of like Emma's word *hope* worked into her art.

Chapter Ten

Emma was so edgy she could hardly sit still. She had never sold anything, and Sophie had said that Leo was a big man. Could she even look at him without remembering the smothering pressure on her body when Terrance raped her?

Sophie explained that Leo always went to Arty's place first and loaded up whatever metalwork pieces Arty had ready. Then he made a stop at Filly's trailer and came out with a box of jewelry that he put into his truck. After that, he came to Sophie's trailer to try to talk her into letting him have something she had done, and then he went to Josh's place.

Emma watched the process from the living room door. Leo was as big as a refrigerator, but nothing about him reminded her of Terrance. She had convinced herself that everything was going to be all right until he started toward their trailer.

"I don't know . . . ," she whispered.

"Don't be nervous. He's going to love your work," Sophie said. "But if this is too much, I can always negotiate a price for your two paintings."

Emma took a deep breath and let it out slowly. "He's huge, and I *am* nervous, but I have to do this. I don't want to, but I need to. You aren't always going to be here, and I want to be independent."

"I can guarantee you that he's harmless." Sophie gave her a brief hug and then opened the door. "I've got a surprise for you today, Leo. Come in and meet my best friend, Em."

"Filly told me that you brought a friend with you this year." Leo's presence filled the small room. He stood well over six feet tall and had shoulders and a chest that covered acres instead of inches, a big bald head, and a curly red beard that was twisted into two braids with beads.

Emma had started to twist her hands, but when she heard his high, almost feminine, voice, she dropped them to her sides. She stuck out her right hand and said, "Hello, I'm Emma Merrill. It's nice to meet you, Mr. Leo."

"Just Leo." He smiled as he shook with her and then turned his attention back to Sophie. "I'll give you top dollar for that rain picture right there, girl."

"Can't do it. It's part of a collection for an upcoming showing," Sophie said, "but Em has a couple of small works over there on the bar you might look at. She's dreamed of painting for these new small houses that folks are building. It's a brand-new market that you can swoop into on the ground floor if you're interested."

Leo stared at the two small paintings and the

half-finished one beside them for what seemed like hours; then he shook his head slowly from side to side and turned around to focus on Emma. "Where have you been hiding? How come I've never heard of you? These are amazing. I can already name six clients who will be interested in them if I even want to sell them right now. I may hang them in my gallery and tease my customers with them until they are all itching to own an Emma Merrill original."

"We're calling them the MM originals," Sophie said. "Those are the first two that she's done since she left college more than ten years ago."

"I just saw the word *hope* in the cardinal's feathers. Can we call this the Hope period of MM's works?" Leo went back to studying the paintings.

"Yes, you can." Emma had to remind herself that she needed to breathe. She sucked in a lungful of air and wanted to pinch herself to be sure that she was awake.

"So, what are they worth?" Emma asked.

"Honey, I'm an honest man, so I'll make you a deal. I'll give you a choice of paying you outright for them or taking them on commission and giving you seventy-five percent of what I can sell them for," Leo answered.

Emma looked over at Sophie.

"It's your decision," Sophie said, "but I'd take the commission thing. If they have a bidding war to get one of your first works, then it could amount to thousands."

Emma's eyes grew wide. "Are you kidding me?"

"No, she's not kidding you one little bit." Leo pulled a red bandanna from his pocket and wiped his bald head. "You've got talent like I haven't seen in a while, and I love the idea of selling for the new smaller houses people are building. I've got a contract out in my truck that we can both sign, and I'll take pictures of the paintings, print them out, and attach them, so everything is legal. I can't wait to be known as the guy who discovered you, Miss Em."

"Then I'll do what Sophie says," Emma agreed, "but why do you think they're that good?"

"Because there's heart and soul in them," Leo told her, "just like Sophie's paintings. I see pain, heartache, and fear, and yet there's a ray of hope hiding in the background. Folks are going to go crazy for these things."

"Thank you." Emma couldn't help but wonder what her mother would have to say.

Leo stuffed the bandanna back in his pocket. "I sweat when I get excited. When can you have more? I'd like to see half a dozen a month, if that's possible."

"When will you be back?" Emma asked, a little proud of herself for having the courage to ask the question.

"I come by here sometime in the middle of the month. Never know what exact day," he answered as he picked up the paintings as if they were gold.

"I can have six ready to go by then, maybe even seven or eight," she said.

"That's great. I'm going to take these to my truck and bring the contract back in," Leo told her as he headed toward the door.

The second he was outside, Emma plopped down on the sofa and put her hand over her eyes. "If I'm dreaming, don't pinch me. I don't want to wake up."

"I told you that you're fantastic." Sophie sat down beside her. "And I'm never wrong about good art."

"Thousands? For real? For those small canvases?" Emma whispered. "How much . . . no, that's personal . . ." She frowned.

"Six figures at the very least for each one that I do." Sophie smiled.

"Who needs oil wells when we've got paintbrushes?" Emma giggled. "Answer me truthfully. Am I really awake?"

Sophie draped an arm around her shoulders. "Darlin', we just proved what I've said since we were kids. You *are* an exceptional artist, and yes, we are awake."

Josh sat on the porch and watched Leo go into Sophie's trailer. He remembered the very first drawing that he sold to Leo. It had been a picture of two ring-neck doves with their outspread wings flying above a band of coyotes. Leo had asked to see more of his work right then, and Josh had brought out a piece he had done before he came to the trailer park. That one had a barn in the background and a mare with her colt beside her in the foreground. Leo had bought them both in that moment and asked if he could have more done in a month. Josh didn't tell him that there were probably twenty in his closet, or that he was producing at least two to three a month. He had just agreed to do more and then fell back onto the sofa the minute Leo left the trailer.

He hoped that Emma was having a similar experience and that Leo echoed all the trailer family's praise for her works. She needed to hear that even worse than he did back when he moved to the park.

He heaved a sigh of relief when Leo carried the two paintings out to his truck and then took a clipboard with papers back into Sophie's trailer. Evidently, Leo had seen that Emma was an outstanding artist, just like the family there in the park had realized.

"Hey, Josh." Leo waved as he started across the yard. "What have you got for me today?"

"Just a couple of things." Josh stood up and shook hands with Leo. "Come on inside and have a look."

"I will, but you know I'll buy anything you produce. I've got a waiting list to look at whatever you do. You really should let Sophie take you on a tour with her." Leo followed him into the trailer. "And by the way, that Emma is going to be a star."

"She's a little shy like me, but she really puts heart and soul into her work."

"The better the artist, the more temperamental," Leo said and then stopped in his tracks. "I want that one." He pointed at the drawing of Emma. "I'll keep it for my own private collection."

"It's not for sale," Josh said.

"Everything is for sale," Leo chuckled. "Name your price."

"Some things are priceless," Josh told him. "You can have those two"—Josh pointed at the eagle and a drawing of a fox—"but that one will never be for sale."

"It's Emma, isn't it?" Leo's eyes never left it. "That's your first work ever with a bit of color. It's absolutely stunning."

"Yes, it's Emma," Josh answered.

"Will you promise me that you won't sell it to anyone else if you ever do decide to put it on the market?" Leo asked.

"I can do that, but I assure you, it won't be sold," Josh agreed.

"All right, then, can I talk you into putting just a touch of color into another one?" Leo turned away from the drawing. "The eagle is fantastic, and that mama fox with her babies will sell fast. What's next?"

"Whatever hits my fancy, I guess," Josh told him. "Maybe I'll work on a black hawk. I saw a pair last week sitting in an old cottonwood tree."

"I wish you'd do another one of Emma. That one of her sitting on the back porch with the wind blowing her hair is mesmerizing, but I can so see her in other settings. You could call it your MM period," Leo pressured.

"I'll let Em have her own MM period," Josh said. "She is one of a kind and deserves to own her brand. I will think about putting a little color into a couple more this next month." Josh glanced over his shoulder at the drawing. Folks might call him crazy, but he had told the image good night before he went to bed the night before.

Leo handed Josh a check for what had sold in the last month. "This little trailer park is the best-kept secret in the whole state of Texas," he said.

"I think so, too." Josh smiled as he put the check in his shirt pocket.

"Folks who buy all you folks' art wish they could meet you." Leo chuckled. "I tell them that you are all recluses, but they don't believe me. I've even had some magazine editors call me to set up interviews."

"Not interested in either." Josh smiled. "We just

want to do what we love, sell it, and live simply out here in our corner of the world."

"I understand," Leo said. "I'll see you next month."

"You should come around in the evening sometime and have supper with all of us," Josh offered.

"Can I bring a newspaper reporter?" Leo grinned.

"Only if you want to die," Josh answered.

Leo laughed out loud, picked up the two canvases, and in two strides was at the door. Then he turned around. "Does Emma know how you feel about her?"

Josh's cheeks burned. "What do you mean?"

"Anyone who can make that"—Leo nodded toward the picture—"has feelings for the subject. There's pain and love both featured there."

"I'm not sure that I know how I feel about her," he said. Just the thought of a relationship with Emma made him nervous, and yet the idea of her leaving made him so sad that he wanted to cry.

"Well, when you figure it out, don't be too shy to tell her," Leo suggested.

When he was gone, Josh picked up the picture of Emma and carried it to his bedroom. He hung it on the only wall big enough to support it and then sat down on the end of his bed and stared at it. "Why would I tell her anything? It might just scare her away," he whispered.

• • •

Emma was about to be all alone for the first time since she left her college apartment. She'd told Sophie that she would be fine, but now she had doubts. What if she had another nightmare? What if more than the rape had happened, and it all came to the surface? She wouldn't feel right calling Sophie in the middle of the night or waking Filly up, either. She tore into a bag of chocolate doughnuts and ate a few straight out of the bag for breakfast. "Will you call me when you get to Del Rio and tell me what all this big talk is about?"

"Of course." Sophie put another shirt into the open suitcase on the sofa. "To tell the truth, I'll probably need you to help me sort out whatever is going on."

"You don't think he's about to break up with you, do you?" Emma asked.

"It's crossed my mind. He's always said that he wants a family, and I'm not sure if I do," Sophie answered.

"Well, I'd think that's something that you should definitely agree on." Emma wondered if she should even think about children. Getting pregnant involved sex, and she wasn't sure she could ever do that after what had happened. Maybe she should talk to a therapist about that sometime.

"You'll be okay, right?" Sophie stopped

packing and joined Emma at the bar. "I don't care what time of day or night it is, if you need me, you call."

Emma shoved the bag of doughnuts over toward Sophie. "I will, and you do the same. I'll work every day until you get back to pass the time. I still can't believe that I've sold two paintings. Well, not sold, but they *are* out on commission. What if no one likes them or buys them?"

Sophie ate a third tiny doughnut. "Since you're a newbie, I wouldn't be surprised if Leo calls you when they sell. He's a good man, and he runs a really neat little store and gallery over in Terlingua. Maybe someday we can drive down there and you can see for yourself."

"How big is that town?" Emma asked.

"It's almost a ghost town, but there's a few little shops, and folks come from miles around to go to Big Bend park. Leo's place has a reputation that's known all over the world, and lots of buyers come from the big cities like New York City and Los Angeles. If he puts your stuff in his shop, it's a big step up, believe me," Sophie answered.

Emma took a sip of her coffee. "No pressure."

"He's also brutally honest. If he hadn't liked your work, he would have said so." Sophie slid off the barstool and took a pair of jeans from the dryer, folded them, and laid them in the suitcase.

"I'm never sure what all to pack for a trip, and this is all the way to Europe."

"What do you mean? Don't you and Teddy take several little vacations a year?" Emma moved from her barstool over to the sofa.

"Yes, but . . ." Sophie went to the refrigerator and got out milk. She poured two glasses full and set one down in front of Emma. "Usually we go somewhere, and I paint all day. Then we go out in the evenings or else cook at home if we've rented a condo. But this time Teddy asked me to leave my work behind. We're staying in a house in Del Rio for one night and then we're flying to London, where the first showing is to be held, and he wants to talk about something serious. What if he proposes?"

"Do you love him?" Emma finished off the last of her coffee and took a sip of the milk. "Why are you afraid of marriage, anyway?"

"Yes, I love him," Sophie answered, "but in my experience, married men can't be trusted."

"In mine, men can't be trusted, married or not," Emma said, "but it's not fair to Teddy for you to judge him by other guys."

Same goes for you. Don't judge Josh by other guys, either. Rebel's voice in her head was loud and clear.

"You're right," Sophie sighed. "Man, I hate surprises! I'd rather know what's comin'."

"Amen and amen," Emma said. "But sometimes

217

surprises are downright wonderful. Like when you walked into my room after all those years. Like Leo loving my work. Like me getting to come to this place."

"Okay." Sophie smiled. "You've made your point. Teddy has a surprise for me, and I'll enjoy it every bit as much as you did all those things. Still no regrets?"

"Only that I didn't have the courage to do it on my own. But if I had, I wouldn't be where I am right now. With that in mind, I wouldn't change a single thing in my past," Emma said.

Sophie raised an eyebrow.

"Not even the rape. It devastated me and made me hit rock bottom for a long time, but I'm coming back with strength I didn't even know I had," Emma said. "And I want you to have a good time with Teddy. Call me when you have time, and especially when you find out what the surprise is, but please don't worry about me. I feel like nothing can hurt me here in this place. I'm safe and at peace."

Sophie sat down in the rocking chair. "I worry you'll go backward and hit bottom again if I'm not here."

"Only way I'm going is forward." Emma held up her glass. "Like you said, it won't happen overnight, and I might have more nightmares." She shuddered at the thought of going through that experience again, even in dreams. "But if

I do, I can call you and talk to you, or like you and Filly both have said, I can march across the yard and knock on Filly's door. I have a support system here like I've never had before."

Sophie swiped a tear from her cheek. "God, Em, I feel so bad that I wasn't there for you, but none of what happened is your fault. Not then. Not ever, so don't blame yourself."

"If I'd been more street savvy, I would have known better than to go with Dallas to a strange guy's apartment. I'm so glad you're here to help me get through all that, Sophie. My road to recovery might take a while longer than I want, but I'm going to get over this horror," Emma said with so much confidence that she honestly believed what she was saying. "Hey, I didn't run and hide under the bed today when Leo came into the house. Lord, have mercy!" She fanned herself with the back of her hand. "I thought for a minute I might faint dead away, but then he spoke, and you were right. His voice didn't sound like it should come out of a man as big as a refrigerator."

Sophie laughed out loud. "Josh says that he's the Hulk with a red beard."

"The Hulk isn't even that big," Emma whispered. "My chest tightened up, and it took every bit of my courage just to shake hands with him."

Sophie nodded and took another sip of her milk. "I felt the same way the first time I met him."

"On a different note," Emma said, "do you believe all that stuff Filly said when she read our palms or was it just a line of bull crap? I want to believe every bit of it. It gives me hope and courage, but what do you think?"

"I think Filly has the ability to read people," Sophie answered. "Kind of like a sixth sense. I don't know if palms really figure into it all that much, but what she said about our hands sure made me feel better."

"I'm going to believe that she's got the gift of seeing beyond today because I want to," Emma said. "I want to get past all that stuff I've buried and move on with life. Now, enough of this, let's get you packed up. What time will Teddy be here tomorrow?"

"Right after breakfast," Sophie answered.

Emma stood up and touched her milk glass to Sophie's. "To a bright future for both of us, just like Filly said."

"To us!" Sophie said.

Chapter Eleven

Sophie was up at the crack of dawn, made coffee, and took a cup to the front porch. Teddy wouldn't arrive for at least a couple of hours, but she was too excited to sleep. Tonight she would fall asleep in his arms, and tomorrow morning they would have breakfast together. That was, if he wasn't breaking up with her. He had never given her a reason to even think that was the case, but if he did, she wasn't sure she could handle it. He'd been her rock as well as her manager for years. She didn't want to lose him in either way.

"Good morning," Emma said behind her.

"What are you doing up at this time of day?" Sophie moved over to give Emma room to sit beside her.

"Wanted to watch the sunrise this morning. I'm glad I get to see it with you. I had another dream last night." Emma eased down on the porch so that she wouldn't spill a drop of the full mug of coffee in her hands.

"Why didn't you wake me?" Sophie asked.

"I stood up to my mother in the dream," Emma said. "I told her that this is my life, and I'll live it however I please. She started to tell me how foolish I was and said I was too delicate to know how to run my own business."

"What happened?" Sophie was having even more second thoughts about leaving Emma alone.

"I said I might fall," Emma said, then grew serious. "But if I did, I'd get up with the help of all my new friends, pull the cactus needles out of my ass, and try again. Then I picked up my suitcase and carried it out of the house. I told Jeffrey to take me to the bus station, and he nodded. That's when I woke up. What do you think it means?"

"I'll go back to one of the therapists' lines and ask, 'How did it make you feel?' "

Emma blew on the top of her coffee and then took a sip. "Free at last. Kind of like the words of that song say: 'Free at last, thank God Almighty, I'm free at last.' "

"Well," Sophie said, "I think the suitcase symbolizes the baggage that you're carrying with you, and the fact that you're willing to take it with you and own it as yours is a good sign. You aren't hiding anything anymore, and you don't care what Victoria thinks."

"That's easy to say when I've got this perfect hiding place away from her right now." Emma sighed. "But when the time comes that I have to face her in person, will I cave in, or will I be able to tell her to go to hell?"

"You're gaining more and more independence every day, Em, but when that time comes, I'll be standing right behind you. Victoria has lost her power. Just remember that," Sophie told her.

"I hope you're right," Emma said and then pointed at the eastern sky. "Look at that gorgeous sunrise. This is going to be a good day. I haven't had this feeling since we were kids and it was the day for Rebel to come clean our house. That always meant she would bring you with her, and I couldn't hardly sleep the night before."

"Then you're not going to miss me?" Sophie teased.

"Not in the least," Emma told her, "and if you believe that, I've got some oceanfront property in New Mexico that I'd like to sell you."

"We've made some good memories," Sophie said.

"But none of them are as good as what we're making these days." Emma grinned. "We shouldn't be talking. We should be painting that gorgeous sunrise. I've never seen so many brilliant colors. How many have you painted?"

"Not many, but I do plan on doing at least one somewhere in the Big Bend park this summer. There's this place . . ." Sophie pulled her phone out of her hip pocket and flipped through her pictures. When she found the one of two enormous rocks with a big round one cradled between the two like the hand of God had laid it right there for them to hold up, she handed the phone to Emma.

"That's awesome," Emma said.

"See that hole at the bottom of the round one?" Sophie pointed. "I want to put the rising sun right there, with maybe some dark clouds all around it. What do you think, Em?"

"That would be surreal, as if nothing, not even evil, can stop the light from shining through," Emma answered.

"I just have to be there when the sun comes up to get the essence of the whole thing, to feel it down deep in my soul," Sophie said. "I'd forgotten how much I missed talking art with you. I wish I'd plowed right through Victoria and come to see you."

"She'd have had someone toss you out on your ear." Emma's tone was dead serious. "She *will* have her way. If she can't control me, then she'll cut off my money, hoping that I'll starve, but I won't now that Leo is buying my work." She cocked her head to one side and said, "I hear a vehicle coming. I thought Teddy wasn't arriving for another couple of hours."

"Sometimes folks make a wrong turn and—" Sophie gasped. "It *is* Teddy. He's early."

She was halfway across the yard when Teddy parked his truck. He got out and opened his arms, and she ran into them. His eyes sparkled, and he held her tightly for a few seconds before he tipped up her chin and kissed her long and passionately. How could she have ever thought he was going to break up with her? Her heart pounded in her chest, and every nerve in her body wanted more than a kiss, even if it was steamy hot. If Emma hadn't been sitting on the porch, she would have pulled him inside and dragged him back to her bedroom, but today the sex would have to wait until they were in the house he'd rented.

"You're early," she panted when he finally pulled away from the kiss.

"I couldn't wait to see you, so I drove longer yesterday and got up at three this morning. Couldn't sleep anyway. I'm tired of us being apart, darlin'," Teddy whispered.

"Want a cup of coffee before we go?" she asked.

"No, I just want to meet Emma and then get to the house in Del Rio, leave our clothes in a heap by the front door, and fall into bed with you," he said.

"Me too." She buried her head in his shoulder for an extra minute, then laced her fingers in his and led him to the porch. "Teddy, this is my best friend, Em Merrill. Em, this is Teddy."

Emma stood up and nodded. "I'm glad to finally meet the man who puts a smile on Sophie's face every time his name is mentioned. We can even tell when she just thinks about you!"

"The pleasure is all mine. She's told me all about you. Congratulations on the paintings that Leo took yesterday," Teddy said.

"Are you sure about me going away for a whole week?" Sophie asked one more time.

Teddy held up two fingers. "Ten days or two weeks. One of my surprises is that we got a showing in Rome as well, so we'll be staying over a few extra days."

"Oh. My. Sweet. Lord!" Sophie's hands shook like Emma's did when she was nervous. Two whole weeks away with Teddy would be heaven, but then she heard Emma's quick intake of breath and felt guilty.

Emma smiled so wide that you could see her back teeth. "You've earned this, Sophie. Congratulations! Take lots of pictures to share with all of us when you get home."

Sophie hoped that she had mistaken Emma's reaction for fear when it was really happiness for her that she'd also been booked in Rome. "My phone number is on the refrigerator. Use the landline all you want and call me anytime, night or day."

"Here's your suitcase." Emma handed it to her and then gave her a hug. "Now, get out of here, and don't worry. Teddy, get her out of this place before the waterworks start."

Teddy took the suitcase from her and then draped his arm around Sophie's shoulders. "No tears from either of you or you'll make me cry, and then Em will think I'm a big wuss."

"All right, then, I guess we should go, but . . . ," Sophie started.

Teddy gently pulled her toward his truck. "Goodbye, Em. We'll see you soon."

"Get on out of here so I can paint something with that beautiful sunrise in the background," Emma scolded with a big smile on her face.

Emma stood on the porch and waved until the vehicle was out of sight. Sophie kept one arm out the window of Teddy's truck and waved back at her until they made the first curve in the dirt road and she couldn't see the park anymore.

Teddy laid a hand on her shoulder. "She's going to be fine, but I'm a little worried about you."

"We were friends of the heart." Sophie sighed. "Do you know what that is?"

"Nope, can't say as I do," he answered.

"Neither of us was popular. We weren't accepted in school. I was poor and she was rich, but neither of us fit in with the other kids, not even the nerds. But . . ." Her voice cracked.

"So you bonded and then you were ripped apart. Knowing that you were in the same area and yet not being able to see each other anymore would be worse than if one of you had died." Teddy gave her shoulder a gentle squeeze. "I love you, Sophie Mason."

"I love you right back, and thanks for understanding. I feel so guilty that I didn't try harder to stay in her life. She's coming out of her shell so well now that she's away from her mother and those awful institutions. I'm just afraid that she'll . . ." Sophie wiped a tear away from her eye.

"If she does, she will call," Teddy reassured her. "She wouldn't want you to fret like this, and she sure wouldn't want you to feel guilty over things you couldn't control in the past. You've stepped up now, and that's what's important."

Sophie took his hand in hers and held it close to her cheek. "Thank you for always knowing how to make me feel better."

"That's my job." He wiggled his eyebrows. "Of course, I have other, more important jobs, like taking you straight to bed when we get to the house I've rented."

"I thought that was my job." She finally let go of the sadness and laughed.

"I think I remember Rebel telling us years ago that the best way to get to know someone was to work together, so . . ." His eyes started at her toes and went to her head.

"Keep your eyes on the road or we'll never make it to that bed," she teased.

"Blessed are they who wait, for they shall . . . ," he began.

"Make love," she said, and then quickly fastened her seat belt. "And we both better watch for lightning bolts to jump out of the sky and fry us for being sacrilegious."

Later that evening, Sophie propped herself up on an elbow and stared her fill of Teddy. He looked so much younger than his thirty-five years when he was sleeping. His heavy lashes fanned out on his high cheekbones, and he was so much at peace. She rolled out of the king-size bed on the other side, picked up his plaid shirt, and buried her nose in the collar. She loved the woodsy aroma of his cologne and wished that she could always go to sleep in his arms and wake up in them.

Where did that come from? that pesky voice in her head asked. *You're the first one to admit that you are afraid of commitment.*

She slipped her arms into the shirt, buttoned it up, and eased the door shut when she left the room. The house was exactly what she would want in a home if she ever gave up her loft and bought a place. The front door opened into the open living space—a living room, kitchen, and dining area all in one. A hallway led to a master bedroom with a huge walk-in closet and a private bathroom. Stairs led up to two more bedrooms and a bathroom on the second floor. Roses were already blooming at the edge of a wide veranda that had a porch swing back in the shadows.

Teddy came out of the bedroom and slipped

both of his arms around her waist. "Now, I'd say after that amazing lovemaking that we've been working together in the best way possible."

"If we were judging, I'd give it a ten out of ten." She flipped around and put her arms around his neck. "And now I'm starving."

"Supper will be delivered pretty soon." He had pulled on a pair of pajama pants and a tank top, but the clothing that they'd worn into the house was scattered from the door all the way down the hallway.

"Oh, really? And what's for dessert?" she asked.

"That's your department." He grinned.

"Then ice cream it is," she teased.

"We'll need it after Mexican food and before another round of hot sex." He slid a sly wink her way.

The doorbell rang, and Teddy picked up his jeans from the floor and slipped his billfold from the hip pocket. Sophie took down a couple of plates from the cabinet and some cutlery from a drawer and had the table set when he brought the sacks of food into the kitchen area. While he opened the covered containers, she got two beers from the refrigerator. He pulled a chair out with a flourish and motioned for her to sit down.

"You are lookin' lovely tonight, my darlin'," he whispered.

"You don't look so shabby yourself." She

smiled up at him and put two chicken enchiladas on her plate.

He picked up her hand and kissed her knuckles. "Be honest with me, Sophie. What do you think of this house?"

"If I ever leave my loft in Dallas, this is exactly what I'd want," she answered.

He let go of her hand. "It's going up for sale in another week. If you like it, we might put in a bid on it."

"Are you serious? Why would we live in Del Rio?" She could tell that he was about to burst with excitement, but in a far different way than she was. Her head suddenly throbbed. He was going to propose and ask her to move in with him. The next thing would be marriage and then babies.

"I'm ready for a life change, and I want you to be with me all the time."

Sophie was stunned speechless.

"Is that a no?" Teddy asked.

"It's a give-me-a-minute-to-catch-my-breath-and-think-for-a-second." She dropped her fork on the table.

"Then is it a yes?" he asked. "You can work anywhere, and you must like this area, because you come down here every year to paint."

"Teddy, I've got a hefty savings account, but can we afford to do something like this?" she whispered.

"Remember that trust that my father left me? I'm thirty-five, so it's mine now, and, honey, we can afford to do anything we want," he said. "I can't see myself not working, but I'm tired of traveling. I want roots, and I want to put them down with you. And the rest of the surprise is this . . ." He took a long drink of his beer.

Her head was spinning. Good God, was he about to propose? Was that the rest of the surprise?

"I want to use some more of my trust fund to buy an old store on Main Street. It was built back in the days when owners with a place like that would put a furniture store on the ground floor and a funeral home upstairs. There's still a service elevator where they took the caskets up to the parlor. The last folks that owned it had an antique store in it, but I . . ." He took another long drink of his beer.

She had been in an old store like that in a little town in the northern part of the state and loved the feeling she got when she was inside it, surrounded by all those old dishes and antiques. Each one had a story to tell, if they could only talk.

"I want to put a gallery in the downstairs and turn the loft into an area for you to paint. I'll run the gallery while you paint, and then we'll come home to this house," he finally spit out.

"Have I reached a place in my career that I

should do that?" She had to give him an answer. She couldn't break his heart, but . . .

There are no buts in love, the voice in her head said. *If there are, then you need to end this relationship right now and let Teddy find someone who will give him what he needs and wants.*

He laid a hand on hers. "Honey, you saw that place where you were just a struggling artist in the rearview mirror years ago. You are known internationally, so yes, you are ready. We can do the Europe thing and come home to settle down into our own place, with our own store."

Sophie's eyes filled with tears. "This is too much to take in all at once."

"The last thing is that I want us to get married. I want to know that you are mine forever," he said.

And there it was. The very thing that she had dreaded.

"First, I have to tell you something that I've never told anyone else," she whispered—could she even say the words? Her emotions zoomed as if on a roller coaster that sucked her breath right out of her chest. Her hands trembled so badly that she laced her fingers together and held them in her lap. She opened her mouth, but nothing came out.

"Spit it out and then say yes to everything I've suggested." He took her hands in his. "You are shaking, darlin'. Talk to me. There's nothing we can't get through together."

"I . . . there was . . . ," she stammered.

"Is this something that happened before I met you?" he asked.

She nodded.

"Then it doesn't matter," he said.

"Yes, it does, because it's my biggest fear. I know you want children, and I'm terrified that God will punish me and never let me have kids, or if I do, I'll be a terrible mother." Tears streamed down Sophie's face.

"Why would you even think that?" he asked. "Rebel is a fantastic mother, and she'll make an amazing grandmother. You'll be more like her, I'm sure because she was your role model, not Victoria."

"I got pregnant my first semester in college," she said in a voice so low that she could barely hear herself speak.

"You had a baby?" Teddy's expression went to sheer shock.

"No, I lost it." She sucked in a lungful of air. "I didn't do anything to cause it, but I always felt guilty because I didn't want a baby at that time in my life. The father was a substitute art teacher, and I didn't know until he'd already gone back to Chicago that he was married and had children. Victoria didn't want children, and look what she did to Em. What if . . ."

"Good Lord, Sophie, why didn't you talk to me about this before?" Teddy scooped her up in his arms and carried her to the sofa. He sat down with her and kept his arms tightly around her. "You shouldn't have carried this burden all alone."

She shook her head. "I was afraid of losing you. I'm terrified of getting married because look what my father did, and then that substitute teacher cheated on his wife with me. I've always been afraid that . . ."

"That marriage would change what we have?" he asked. "Darlin', that will never happen, whether we have a conventional marriage or just a commitment ceremony."

"Or jump the broom?" She smiled through the tears.

"What's this about jumping a broom?" He tipped up her chin and brushed a soft kiss across her lips.

She told him the short version of what Filly had said.

He chuckled and pressed his forehead against hers. "I would be honored to say my vows and jump the broom with you if you are proposing to me."

"Then I think I am," she said. "Are you sure you're all right with what I told you?"

"Honey, that happened before I was part of your life." He hugged her even tighter. "And you need to give up that guilt trip right along with the one about Em. You are an amazing person, and when we're ready, we'll be wonderful parents. But first we've got a trip to Europe, a business to put in, and a broom to jump. Just when is this ceremony going to take place?"

Sophie thought maybe she was dreaming and started to pinch herself. But this was real, and she wasn't sure whether to be relieved that she had finally told someone about her baby, or skeptical that she could be absolved in the blink of an eye. She'd carried the burden, as Teddy called it, for seventeen years. How could she just shake it off now? She immediately thought of Emma trying to get past what she had endured.

"Well?" Teddy asked. "Do you want to jump the broom as soon as we get back from Europe or wait until we get established here in Del Rio?"

"July Fourth," she blurted, "at the trailer park. That way my friends can be at the ceremony, and it's the last week I've got the trailer rented. We'll have a weeklong honeymoon right here in our own house before we settle down to a nine-to-five job of running our new gallery."

"I love it, and I love you. For this broom-jumping business, do I buy you an engagement ring?" he asked. "Or a small dustpan and broom first?"

"Just a plain gold band, please," she suggested with a laugh.

"Consider it done. Are we in agreement about

everything—the house and the business?" he asked.

"Yes! Yes! Yes!" she squealed. "When can I see the building?"

"Tomorrow morning at eight, and then we go straight to the airport," he said.

"Can we put Josh's and Em's and Filly's and Arty's work in the gallery?" She could already visualize paintings hanging on the walls, jewelry in glass cases, and Arty's metal art displayed on pedestals.

"I would like to if they're willing," Teddy answered. "But right now, our supper is getting cold, and you're supposed to be in charge of dessert. Have I told you how sexy you look in that shirt?" He pulled her close and kissed the side of her neck.

"If you don't stop, we'll have dessert first and then reheat supper in the microwave." Her knees were getting weaker with each kiss.

He scooped her up and carried her down the short hallway to the bedroom. "Best idea I've heard since you said yes to my proposal."

"I thought you said yes to mine." She nibbled on his earlobe.

"I guess I did." He closed the door with his bare foot.

Chapter Twelve

Emma wandered through the trailer that evening before supper. She was dressed in one of her long skirts and had flip-flops on her feet. She had slept well the night before, but she missed having that first cup of coffee in the morning with Sophie. By suppertime that evening, Emma was in a funk. She knew the difference between what she was feeling at that time and the down-and-dirty depression she had known for the past years, and this was not the latter. It wasn't as bad as the blue mood she had sunk into when she and Sophie had to part when they were twelve years old, but it was a similar feeling.

Craving company, however, was a whole new feeling for her, and that evening she was sitting at the picnic table before Arty and Filly brought out the food. She was so hungry and nervous after spending that first night alone in the trailer that she didn't even realize Josh was anywhere around until he slid onto the bench across from her.

"Hey," he said.

"Evenin'," she gasped.

"Did I startle you?" Josh asked.

"Little bit," she admitted. "My mind was a million miles away."

Filly set a two-layer lemon cake on the end of the table. "How you holdin' up, darlin' girl? Missin' Sophie?"

Arty put a platter of smoked pork chops in the middle of the table. "That's a stupid question. Of course she's missin' Sophie. We all miss Sophie every time she leaves us." He headed back inside the house and returned with a container of cheesy potatoes and a bowl of salad.

"Amen," Josh agreed. "These two"—he pointed at Arty and Filly—"get downright cranky when all they have is me."

"Arty just brings out the worst in me," Filly grumbled.

Arty shot a dirty look her way and then bowed his head. He said a quick grace and then passed the pork chops to Filly. "This is me being nice. You should appreciate it."

Filly put a chop on her plate and sent the platter to Josh. "Well, thank you. I'll remember to write it down in my diary tonight that Arthur must be sick because he was nice."

"You're an evil woman," Arty chuckled.

"See what I mean?" Josh said. "They're worse than raising teenagers. Have you heard from Sophie?"

Emma nodded. "She called last evening, but

we only talked a minute or two. They're having a great time, and she said that she's got a surprise to tell us all about when she gets home. Next time y'all go to the store, I want to send some money for you to buy me one of those prepaid cell phones so she can text and send pictures to me."

"I wonder if she and Teddy got married?" Filly sighed.

The idea that Sophie would get married and not tell Emma—that just couldn't happen. Maybe engaged, but not married. No, sir!

"Not without us," Arty growled. "She wouldn't do something that big without inviting us to the wedding."

"What if she gets married in Dallas in a huge church with lots of people?" Josh's eyes were wide with worry.

Emma could feel his pain, because she shuddered at the thought of possibly being one of several bridesmaids at such an affair.

"Would y'all go to that wedding? The one in a huge church with all kinds of people around?" Josh asked.

Emma sure couldn't answer yes to the question.

"Of course, but only if I could wear my bibbed overalls and give away the bride." Arty chuckled.

"I'd go, but I would go as myself, not a silly dressed-up version," Filly agreed, "but I'd sure hate to make that drive. I don't even like to ride an hour up to the grocery store."

"You haven't in over a year," Arty reminded her. "You just make out a list for me and Josh to take care of."

"Well, I'm going next week," Filly said. "It's time for me to get some things that I don't want y'all to see, and, Em, I'll be glad to get you one of those phones. I keep one handy for when we lose power out here"—she pointed at Arty—"and I need to check on this old smart-ass right here and make sure he didn't get struck by lightning."

A feeling of contentment replaced Emma's burst of fear over having to walk down an aisle with a bouquet in her hands. If she had Arty, Josh, and Filly with her, she could survive the biggest wedding in the whole state of Texas.

How would you feel about some guy asking you to marry him? Her father's voice popped into her head.

Scared out of my mind. She had no trouble answering that question.

She looked up and locked gazes with Josh. Her heart threw in an extra beat, and her pulse jacked up a notch or two. Surprisingly enough, she didn't want to wring her hands and didn't even blink. She might even say yes if it was Josh who proposed—someday, not right then.

"So, what did you paint today?" Josh asked.

"I started a picture of that beautiful sunrise yesterday morning, but I had no idea what to do with it until I saw a turkey with his tail all fluffed out. I walked out to the spot where he had been and found a small feather. I painted him looking at the sun as it rose, like he was scaring away the dark night," she said. "I used an eleven-by-fourteen-inch canvas, which is as big as I ever intend to do. What about y'all?"

"Can I see it?" Josh asked.

"Sure. Y'all can come over and see it after we eat." Emma hoped that maybe they'd even sit awhile and visit with her so the evening wouldn't be so long.

"I haven't seen an old tom turkey in a couple of years, but I think I may do a metal piece of one when I finish the replica of this old live oak tree we're sitting under," Arty said. "It's been giving me fits with all the intricate limbs and the twisted trunk."

Filly laid her hand on his shoulder. "I've got faith in your artwork."

"Sweet Lord!" Arty laid a hand over his chest. "The world is coming to an end. This darlin' woman said something nice to me."

"Oh, hush!" Filly slapped him on the arm. "Ignore him, Em. He's being a smart-ass again, and to answer your question, I've been working on a necklace made of tiny wood pieces woven into leather. I'm going to paint rosebuds on the wood when I get the first phase done, and I think I'll make a matching bracelet."

"That sounds beautiful," Emma said. "What about you, Josh?"

"I saw that same turkey, and like Arty, I hadn't seen one in a couple of years, so that inspired me to draw one. Leo mentioned something about me working a spot of color into a painting, so I thought I'd give that little mesquite grove some green leaves," Josh answered.

"Well, I can't wait to see that one." Filly winked at Josh.

Emma noticed that his cheeks turned scarlet and wondered what the inside joke was. If she had learned anything from living in a dysfunctional family, it was to watch her parents' expressions. When she came home from college, she could read Victoria's and Wyatt's moods simply by looking at them. Something had caused Josh to blush, and she couldn't help but wonder what it was.

"Maybe instead of rosebuds on my necklace"— Filly abruptly changed the subject—"I will paint small feathers on it. That would give it a more southwestern feel with the wood and leather, and y'all are all working with turkeys, so we could make it a family thing."

A family thing. Those three words stuck in Emma's mind. She had had many dinners with her mother and father, but not once had there been anything like game night, or even vacations. They were both too wound up in their jobs for such tomfoolery, as Victoria called it. The closest thing to a vacation that Emma ever had was when Rebel asked if she would like to join her and Sophie on a Saturday trip to Six Flags.

The happiness she had felt that day rushed over her as she remembered the fun of riding the roller coasters, eating hot dogs and cotton candy, and getting to buy souvenirs to take home. But the shadow of Victoria's attitude came back to ruin the moment of euphoria. When Emma had handed her a tiny shot glass with the Six Flags logo on it, she had frowned and said, "This has to be the tackiest thing I've ever seen."

At least Daddy pretended to be proud of the one I gave him, and he put it on the desk in his office, she thought. *I kind of feel sorry for him for having to put up with Mother.*

Josh would have liked to stay longer at Emma's that evening, but after everyone had seen her new painting, Arty and Filly both wanted to get back to their houses to watch their favorite reality television show. The air in the trailer grew heavy, the awkwardness stretching between them, so he made an excuse and hurried outside. Back at his trailer, he hooked up his little square record player on the back porch and sat down on the steps to listen to some of his vinyl collection—

while he scolded himself for not taking advantage of the situation and talking to Emma.

When Simon and Garfunkel started singing "Bridge Over Troubled Water," he closed his eyes and let one of his favorite songs sink deep into his soul. He was thinking that this song could so easily be his song to Emma and didn't even realize anyone was close by until she spoke his name.

His eyes popped wide-open and he stammered, "You startled me."

"Then we're even. You gave me a start at supper," she said. "I was lonesome, so I came out for a walk. That's one of my favorite songs—I didn't know anyone even had records anymore. I thought everyone had gone to using their phones to bring up music."

"Got time to sit down for a little while?" He moved his legs to give her space.

"Sure." She nodded and took a seat. "I used to listen to this song over and over. Mother said the music I liked was depressing."

Josh's folks fussed about his obsession with art, but they gave up trying to transform him into a brain surgeon or a nuclear physicist when he was eighteen and refused to go to college. "What other songs did you listen to?"

"I like the older country music and jazz," she answered. "Especially Etta James and Sam Cooke, and some Cajun. But after the second round of being in an institution, I quit listening to anything except what Mother thought was appropriate for me."

"Why would you do that?" Josh asked.

"My therapist agreed with Mother and thought that maybe the music was depressing me even more, so . . ." She shrugged.

The song ended, and the needle came back to rest in the right place. He didn't want her to go, so he asked, "And now?"

"I would listen to all of it now, but"—she blushed—"I got mad and threw my phone away the first day I was here. Mother could trace me with it, and she was really angry, so I knew she would come down here and make me go back to a long-term care center."

"Well, you are welcome to come listen to my vinyls anytime you want," he said. "I've got an Etta James and also a couple of George Jones. We could just sit here and listen to them this evening if you want to."

"I'd like that." She smiled.

He made a mental picture of the way her eyes lit up. Sometime that week, he was going to draw her again—this time from the waist up, with her hair in braids and Filly's necklace hanging down between her breasts. A fiery heat started on his neck at the thought of drawing something that close to an intimate part of her body. He jumped up and hurried into the trailer so Emma wouldn't see him blush. While he was inside, he splashed cold water on his face and picked out half a dozen records.

That was Emma out there on his porch. Sure, they'd taken walks together and even spent a day working on their art, but that wasn't like a date. This was—at least to him it was. He'd never been on a date, and he wasn't sure how it should all go. Didn't most of them involve dinner and a movie?

You are both artists. His grandfather popped into his head with a chuckle. *You don't do things like other people. Evidently, she likes spending time with you or she wouldn't be waiting for you. Now get it in gear and get back out there with her. She might not want to wait forever.*

"Sorry I took so long," he said when he carried the records out to the porch. "I should have asked you to come in and pick out whatever you like. I have a really big collection. Would you like a beer or something to drink?"

"I'm sure whatever you've got is fine, and I don't need anything to drink right now," she said.

He removed the record on the player and put on a George Jones. "We had this elderly guy who was my grandpa's friend. Harry was his name, and he and his wife, Sally, lived down the street from us. When Harry's wife died, he spent even more time with me. We used to listen to his vinyl records and go fishing together. Then a year later he passed away and left a big chunk of his money to me. Before that, though, Harry gave me that old record player right there and all his vinyls. I've got a fancy stereo setup in the house, but I bring this one outside and listen to the music, like we did back when . . ." He choked up at the memory.

"Sophie and I used to listen to music together. I missed that when she wasn't there anymore," Emma said.

"I still miss him"—he swallowed hard—"a lot."

"I'm so sorry. I can't imagine losing Sophie. We hadn't talked in years, but friendship like we have and what you had with Harry doesn't need words every day. It's just knowing that that person is there," she said. "But your friend is gone, and that has to leave a hole in your heart." She slapped a hand over her mouth. "I'm so, so sorry. That came out wrong. I would never . . ."

He reached over and removed her hand. "It's okay, and you are right. It did hurt for a long time, but now I just think of all the good memories and let go of the pain. I do feel bad that I didn't go to his funeral, but I couldn't bear to see him in a casket. I wanted to remember him sitting in his living room with me while we listened to his records."

"Then you did what was right for you," Emma said. "That's all any of us can do when it comes right down to it. I've tried for all my life to make my mother happy, but it's only been since I came here that I've realized that's impossible. She doesn't like me or my father. She only likes her fancy friends, her money, and her job. And even at that I wonder if she even likes herself. How could anyone so calculating and self-centered like themselves?"

"I think my folks like me," Josh said, "especially now that I'm getting a name in the art world, but I've always felt like I disappointed them. I hated school, so that put an end to me becoming something they understood and could be proud of. My dad wasn't real happy when Harry named me as the heir to his estate. He and Mother have only visited me a couple of times here at the trailer park. They both thought I was crazy for buying it, and for not moving into my grandpa's big mansion. But before he died, Harry told me that I should make myself happy. This place makes me happy."

"Artists are often . . ." She shrugged. "You know."

"Yes, I do." He sat down beside her on the top step but kept his distance.

Sophie had told them when she first brought Emma to the park that she was a little like Coco.

Josh understood that it would take time for her to be comfortable with him, but he had hopes that someday she could see him as a real friend—and maybe more.

Chapter Thirteen

Sophie stood in the middle of the building that might be the art gallery and let the spirit of the place talk to her. That would sound crazy if anyone else felt that way, but she was an artist, and to be able to work in a place, she had to be at peace in it.

The old building had such character, with its high ceilings that were covered in copper tiles. True, they'd been painted pale blue, but the detail was still there, and someday if Sophie and Teddy wanted to have them stripped, there was that possibility. The walls needed a fresh coat of paint, but the black-and-white floor tiles, so evocative of the seventies, would be perfect once they were cleaned and waxed to a shine.

"Oh," Sophie gasped when she saw the loft where her studio would be. "Once those windows are cleaned, there will be light and"—she stopped and wrapped her arms around Teddy's neck—"is this really going to happen?"

Teddy removed his glasses and cleaned them on the tail of his shirt. "I see us being happy here, don't you?"

She pulled him to her lips for a long, steamy

kiss. They were both panting when she took a step back. "This building loves us, but this is all so perfect that I feel like the other shoe will drop any minute. Are you sure you are ready to settle into one place and to be committed to store hours? You won't regret this decision in a few years, will you? You're used to traveling and setting up shows for artists—to wheeling and dealing and selling their things. Are you going to be happy just working with me and selling art out of this place?"

"I will absolutely never regret it. Knowing that between customers I can run up those stairs and make out with you through the day, and have lunch with you, go home with you, sleep with you every night. You want me to yell *yes* from the rooftop of this building?" Teddy grinned.

"Just from the depths of your heart," Sophie answered.

"You got it, darlin'. Shall we go downstairs and make an offer on the place?" He tucked her arm into his.

"Yes, please, and thank you." This was happening way too fast, but then perhaps that's the way it had to work or else she would go insane with worry over every little decision.

"Hey, don't thank me. This is a joint effort. You are going to have to keep the work coming to hang on the walls, and"—he escorted her down the stairs—"talk your friends into letting us display their art as well. You've got your job cut out for you as much as I do. And, honey, if you need to go off to the wilds to paint for a couple of days now and then, I might pout, but I'll understand."

"I love you more every day," Sophie said.

"Of course you do. I'm your soul mate." He gave her a squeeze as they headed toward the front of the building, where the Realtor waited.

There was no doubt about him being her soul mate, but there was still just a little something hanging on in her heart that worried that she might be caving in because she didn't want to disappoint Teddy. She would have to get rid of it—somehow, some way—before they had the broom ceremony.

Emma had worried about how much the phone that she'd asked Josh and Arty to pick up when they went to town would cost. She had little to no idea what the price of anything was these days, and she only had a hundred dollars in her purse. "Dammit!" she swore as she stared at a hummingbird flitting around the red flower on a cactus not far from the back porch. "No mother should treat her child like this. Even a teeny-tiny hummingbird protects its babies. They don't mentally abuse them, and they damn sure don't take away their money so they can't even buy a phone."

She was still keeping an eye on the bird when

the landline rang. She rushed inside and caught it on the fourth ring.

"Hello," she panted.

"Hey, girl, did I get you out of bed with some handsome guy?" Sophie teased.

Emma's face went up in a red-hot blush. "I might ask you the same question."

"Not right now, but if you'll call in about an hour, you'll hear me trying to catch my breath for sure," Sophie said. "I've got so much to tell you that I don't even know where to begin. I have to talk fast, because we're about to board the plane."

Emma sat down on the floor, leaned back against the bar, and sincerely hoped that the excitement in Sophie's voice meant it was good news. "Start at the beginning."

"First of all, the house that Teddy rented is going up for sale, and we're going to buy it and move in together. He's going to change jobs, stop traveling, and—"

"You're going to live in Del Rio," Emma butted in. "Isn't that closer to this place than Dallas? If I stay here, we won't be so far apart. Tell me more."

"Yep, and there's two extra bedrooms upstairs if you want to live here with us," Sophie offered.

"No, thank you," Emma said. "I love you, and I appreciate the offer, but you and Teddy need to live your own lives. I never want to live in a city again, but I'm happy you'll be closer than Dallas. I'm still hoping that Josh will rent me this trailer on a permanent basis."

"Have you talked to him about that?" Sophie asked.

"Not until I see if I can sell enough paintings to afford such a thing. I told Josh to get me a phone when he and Arty go to town. Filly's going with them this time, and she said she knew just what kind to buy me, but now I'm worried that I won't have enough money to pay for the damn thing. Mother sure screwed up things when she froze my accounts," Emma said.

"Well, you've got a while to figure that out, because that rent is paid up through the week of July Fourth," Sophie told her. "And, honey, I talked to my lawyer, and he's looking into that business. I don't think she can legally do that."

"Thank you! I hate to ask, but if that phone is more than what I have . . ."

"There's money in the coffee can in the freezer, and two envelopes with our grocery money on top of the fridge. Give Josh an envelope a week while I'm gone and use what you need from the freezer. You can pay me back anytime you want," Sophie said.

"Thank you, again, but I thought we were only going to be here a couple of months."

"Nope, I pay for April through July. But this year is special. Teddy and I are going to have a broom-jumping ceremony on July Fourth." Sophie was almost breathless.

"You are engaged!" Emma squealed. "You committed!"

"I did, but"—Sophie lowered her voice—"I'm still a little worried that maybe I'm just agreeing so that I won't hurt Teddy's feelings. We need to have one of those all-nighter talks when I get home."

"We can do that. But if you love him, and you know it in your heart, what's there to be worried about? Can I please decorate the broom?" Emma asked.

"Ask Filly if that's what the maid of honor does. We are only inviting my mother, his dad, and the folks at the park. Then we're coming back here to Del Rio to honeymoon in our own house while we work on getting the gallery ready to open," Sophie said.

Emma heard what Sophie said, but she could hardly believe it. "Gallery? You're opening your own gallery? Oh. My. God! Sophie, this is what we always dreamed about doing when we were young. You will continue to paint, right?"

"Of course. I'd die if I couldn't smell paint every day." Sophie laughed out loud.

"Tell her the rest now." Teddy's voice was faint, but Emma heard it very well.

"We're buying this old building here in Del Rio," Sophie said. "I was saving the best until last."

"Why would you do that?" Emma asked. "And your engagement is the best anyway."

"It's got an upstairs loft where I can paint, and we want to sell your paintings, too, and I want to bring in Josh's work, and Arty's and Filly's. We are only going to sell Texas art, and we'll promote and advertise, and . . ." She stopped to catch a breath.

"Are you kiddin' me? For real, your own place to sell your work?" Emma was glad she was sitting on the floor. "And you really want to display my little paintings?"

"You promised Leo six paintings, but after that, I want you to sign with us exclusively," Sophie told her. "I can't expect Arty and Filly to give me an exclusive since they've been working with Leo so long, but I sure want your things. We'll drive up there once a month to pick up whatever y'all will let us have, and that way I can have a visit with you. Or you can bring it down here to me and spend a few days in our house."

Emma shook her head even though she was aware that Sophie couldn't see her. "And what would I drive? I don't have a vehicle anymore, and unless your lawyer can figure out a way to get Mother to unfreeze my accounts, it will be a long time before I have one again."

"Honey, pretty soon you will be able to buy any type of car you want," Sophie said. "Leo knows paintings, and those two you sent with him are going to sell high, believe me. Then when we open this place in the fall, you'll be raking in the money."

Sophie was a lot more confident than Emma could ever be. She wouldn't let herself think in terms like that. She just hoped that she could make enough money that she would never have to leave Hummingbird Lane, and that Josh would rent the trailer to her on a permanent basis.

"Are you still there?" Sophie asked.

"I'm here, but I think I must be having a dream. This can't all be real. My heart is thumping around in my chest like a bass drum," Emma said. "To think that only a little while ago I was trying to figure out what exactly I was repressing and how to remember so I could stop going to institutions."

"Stick with me, my friend, and there might be more on the way," Sophie said.

"Can I tell the rest of the family?" Emma asked.

"Of course, and ask Filly to tell you even more about jumping the broom," Sophie said. "Em, I'm so happy and so excited that I think I'm the one having the dream."

"We have to have a cake and wine, and . . . ."

"Nothing big or fancy," Sophie laughed.

"And a dress," Emma finished.

"We'll talk about all that when I get home," Sophie said. "Right now, they're calling us to board the plane. See you later." Her voice dropped to a whisper. "And if you've got a hot-line to heaven, pray that this fear that I'm rushing into this will go away."

"You got my prayers, my positive thoughts, and love. See you later." Emma held the phone in her hands for a few minutes before she stood up and put it back on the base. When she and Sophie were little girls, neither of them liked to say goodbye, so they just said *see you later.*

"Hey! You ready for supper?" Josh's voice floated through the open back door.

"Be right there." She slipped on a pair of flip-flops and went out the front door.

Josh met her halfway across the lawn. They fell into step together, and her hand brushed against his. A strange feeling wrapped itself around her at just that simple gesture. Was that what Sophie had been talking about in college, one of the last times they had met for ice cream? She had said that there were sparks or vibes between her and her newest boyfriend, some substitute professor. Emma stole a few glances at Josh. He was handsome, and kind, and funny, and she was comfortable with him, but what they had was friendship—not unlike what she had with Filly and Arty.

Did touching Arty's hand when he passed the biscuits at the supper table ever give you a little jolt? Sophie's voice was in her head.

Of course not! Emma pushed the crazy thought aside.

"I've got news from Sophie," she said when she took her seat across the table from Josh and Filly.

"Arty, hurry up and say grace," Filly said. "And make it a short one, because I want to hear what Sophie said. It must be good news, since Emma looks like she's about to dance a jig."

Arty bowed his head and said, "Lord, thank you for this food. Amen." Then he looked over at Filly. "That short enough?"

"It'll do." Filly nodded. "Now pass the potpie, and, Em, you start talking."

Emma wasn't sure where to begin, but the most important thing in her mind was Sophie's happiness, so she said, "Teddy and Sophie want to have a commitment ceremony right here in the park on July Fourth, and they want to know more about how to jump the broom, so, Filly, what can you tell me that you haven't already?"

"Are you serious? That's fantastic," Josh said.

Emma almost reached across the table and laid her hand on his. Just that thought shocked her. She hadn't even wanted to be in the presence of a man after the rape. She could tolerate her father, though he'd never visited to test that point. She wondered if him not coming to see her was due to something her mother had said—or threatened.

Good God, you aren't a child, girl. You can

have friends, both male and female. Sophie scolded her in her thoughts.

"Well, now, that's good news, but this is a long way from anywhere for the guests," Arty said.

"Don't be a killjoy," Filly fussed. "Folks have cars. We can have an early evening ceremony and hang twinkle lights in this tree. I'll make the cake, and we'll fix up this old table with a pretty white cloth. How many folks will be attending?"

"No more than ten, I would guess." Emma noticed that Josh finally smiled. "The bride and groom, Rebel, Teddy's father, and us. Now, about that broom thing?"

"Rebel could stay in one of the empty trailers, and Teddy's dad could stay in the other one," Josh offered. "Rebel has been down here before, so we know her."

"I've told you everything I know about the ceremony. The bride and groom say their vows, give each other a ring if they want to, and then they join hands and jump over the broom. And that's that. We'll decorate it up real pretty," Filly gushed. "I'm so dang happy, I could dance around a bonfire."

"Please don't." Arty dipped deep into the chicken potpie and put several spoonfuls onto his plate. "I don't have enough burn medicine to cover your body if that big floppy skirt of yours went up in flames."

"Oh, hush!" Filly slapped him on the arm.

261

"We've got time to plan the ceremony and think about an appropriate wedding gift. Do you think they'll come back here every year once they're married?"

"There's more," Emma said. "They're going to buy a house in Del Rio and live there permanently. This trip to Europe will be Sophie's last big gallery showing."

Filly threw a hand over her heart. "She's not going to stop painting, is she?"

"I asked her the same thing, and she says she'll *never* quit painting," Emma said. "But there's still more."

"She's pregnant?" Filly clamped a hand over her mouth. "Are we going to be grandparents?"

Emma shook her head. "No, but it's almost as big as that. She and Teddy are buying an old store building with a big loft. He's going to run a gallery, and she'll use the loft for painting. And . . ." She still had trouble believing the rest herself. "And she wants all of us to let her put our work in the gallery. They'll open in the fall, and she asked me for my work exclusively at that time. You all can talk to her about that part when she gets home, but she wants some of your work to go in the gallery, too. I'll sell some stuff to Leo until then, but—"

"That's huge!" Josh said. "But we can't cut Leo out altogether. He's been too good to us through the years."

"We can sell to both places," Filly said, "but you make a good point. Leo depends on us, so we'll need to share between the two."

"Sophie will come up here once a month to get whatever we've got for her, so we'll get to see her pretty often." Emma didn't realize that she'd included herself in the future plans until the words were out of her mouth.

"We?" Arty raised an eyebrow.

Emma frowned. "About that? I know I've only been here a few weeks, but I love this place and . . ." She paused, trying to figure out a way to ask to rent Sophie's trailer on a permanent basis. "I'd like to stay on after July."

"You don't want to move to Del Rio to be closer to Sophie?" Josh locked gazes with her across the table.

She felt like his eyes could see right into her soul, but it didn't make her uncomfortable. Instead there was something exciting about sharing the moment with him.

"She offered to let me move into the house with her and Teddy, but they need their time to be together," she said, "and I'm"—she blinked and looked down at her plate—"I know in my heart that I may never be ready to live in a big city. So, Josh"—she raised her face—"can I rent Sophie's trailer, or will you sell me a little land when I can afford it to build a tiny house on? I prefer having the trailer because it's home now, but I understand if you don't want to tell the snow-birds that rent it that it's taken on a permanent basis."

"You can have the trailer for as long as you want it," Josh said without hesitation.

To Emma, that was even better news than having her paintings displayed in Sophie and Teddy's gallery. Tears dammed up in her eyes, but she refused to even shed happy tears. Sophie said that she was strong and could make her own decisions, and she'd just managed to do both. She didn't have to leave Hummingbird Lane. If she could only make enough money with her artwork to pay the rent and feed herself, she could be happy there forever with her little newly found family.

"Well, hot damn!" Arty clapped his hands. "Every bit of this is the best news ever. If we had a bottle of champagne, we could celebrate."

Emma shuddered at the thought of champagne. She filled her mouth with potpie to quash the memory of the taste.

"I've got some beers in my fridge," Josh offered. "After we finish supper, maybe we could raise a bottle and have a game of cards."

"Yes!" Filly said. "Em, I was going to tell you that you could live with me if Josh wasn't comfortable telling the folks they couldn't rent the trailer. We just love having you here with us."

Emma couldn't help but compare their enthusiasm with the blunt statement her mother had made that day when Victoria told her she had never wanted children.

Chapter Fourteen

For the next week, Emma and Josh spent almost every evening on his back porch listening to his records. She painted through the day and had supper with the folks in the evenings. Filly ran in and out of the trailer throughout the days to show Emma the jewelry she had made, to check on her progress with her pictures, and to write down plans for Teddy and Sophie's marriage ceremony.

Emma could hardly believe it when she looked at the calendar that morning. It seemed like she had lived at the trailer forever, and now could live there as long as she wanted. She had finished five paintings for Leo since Sophie had left. She had even caught herself humming and singing while she worked. But that day was going to be a test for her. She would be left alone at the park for most of the day. The last time she talked to Sophie, she had said that her lawyer had checked into the money situation and was thinking that he might be able to settle things with Victoria.

Emma wasn't holding her breath. She'd even considered calling her father to see if he could talk sense into her mother, but she couldn't bring herself to do it—not yet, anyway.

"I'm going to be alone today," she whispered, "and I'm not even scared. Is that stupid or am I making more progress?"

Filly had asked her to go along with them, but she had a couple of ideas for the last things she wanted to do for Leo, and then she would work the rest of the summer on pictures for the new gallery. The quiet would be nice.

Emma had slept through the nights without nightmares, but she did lock the doors. That morning, she had forgotten about the locked door until someone knocked, and she had to run from the back porch to open it for Filly.

"Sorry about that," Emma said.

"Honey, if it makes you sleep better, then it's no big thing. We're about ready to leave. Have you thought of anything else you might need this next week? Need me to pick you up any feminine products?" Filly asked.

Emma hadn't thought of that in months. With her depression and the medicine, she had a period about every three to six months, but she was happy these days, so maybe her body would begin to work like it should. "Yes, please," she said as she grabbed a notepad and wrote down what she needed.

"You sure you'll be all right here by yourself until midafternoon?" Filly asked. "I can stay home if you're not comfortable with us all going."

"I'll be just fine," Emma replied. "I've got lots of work to do, and the time will go by fast."

"All right, then, we'll see you later." Filly gave her a quick hug. "I know you and Josh have been spending a lot of time together, but if you ever want to talk about anything, I'm just across the yard. My door is always open."

"Thank you." Emma nodded. "You'll never know how much I appreciate that."

Emma followed her outside and waved from the porch as they drove away in Josh's black SUV. She popped a breakfast pastry into the toaster and poured herself a glass of milk. She'd just put the steaming-hot tart onto a paper towel and taken the first bite when she heard the crunch of tires on gravel outside. Thinking that Filly had forgotten something, she didn't even go to the door to check on things. Then she heard a faint pounding on a door, and then another one. She took a drink of the milk and tiptoed to look out the storm door. She had to blink a dozen times to be sure that what was in front of her wasn't a figment of her imagination.

"Jeffrey?" she whispered as she squinted against the morning sun.

There was no doubt that was her mother's driver out there pounding on trailer house doors. Then he was coming up on her porch and knocking on her own door.

Emma stepped out onto the porch wearing a

pair of Sophie's bibbed overalls with the legs cut off to make shorts, a bright-turquoise tank top with paint stains scattered over it, and no shoes on her feet. "Are you looking for me, Jeffrey?" she asked.

"Your mother has sent me to bring you home," he said. "Go get in the car. It's time for you to end this folly and come home. Those are her words exactly."

Emma opened the door. "Come inside, Jeffrey. Would you like some breakfast? I was just having a Pop-Tart and some milk. I'm sure you'll find it delicious."

Jeffrey crossed his arms. "I do not want food. You've had your fun. Now you will be going home and getting the help you need at a center where they know how to treat your problems. Again, I'm delivering Victoria's words."

"Do you ever have a thought of your own, or are you just Mother's little lapdog?" she asked. That wasn't very nice of her, but it felt damn good to say it.

That seemed to strike him speechless, and he blinked several times. His mouth opened, but no words came out.

"Either come in or leave." Emma's hands shook as she held the door open. "But I'm not going anywhere with you, no matter what Mother says." She had never been afraid of Jeffrey, but he was a big guy, and she wasn't sure she would

269

come out on the winning end if he decided to manhandle her into the vehicle.

"All right, I'll give you ten minutes, but then you will be leaving," Jeffrey said. "I can't believe that you are living in a place like this. Your mother has your best interests at heart. You should be in a place that would care for a person like you properly, not living out here in the slums."

"One man's slum is another man's castle," Emma said.

With his head held high, and his back ramrod straight, Jeffrey marched across the porch and into the trailer. "This place smells awful and looks even worse."

Emma swept a hand around the room to take in the sofa, the barstools, and the rocking chair. "Have a seat, Jeffrey."

His nostril twitched, and he shook his head. "I'm not sitting anywhere in this place."

"Have it your way." Emma sat down on the sofa. "You know, I used to feel sorry for you. Mother has always talked down to you like you were something she tracked in on her shoe, but the way you're acting now, I think you're on her side. Are you in love with her or something?"

His jaw dropped, and he glared at her. "You aren't worthy to be her daughter," he hissed.

"I always liked you, Jeffrey, but you're just like her." Emma sighed.

Coco came through the open back door and jumped up in Emma's lap. "This is Coco. She's kind of the trailer park community cat."

"I hate cats and so does your mother." He checked his watch. "Your time is running out."

"No, *your* time is running out," Emma said as she stood up and crossed the room. She picked up the house phone and dialed her mother at the office.

"Is Jeffrey there?" Victoria asked without saying *hello, how are you,* or *kiss my ass.*

"Yes, he is, and I've got something to say that should have been said when I came home from college. You never even asked me why I was a wreck. You just put me in that first miserable therapy center and forgot about me. I was raped, and I couldn't tell you because—"

"What did you do?" Victoria's tone turned as cold as ice. "Go out to a bar and go home with the wrong guy?"

"That's exactly why I couldn't tell you," Emma said. "I knew you'd blame me and call me stupid, which I was for trusting my friend." She went on to tell her the whole story. "Trusting him is on me. But you let me think I was delicate and hid the way the world worked from me, so that's on you. I was raped and humiliated, and I repressed the memories rather than tell you, and now I'm not leaving this trailer park. I intend to live here the rest of my life."

"You've always been a weakling like your father, who, by the way, has filed for a divorce from me, and just so you know, my lawyers will be crushing that lawyer that Sophie hired. I'll fight you to the end for the money. If you want to be your own boss, then you can find your own money," Victoria hissed into the phone.

"Frankly, I don't know why Daddy has stayed with you as long as he has. Did you finally drive him as crazy as you tried to do with me?" Emma could hardly believe that she was standing up to her mother, but it felt damn fine.

"Don't be curt with me." Victoria had gone from cold to demanding. "I took him out of the gutter and gave him a good life, but I'm glad he's filed. I would have done it right after my mother died, but well"—she paused—"I wanted you to have a father."

"I'm calling bullshit on that, Mother. I lived in that house. You didn't give a good hot damn about Daddy—or me, for that matter," Emma said.

"Don't you use that kind of language with me," Victoria growled.

Usually, when her mother lowered her voice, it meant that she was really angry, and Emma went into a panic mode. That was when she tried to fix whatever she'd done wrong, and as usual, she felt her chest begin to tighten. She made herself breathe and remember that she was strong, and she had a good future ahead of her like Filly said.

"It's the truth, Mother. I've been a bother to you from the day I was born, maybe even before, so why would you want me to come back to Dallas now?" Emma asked.

"It's where you belong," Victoria said. "My daughter doesn't live in a hovel like this. What would I ever tell my friends? And you can tell Sophie to call off that damned lawyer. My name was on those accounts, and there's nothing you can do about it."

"You can tell your friends that I'm alive and happy and starting to make a name for myself in the art world. I sold two paintings last week, and that should pay the rent on this trailer after July and buy whatever food I need. And, Mother, I'll face you in court if I have to over the money that is mine. I don't give a damn about the company, but the money that my grandmother left me is mine. I'm just not afraid of you anymore." She was stretching the truth. Those two paintings might not sell for months, but Victoria didn't need to know that. "I really don't care what people think of me anymore, Mother. Not even you. Sophie has shown me that I can make my own decisions and my own way now. And I got far enough away from your control to remember those repressed memories. I'm dealing with them without institutions or therapists, and I'm getting stronger every day."

"You should have been smarter than to go with

that kid to the apartment of someone *I* didn't know. You've always been gullible, just like Wyatt. Sophie has bewitched you, just like Rebel did Wyatt all those years ago."

"Why are you like this?" Emma asked. She could hear her mother tapping her foot on the hardwood floor of her office.

"Like what?" Victoria tapped her foot.

The tapping of the foot was one of her last resorts to bend Emma to her will. It meant time was running out, and Emma had better agree to do whatever Victoria wanted her to do.

"Like controlling. Like so cold. Like you hate me." Emma asked, "What happened to you that you didn't want kids and made you give me to the nanny to raise? You must have a demon in your past, too."

"I raised you like my mother raised me," she said. "I grew up to be the businesswoman that Mother was, and she was proud of me. I might have had some pride in you if you hadn't turned out to be so much like your father."

"Daddy has worked for you all these years and has done a good job. He's stood beside you at whatever you wanted—dinners, trips, all of it," Emma reminded her.

"But he wasn't the one I loved," Victoria said. "The man who should have been your father was strong, and I loved him. Your father was just a means to an end."

Emma was the speechless one now. Her mother had been in love? Was that why she was so bitter?

"Why didn't you marry that man?" Emma whispered.

There was a long silence.

"You didn't mean to say that, did you, Mother?" Emma said. "You've always been so close-mouthed about everything that I don't even know you. What happened that the love of your life didn't marry you?"

"My mother happened," Victoria answered. "She said he wasn't good enough for me, but she said I had to have a child to leave the family business to, so I married the worst guy I could find. Every time I looked at you, I thought of what I should have had, and I hated you. At least you were too backward to ever run the business, so I can sell it instead of passing it down to you."

"I'm sorry you've had such a miserable life," Emma said, "but you are not controlling mine anymore. Why don't you just do what's right and unfreeze my bank accounts? For once have a heart."

"I'm not having this conversation with you. My company will never be in your hands, or any of the money from it. I have a buyer for it, and since you aren't mentally stable, you don't get a dime of that money, and I'm not giving you a dime of that money that my mother left you. Time's up. If you come home, I might let you live in a decent permanent-care facility."

"Mother, I wish you all the best in your retirement, but I don't give a damn about the company, and there's no way you can put me in an institution. I'm an adult, remember? That's why you always made me sign myself into those places. If I've got enough to make rent and put food on the table for myself, that's all I need," Emma said. "And maybe a fancy new flowery skirt every so often. I do like the way I dress these days."

"Why couldn't you have had a backbone when you were a little girl?" Victoria sighed.

"I was afraid of you back then, but I'm not anymore. I've come to realize what is important," Emma said.

"And what's that?" Victoria's tone went icy cold.

"I woke up after a horrible nightmare about that rape, Mother, and Sophie was here for me. She has helped me get past the guilt and the pain. After that night, something just clicked, and I realized that I care less about what other folks think of me and more about what I think of myself. I have come a long way in these past few weeks. I thought my life was such a mess that I would never recover, but this little family I have here supports me with love and kindness. I can smile again and put all those horrible memories behind me, and I'm proud of my strength and the person I'm becoming," Emma said.

"That sounds like a bunch of psychobabble," Victoria said.

"You should know the sound—it's from all those institutions you sent me to. I'm sorry you feel the way you do. I'm sorry you couldn't hang on to the love of your life. I'm sorry I couldn't be the person you wanted me to be, but I'm not sorry that I am the person I am right now. If you ever change your mind, you know where I am," Emma said.

"Goodbye," Victoria said, and hung up.

Emma's head pounded so hard that it would take more than two aspirin to make it better. She just wanted to be alone—no, she *needed* to be by herself for a little while so she could cry or throw things or just scream to get out the rage that she felt. Her time was her own.

She pointed at the door. "You can leave now, Jeffrey. I'm not going with you."

"Please come home with me." He'd resorted to begging. "I simply can't go back there without you."

"Like I said, I liked you, but I'm not leaving this place," Emma told him.

Jeffrey's face looked like he had eaten green persimmons, but he gently closed the door when he left.

"Well, that went well," she told Coco. "And

poor old Jeffrey is still a gentleman, even though he's been in Mother's presence so much that he has a little mean streak. He didn't even slam the door even though I know he was so mad he was humming."

The cat opened one eye and meowed.

"Don't take it personal. Jeffrey is just like Mother. Neither of them likes kids or animals." Emma picked up the phone and called Sophie.

"Hey, girl, how's it going? Are you all right there by yourself?" Sophie answered.

"Jeffrey just left, and I called Mother," Emma answered.

"Holy crap!" Sophie gasped. "What happened?"

"I'm fine, and I mean it this time," Emma said. "I love you, Sophie. You are my best friend, but I've just figured out that I can stand on my own two feet. I can make it on my own, so I. Am. Fine. I'm not just saying that this time. She spoke her mind. I spoke mine. I may be poor the rest of my life, but in a lot of ways I'm richer than I've ever been." She told Sophie the rest of what had happened.

"I'm proud of you and so sorry that you can't have a relationship with her like I have with my mama," Sophie said. "And I'm so glad you called because I just talked to my lawyer. He had your mother served with papers. We are suing her for what is rightfully yours. I'll testify for you, and I bet Arty and Filly will, too. And Josh will even come out of the park if we need him to, I just know he will."

"It wasn't easy, Sophie, but I feel stronger for having told her about the rape." Emma's voice almost broke, but she got it under control. "You told me I was strong and that I can make my own decisions. I leaned on that thought pretty heavy while I was talking to her. Now tell me about the showings. How are they going? Are you going to come home with a million dollars in your pockets?"

"I just might if we have another sale like this when we get to Rome," Sophie laughed. "This has been an amazing experience, but I'm so ready to be home."

"I'm so proud of you and for you," Emma said. "You're carving out a place in the world. But for now, you should go enjoy being with Teddy. We'll see you in a few days."

When the call ended, Emma got out her brushes, paints, and a canvas and carried them to the table behind Filly's house. Hummingbirds were fluttering around the feeders, their long bills acting like straws to suck up the sweet red water.

She painted in a blue sky and then added some fluffy white clouds. After that, she laid in just enough of the edge of a feeder to catch a little of one of the yellow plastic daisies around the glass.

"And now the bird." She smiled. "No darkness anywhere today, just a bright picture. Hello,

Coco!" she said when the cat walked across the table. "What do you think, girl? Shall we defy all logic here and dress the hummingbird in bright colors? It's not a purple lizard, but we can give it some extra help."

Coco gave her a pitiful meow.

"Does that mean you want me to paint it as I see it or as I see the hope of a brighter future?" she asked.

Coco yawned and curled up on the end of the table.

She laid in the general outline of the bird with his wings outstretched. "I feel like I opened up my own wings today, and now I can fly."

She painted his chest bright red, added a bit of turquoise to his tail and back, and, as a final touch, put just a hint of purple on his bill. With a few strokes, she made him come alive with yellow in his wings, and with the smallest detail brush she had, she wrote the word *hope* into the lines of his tiny feet and signed the work in the bottom right-hand corner.

"An artist can make the hummingbird any color they want, just like a lizard," she whispered to Coco.

"Yes, they can," Josh said from behind her.

"Sweet Lord!" She gasped and almost dropped her paintbrush in the dirt. She'd been so involved with reliving the phone call with her mother that she hadn't even heard a vehicle drive up in the front courtyard. "You startled me. I wasn't looking for you to get home for a couple more hours." She held up the painting. "What do you think?"

"It's my favorite ever. If I can have it, I'll give you free rent for the month of August on the trailer," he said. "I see happiness, and I love the color."

"It's yours." Emma extended her work toward him. It was hard to believe that one little painting had netted her another month in the trailer. Maybe by the time that month was up, this thing with her mother and the money would be settled.

He's a sweetheart for doing this, she thought as she stole a long look at him while he was studying the picture in his hands.

"Thank you," Josh said. "We brought sub sandwiches. Come on around to the table and have one with us."

Emma nodded. "I'm starving, and I've got a lot to tell you all about what happened today." She was so happy that the family was home and she could share everything that had happened that day with them. The news wasn't as big a thing as when she got to tell them about Sophie's engagement and the new gallery. But just knowing that she was getting stronger every day made her feel closer to Josh—closer to them all.

Chapter Fifteen

Depression was nothing new to Emma, but sheer restlessness was. Her days had been planned from the time she woke up in the morning until she went to bed at night for so long that she loved her newfound freedom. But this antsy feeling down deep inside her was something she had never experienced.

She watched the sunset that evening from her back porch, but it wasn't nearly as pretty as the sunrise had been that morning—before the showdown with Jeffrey and her mother.

"That's it!" She snapped her fingers. "I so wanted her to be sympathetic and say that the rape wasn't my fault, that maybe she shouldn't have kept me away from the world so much as a child. I could actually have developed some street smarts. Instead, she excused herself. Nothing has ever been her fault."

Josh rounded the end of the trailer. "Hey, want to listen to some music this evening?"

"I think I'd rather talk," she said. "Want a beer or a glass of sweet tea?"

"Beer would be great." He smiled.

"Come on inside," she said as she stood up and headed for the door.

She took two bottles of beer from the fridge and handed one to Josh, then motioned for him to sit on the sofa. She took a seat on the other end and sat cross-legged. "I can't decide if I'm jittery or antsy or what the deal is tonight. I already told you about what happened when Mother called, but I just realized that she's been unhappy for most of her life. And yet she's never taken any responsibility for her unhappiness. When something was her fault, she blamed someone else every time. It would be good for her to have to go to court and tell them that she's robbing me," she blurted out as she twisted the top off her beer and took a sip.

"I'm not sure I could have faced my father in court if he had decided to protest Harry's will, but if you have to do that, then I'll be there for you," Josh said.

Emma smiled. "That means a lot to me. What if she wins?"

"Then I'll whisk you out of the courtroom and bring you home to the trailer park." He grinned.

"You're funny, but, Josh, I'm really kind of scared about it," she said. "I was pretty brazen on the phone, but facing her in a court of law is another thing."

"Sometimes you have to fight for what you

283

want, or what is yours," Josh said. "You can do this, Em. I know you can."

"Thank you," she said. "That gives me confidence."

"I'm sorry your mama said those things to you," Josh said. "I know what it feels like to be different in a world of really smart people, but my folks did want a child. Of course, they wanted me to grow up to be something like a nuclear physicist. So, there you go. Hearing your mother say that had to sting, but not spending time with you is her loss."

Emma glanced over at the exact spot where Jeffrey had stood. Could it have really been just this morning? It seemed like the visit had happened years ago. "It did hurt to hear her say it again, but not as much as it did when I was about twelve years old. Down deep I think I knew it even as a toddler. Pretty often, days went by when Mother didn't even come into the nursery. Daddy popped in every evening, but he only stayed a little while. When I was little, he'd read a book to me. When I got older, he would play a board game with me. He'd grown up in foster care, so he can't have had many role models when it came to being a dad."

"What happened to his parents?" Josh asked.

"They died when he was a little boy. He had no living relatives, so he was put into the system, but at least Daddy tried." She sighed. "I told her something this morning that"—she paused—"I was hoping she'd react differently to. Rebel would have shown sympathy, but Mother . . ."

"Want to talk about it?" Josh asked.

"Yes, I do, but it's bad," Emma said. "And I'm afraid it will affect our friendship, and I don't ever want that to happen." She began to wring her hands together. *I have to stop this,* she thought. *He needs to know why I am so scared of relationships.*

"Can't happen." He smiled.

Just those two little words and his smile filled her with the confidence to go on. She took a deep breath and spit out the story of the rape and the nightmares, and even told him how she thought that she'd killed both guys. She kept her eyes on her beer bottle and didn't look up at him until she finished. When she finally did glance his way, he had taken his glasses off and was wiping away tears with the back of his hand.

Other than Sophie and Rebel, no one had ever shown her that kind of empathy. She could tell that what he felt wasn't pity but sincere, and it warmed her heart so much that she reached over and took his hand in hers. "Thank you for listening and for not looking at me with disgust right now."

"I'm so, so sorry that you had to endure that, Em." He laid his free hand on top of hers. "But most of all, I'm sorry that you had to carry that around with you all those years. I wish I had known you then so you would have had someone to talk to about it."

"I should have called Sophie, but I just thought if I didn't admit that it happened, then it would go away." She liked the feel of his hand on hers. "I wish I had known you then, too, Josh. We're so much alike that it would have been nice to have had a friend like you."

"You've got me now." Josh freed his hands from hers.

"Thank you." One more little obstacle conquered. She liked to be touched by a man, even if it was just holding hands.

He worked on his glasses with the tail of his T-shirt and then put them back on. "Hey, I almost forgot. You told us to get you a pay-as-you-go phone, but I just got you one like mine and put you on my plan." He pulled the phone out of his shirt pocket and handed it to her. "I took the liberty of setting it up to the Wi-Fi we've got here at the park, and"—he ducked his head—"I made a playlist so you can have music while you work."

When she took the phone from him and his bare fingers touched hers, it excited her. The warmth of his hands on hers, even in a simple gesture like a brush, was so different from anything she'd felt from a man in the past, and she liked it—a lot.

"I can't thank you enough," she said, "but you didn't have to do something like this."

"You need a phone when you go out there"— he motioned with a flick of his wrist toward the outside—"to scout for new ideas. Want to listen to the music I put on there? Or would you rather go down to my trailer and listen to records?"

"We wouldn't have to keep changing the records if we just listened to the playlist here, and besides, I'm anxious to hear what you put on it," she said.

"If you don't like any of them, you can redo it," he suggested. "The first one is 'Bridge Over Troubled Water,' because that's the first song we heard together."

Emma started the list and laid the phone on the rocking chair. "That is so sweet. I love this song so much. Like the words say, when I'm weary and feeling small, I know I have friends right here that will help me get through the tough times."

"Just know that I'll always take your part if things get dark, Em," Josh said. "I'm here for you anytime you want to talk."

Emma knew that he meant every word, but was it just as a friend? She'd begun to look at Josh with new eyes lately and was beginning to yearn for something more—something like what Sophie and Teddy had.

"You don't think I'm damaged goods since"— she winced—"you know."

"I'm sorry that happened to you, but here at Hummingbird Lane, we all respect you, Em." Josh slipped his arm around her shoulders and gave her a hug. "You will work your way through this, and I'm always here for you if you need me."

"Thank you, again, for everything." Emma leaned her head over on his shoulder and listened to Chris Stapleton singing "Millionaire." The words talked about love being more precious than gold. She could believe that with everything in her heart, body, and soul. Whether it was the love of a companion, a friend, or a parent, that's what made a person a millionaire, not dollars or dimes. Love—the real thing—was what she wanted.

What is the real thing? the voice in her head asked.

It's trusting whoever you are in a relationship with to love you unconditionally even if you're damaged, she answered.

Warm sunshine on his face woke Josh the next morning. He could feel someone staring at him and opened his eyes slowly to find that he wasn't in his bedroom. Coco was staring at him from the arm of the sofa in Emma and Sophie's trailer. Emma's back was spooned right up to him, and he held her safely with an arm around her.

He started to jump up, but he was afraid he would wake her. The playlist must have started all over again when it reached the end, because Simon and Garfunkel were singing the bridge song again. Coco meowed loudly, and Emma wiggled in her sleep.

Josh tried to figure out a way to get up without pushing Emma off the sofa, but when the front door flew open, she solved that problem in a flash. She was on her feet and staring first at him and then at Filly, who was standing just inside the door with a plate in her hands.

"Good morning," Filly said with a grin.

Emma's hands went to her chest and then down her arms. "I'm dressed," she said.

"Yep, you sure are. You kids fall asleep listening to music?" Filly carried the plate over to the bar.

"We must have," Emma said.

"I knew that fancy phone Josh got you would be just the thing. Thought you might like some of my blueberry scones for breakfast," Filly said. "I'll leave y'all to them. Got another plateful out on the table that I'm sharing with Arty this morning."

"Thank you." Josh sat up on the end of the sofa and fumbled around on the floor for his glasses. When he put them on, he slowly scanned the room. "I thought I was dreaming."

Filly giggled and waved as she stepped outside.

Emma turned around to face him. "What happened?"

"We fell asleep. I don't remember us stretching out together, but we must have gotten comfortable sometime in the early hours of the morning," he answered. "Are you mad at me?"

"Why would I be angry?" She crossed the room and started to make a pot of coffee. "You kept me from falling off the sofa. Come on over here and have some scones with me. Want a glass of milk to go with them?"

"Love one." He was so relieved that she wasn't angry with him or uncomfortable that he crossed the short distance from sofa to the bar and sat on one of the barstools. "I didn't intend to stay the whole night."

"I liked having you here." She set two mugs on the bar and then rounded the end to sit down beside him. "I slept really well, even if we were sharing the sofa. Now, what were we talking about when we fell asleep?" she asked.

"Music," he answered.

"That's right." She nodded. "We were discussing how the songs on the playlist seemed to fit my situation."

"Kenny Chesney and David Lee Murphy singing 'Everything's Gonna Be Alright.' " He grinned. "It will be, you know. You're going to be fine, Em, I promise. Sophie's lawyer will take care of your financial stuff, and even if you have to go to court and lose the case, you can make money on your own selling your art."

"I hope I can live by my own wits. We heard a Rascal Flatts song last night that kind of fits my situation. It talks about a broken road that led me to this place in my life. Looking back at all the bad things—like when Mother fired Rebel, the rape, and the repressed memories—I'm glad that I'm right here today, Josh. I don't think I've ever been this happy in my whole life."

What if this is all you ever get? the voice in Josh's head asked. *She's experienced trauma in ways that she has to fix on her own. You can be here to help her if she needs to talk, but there are things you can't fix.*

I would if I could, Josh thought as he picked up a scone and bit it. The buttery layers and bits of blueberries tasted sweet in his mouth. Sweet like Emma had been to make him feel less awkward about staying over. He wanted her to be more than a friend, but he didn't have any experience with women, and what she'd had with men was downright horrible.

Just be yourself, and spend time with her. His grandpa's voice was clear in his head.

"Hey," he said, "I'm taking my four-wheeler out this morning. Want to go with me?"

"Where are we going?" she asked.

"I thought I'd ride out to the base of the mountain for some inspiration on what to do next. We've got to work on some pieces for both Leo and Sophie now."

"I'd love to," Emma said, but she had doubts. Could she really crawl on the four-wheeler behind him? She had cuddled up next to him on the sofa, her back against his chest, but she didn't remember how they'd gotten in that position. Her mother would have a fit if she knew that she'd slept with Josh or that she was going out into the desert with him on a four-wheeler. Even though he had money, he would never be good enough for a Merrill daughter, not even an unloved one.

Whoa! she thought. *It's not Mother's business what I do anymore. I have to get past thinking like that.*

And the dependence on Sophie? Victoria's whispers were so icy that they gave her a chill even though the woman wasn't there.

"Great," he said. "I'm going home to get my supplies ready. I'll make us sandwiches in case we want to stay out past lunchtime. Be back in an hour." He disappeared out the door, and Emma reached for the cordless phone.

"I realize I'm depending on Sophie, but I need advice." Emma poked in the number for Sophie, and then she hung up.

She paced the floor for five minutes. "I can't do this on my own today. I need help," she declared.

"Admitting that you need help is part of the healing process," Nancy had said in a session. "Let me help you remember what you have locked away, Emma. Tell me why you left college and never went back. What happened to you there? It's all right to talk about it and to ask for help when you are overwhelmed."

She carried the phone over to the refrigerator, where Sophie had written down the phone numbers for Filly, Arty, Josh, Rebel, and herself. She started to call Sophie again, and then remembered that she would probably be getting things ready for her next showing. She should be thinking about that, not giving Emma dating advice. She was still thinking about calling Sophie when the phone rang. The noise startled her so badly that she dropped the receiver on the floor and had to scramble to pick it up. She finally answered on the fourth ring.

"Good morning again, Em. I wanted to tell you that I didn't mean to embarrass you kids this morning," Filly said.

"Lord, I'm glad you called," Emma said.

"Honey, I'm not the Lord, but what's going on?" Filly giggled.

"I just need to talk to someone. I've got all these strange feelings and . . ." She sucked in a lungful of air.

"I'll be over there in two minutes," Filly said, and the line went silent.

"Thank you," Emma said with relief and went to the door to watch for Filly. Sure enough, in a few seconds, she came out of her trailer. Her bare feet peeked out from under her flowing skirt as she hurried across the yard. When she was on the porch, Emma threw the door open.

The first thing Filly did was stop and hug her tightly. Then she took her by the hand and led her to the sofa and pulled her down beside her. "I'm here, honey. Tell me what's happened."

"I thought when I remembered what happened in college, it would all be over, and I would be a whole person again, but here I am needing help."

Filly patted her on the arm. "We all need help. Talk to me."

"I like Josh, but I'm afraid to like him," Emma said.

"Why? He's a good man, independent, solid, upstanding," Filly said. "I could go on and on, but you know him, Em, so what's the problem?"

"It's not Josh, it's me," Emma whispered.

Filly slipped an arm around Emma's shoulders and hugged her. "You are a good woman. You and Josh have a lot in common, and you—"

"I have stuff in my past." She frowned. The nightmares had brought out the story to Sophie, and Emma had told Josh because she wanted him to understand her issues.

"Talking about it will help you face it, so try to remember," Nancy had said.

She kept her eyes on her hands, folded in her lap, and said, "I had one guy that I thought was my friend when I was in college. We sat by each other in art classes and talked every day that semester. He betrayed me." She paused for a moment. "He let another boy drug and rape me. The therapists tell me I have repressed memories, but it goes deeper than that. Mother never wanted me, so it stands to reason she wouldn't want me to inherit the company. She's been destroying me so that I wouldn't be fit to run the precious company that means more to her than I ever did."

"Oh, honey, that's what you call gaslighting. Take a breath and sit here with me for just a minute or two before we go on." She reached over and took Emma's hands in hers.

That calmed Emma's racing thoughts and turmoil, but after a few seconds, she blurted out, "What am I going to do?"

"About you? About Josh? Or about both of you?" Filly asked.

"It has to be about me before it can be about anything or anyone else," Emma said.

"Then you've answered your own question," Filly said. "Straighten you out so that you don't need anyone to complete your life or heart."

"Sophie needs Teddy," Emma said.

"No, Sophie *loves* Teddy. She is complete in her own self. She can survive without anyone. Think about it like this: If you had to have Josh to live or function, what would happen if he died? You would be right back where you were when you depended on your mother for everything. Work on getting where you need to be within you, and then you can think about what happens with you and Josh," Filly said.

"Like you, huh?" Emma said.

"I wasn't always like this." Filly smiled. "There was a time in my life when I thought I had to have a certain young man in my life to make me whole. I got him, and everything was rainbows and unicorns until he decided to leave the carnival with another woman."

"What did you do?" Emma asked.

"I went to pieces, of course, and that's when I realized that it was all right to grieve, but it was not all right to depend on someone to define who I was. It took several months, but I came out on the other side a stronger person," Filly told her. "You will, too, but you have to hunt for yourself before you do anything else."

"Hunt? That's a strange word," Emma said.

"Honey, we are hunting our whole lives. As women, we hunt for love. As artists, we hunt for inspiration. As people, we hunt for truth. You've been on a quest to find out what happened to you to make you so dependent on others, and you've found it, but now you have to hunt for your own inner peace. Remember what I told you when I read your palms? You are a strong person who will influence others. You want that, but you want someone who will influence you in ways that will balance your relationship." Filly dropped her hands.

"Did you ever find someone like that?" Emma looked down at her hands and felt just a little empty without Filly's touch.

"Sure I did," Filly said. "Arty is my partner. We balance each other."

"Really?" Emma could feel her eyes widening.

"Oh, yeah," Filly answered. "Years ago, when we were younger, it was physical, but now that we're older, that part has begun to fade and we're just the best of friends. We've had an amazing journey together."

"But you argue so much," Emma said.

Filly chuckled. "That's just our way. Be true to you, and the rest of the world, including Josh, will love you."

"But what if . . . ," she started.

"Worrying about *what if* ruins your day," Filly said.

"I'm thirty-five years old, and I don't even know how to kiss a man," Emma admitted and felt her face burn with a blush.

Filly's chuckle turned into a giggle. "Honey, kissing comes as natural as breathing. Just let nature take its course and don't overthink anything."

"I must sound like a fool," Emma whispered.

"Never." Filly patted her on the knee. "If you have questions, feel free to call me. I'm glad you feel close enough to me to feel like you can ask me anything."

"Thank you, Filly." Emma smiled.

"Now, stop worrying and enjoy this beautiful day. I hear Josh's four-wheeler coming this way. Are you kids going out today?"

"We're going out to"—Emma's smile got even bigger—"hunt for inspiration."

"Then you should be going, and so should I. I've got jewelry to make and dessert to think about for supper tonight." Filly got up and slipped out the front door just as Josh rapped on the back one.

Chapter Sixteen

Emma had been nervous the first time she rode the bike she got for her eighth birthday, but with Rebel's help and a lot of encouragement from Sophie, she had mastered the thing in a few tries. She grabbed up her backpack and was heading toward the door when Josh knocked.

"I'm ready," she said.

"Great." He slid the door open for her and stood to one side. "It's a nice, sunny day for writing down ideas and maybe even doing some rough sketching."

That same feeling that she had had the day she rode the bike—fear that she couldn't do it—knotted her stomach into a pretzel when she looked at the four-wheeler.

You don't have to drive the damn thing. Sophie's giggles were so real that Emma glanced over her shoulder to see if her friend had come home early.

Josh slid out of the seat and stowed her backpack in one of the saddlebags attached to the sides of the machine, then got back on and slid forward. "Have you ever ridden on one of these before?" he asked.

"Nope," she answered. *Or sat behind a hand-some guy on one, either,* she thought.

"Just get on behind me." Josh patted the back of the seat. "I'll go slow and try not to hit too many gopher holes."

She slung a leg over and settled in behind him, but there was no way she could keep any distance between them. Her front was plastered against his back, and her legs were against his. Every nerve in her body tingled, her breath shortened, and her pulse raced. She wasn't sure what to do with her hands. Should she wrap them around his waist or hold on to the sides of the seat?

"I've never had anyone ride with me before, Em, but I think you'd feel more secure if you hold on to me," Josh said.

"All right." She wrapped her arms around him and then didn't know whether to clasp her hands together or splay them out on his chest. She finally opted for the latter. He revved up the engine a little, and they were off.

True to his word, he did not go fast, but the wind in her hair and the instant feeling of total freedom were like nothing she'd ever felt before. If she ever made enough money with her artwork, she was going to buy one of these things for herself. Riding in or even driving a car had never made her feel like this, but then the only time she'd been this close to a guy before was in the halls at the elementary school as all the kids rushed from class to class.

Your father hugged you and kissed you on the forehead before he told you good night, the voice in her head reminded her.

That's different, she argued.

And then there was the rape. You were close to Terrance during that horrible ordeal, the pesky voice reminded her.

Don't ever compare Josh to that monster, she said silently.

"Are you all right?" Josh yelled over the roar of the engine and the wind. "I can feel your heart racing."

"I'm fine," she answered. "I can feel your heart doing the same." She amazed herself when she tapped her fingers on the left side of his chest. She was flirting, and it didn't feel weird.

"Only other time I've had a girl pressed up against me was when I woke up this morning," he admitted.

"You've never dated?" she asked.

"Nope." He stopped the vehicle and turned off the engine. "Don't get off. I just wanted you to see the cottontail rabbit over there against that big cow's tongue cactus. He'd be a real cutie for one of your paintings."

The bunny was sitting up on his hind feet and staring right at them. She took her new phone from her hip pocket and took a picture of him. "I can see him sitting at the end of a rainbow," she whispered.

"Or maybe with a stylized cactus behind him. He'd be the only real-looking thing in the picture," Josh suggested.

"Purple cactus with pink spines." She thought again of what Sophie had said about the liberties an artist could take with her work.

"Might be interesting." Josh fired up the engine.

She tucked the phone back into the hip pocket of her jeans and wrapped her arms back around him. Then they were off again. The mountain range didn't look nearly as tall when Emma viewed it from the trailer, but the closer they got to the shade that it threw, the bigger it was.

Josh parked the four-wheeler under a big scrub oak tree. She moved her arms so he could hop off, and then she slung a leg over the seat and did the same. He got out their supplies and a quilt from the saddlebags.

"You thought of everything," she said.

"This ain't my first time to come out here. I even discovered a cave about a quarter of the way up the mountain." He grinned. "We'll spread this out and have a little snack. Then we'll just let the ideas for future projects come to us."

"How do we do that?" Emma asked.

"The ideas?" Josh whipped the quilt up into the air, let it fall, and then smoothed it out. "You just lay down on your back and stare at the tree limbs and leaves and even the clouds. You clear your mind of everything and wait. When you get an idea, you write it down. I brought two small notebooks—one for you and one for me."

"Couldn't we just make a note in our phone?" she asked.

"Of course, but I always back up everything with notes in case I lose my phone. You can use the notes app on your phone, but there's no service when we're this far out. That picture you took of the bunny was about the last place that got reception," he explained. "We can spend the whole day until dark, or if nothing comes to mind, we can go home anytime we want."

She opened her backpack and brought out two bottles of water and some snacks that she'd packed, thinking the whole time that she should have tucked in more. But then, she hadn't figured on spending the whole day. And ideas about painting? Forget that when she was stretched out beside Josh on a quilt all day. Her mind would be going in circles about him and what Filly had said about hunting for truth, love, and inspiration, not thinking about pictures to produce for Leo and Sophie.

Josh handed her a protein bar and a bottle of apple juice. "There's"—he blushed—"I don't know how to say this"—he rolled his eyes up toward the sky—"but if you need it, there's toilet paper and a small trenching tool in my backpack."

"I brought some, too, but I didn't think of a little shovel." She'd lay dollars to doughnuts that Sophie never had to discuss such things on her first date with Teddy. She opened the protein bar and took a bite. *Forget love, inspiration, and truth. I'm hunting for the new me.*

Josh handed her a small notebook and a sharpened pencil, finished the last of his snack, and stretched out on his back. "Those clouds look like an angel. I wonder if I could do justice to them in a drawing, maybe with just a hint of color in them from the sun rays."

Emma never wanted to paint angel clouds again. Just looking up at them made her skin crawl and her stomach almost rebel at the small protein bar she'd been eating.

"I don't paint clouds that look like angels' wings," she said.

"Why?" He turned his head to look at her. "You know you can talk to me, Em. I'm a dang good listener."

She thought of all the times that Nancy had tried to get her to open up about her memories and she couldn't. Maybe she should call Nancy and talk to her on the phone about some of this. Sophie and Josh, along with Filly and Arty, *were* her friends. She could talk to them, and they would help her, but maybe Nancy could help even more.

"I'd just finished the painting a day or so before

and gotten my final grade on it," she sighed. "Rebel used to tell me and Sophie that we had guardian angels that would wrap their wings around us and protect us. That's what I thought about when I was working on it. Then no one, not a guardian angel or a real person, was there to protect me when I was raped." She told him about how she felt at the hospital and how she had sneaked out. "I took a knife from the kitchen and destroyed the painting because my guardian angels had forsaken me."

Josh reached across the distance separating them and laced his fingers with hers. "I understand, but someday you might be ready to paint angel clouds again."

"Thank you, but what I really need to do is figure out who I am right now," she said.

He pulled his hand free. "How long do you think that will take?"

Suddenly she felt pressured to figure things out in a hurry, and yet she needed the time to work through it all. Would Josh be willing to wait, or did he want a relationship now?

"I have no idea. It took my whole life in some ways to get me in the shape I was in before I came to the trailer park, so I expect it will be a slow process. I'm sorry if . . ."

He turned his head and reached for her hand again. "I didn't mean to pressure you. Take all the time you need."

"Seems that I'm always saying it, but thank you, Josh." The antsy feeling of being pressured to rush was gone in the blink of an eye.

"Look at those birds, Em." Josh turned back so he could see the sky again. "They're flying close to us, but you could paint them in the middle of that heart-shaped cloud." He was a little disappointed that she wasn't as ready as he was to be more than just friends.

What makes you think you'd even know how to have a relationship? Maybe you need to work on your social skills before you think about a girlfriend. You couldn't even keep it together enough to go to public schools. This time it was his mother talking to him.

Emma broke into his thoughts before he could argue when she asked, "What kind of birds are they?"

"Mexican jays," he said. "The blue on them is so brilliant that they . . . oh!" He sat up and grabbed his notepad.

"What?" She popped up to a sitting position right beside him just in time to see a lizard crawling onto their quilt. "What is that ugly thing?"

"That would be a Texas toad, or what folks around these parts call a horny toad. I haven't ever done a drawing of one of those," he said as the round thing that looked like it popped out of a sci-fi comic book made its way across the quilt.

Emma giggled. "If Sophie was painting that thing, it would be purple."

"What if I draw it with a cactus off to the side of the canvas and put just a tiny bit of purple in the cactus flower?" Josh finished the rough sketch and laid his notebook back down.

"I can't wait to see it. I think I'll do one of it all stylized with purple horns and maybe blue eyes." She made notes until the reptile scurried away.

"Now the day hasn't been totally shot." Josh grinned. "If I get even one idea when I come out here, I feel like it's profitable." Mentally, he was making notes about his next drawing of Emma's face with the sunlight filtering through the oak leaves onto it.

Josh loved the peace of this place, with the birds singing, crickets chirping, and the occasional coyote adding his voice to the mixture. But he had never liked it nearly as well as he did when he shared it with Emma.

"Is that thunder?" she asked when a low rumble sounded on the other side of the mountain.

"It's not supposed to be stormy today." He stood up and walked out past the four-wheeler. Sure enough, dark clouds were gathering and moving toward them from the southwest, pushing all those puffs of white to the side as if they were nothing but marshmallows. "But I guess it is. We'd better cut our trip short or else we'll be dodging lightning bolts here in a little while."

Dammit! he thought as he put everything back into the backpacks. He'd looked forward to a whole day with Emma, and a damned storm had ruined it.

She grabbed one corner of the quilt, and he got the other end. Together, they folded it and loaded their backpacks into the saddlebags. Then Josh hopped onto the four-wheeler and tried to start the engine, but it only made a grating sound. The noise when lightning struck a nearby tree deafened them. The thunder that followed compounded the racket, and Josh jumped off the vehicle.

"What's the matter with it?" Emma's eyes had gone wide with fear.

"We're going to be fine," Josh tried to reassure her. "I've had to spend some time out here before. Remember me telling you that I discovered a cave just a little way up the mountain? Well, we should be heading that way if we don't want to get soaked."

"I've never been inside one, but it sounds better than this. How far is it?" she asked.

"About a quarter mile up that mountain." He tossed her backpack to her.

She caught it and slung it over her shoulder while he strapped his on and tucked the quilt under his arm. "I already smell rain, and it's a steep climb, so we should hurry."

"Lead the way," Emma said.

The path that he'd used to go from the base of the mountain to the cave had grown over and gotten tangled since the previous fall, but it was still passable, even if they did have to sidestep a few cacti. "I found this place the year I bought the trailer park," he said. "I was following a rare kit fox up here and happened upon the cave. I was kind of scared to go inside it at first—bats scare the bejesus out of me—but I forced myself to face my fears and go inside. There were no bats or animals of any kind, thank goodness, but I did find where my fox had probably had a litter of babies. I guess I tainted the cave, because I've never seen any other foxes or animals up here."

Lightning zigzagged out of the sky and seemed to land only a hundred feet off to the side of the pathway. Thunder followed so low over their heads that Emma stopped and covered her ears.

"Just a little farther," Josh yelled over the din just as the first drops of rain splattered on his glasses. "See that big cedar tree? It's a few steps beyond that. Take my hand. It's steeper from here to there."

She grabbed for his hand without hesitation. "What happens when it all ends? We don't have phone service to call for help. Will Filly and Arty come looking for us?"

"Not until morning," Josh said as he pulled her inside the opening to the cave. "I told them we might not be back in time for supper, but when we aren't there in the morning, Arty will come this way." He went straight to a lantern and lit it.

"Oh, my!" Her eyes grew wide again as she took in the cave.

"After the first time I got stuck up here, I got prepared. There's dry wood back there for a fire." He pointed to the circular pit outlined with rocks. "Over there on that big rock are a few cans of beans and a couple of flashlights. Even if I don't have to stay here, I check on the place a few times a year and make sure firewood is ready if I need it."

"Well, thank you once again," she told him just as the wind picked up and the rain fell outside the entrance in gray sheets. "We sure wouldn't want to be huddled up under that tree with this much lightning."

Josh dropped his backpack and spread the quilt out near the firepit he'd circled with rocks a few visits ago. "I'll build us a little fire to warm this place up."

Emma shivered. "What can I do to help? Is that hail?"

He turned and looked at the cave entrance. "Yep, and that would be why it's gotten so cold. If you'll sit down right here in the middle of the quilt, I can wrap the edges up around you. That will keep you warm until the fire gets going." She sat down, and he pulled the edges up over her shoulders to make a shawl. "The fire will take the damp off the cave in a hurry."

"I didn't even think about a jacket," she told him.

"These storms come up fast out here in the desert," he said as he laid kindling in the firepit. Once that was burning, he put a few small logs on top of the embers. "First time I did this I was afraid the smoke would run me out of here, but this place has a natural vent up there to get rid of the smoke. I'd love to know the story of why that's even there."

"I'll make up a story for you." She smiled.

"I'd love to hear it," he said as he got a good blaze going.

"Once upon a time, a princess lived in this area in an adobe castle with her parents, the king and queen of Hummingbird Lane. She fell in love with a young man, but he was a lowly blacksmith," Emma said, "and the king would never consent to her marrying the man. Jeremiah, the blacksmith, found this cave when he was running away from the princess's brothers late one night. He pulled some brush over the opening, and they never found him, so it became the place where he and the princess could meet."

Josh pulled back the quilt on one side and sat down. "You should have been a novelist as well as an artist."

"When I was a little girl, I spent lots of hours

entertaining myself with made-up stories. Mother fussed at me for spending more time with my stories and pictures than I did with math and history. Truth is, I never wanted to do anything but paint anyway, and I would much rather have cleaned houses like Rebel did than run a big oil company like Mother. Rebel was my hero," Emma said.

"Tell me more of this story that you just made up." Josh could have listened to her soft voice all night.

Emma turned her head slightly and smiled.

"Her name was Rachel, and his was Jeremiah. She was a beautiful woman and he was a very handsome man, but he was just a poor man. They knew they could never be together, so after a very long winter, they decided to run away together. They traveled all the way to the shore and lived happily ever after," she said.

"And it all started right here in this cave?" Josh asked.

"Yes, and it was raining the night they made plans to run away together, just like it is now," Emma said. "The end." She had moved closer to him and wrapped a part of the quilt around him.

"But I wanted a whole long family saga that brought the story right up to this century," he protested, hoping that if she kept talking she would stay right beside him.

"Maybe you are a descendant of one of them—

either the blacksmith or the princess. One of their spirits led you to this cave because they knew that someday, you would need protection." Emma spun more of the story.

"I would rather share genes with the blacksmith. They were artists of a sort." He stretched out his hands to warm them over the fire.

"Then that's who you will get your DNA from in my story. He had a strong, square jaw and brown eyes," she told him.

He blinked several times. "My eyes are hazel, which is pretty common."

"Rachel had very light brown eyes, and down through the ages, there were some blue-eyed people in my story." Emma smiled.

"Do you think I've saved a princess from getting wet?" he asked.

"No, you've saved a commoner from getting hit by lightning. I don't want to be a princess. I just want to be a common woman who lives in a trailer, goes out into the desert on adventures, and paints pictures of horny toads with purple spikes on their ugly little heads," she told him.

"You can be anything or anyone you want to be in this part of the world," Josh said. "Did your mother or father tell you bedtime stories when you were little? Is that where you got your ability to make up fascinating tales?"

"Mother didn't have time for that. Daddy used to read to me sometimes, and I looked forward to the evenings when he read to me, but after I learned to read for myself, that ended. Rebel used to make up tales for me and Sophie, though. She would entertain us girls when she took her lunch break, and I would sit almost in a trance listening to her."

The wind blew a few hailstones the size of golf balls across the floor of the cave. The storm had settled right over them, and it was beginning to look more and more like they would be there the rest of the day and probably through the night.

Josh didn't mind that idea one bit. He could have lived in the small cave for the rest of his life with Emma. "You really love Rebel, don't you?"

"Oh, yeah!" Emma nodded.

"Then why didn't you call her when"—he stammered a little—"when that happened?"

"I didn't want Rebel to think I was a complete idiot," she answered. "Locking it away in a box and throwing away the key was easier than talking about it to anyone until now."

"Well, I'm glad you can talk about it," he said.

"Me too. Did your parents tell you bedtime stories?" she asked.

"My grandfather's friend, Harry, kind of filled in with that role. He spent a lot of time with me, but his stories were more like fishing stories," he said. "Mother and Dad were pretty wrapped up in their careers, and still are."

"Well, I love stories," Emma said as she looked

around the tiny cave. "And I like this place. I'm glad you found it."

Josh's heart swelled. Emma liked his cave and had told stories that made him look like a warrior. He wouldn't mind if they had to stay in the cave for the night—not one bit.

Chapter Seventeen

The story had been just a tale that Emma made up to pass the time when she and Josh were in the cave. The characters weren't real, and she'd made up the names in her rendition of *Romeo and Juliet*. But when she awoke for the second morning with Josh spooned up against her back and his arm around her, she wished that it were real. As the characters, they would have already had a first kiss, and most likely even slept together—as in real sex. That terrified Emma more than she would like. What if when she finally did get past the kiss, maybe even the making out, she froze when it was time for sex? She had told her therapists in the counseling sessions that having a relationship terrified her, and they had assured her that when the right time came for that step, she would probably be comfortable with it.

"Yeah, right," she murmured. *I couldn't even remember why I felt that way, so how could they know how I would feel?*

"Did you say something?" Josh tightened his hold on her.

"I was just mumbling," she whispered. "Oh. My. Gosh!"

"What?" He started to jump up but got tangled in the cocoon they'd made with the quilt tucked in around them.

"Shh . . ." She put her finger over his lips and pointed toward the cave entrance.

"Is that real or are we dreaming? Is that really bright sunshine I'm seeing?" He sat up and untangled the quilt.

"The storm is over." Emma pointed to the firepit. "There's nothing left but embers, and I'm starving. Think we could break out the last of those energy bars?"

"Or I could build a fire and warm up a can or two of beans," he suggested.

"Then we'd have to make sure the fire was put out before we left. How far is it from here to home?" Emma asked. "If we have to walk, can we get there by noon? That's when Sophie gets back. I'm dying to hear more about her trip. We've talked on the phone, but it's just not the same."

When they had packed everything into their backpacks and stepped out into the sunshine, Emma noticed that raindrops were still hanging on to the oak leaves, and she took her notebook out of her hip pocket.

"I want to paint that leaf," she said.

"That would be a great picture for your Hope

collection." Josh carefully buckled the front of his backpack over his chest. "Ready to go forth and overcome the obstacles?"

"What's that supposed to mean?" Emma asked.

"We came up the mountain on dry ground. Going down is going to be on a slippery slope, but we have lots of saplings to hang on to," he explained. "I've only made this trip once after a hard rain, and I rolled most of the way to the bottom. Course, only my pride got hurt. I'll lead the way, and we'll go slow."

"I can't imagine life without art now that I've found it again. I love doing the small things." Emma inhaled the clean morning air and felt happiness surge through her—real happiness. She took the first step and her boot sank down into at least an inch of mud, and even that didn't spoil the joy in her heart.

A sucking sound came from Josh's boots every time he moved forward. Emma grabbed a small tree trunk for support with each step. She slipped a couple of times, but she was able to get her balance before she took a tumble or sat down flat on her butt. But near the bottom of the slope, there were no more trees to hang on to, and the mud was even deeper. Josh went even slower at that point.

Emma kept her eyes on the ground and took one step at a time—right up until a big black snake slithered out of nowhere. She froze. Her breath stuck in her chest. Her hands trembled when the thing crossed right over the top of her boots. She tried to scream, but nothing came out. She shivered so hard that she lost her footing and fell forward, bumping into Josh on the way. Together, they tumbled, ass over teakettle, all the way to the bottom. When they finally stopped rolling, she was lying on top of Josh, and they were both covered in mud.

"I'm so sorry," she apologized. "Snake . . ."

"Where? Are you all right? Did it bite you?" Josh wrapped both arms around her and sat up with her in his lap.

"It's gone now," she panted, "but it crawled across my boots. I hate snakes."

"Me too." His breath came out in short gasps. "Are you sure you aren't bit?"

"I'm fine, but I lost my backpack." She realized at that moment that they were sitting in a mud puddle that was at least six inches deep with cold water. When Josh gazed into her eyes, she wouldn't have cared if the water came up to her chin. She didn't even realize that anyone was nearby until Arty chuckled. She looked up to see him holding her soaked green backpack. "You kids doin' some mud wrestlin' or something?"

His voice startled Emma so badly that she tried to jump up but only fell again and landed on top of Josh a second time.

"Do I start countin' now to see who's the winner?" Arty laughed out loud.

Emma looked up at him. "Why would you count?"

"Haven't you ever seen a wrestling match, girl? Got to count to ten or you don't win this match. Hold him down and you can get the golden buckle." Arty pulled a snow-white hankie from the bibbed pocket of his overalls and wiped his eyes. "Filly will be jealous that she didn't get to see this."

"Where did you come from?" Josh sat up again.

Emma stood up and stepped away from the puddle. "I'm just glad my mother isn't here to see it."

Josh got to his feet. "I wish she was here so she could see that her daughter has chosen to be a mud-wrestling queen. She might begin to believe that you are going to be yourself no matter what."

"Well, thank you." Emma did a curtsy.

"If you two are through flirting, we should get on home," Arty said.

"I wasn't flirting." Josh blushed.

"We're covered in mud. How can that be flirting?" Emma tried to wipe the mud from her jeans, but it just smeared.

"Yep, you were, and right there in a mud puddle." Arty chuckled again. "Right now, we need to get you home and cleaned up."

Home! Emma liked the sound of that. That's

what had been missing in her life. All she had needed to find herself was to find a home first.

"I've got the four-wheeler on the trailer, and Filly is worried about y'all. She went over to take some waffles to Em this morning and found her gone. Then when she stopped by your place, Josh, and you were gone, we pretty well figured y'all got caught in the storm. But y'all ain't getting into my truck looking like you do. You can ride in the back."

"Fair enough." Josh nodded. "I've got to retrieve my quilt. I lost it on the way down." He jogged back to the place where the fall had begun, picked up the poor muddy old quilt by the corner, and dragged it along behind him.

"You look like Linus from the Charlie Brown cartoons," Emma said.

"We both look more like Pigpen." Josh threw the quilt into the back of the truck, unhitched his backpack, and tossed it over, too. He hopped up on the trailer and extended a hand to help Emma.

"I can do it by myself, but thank you," she said.

"Yes, ma'am." He inched his way around his four-wheeler that Arty had already strapped down and sat down with his back to the cab.

Emma crawled up on the trailer and followed his lead.

"Everyone ready?" Arty called out the window.

"Yes, sir," Josh yelled back.

"Well, that was an adventure like none I've ever been on before," Emma said. "Not even Six Flags was that much fun."

"How did you ever endure Six Flags?" Josh asked.

"Rebel was there. She always made things easier." Emma remembered the day very well. The excitement of getting to go and riding with Rebel in her car with no air-conditioning. Sweat sticking her hair to her face. Eating hot dogs on the go. Picking out souvenirs for her mother and father. But most of all she remembered giggling with Rebel and Sophie.

"Did you ever go?" she asked Josh.

"When I was still in public school, they took us on a field trip to that place. I made it through the gates, saw that crowd, and spent the rest of the day in the bus with my sketchbook," he answered. "I wanted my grandfather to go with me, but he couldn't take off work. I asked if Harry could be a chaperone, but Mother said I needed to grow up and be a big boy."

"Well, you are a hero in my eyes," Emma said. "You took me to the cave and even let me win at mud wrestling. When we get home"—she smiled at the way the word rolled off her tongue—"we should ask Filly or Arty to take a picture of us so I can show it to Sophie."

"We could take selfies now." He pulled his phone from his hip pocket. "I'm glad we have waterproof cameras. Let's see if they're mud-proof as well."

The past days had gone by so fast that Sophie couldn't hardly take it all in. Her showings had all been very successful, and in a few short hours, they would be home. She couldn't wait to see Emma again, and yet there was an underlying sadness in her heart and soul.

"We should be at the trailer park by noon," Teddy said as he loaded their luggage into the back of his truck.

Sophie wrapped her arms around his neck. "Just think, in just a couple of weeks, we won't have to leave Texas again. If anyone wants one of my paintings or anything we sell in our gallery, they can come get it. I love you, Teddy."

Teddy tipped her chin up, and their lips met in a string of steamy kisses that made her knees go weak and every nerve in her body tingle. When the kisses ended, he held her close to his chest for a few more minutes, their hearts pounding together at the same rate.

"I hate goodbyes," she whispered.

He buried his face in her blonde hair. "We're working on never having to say that again. For right now, we'll focus on a day at a time, and today we're on the way to see Emma and the rest of our friends."

"I'll need to come back to Dallas that last week

and get my loft cleared out. I called my landlord yesterday and told him that I'd be out before my rent is due on the fifteenth of the month. So, we can spend that week together." Sophie wanted to focus on the logistics of everything rather than saying goodbye to him.

"I'll keep the bed in my apartment until the last minute." He opened the door for her. Once she was settled, he rounded the truck and slid in behind the wheel. He started the engine and drove away from the airport. "I'm so glad that Em has done well while we've been gone, so you won't worry about leaving her for another week."

"Me too," Sophie answered. The trip was supposed to erase all her doubts and fears about making such a rushed decision to leave her Dallas loft and move to Del Rio, but it hadn't.

Her phone pinged, and she dug it out of her purse and smiled when she saw that it was a FaceTime call from Emma. She hit the accept icon and gasped. "Holy crap on a cracker! What happened to y'all?" She held up the phone so Teddy could see the screen.

"Looks like we missed a mud-wrestling event," Teddy laughed. "Who won?"

"I did," Emma giggled. "I pinned him in a mud puddle when we lost our balance coming down the mountain. You should have seen Josh dragging the quilt behind him. He looked like a cross between Pigpen and Linus from the Charlie Brown cartoons."

"I was just offering Em a fancy spa mud bath. Don't ever say that the Hummingbird Trailer Park doesn't have amenities, especially when it rains." Josh chuckled.

"I can't wait to hear this story," Sophie said.

"Not over the phone," Emma said. "I'll give you all the details when you get home. See you in a few hours." The call ended, and Sophie laid the phone on the console.

"Em is going to be all right," Teddy said with confidence in his tone. "We've both worried for nothing."

"Looks like it, but why does that make me sad?" Sophie sighed.

Teddy laid a hand on her shoulder. "I imagine it's kind of like when the first child goes to kindergarten and doesn't cry for their mommy. You've rescued Em, brought her into a healthy environment, and now she's flourishing. But up until last week, you and the folks at the park have been her sole support system. That eased the guilt you had in your heart because you didn't make a bigger effort to keep in touch with her."

"Will you send me a bill for this therapy session?" Sophie laid her hand over his and squeezed.

He slid a sly wink her way. "Yes, I will, but don't expect it to be for dollars."

• • •

Filly came out of her trailer the minute she heard Arty's truck on the gravel. The wind had dried the mud on Emma's face, and now it was cracking, so she wasn't a bit surprised when Filly's eyes got wide and she hurried out to the edge of the truck.

"What in the hell happened to y'all?" she asked. "Are you all right? Are you hurt?"

"They played in a mud puddle," Arty said as he stepped out of the truck.

"We might've been able to outrun the storm, but the four-wheeler wouldn't start, so we took shelter in my cave," Josh explained as he stood up and offered his hand to Emma.

"Why didn't you call?" Filly fussed. "I would have sent Arty sooner than this to get you."

"No service." Emma took Josh's hand and let him help her up. "But I FaceTimed Sophie so she could see us. She'll be here in a few hours. They were just leaving the airport."

"Why isn't it all soggy here?" Josh asked.

"We only got a little shower, not a downpour like you must've gotten near the mountain range," Arty said. "We just got enough to cool the temperature down a little and water Filly's rosebushes. We're supposed to have sunshine for the next week, so Sophie's homecoming today will be nice."

"You two get on home and take a shower, and then I want Em to come straight to my trailer and

326

work on decorations. Josh, you are to help Arty with the outside stuff," she bossed.

"Yes, ma'am." Emma nodded. "But first, will you take a picture of me and Josh with my phone? I don't ever want to forget this adventure, and if my mother gets hateful with me again, I will send it to her."

"Of course," Filly agreed.

Emma took her phone from her hip pocket and handed it to Filly. "I want one of each of us, and then one of us together."

"Good Lord, darlin' girl, did you drop this in the mud puddle? The only thing clean on it is the camera lens."

Arty whipped a red bandanna from his hip pocket and tossed it to her. "Wipe it all off before you take the pictures."

Filly caught it midair, wiped most of the now-dried dirt from the phone, and took several pictures of Emma and then a few of Josh. "Now, the two of you together."

Emma wasn't quite sure what to do since this was her first picture with a guy. Josh had sat down on the tailgate of the truck and patted the place next to him. She eased down beside him, and he scooted over closer to her. Then he draped an arm around her shoulders and said, "Say *cheeseburger.*" She giggled but said the word, and Filly snapped half a dozen pictures of the two of them covered in dried mud.

"One of those will definitely send your mama into a cardiac arrest if she ever sees it." Filly handed the camera back to her.

"Thank you so much," Emma said. "Now, I'm going to go get cleaned up. I'll be over to your house as soon as I get all the dirt and mud off me."

Josh walked beside her to the end of the porch steps and said, "Thanks for being such a good sport about everything."

"I was serious when I said this was an adventure," Emma told him. "I never got to play in the mud when I was a child. Sophie talked about making mud pies, and she told me about her and Rebel taking off their shoes and wading through puddles. Yesterday and this morning have been the stuff dreams are made of, even if I am past thirty, and, Josh . . . ," she started.

She glanced down at his lips and then back up at his eyes. He was going to kiss her, and her lips and face were still smeared with dirt and mud. She wanted him to kiss her, but her first kiss ever should be special—something that dreams were made of, not just the taste of dirt in her mouth when it ended.

"I know," he said, and then brushed a soft kiss across her forehead. "I'll give you the space to find yourself."

"Thank you," she said.

She floated into the trailer and went straight to the bathroom, wondering if it would be possible to clean her face without washing her forehead.

Chapter Eighteen

Josh had wanted to kiss Emma for days. He had envisioned all kinds of scenarios and hoped that he would have the nerve to actually kiss her when the opportunity arose. When it came right down to it, everything happened in a split second, but it did not take one thing away from the effect it had on Josh.

"I'm thirty-two years old," he grumbled as he kicked off his boots on the porch of his trailer. He went straight to the tiny laundry area in the hallway and put his dirty clothes in the washer. "I should have kissed lots of girls before now. Kiss nothing—I should have had sex by now, too." He continued to fuss at himself as he got into the shower. "But I've been afraid to even talk to girls until Em came into my life. Besides, it wasn't a real kiss on the lips."

Has any other woman ever made you feel like Emma does? The voice in his head sounded a lot like Filly.

"No," he answered out loud.

His heart had quit doing double-time when he turned off the water and wrapped a towel around his waist. He shaved, brushed his teeth, and grinned at his reflection in the bathroom mirror. "She makes me feel like a superhero, like I could move mountains and wrestle with a bear and win," he whispered.

He dressed in a pair of denim shorts and a bright-blue polo shirt and combed his hair. He didn't like going to the barber with all those other people around, so he cut his hair himself and kept it just long enough to slick back into a short ponytail.

He and Emma came out of their trailers at the same time. Josh stopped and watched her cross the courtyard to Filly's place. She'd gained a little weight since she'd been at the park, and it looked good on her. Her dark hair was pulled up into a high ponytail, and the sun's rays appeared to give her a halo.

She turned around when she reached Filly's trailer and waved at him. The smile on her face made her appear even more angelic, and Josh felt like a king when he waved back at her.

Emma knocked on the door and then stuck her head inside and called out, "I'm here. What can I do to help? I'm hyper, so please give me something to do to keep me busy." She truly felt like she was floating on clouds—Josh had kissed her on the forehead and Sophie was coming home.

"Come on in. I've made the engagement cake

and it's cooling. Arty is going to grill steaks for us and make baked potatoes. My bread dough is rising, and I'm right with you, girl, on this excitement thing." Filly talked as she worked. "I want to really surprise Sophie and Teddy with this party. Of course, they've had all kinds of fancy things in Europe."

"This is family and home," Emma said. "I can almost hear her squealing when she drives up and sees everything."

"I hope so, but now I'd like to know what happened last night with you and Josh," Filly said. "Are we going to have another engagement sometime in the future?"

Emma blushed. "I guess we never know what the future holds, but right now I'm still hunting for me. I did figure out that I'm sneaking up on it pretty good, though. Last night we wound up sleeping together for the second night, but that's all we did." Her cheeks turned red a second time. "But he did kiss me on the forehead before we went to clean up."

"I was hoping to hear something a lot more romantic than that," Filly said.

"In my world, that was very romantic," Emma said. "Even falling down the hill and landing in the mud puddle was romantic." She giggled. "Words can't describe the look on Arty's face when that happened or on your face when you saw us."

Arty came through the back door and chuckled. "I heard that last bit there about Filly's face, and it's the God's honest truth. I don't think I was even as shocked as she was, but then, I saw the fall from where I was standing. Lord, I'm glad I didn't have to start up that slippery slope to find you kids. That could have been *me* slippin' and slidin' like I was a greased pig."

"You would have been rolling like a basketball," Filly teased.

Arty cocked his head to one side and gave her a long sideways look. "I guess that's the pot calling the kettle black, isn't it?"

In the blink of an eye, Filly rolled up a tea towel and snapped it right over Arty's head. "Next time you call me fat, that's going to pop your arm—or your butt, if you've got the good sense to run."

"Oh, honey, I can outrun you any day of the week." Arty stepped back closer to the door.

This was what Emma wanted in a relationship—fun and bantering as well as all the rest.

"Josh is hanging the lights from a couple of tree limbs, and he wants to know if you have any more."

"Oh. My. Goodness," Emma said. "You really are going all out."

"Of course we are. You finish stirring this frosting while I locate the lights." She started back down the hallway. "Sophie is like our granddaughter, and, honey, you and Josh are like our grandkids, too. Besides, we love a party."

Filly returned in a few minutes with a box and carried it out to the porch. When she came back inside, she put a small amount of the frosting into a bowl, added a few drops of blue food coloring, and motioned toward two dozen sugar cookies. "You can put a thin layer of icing on each of those. Something old is the hanging lights. Something new is the cake. Something blue is the cookies, and something borrowed is Arty's fancy tablecloth that we normally only use on Christmas Day."

"But this is an engagement party, not a wedding," Emma said.

"Oh, honey, we'll have something even bigger at the commitment ceremony. Arty and I will both cook for a week, and this park will look like a wedding chapel," Filly giggled, "with a broom in the middle, of course, and we'll send them off with fireworks."

"I love this place," Emma said with a long sigh, "and I love every one of you all."

Filly patted her on the shoulder. "And we love you, too, girl, and you've made us so happy by talkin' about stayin' on with us. We need you. Josh gets lonely with just us old people, and me and Arty get cranky in the summer without a few more folks around us."

We need you.

Those words kept going around in circles in

Emma's head. She'd never had anyone tell her that they needed her. She had always been picked last.

"Thank you," Emma whispered.

"Nope, darlin' girl, it's us thanking you." Filly stopped and gave her a side hug and then went right back to work on the cake.

Sophie was glad to see sunshine and a blue sky on the trip from the airport to the park. Emma had mentioned that they were planning a little party. Sophie just hoped that they weren't going to too much trouble since Teddy would only have a couple of hours before he had to leave.

She always hated to see him leave, but this time it was going to be doubly hard. After the amazing time they'd had together, she couldn't imagine telling him goodbye. Maybe that's why she had this feeling of dark doom floating over her head.

Everything is perfect. Why are you sad? the annoying voice in her head scolded.

Because nothing is ever perfect, and that scares me, she thought. *And I don't deserve a perfect life, or perfect showings like I just had.*

"Darlin', we're almost there," Teddy said.

She turned to face him and realized that they had turned off the highway onto the dirt road leading back to the trailer park. "I'll miss you so much, but I'll paint from daylight to dark to make the time go by faster." She leaned over the console and kissed him on the cheek.

"I may not wash my face or shave for a week," he teased.

"Oh. My! Look what they've done," she squealed.

"What?" Teddy asked.

"Look at the park and all those lights. It's broad daylight, and the sun is shining, but just look at what they've done for us."

"Holy smoke," he gasped. "We're not having the commitment ceremony today, are we? I haven't even bought the wedding bands or written my vows."

"No, I made it clear that the ceremony would be on July Fourth. That way you won't ever forget our anniversary, and there'll always be fireworks," she said.

"Honey, there will be fireworks between us until we dance across the clouds into eternity," he told her.

"Keep telling me pretty things like that even when we're old and gray." She laid a hand on his cheek. His sweet words helped chase away part of the heavy feeling, but not all of it.

"You'll still be hot to me when your blonde hair is gray, sweetheart, and I bet the twinkle in your eyes will always be there just like it is today." He parked the truck in front of her trailer.

Filly, Arty, and Josh all waved from the table.

Emma came out of the trailer wearing one of her flowing skirts and Filly's jewelry. Her dark hair was piled up on top of her head in a ponytail, and she was smiling even brighter than the sun and the flashing lights hanging from the trees. Suddenly, Sophie couldn't wait to get her alone and get all the details of what had happened while she was gone.

Teddy unfastened his seat belt, got out of the vehicle, and jogged around the front end to help Sophie. They started toward the table together, but when the hugging, hand shaking, and back patting started, they were soon separated.

"We are so happy for you kids," Arty said. "Come on around and take your places at the table. It's ready and waiting for you to dive in."

"Y'all didn't need to go to all this much trouble," Teddy said, "but those steaks sure smell good."

Emma gave Sophie a second hug and whispered, "I'm so glad you're home. It'll take hours and hours to tell you everything."

"I know, and then I'll tell *you* everything," Sophie said.

Teddy reached out and took Sophie by the hand, tugging it gently. "Shall we, darlin'?"

"Of course." Sophie flashed a smile at him and stepped out of the hug. "This is absolutely amazing. Em, you should have told me. I would have dressed up."

"And ruin all the surprises?" Emma winked.

"As in more than one?" Sophie asked.

"Wait and see," Filly told her.

A lovely white cloth covered the table. Sophie had never seen the real china plates on the table, but there they were today—white with a shiny gold edge—and sparkling silverware also. Gorgeous cactus flowers floating in a crystal bowl served as a centerpiece. The place looked like something Sophie would have expected to see at an outdoor party in Paris.

Teddy waited for her to be seated on one side of the rectangular picnic table, and then he sat down on the bench beside her. He took her hand in his and gave it a gentle squeeze. "This is awesome," he whispered just for her ears.

Arty's prayer was a little longer than usual because he said a blessing for the newly engaged couple. Tears welled up in Sophie's eyes. These folks were more than just friends—they were family.

Arty said, "Amen," and immediately picked up the platter of thick steaks and passed them to Sophie. "I hope everyone likes their T-bones medium rare."

"Arthur Crawford!" Filly's tone scolded.

"Oh, don't get your granny panties in a twist. The one on the right"—he pointed—"is burned black just for you."

"Well done, not burned," she corrected him with an evil look.

"Same difference," he chuckled.

Sophie forked a steak onto her plate and passed the platter on over to Teddy. "Thank all of you for this magnificent party, and, Arty, everything looks delicious." She glanced toward the end of the table, expecting to see a pie or one of Filly's famous chocolate sheet cakes.

"Dessert is staying in the cool house until we are ready for it." Filly held up a bottle of red wine and a pitcher of sweet tea. "Tea or wine? I know it's not five o'clock, but this is a celebration."

"Wine, definitely wine." Sophie picked up a stemless wineglass and handed it over to Filly. "I've never seen these fancy glasses or china before."

"We only get them out at Christmas. Since y'all are going to live in Del Rio, maybe you can join us for all the holidays," Filly said.

"I'd love to spend Christmas here." Sophie could already imagine buying presents for everyone and opening gifts with them.

"I'll have tea," Josh said.

"Me too." Emma nodded.

"I'll take both." Arty winked at Emma.

Sophie ate slowly, sipped at her wine, and tried to make the moment last forever. When it had passed, Teddy would leave, and telling him goodbye put a lump the size of an orange in her throat.

When they had finished the meal, Filly and

Emma left their places across the table from Sophie and Teddy and made short work of crossing the yard. Taking short steps and balancing it carefully in both hands, Filly brought out a triple-layer cake decorated with blue piping the color of a summer sky. Emma carried a platter of cookies with the same color frosting. When they set both on the table, Sophie realized there were entwined hearts on the top of the cake with an *S* in one and a *T* in the other. The cookies had the same decoration on each one.

"Hawaiian wedding cake with cream cheese frosting," Filly said. "This is the cake we always served at the engagement parties when I was in the carnival. It's supposed to bring the best of luck to the future couple. Sophie, in keeping with tradition, you should cut and serve it. First to Teddy and yourself, and then I'll take over the duties."

"This is too much." Sophie blinked away the tears. Everything was absolutely perfect, so why should she cry?

"Ah, shucks." Arty smiled. "We do what we can for our kids."

"Yes, we do." Filly smiled back at him.

"We want to hear more about your new gallery before we all get emotional and can't enjoy that cake and those cookies," Arty said. "Filly ain't made iced sugar cookies since Christmas, and she's never made one of those cakes."

"This cake is special for weddings and engagements. You don't get it at Christmas, and if I made iced sugar cookies every week, they wouldn't be special for the holidays, now would they?" Filly smarted off as she served the rest of the group slices of cake.

The thought of leaving this special group of people made Sophie even sadder than she'd been before. How could she ever move to Del Rio and not see Emma and the others for a whole month at a time?

You went for months without seeing Arty, Filly, and Josh, and years without seeing Emma.

That was different, she argued with the voice in her head.

Josh took a bite and groaned. "Do I get one of these when I get engaged?"

"Of course you do"—Filly flashed a bright smile—"and so does Em."

"What about the leftovers?" Emma asked. "Is it bad luck to eat every single crumb?"

"No," Filly answered, "and according to tradition, it must all be eaten before midnight to bring good luck, so everyone will take a portion home and have it for a bedtime snack."

Good God Almighty! Sophie thought. *I don't need the idea of bad luck hanging over my head right now when I feel like something isn't right.*

"The cookies? Is it bad luck or good luck to

leave a few of those until tomorrow?" Teddy asked.

"No time limit on those," Filly told him.

When dessert was finished, Teddy stood up and held up his wineglass, which only had a sip left in the bottom. "A toast," he said, "to good friends who make us feel special."

All six of them touched glasses, and Emma got to her feet. "Another one. To Sophie and Teddy. May your life be filled with sunshine to warm your faces, laughter to feed your soul, and happiness every single day."

"Hear, hear!" Josh raised his glass with the rest of them.

"Thank you." Sophie suddenly wanted this party to be over so she could think. Sure, she'd be sad when Teddy left, but she felt like she was on an emotional roller coaster that was about to spin off the tracks.

Teddy finished his cake and gave her a sideways hug. "I'd love to stay all afternoon, but I should really be going. Walk me to the car, Sophie?"

"Of course, but don't ever expect me to do it again," she teased. "Y'all save me another piece of that cake. It's better than all the fancy pastries in Paris."

They walked arm in arm to his car, and he kissed her goodbye. "I don't want to let you go," he whispered.

"Me either," she said, but deep down inside she really needed to analyze everything from the moving business to the fantastic gallery showings they had had. He took a step back, retrieved her bags from the truck, and set them on the porch.

Sophie felt like an emotional train wreck, and she couldn't even figure out exactly why. She'd always felt like Teddy deserved more than she could give him, but it went deeper than that—deep enough that tears spilled down over her cheeks.

He kissed her wet cheeks. "You've never cried before. Are we all right? Something seems off with you."

"I'm just fine." She thought of the times when Emma had said that and yet, like her, she was anything but fine.

After one more long, lingering kiss, he got into the vehicle, and she closed the door. She waved until he disappeared around the first curve. Emma walked up behind her and slipped an arm around her waist. "Filly says they can take care of cleanup. I'm supposed to go with you and help you get unpacked. Are you going to be all right?"

"Yes, but not without tears, and I don't even know why I feel like crying. This is our last goodbye, and I've never cried before. Everything is perfect, Em, but I feel like I'm smothering, like

I can't breathe. What's wrong with me?" Sophie answered.

"I don't know, but together we'll figure it out," Emma said and led her into the house.

Chapter Nineteen

Emma made sure there was not one single smidgen of cake left and then snuggled down into her bed. After a night on the sofa and one on the hard ground, she thought she would be happy to be in a nice soft bed and under her own covers, but she missed Josh. Six months ago, she would never have thought, not even for a split second, that she would toss and turn because a guy wasn't lying next to her.

She sat up and beat her pillow, flopped back down, and covered up with a sheet. Then she heard a strange, muffled sound. Thinking that maybe Coco had gotten shut inside and wanted out, she threw back the covers and padded through the dark trailer to check both doors. No cat to be found, but the sound was still there. She tiptoed down the hall, noticed a light coming from under the bathroom door, and finally recognized the noise as crying, not a cat's meows.

She eased the door open to find Sophie curled up on the floor, her hands over her face, crying like the end of the world had come. Emma eased down beside her and wrapped her arms around her. "Has someone died? Is Rebel all right? Did Teddy have an accident?"

"I had a fight with Teddy on the phone," Sophie answered between heartbreaking sobs. "Teddy even ate all his cake, and this still happened."

"What about? Is the wedding ceremony off?" Emma pulled Sophie up to a sitting position and kept her arms wrapped tightly around her.

"It was a silly fight. He wanted to take his sofa to our new house, and I told him I wanted to take mine because his was ugly," Sophie said. "We wound up arguing, and I told him that he should have asked me before he went looking for a house and a gallery, and then he said I would have never picked anything out because I have these commitment issues, and . . . it went from there." Sophie wiped her eyes on the tail of her nightshirt. "We had a wonderful time in Europe, but I was"—she hiccuped—"sad and anxious most of the time." She buried her face in Emma's shoulder. "I'm the strong one. I shouldn't be carrying on like this, but I don't deserve to be happy."

"Why would you think that you don't deserve to be happy?" Emma asked. "You've worked hard for years to get to where you are now, and you love Teddy and he loves you. This is a stupid fight that can be fixed."

Sophie rolled off a fistful of toilet paper and blew her nose.

Emma took Sophie by the hand and stood up, pulling Sophie with her. "Let's sort this out in the living room with some yogurt and two spoons." She had to be strong for Sophie. She owed her that much, but Emma wasn't an expert on relationship advice.

"Just let me wallow in misery for a while," Sophie said.

"You need to pick up your brushes and get busy, not go into a depression like I did all those years," Emma said.

"I can't, Em. Whatever this is started on the way home in the airplane, and I can't shake it," Sophie said.

"Let's eat all these cookies and watch a movie. Neither of us can sleep anyway. We don't have a man in our beds," Emma told her.

"You want to explain that?" Sophie asked.

"Not tonight. Maybe later," Emma replied as she turned on the television and put the first season of *Castle* into the DVD player. She hoped that would cheer Sophie up a bit.

It didn't work, but just as the sixth episode ended, Sophie fell asleep on the sofa. Emma threw a blanket over her, went to her bedroom, and pulled the spread off the bed. She tucked it under one arm and a pillow under the other. She tiptoed back to the living room and made a pallet on the floor right beside the sofa. When Sophie groaned, Emma reached a hand up and laid it on her shoulder.

"It's all right. I'm right here," she whispered. This was the first time that Emma had had to be the strong one, and she hoped she was doing a decent job of helping her friend. Even though she was sad for Sophie, it was an amazing feeling to be needed. She wasn't an expert on relationships, but she could be there for her one hundred percent.

The clock on the stove said that it was after ten when Sophie awoke. Rebel used to say that everything, no matter what it was, looked better in the light of day. She was wrong this time. Nothing was better.

With a long sigh, she started to get up and realized that Emma was sleeping on the floor right beside the sofa. Anyone who would sleep beside her on the floor was a friend indeed. Suddenly, tears were flowing down Sophie's cheeks again. She didn't deserve a friend like Emma, one who would give up sleep and then stay right by her side the whole night through. After the way she had felt about the baby that she lost, she didn't deserve anything. Her negative feelings had caused her to lose the baby. Maybe she shouldn't be with Teddy after all.

"My baby would have been a happy child. He

would have had Rebel for a grandmother, and once I got over the shock, I could have cleaned houses with you and worked nights on my art." Sophie eased off the sofa and made her way to her bedroom, where she crawled into bed and pulled the covers up over her head. Just saying that out loud made her a little less sad.

Her phone pinged, so she reached out with a hand and felt around on the nightstand until she located it. When she had a hold on it, she brought it under the covers to discover several messages and two missed calls from Teddy.

She dried her wet cheeks on the sheet and called him.

"Are we okay?" Teddy asked.

"I'm fine," she said.

"You're saying the words, but your tone isn't agreeing with them," he told her. "I can be there in a few hours."

"No, don't. I don't deserve for you to love me or to come down here and comfort me. I don't even deserve to know someone like you. Do you even realize that there must be something wrong with you to want to spend the rest of your life with someone like me?"

"Good God, Sophie!" he said.

She could imagine him running his fingers through his hair.

"What's gotten into you? Have you lost your mind? We were so happy right up until I left. This is more than a fight about a sofa. What's wrong with you?" he asked.

"Nothing is wrong with me. I just need to be alone," she said and ended the call.

She turned the phone off and laid it on the bedside table. She could call her mother, but Rebel would throw a suitcase in her car and be there by suppertime. Sophie couldn't face her, not with these feelings that had come over her.

"Would I have been that way with my baby? Would I have been a smothering mama?" she whispered as she closed her eyes and went back to sleep.

Three sets of eyes full of questions met Emma when she went to the supper table that evening. She wasn't sure what to tell them. In what should have been the happiest time of her life, Sophie had hit rock bottom. She hadn't been out of bed all day, except to go to the bathroom. She hadn't eaten a single bite of food, and when Emma tried to talk her into getting out of bed and going to supper, she refused.

Arty said a quick grace and then raised an eyebrow toward Emma.

"I don't know what to do for her," Emma said. "She's always been the strong one. Now all she will say is that she doesn't deserve to be happy. She and Teddy are fighting over something as silly as which sofa to take to their new house. She had a great showing and sold a lot of pictures, but that didn't make her happy. I don't know what happened or how to fix it, but I feel like it's up to me to take care of it."

"Usually when she comes home from a few days with Teddy, she's whistling and all fired up about getting back to work," Josh noted.

"Is she sick?" Filly asked. "Maybe she's pregnant."

"She's sick, all right," Emma said, "but not because of a baby." She held her plate out for Filly to dip chicken potpie onto it. "I see the signs of deep, major depression. She won't eat, and she's holed up in her bedroom under the covers."

"You can rescue her like she did you," Josh suggested.

Good grief! Emma thought. *I'm barely taking baby steps in this hunt to find myself. How can I ever rescue someone as strong as Sophie has always been?*

"How would I do that?" Emma asked. "I can't imagine being in a better place than right here to heal."

"For *you*," Arty said. "But Sophie needs to get her own mojo back. She used to disappear into the Big Bend park while she was here, and that seemed to make her happy. Take her there, and don't come back until she's healed."

"I've got a couple of sleeping bags you can use," Josh offered.

"I'll pack food to last a few days," Filly said.

"I'll help Filly with that food idea. We can combine what we've got in our trailers so y'all won't starve," Arty said. "When are you leaving?"

Emma felt like a whirlwind had just hit her. She wasn't sure how to even get to the park, much less camp out for days, or until Sophie got her mojo back, as Arty put it.

"Who's going to help me carry her out kicking and screaming?" Emma asked.

"That part is your job," Filly answered. "Did *you* kick and scream when she rescued you?"

Emma served herself another helping of the chicken potpie. "Not so much, but I *was* worried about Mother and what she might do."

"Well, your job with Sophie is easier than she had with you, then," Arty said. "Rebel won't give you any trouble."

"What's in the park?" Emma asked. "Do they have places to buy junk food and stuff like tourists want?"

"Just mountains, rocks, and lots of cactus," Josh said. "There's a small convenience store at a junction. Fuel is expensive in the park, so fill up the gas tank in Sophie's vehicle before you enter. You can get ice, drinks, and the essentials there, but they close early in the evening. You'll need to take toilet paper, paper towels, and . . ."

"What about showers and bathrooms?" Emma asked. She'd just spent the night in a cave, but she couldn't imagine living like that for days on end.

"Got several bathrooms along the way, but sometimes they're out of toilet paper, and they're mostly outdoor toilets—no flush. They do have picnic tables scattered around," Josh answered. "A couple of places offer showers, but pack your own soap, of course."

There had been a sign on one of Emma's therapists' desks that said SOMETIMES WHEN THINGS ARE FALLING APART, THEY ARE ACTUALLY FALLING IN PLACE. Emma had thought about that often, but it never made as much sense as it did that evening. She had been falling apart, and Sophie had arrived to help her. Now it was her turn to help Sophie find her inner strength again.

Emma took a deep breath and nodded toward Josh. If she had to stay in the desert with no showers for a week and use smelly potties, then that's exactly what she would do. She owed Sophie that much and more for helping guide Emma back to her own life.

"All right, then, when should we leave?" Emma asked.

"As soon as possible. Tomorrow morning would be good. How long did Sophie give you to make up your mind about leaving?" Arty asked as he spooned up a bowl full of peach cobbler.

"About two minutes," Emma answered.

"Then don't give her more than that," Filly said.

"We can start loading the SUV tonight," Josh said. "Take at least three canvases for her and a few for yourself. Watching her paint was inspiration for you to start, so give her a dose of her own medicine and inspire her with your eagerness to work."

Emma finished off her food and then dipped up her own peach cobbler. "I guess we should have it loaded and ready or she'll make a hundred excuses as to why she can't go. So how many canvases do you think it will take before she's cured?"

"Take four," Arty said. "Better to have too many than not enough."

And she may slice one to ribbons.

"Good cobbler and great supper, Arty," Emma said. "Maybe I could take a plate in to see if I can entice Sophie to eat. If she will get up out of bed, maybe we won't need to leave."

Emma knew the moment the words were out of her mouth that wasn't the case. She had spent the better part of a week hiding in her bed after the rape, and then another week at home before Victoria checked her into the first institution because she couldn't come out of a deep depression. That's where she'd learned to say, "I'm fine," just like Sophie had told her a dozen times. Now that she was on the other end of the conversation, she understood why the therapists never believed her. Saying the words did not mean anything when the tone was graveyard dead.

Filly got busy loading up a plate with potpie and salad and a bowl with peach cobbler. "If anything will get her up and going, it'll be food. She loves to eat."

"I'm going to box up some grub," Arty said, "and get out the cooler to put some frozen meat in. To cook over a campfire, all you girls need is a skillet and a coffeepot. I've got extra of both."

"We'll have you all loaded up and ready to get out of here by daylight." Filly began to clean up the table. "She'll get over this with you by her side."

"We'll miss you girls. When you have reception, we'll expect a report every evening," Arty said. "I'll tuck in my little .22 pistol in case you need it for snakes."

"Either two-legged or the slithering kind." Filly winked.

"You probably shouldn't do that. If a two-legged one came sniffing around, I might shoot first and ask questions later," Emma told him. "Did Filly tell you—"

Arty slammed a fist into his open hand. "She did, and I just want to know if your mama or daddy killed those sorry bastards."

"I didn't tell them until Mother sent Jeffrey to take me home a few days ago. I told her over the

355

phone, and she responded just like I thought she would. She asked me what I'd done to provoke the attack and called me stupid for being so naive. At the time, I just figured if I ignored it, everything would be all right, but it wasn't. I haven't told my father yet, and I don't know if Mother will even bother to tell him. Sophie and you all have helped me realize that ignoring something doesn't make it disappear, and now I have to help her see the same thing. No matter what happens to us, we can't let it define the rest of our lives," Emma said.

"Amen to that, sister," Arty agreed.

"Your mother said that to you?" Filly laid an arm around Emma's shoulders. "I shouldn't talk ugly about your mama, but, honey, that ain't normal. She should have gone gunnin' for those sumbitches even after all these years."

"Mother isn't capable of loving anyone but herself—at least that's the way I see it," Emma explained.

"Guess you're showin' her that you're nothing like her, ain't you, child?" Arty said. "And, honey, I'm still tuckin' in that little gun. If you have any doubts, you just flick the safety off and shoot! You are not stupid and you're damn sure not delicate. And that horrible thing that happened to you wasn't your fault. You are an artist, and that makes you different and special. Don't ever forget it."

"Thanks, Arty." Emma felt empowered by his words.

Arty nodded. "You two kids go get the sleeping bags and whatever else Josh can think of. Tuck in her art supplies, and me and Filly will have the food ready to load at dawn."

"Thank you." Emma smiled. "For everything. And if you've got any connections"—she rolled her eyes toward the sky—"you might put in a word for me. Other than a night in Josh's cave, I've never spent a night out under the stars."

"You're goin' to love it," Josh said. "Even though you need to get her out and painting again, I'll miss you, Em. Take the food inside and grab Sophie's keys and an armload of canvases. I'll meet you there in a few minutes."

His words put an extra beat in Emma's heart, and knowing that she would be missed sent a surge of happiness through her. "One more time, thank you, Josh," she said.

He eased out the door, and she grabbed a fork and carried the food back to Sophie's room. "Hey, it's time to wake up and eat something. You'll be sick if you don't start—"

Sophie waved her away with a flick of the wrist. "Go away, I'm fine."

"No, you are not," Emma told her, "but you will be. If this food isn't eaten by morning, I'll call Rebel."

"I already did," Sophie said. "I told her I was

just fine and that you would take care of me."

"Well, since you told her that, then I suppose it's my job," Emma said. "Eat your supper."

"Later," Sophie said.

"Okay, have it your way." Emma left the room and went straight to her bedroom. She packed a tote bag with two changes of clothing for each of them, took the SUV keys from a hook beside the kitchen door, and headed outside with canvases under one arm and the bag slung over her other shoulder. Josh met her at the back of the car with two sleeping bags and a lantern of some kind that she hoped Sophie knew how to light. She hit the button to open the hatch, and he began to load things.

"I'm putting these matches"—he held up several small books—"in the glove box. You'll park close to your campsite, and if it happens to rain, you don't want them to get wet."

"You thought of everything," she said.

"I've been out in the desert a lot at night," he explained as he took the bag and canvases from her and loaded them. "I learned by my mistakes. Can I help you carry anything else?"

"Yes, and thank you." She nodded.

"Want to have a beer with me on my back porch when we get done?" he asked.

She wished that she'd known him before she went to college, that they'd gone to the same high school together and maybe even dated.

Everyone knew her story now, and no one seemed to be ready to send her packing for being stupid. Knowing that someone believed in her, and that Josh would miss her even when he knew what had happened, made her feel like she was walking on air.

"I'd better take a rain check, so I'll be close if Sophie decides she wants to talk," she answered.

"Don't forget to take your pillow in the morning," Josh said as they went into the trailer. "Just grab Sophie's and yours and take her to the vehicle. I'll put Arty's and Filly's stuff inside for you and leave the keys in the ignition. The less you have to do, the more likely you'll get her out of the house."

When they finished taking out the last load, he walked her back to the porch. He brought her hand to his chest and held it over his heart. "Feel that?" he asked.

In her mind, she could see fireworks all around them. "Feel what?"

"That's my heart. It likes you a lot, Em, and it's going to miss you terribly. Come home to it when you get done taking care of Sophie," he whispered.

Lord, have mercy! She'd never heard anything so romantic in her whole life. "I will, Josh. I promise."

He dropped her hand and cupped her face in his hands; then his lips met hers in a fiery kiss that left her panting when he took a step backward. "Take that with you and know that I'll be right here waiting for your call each evening."

"I'm going to miss you, too," she whispered.

He brushed a soft kiss across her forehead. "I hope so, Em. I really, really hope so, and while you are rescuing Sophie, I hope that you find you out there in Big Bend."

She floated into the house, checked on Sophie, and took the plate of untouched food to the trash can. Then she took a long, hot shower, since she knew she might not get one for a couple of days. When she crawled into bed, she realized that Josh had really kissed her—and that she wanted more.

"I feel like the high school student I never got to be," she giggled.

Chapter Twenty

Emma made sure everything was ready and loaded the next morning. Filly had even thought to include two travel mugs of coffee and a box of breakfast bars. All that was left was waking Sophie and demanding that she get dressed. She opened the bedroom door, hoping to find that Sophie was up and getting around, but no such luck. There was the same old heap of covers and nothing else. She tiptoed across the room and picked up Sophie's phone to find that it had been turned off.

"Go away," Sophie said. "If you were my friend, you'd leave me alone."

"This is called tough love." Emma ripped the covers away and tossed them in the corner. "Get up and get dressed."

Sophie didn't even open her eyes. "I'm fine. Go away. I don't want to eat."

Emma untucked the bottom sheet on all four sides, grabbed the edge, and gave it a jerk, landing Sophie on the floor. Her eyes popped wide-open. "Dammit, Em! I said I'm fine. I just need to wallow in guilt for a few days."

"You've had more than twenty-four hours of

wallowing, and that's enough. Either get dressed or go like you are. It makes no difference to me, but you look like shit." Emma crossed her arms over her chest and tapped her foot. "And you might want to wear boots."

Sophie rubbed her swollen eyes. "I'm wearing what I have on, and I'm not putting on boots."

"Fine by me," Emma said. "Stand up."

"What for?"

"I'm rescuing you just like you did me."

"I don't need rescuing. I'm fine," Sophie argued.

"If I had a nickel for every time I said that I was fine, I'd be a rich woman. That's the first sign that you are not fine. Stand up or else I'll go get Arty and Josh and we'll carry you outside." Emma's voice sounded just like Rebel's in her own ears, and that made her happy.

"I'll stand up, but I'm not going outside. I have to go to the bathroom, and then I'm going back to bed." Sophie got to her feet.

Emma picked up her hiking boots from the closet and her purse from the dresser. She carried both out to the vehicle, tossed them inside, and got back just as Sophie was coming out of the bathroom.

"If you don't walk out on that porch, I'm calling Rebel to come down here," Emma threatened.

Sophie whipped around and gave her a dirty look. "You wouldn't dare. I didn't call Victoria to come get you."

"That's a whole different story. Walk outside on the front porch." Emma pointed to the door.

Sophie stomped to the door and went outside. "Now what? Do you have one of your high-dollar therapists out here to talk to me?"

"Now you are going to get in the passenger seat of your vehicle, and we're going for a drive," Emma said.

"You're not driving my car," Sophie declared as she went down the stairs in her bare feet.

"I've got the keys." Emma dangled them in front of her. "Either you go with me, or I'll go by myself and let you wallow in your misery for the rest of the week."

"You wouldn't dare!" Sophie raised her voice. "You don't know your way around these parts. I didn't even know you had a driver's license still."

"Mother didn't think I needed one, but that was the one time Daddy put his foot down and insisted that I have a license and my own car," Emma said. "Now, go get in the car and show me where to go and how to get back here when we finish our drive." Emma marched out to the car, where Josh stood waiting with the door opened for her. She slid into the driver's seat and started the engine. Her hands were all sweaty, and her pulse raced. She hadn't driven anywhere in a very long time.

You are strong, and Sophie needs you. Rebel's voice came to her.

"Yes, I am," she muttered.

Filly and Arty both came out onto their porches and waved. "Have a good time!" they yelled in unison.

Josh rushed around to the other side of the vehicle and opened the door for Sophie, who hadn't moved more than a foot from the bottom of the steps. Emma put the vehicle in park and stomped the gas, revving up the engine. Doing that relieved enough of the nerves that she giggled.

"You're going to tear up my engine." Sophie stormed out across the yard and got into the passenger's seat. She fastened her seat belt and glared at Josh when he slammed the door shut.

"Be careful and call," he mouthed and gestured to Emma.

"I promise I will," she yelled through the closed window, and then focused on Sophie. "Driving is somewhat like riding a bicycle, isn't it? It's all instinct, but I have to admit," she said as she made a U-turn in the yard and started away from the park, "this is the first time I've ever driven on a dirt road."

"Pull over and let me take the wheel," Sophie growled.

Emma shook her head. "Nope. If you do that, you'll go right back to the trailer and go to bed again."

"Where are we going?" Sophie asked.

"We're going to tour Big Bend National Park and look for good places to paint a few pictures," Emma answered. "You just look out the window and see if there's anything we need to stop and take a picture of on the way. Coffee is right beside you, and there's breakfast bars in the console." Emma picked up her silver travel mug and took a sip of coffee. "Good and strong. It'll wake you up, believe me."

"I don't want coffee, and I don't want to eat," Sophie moaned.

Emma took another couple of sips, put the mug back in the holder, and popped open the console. She removed a breakfast bar and used one hand and her teeth to open it. "Then just sit there and pout. I wasn't this cantankerous when you rescued me. Have you been using drugs or something? Is that what you and Teddy really fought about? Did he find your stash and break up with you because he can't stand the idea of being married to an addict?" Maybe that would shock Sophie out of the depression.

Sophie folded her arms across her chest. "No!"

"Then what?" Emma asked. "Talk to me."

"No." Sophie sighed.

Emma braked hard and brought the vehicle to an abrupt stop to let a herd of deer cross in front of her.

"I don't want to talk. I just want to be left alone," Sophie said.

"You'd be better off dead than half-alive like you are right now." Emma eased on down the road and ate the breakfast bar with one hand. "And don't be a back-seat driver. Drink some coffee so you won't be so grouchy."

"You're worse than Victoria." Sophie picked up the coffee and took a few sips, but she didn't say another word for thirty minutes. By then they were passing the tiny community of Terlingua.

"I'm stopping for a bathroom break. If you want to call anyone, like Teddy, and tell him what a jackass you've been, your phone is in your purse." Emma pointed to the back seat.

"What the hell is all that other stuff?" Sophie gasped.

"It's what Josh, Arty, and Filly say we need for a few nights in the park. Are you going with me to the bathroom or not? I thought I'd also pick up some milk and maybe a six-pack of beer while we're here. Arty said he put enough ice in the cooler to last until tomorrow," Emma answered.

"Good God!" Sophie groaned.

"You might want to put your boots on if you need to use the bathroom. Looks like that gravel would hurt bare feet." Emma snagged the keys and her purse and opened the door. She unfastened her seat belt and followed the signs around to the side of the building where the restrooms were located. She wasn't a bit surprised when she finished to find Sophie waiting at the door with her boots on.

"If we were on Facebook right now, I would unfriend you," she fumed with her arms crossed over her chest.

"Good thing we're in the real world, then, isn't it?" Emma flashed her brightest smile. "If you're not ashamed to be seen in the store in your pajama pants and no bra, come on inside and see if there's anything you might like to take with us. I've still got my hundred dollars I left the institution with, so I can get what I think we might need."

Sophie went into the bathroom and slammed the door behind her. "You are a witch."

"I believe it," Emma yelled through the closed door. "I got you out of bed, so I must have super-powers. When we get back home, I'll see if I can make a broom fly and turn frogs into princes. Maybe I'll turn Teddy into a frog and you'll be plumb out of luck."

"Hush," Sophie shouted. "Go buy the beer."

Emma didn't budge. No way was she giving Sophie a chance to hitch a ride back to the trailer park. "If they have whiskey, I might need a bottle of that just to get me through the next few days with an old cranky-butted woman."

Sophie slung open the door. "Don't call me old."

"Well, today you look twenty years older than

me," Emma said. "Your hair is a fright and your boobs are sagging. It's a good thing Teddy can't see you right now."

Sophie crossed her arms over her chest again and stormed back to the car, got inside, and slammed the door so hard that it rocked the vehicle.

"Mission accomplished," Emma singsonged. "Being mad is a step up from being numb." She got two six-packs of beer, a couple of bottles of cheap wine, half a gallon of milk, and, on the way to the register, she picked up two Cherry Mash candies. Emma hadn't had one of those in years, but just seeing the red-and-white wrapper reminded her of the days when Rebel used to give her and Sophie one while they sketched or colored in their books. Maybe just having one would help Sophie get over all this and make up with Teddy.

Sophie was still in a mood when she got back to the vehicle. Emma wedged everything except the candy into a small place in the back, and then got behind the wheel again. "I'm going to turn Lulu off now, and you can guide me through the park and to the best campground."

"Why do you call the GPS Lulu, and what are you hiding in your pocket?" Sophie asked.

"The cleaning lady we had after Rebel got fired was Lulu. She had a voice just like that GPS lady, and she was very blunt, not at all like

Rebel. She never told stories or brought me one of these." Emma tossed a Cherry Mash candy toward Sophie.

Sophie caught it midair. "Don't think because you brought my favorite candy out here that you are forgiven."

"Eat it and drink your coffee and tell me what to do now," Emma said.

"Drive straight into the park, stop at the toll booth, and pay for us to go inside. It's fifteen dollars for each of us," Sophie said.

"Get your purse out," Emma said.

"Oh, no." Sophie shook her head. "This is your party. You pay the cover fee."

Emma did a quick tally. She had more than thirty dollars left in her purse, even after buying what she had, but there wouldn't be much left. Hopefully Arty and Filly had packed enough food to get them through until Sophie's funk ended. Thank goodness Filly hadn't let her pay for the things she'd asked them to pick up at the store while Sophie was gone, or she wouldn't have been able to pay the toll.

They pulled in behind four pickup trucks when they reached the adobe booth with an American flag flying high outside. "Is there a camping fee in addition—" Emma started to ask, but two of the trucks in front of her shoved something out the window and went right on through, so she had to pull up.

"Sixteen dollars a night," Sophie answered. "How long are we staying and which campground are we using?"

The best-laid plans and all that crap, Emma thought as she tossed out the idea of staying until the weekend. She had enough money to get them into the park. They sure wouldn't go hungry, but Sophie had better get out of her mood by the end of the day.

At least you tried, and you got behind the wheel and drove again, and you asserted a little authority over Sophie.

"Yes, I did," Emma whispered in agreement.

"You did what, and who are you talking to?" Sophie asked.

"I got you out of the house. I don't have the money for campgrounds, so you've got until midnight to get yourself back on track," Emma said.

Sophie grabbed her purse from the back seat and fumbled in it. "I need more than one day to be miserable."

The last truck in front of her drove away, and Emma moved up to the window. Sophie shoved two papers at her. "Keep your money and give her these."

"What are they?" Emma handed them to the woman in the booth.

The woman stuck her head out and smiled. "Is that you in the passenger seat, Miss Mason?"

"It's me." Sophie leaned forward and waved. "Good to see you again, Edna."

"Glad you made reservations and got your annual pass in early," Edna said as she handed Emma the tag to hang on the rearview and a pass to Cottonwood Campground.

"I always do. Have a great day." Sophie smiled and waved.

Emma was as surprised about Sophie's fake smile as she was about the fact that her friend had been going to make her use the last of her money when she had a pass to the park. Emma shoved her money back into her purse and tossed it over the seat. "You are evil when you are cranky. You would have let me use all the money I had, wouldn't you? And you can smile for a stranger, but you're fighting me every step of the way."

"You are evil when you won't leave me alone to work out my depression," Sophie said. "I left you alone to take care of your demons. Drive, woman. There are cars behind you. And that woman didn't make me get out of bed and drag me off looking like this."

"Yep, you did leave me alone for about sixteen years, but you would have had to wade through Victoria to help me. Even you don't have that kind of strength." Emma put the SUV in gear and headed down the narrow two-lane road. "I don't have that many years to worry with you."

"So, you're going to toss me away now that you and Josh are flirting?" Sophie asked.

"I swear to God," Emma said as she clenched her teeth in a sudden burst of anger, "you should have been Victoria's daughter, not me. Maybe when Rebel came to clean houses when we were just little kids, the nanny switched us."

"We were already toddlers by then. I'm a blonde and you're a brunette. I don't think anyone switched us," Sophie smarted off.

"Well, I can dream, can't I?" Emma grumbled. "Right now you're acting enough like my mother that I'd like to kick you out beside the road."

"But you won't because you love me like a sister," Sophie said.

"Sure I do. Like a bratty little sister who's spoiled rotten." Emma drove slowly and wondered what was so great about this place anyway. The landscape wasn't all that different from the acreage around the park, and there was no Josh here or Filly or Arty, either—just a pouting Sophie.

"I'm older than you are." Sophie opened the console and took out two breakfast bars.

"Not by much or by actions." Emma was glad to see her arguing and eating. That was much better than lying in bed and refusing to even look at food.

"If I gain forty pounds, I'm going to blame you. When I'm coming down off a pity party, I eat everything in sight," Sophie told her as she peeled the wrapper off a bar.

"I'd rather have you fat and happy than skinny and grouchy," Emma told her. "Where is this Cottonwood Campground, anyway?"

"When you come to a T in the road, turn right and follow the signs. It's pretty close to the Rio Grande. If you don't quit being mean to me, I'll throw you over into Mexico," Sophie said.

"If you're going to act like this, I'd probably be happier there. How many wallowing moments have you had since our freshman year in college?" Emma asked as she made the turn.

Sophie had only had a couple of moments like this before, but they were nothing compared to how she had felt when it finally sank in that she was truly a success, and then when she'd been fighting with Teddy over such a silly thing. He just wanted to surprise her and make her happy, and now she had probably ruined everything between them.

Emma deserved to know why she was acting like this, but she didn't want her to think she was downright crazy, and yet she had to get it off her chest. She had to say the words again, even if they drove her into an even deeper depression.

Finally, she blurted out, "I lost a baby about the same time you were raped. I didn't know the man was married when I slept with him. I didn't want to be pregnant, and I hated the idea of giving up my dreams to raise a child by myself. I've felt guilty as hell since I miscarried. Sometimes I wish I could have repressed the memories like you did, because I've always felt like my negative feelings caused that baby to die. For the past seventeen years, I've seen my child in every kid that would have been her age. Would she look like the little girl in the mall? Would she be a petulant teenager now? Then I think, would my mother be disappointed in me for being so reckless, and with a married man at that? My baby would be alive if I hadn't hated her so much."

Emma pulled onto the gravel area beside the road and turned off the engine. She unfastened her seat belt, threw open the door, and ran around the SUV as fast as she could. Sophie's head was in her hands and she was sobbing when Emma opened the passenger door and reached across her to undo her seat belt. With an arm around her shoulders, Emma guided her out of the vehicle. Together, they slumped down on the gravel side by side.

"I didn't mean to blurt that all out." Sophie continued to weep. "I shouldn't be happy now when I didn't even want my own child. Teddy wants a family, and I would be a terrible mother. I'm no better than Victoria. She didn't want you, and look how that worked out."

"Shh, don't cry." Emma wiped her own tears

with the back of her hand. "I've had the same worries. What if I find someone wonderful and he wants children? What if I'm no good as a mother? At least you had Rebel, and you know how to be a good mother."

A car parked behind their SUV and an elderly guy with gray hair and a beard halfway to his waist got out. "Are you ladies all right?" he asked. "Do you need help?"

"We're fine," Emma said, "but thank you."

"I can call the park ranger if you're sick," he offered.

"No, we're fine, honest," Emma told him.

"All right, then." He nodded. "Y'all have a good day."

"Yes, sir." Emma tried to smile, but it didn't work. "You too."

Sophie pushed her tangled blonde hair away from her wet cheeks. "He must think we're a couple of crazies, sitting in the gravel like this."

"Well, you do look a little insane. Your hair is a fright. You're not wearing a bra, and those paint-stained pajama pants aren't exactly in vogue right now." Emma threw an arm around Sophie's shoulders and hugged her tightly. "Do you really give a rat's tiny butt what anyone thinks of us anyway?"

"Not really," Sophie answered.

"That goes to prove we aren't either one like Victoria, now doesn't it? We're both going to be fantastic mothers if we have kids," Emma assured her.

"Promise?" Sophie hiccuped.

Emma held up her little finger. "I pinkie promise, and if I see you doing something stupid like not letting your kid go to public school, I'll whip your ass."

Sophie locked her little finger with Emma's. "Why would I do that?"

"Oh. My. Gosh!" Emma untangled her pinkie finger from Sophie's.

"What? Is it a snake?" Sophie began to scan the ground. "Or a scorpion?"

"No." Emma shook her head. "Where would my children go to school if I never intend to move away from the trailer park?"

Sophie giggled and then chuckled and then broke into guffaws.

"What's so funny?" Emma asked.

"We're talking about my guilt and me being a horrible mother, and you—" She wiped her eyes and got the hiccups. "You are suddenly worried about where our kids—that we don't have—will go to school."

"Well." Emma shrugged. "Where would they go?"

"They'd attend Big Bend School over in Terlingua. Last time I checked, it had about a hundred students, and that's pre-K through twelfth grade. Are you and Josh that serious?

Have you already named your firstborn? Do we need to have the talk about birth control?" Sophie got tickled all over again.

"No, but he kissed me one time and I didn't panic," Emma said. "And it's not funny."

"It kind of is." Sophie stood up.

"No, it's not," Emma said. "Let's get back in the SUV and find this Cottonwood place. Josh said he packed us a couple of sleeping bags. Is there a place where we roll them out, or what do we do?"

Sophie got to her feet. "I hope he sent a tent, or we might be in trouble with the bears and javelinas."

"Hav-a-whatus?" Emma got behind the wheel and started the engine.

"They're kind of like a small feral pig. That's why we don't leave food of any kind out on the picnic table or in the tent. We'll keep everything in the SUV except when we're cooking or eating."

"Are they dangerous?" Emma checked the rearview mirror to be sure there was no traffic, and then she pulled out onto the road and started driving.

"If you provoke them, they are, but they'll run away from loud noises most of the time. Just grab a pot and bang on it. Stop!" Sophie yelled.

Emma slammed on the brakes. "What is it?"

"Lord, woman! Don't do that. You about slung me through the windshield," Sophie said.

"Well, don't yell *stop* at me," Emma shot back. "Why did you tell me to stop?"

"Right there." Sophie pointed. "That's a javelina. A mama and her two babies."

"Ugly critters. Do people eat them?" Emma's nose curled.

"I've never been that hungry. Go on now. Turn left about a quarter mile up the road and we'll be at the campground. I usually rent an RV when I come here, but as you know, I didn't have time to plan this trip."

"Bathrooms?" Emma made the turn.

"Outside toilets, but they usually don't smell too bad. Biggest problem is that they run out of toilet paper pretty often," Sophie answered. "There. See those two little adobe buildings? Those are the bathrooms. At least when I rescued you, I brought you to a nice trailer with a flushable toilet."

"I've never used a potty that didn't flush in my whole life, but it will be an adventure," Emma said.

Sophie pointed to the right. "That's our spot right there, and there's an RV in it."

"I'm bush broke, as Rebel used to say," Emma laughed. "After we went to the cave, I managed to hold it until we got back home, but before that, I did have to cop a squat behind a bush a couple of times. And I did check for snakes and scorpions."

"Why's an RV in our reserved space?" Sophie stared at the vehicle like it was an alien spaceship.

"I guess the proper thing would be to knock on the door and ask the folks," Emma said. "Or we could just pitch our tent. Maybe back there by the table, and we can share the space with our neighbors."

Sophie whipped around to stare at Emma. Surely she was hearing things. Emma didn't like to be around strangers, and she sure wouldn't want to share a picnic table with folks she didn't know. Where was her Emma, and who was this strange woman occupying her body?

"Well, Miz Social Butterfly," Sophie grumbled. "Why don't you go up there and knock on the door and see if those people have made a mistake?"

"You're the one who reserved the campground." Emma's voice was a little shaky now. "You go tell them to move."

Sophie giggled so hard she snorted. "Would you open the door to someone who looks like me, or would you call the park rangers?"

Emma sucked in a lungful of air and let it out in a whoosh. "I guess if I'm going to have babies and send them off on a school bus, I'd better learn how to ask a few questions."

This can't be much different than watching a child go into a kindergarten classroom all by herself. Sophie thought of Teddy's words as she kept an eye on Emma. But then Emma didn't even knock on the RV door. She just turned around and ran back to the SUV. So much for the child being brave on the first day of school.

Sophie hopped out of the SUV and started across to the RV but stopped when she noticed Emma dragging things out of the back seat. "What are you doing?"

"Read the note," Emma yelled. "None of those pig critters are going to attack us tonight."

Stepping up on the bottom step, Sophie read through the short note twice: *This RV is for Sophia Mason and Emma Merrill's use until Saturday afternoon. Josh Corlen says he forgot to pack a tent.*

Sophie suddenly felt a little better just knowing that the trailer family was thinking about her. She went back to their vehicle and got her phone from her purse. She scrolled down through the list of contacts until she came to Josh's name and then hit the call icon.

"Hey, did y'all make it? I'm sorry about the tent. I called the Terlingua rental right outside the park, and they said they only had one left. I asked them to put a rush on it and have it set up for you when you arrived. The keys are under the bottom porch step," Josh said.

"Thank you, thank you! You are my new hero," Sophie said. "I'll reimburse you when I get home."

"No need," Josh chuckled. "My treat, and it's good to hear your voice. You sound better."

Yes, sir, she was better because so many people cared about her and were supporting Emma in trying to get her over this horrible nightmare of depression.

"I am better," Sophie said. "There's nothing like a friend who'll rescue you, or other friends who help her out with the job. See you on Saturday."

"Bring home paintings," he said.

"And Emma?"

"Yes, please," Josh answered. "See you then. You ladies have a great time. 'Bye, now."

Chapter Twenty-One

Emma carried the first load of food into the small RV. A bench wrapped around a small table on one side of the room. A kitchenette-type area was straight across from that with a tiny sink, dorm-size refrigerator, and stove top with two burners. To the right was a small settee, and to the left, two bunkbeds took up the rest of the space—except for a shower and potty in a room that was smaller than any broom closet Emma had ever seen.

"It beats javelinas and bears attacking us in our sleep or going without a shower for three days," she whispered.

"Pretty small." Sophie brought in another load. "I usually rent one about twice this size, but a rescued princess can't fuss about her living quarters."

"I love it, and I hate to break the news to you, but neither of us are princesses, thank God. If I never see that hideous bedroom at Mother's house again, it will be too soon," Emma said. "This is about the size of the tiny house I've always dreamed of having. And we have a shower, and a flushable potty."

"The potty should only be used at night and the showers kept very short or we'll run out of water." Sophie set her things on the table. "Potty only at night because, even in three days, it will begin to smell. Showers because a trailer this size has a small water tank."

"Still, it's better than being pig food in our sleep." Emma smiled.

"I can agree with that for sure." Sophie slumped down on the settee and scanned the whole place. "It's got more room than a two-man tent, and we don't have to build a fire to cook, so we're good. We'll set up our painting supplies on the picnic table and put them all in the SUV at night."

This was her Sophie—taking charge and making decisions. Emma couldn't help but think about her own journey from institution to standing up for herself. Dragging Sophie away from her pity party was the right thing to do, but Emma was already missing Josh.

Emma searched through the bags on the table until she found the beer. She twisted the top off one and handed it to Sophie. "I was scared out of my mind that I might be pregnant after the rape. I was too scared to go to the pharmacy for the morning-after pill. I stopped by a store on my way home and bought ten tests and took one every week until I finally got my period." She removed the cap from her beer and took a long swallow. "I buried the rest of them in the rose garden out in the backyard. I was afraid that if I put them in the trash, Mother would find them."

"What would you have done if you had been pregnant?" Sophie asked.

"I'm glad I didn't have to make that decision. I would have felt guilty if I had decided to terminate the pregnancy, but"—Emma shrugged—"you know Victoria. She would have insisted I have an abortion or else sent me away to some exclusive unwed mothers' home and given the baby up for adoption."

"What would you have wanted?" Sophie asked.

"I couldn't have raised a child back then, not in the condition I was in, and besides, every time I looked at the baby, I would have remembered that awful night. I just wanted to put it all behind me and never think of it again. That's exactly what I did until you came to the center." Emma touched her bottle to the one Sophie was holding. "To friends who are closer than sisters."

"To us." Sophie's smile wasn't brilliant, but it sure beat the scowls she'd been giving Emma since they had left home. "I'm glad you are here, Em. My heart and mind tell me not to feel like this, but it's so tough."

"Yep, I know exactly what you're talking about," Emma said.

"Couple of basket cases, aren't we?" Sophie sighed.

"Maybe we *were,* but we're two strong women now who have overcome horrible things and lived with the guilt for too long. Did you ever read that plaque hanging on the wall in my bedroom?" Emma asked.

"I noticed it was there, but until you moved into the trailer with me, I probably wasn't in the bedroom you use more than a couple of times," Sophie answered.

Emma set her beer on the floor and hopped up off the settee. She pushed some bags to the side and found her purse, took out her phone, and went back to sit beside Sophie. "Listen to this very carefully: 'Love will put you face-to-face with endless obstacles. It will ask you to reveal the parts of yourself you tirelessly work at hiding. It will ask you to find compassion for yourself and receive what it is you are convinced you are not worthy of. Love will always demand more. Surrender to being seen and being loved. Surrender to the beauty of revealing yourself to yourself, and to the ones who saw you before you saw you.' It was written by Vienna Pharaon, who is a therapist." She took a drink of her beer and then went on, "We have faced obstacles. We have hidden parts of ourselves. We should give up all this baggage and realize we are worthy to be seen and to be loved."

"That's easier said than done," Sophie whispered. "I haven't told my mother about the baby.

What's she going to say? Is she going to be disappointed in me?"

Emma laid her phone in Sophie's lap. "No time like the present. Jump over the obstacle and get it over with. Rebel loves you. She will understand."

"Did Victoria understand when you told her about the rape?" Sophie asked.

"She did exactly what I thought she would do," Emma answered. "And Rebel will do what I figure she'll do. She's not Victoria, and neither are we."

Sophie scrolled down through Emma's contacts and called her mother.

Emma stood up. "I'll go on and finish unloading the SUV."

Sophie grabbed her hand. "You are going to sit right here beside me. This is too much for me to do alone. Mama, I've got Emma here, and I'm putting you on speaker."

"How are you holding up? Did Emma take you to the park?" Rebel asked.

"Yes, I did, but I had to bring her barefoot and in her pajamas, because she refused to get dressed," Emma tattled.

"She can always get dressed later. The important thing is that you've gotten her out of bed and into a place where she's always loved to paint," Rebel said.

"Mama, I need to tell you something." Tears

flowed down Sophie's cheeks again. "It's so hard to even say the words."

"Does Emma know what you're about to say?" Rebel asked.

"I didn't until this morning, maybe an hour or two ago," Emma answered.

"Is Sophie crying?" Rebel asked.

"Yes," Emma said.

"Then you tell me why she's crying. That's what friends are for," Rebel said.

Sophie nodded at Emma. "I just can't do it."

Emma shortened the story, but by the time she was finished telling Rebel Sophie's secret, all three of them were weeping.

"Don't hate me, Mama," Sophie sobbed.

"Hate you?" Rebel blew her nose loudly. "I'm just sorry you didn't come to me and tell me then. You shouldn't have carried this burden alone all these years. Promise me you'll never do something like this again."

"I promise," Sophie agreed.

"Now, I'm going to hang up this phone because all we're going to do is shed tears together if I don't. I love you, Sophie, and I love you, Em, for being there with her. You two should never have been separated. You're like twins, even more than most blood kin sisters are, and you've had to face battles that neither of you should have had to endure, especially alone," Rebel said.

"Love you, Mama," Sophie said.

"Me too," Emma told her and ended the call.

Sophie went straight to the bathroom, brought out toilet paper, and pulled a fistful off before she handed it to Emma. She wiped her face, blew her nose, and tossed the tissue into the small trash can at the end of the table. "We've conquered that obstacle, but when you read that quote, it said they were endless. I'm not sure I can handle too many more as hard as the past two days have been."

"Toad frogs." Emma managed a weak giggle.

Sophie sank back down on the brown-and-orange-plaid settee. "I'd forgotten about that."

"Get up every morning and eat a toad frog. Nothing will faze you the rest of the day," Emma said, quoting something that Rebel had told them when they were girls.

"You ever seen a cat or dog bite into a toad frog?" Sophie asked.

"Of course not. Mama wouldn't allow pets of any kind in or around the house." Emma leaned her head back, resting it on the overstuffed cushion.

"The frog has a protective thing that must taste awful. I saw a big old pit bull grab one up and bite it. The dog frothed at the mouth and howled like it had been shot." Sophie turned up her beer, finished it, and tossed the empty bottle into the trash can. "Three points from this far away."

"That was barely two points. You're not even

four feet from the can," Emma argued. "Are you serious about the frog?"

"Yep, I was about thirteen when I saw it happen. I was sitting on the porch of our trailer. The neighbors owned that dog, and I hated it because it always barked at me, but I felt sorry for it that day."

"What's that got to do with today?" Emma asked.

"We've faced our biggest fears," Sophie said. "They were as bitter as that dog eating the toad frog, but now we are past that and we can move on."

"Yes, we can." Emma felt like she could move on. "What about Teddy? Are you going to make up with him?"

Sophie nodded. "Let's go unload what else we need to bring inside and set up our easels. There's still plenty of light left in this day. I can only handle one thing at a time, Em. Today I told Mama about the baby. Teddy may never want to speak to me again, and I may have to live with that, but I can't face it today. I'm going to get dressed and paint for a while."

"I'll be outside waiting for you, but I'd better not come back in here and find you in bed," Emma said.

Sophie pointed at the door. "I'll be out in a few minutes."

Emma took her phone with her and sat down

on the seat of the metal-and-wood picnic table. The sun was warm, and wildflowers dotted the landscape as far as she could see. Real grass grew in spots where the shade of the trees didn't hinder it, and a nice breeze blew her dark hair away from her face. Everything was quiet so when her phone rang, the noise startled her. She couldn't help but smile when Josh's name popped up on the screen.

"Hello," she said.

"Just making sure that you're all right," Josh said.

"We are here, and thank you for the RV," she said. "I was getting worried when I heard about bears and javelinas."

"Glad you made it safely, but the place seems awfully empty without you and Sophie here," Josh said.

"I miss you." The words were out of her mouth before she even realized she was thinking them.

"Me too," Josh said. "Even though you've only been gone a few hours, I'm realizing how glad I am that you won't be leaving the park when Sophie does."

"Right back at you," Emma said. "I can't imagine living anywhere else, Josh. I'm happy there, and I don't ever want to leave. I'm finding me even faster than I thought I would or could. I'm not sure who rescued who today. Sophie and I both needed help. I drove for the first time in years, and she's already feeling better."

"That's wonderful. I'll go tell Arty and Filly. They're both working behind their trailers today. Call me tonight?" he asked.

"Yes, definitely," she answered.

Sophie got dressed in a pair of her cutoff overalls and a paint-stained shirt and started outside but then stopped and called her mother again.

"Are you really going to be all right?" Rebel asked.

"It's the guilt that finally got to me. I saw a seventeen-year-old girl with dark hair on the plane, and I started thinking about the baby I didn't want and lost. I figured I didn't deserve to be happy when my negative thoughts had killed her."

"That's not the way to think," Rebel said. "Could you have changed the color of your baby's eyes or hair with thoughts? Of course you couldn't, and you were scared out of your mind during those few weeks. Don't blame yourself for what you couldn't help, but from now on, you need to talk about things. Is something else going on?"

"Teddy and I had a big fight, and I don't know if it can be fixed. I said some mean things, and so did he, and . . ." Sophie's voice cracked.

"And is this your first huge argument?" Rebel asked.

"Yes, it is," Sophie answered.

"Then it's a test," Rebel told her. "Time will tell if you passed the test or failed it. Whichever way it goes, you'll have learned a lesson from it."

"Thanks, Mama," Sophie said. "I love him, but I'm just not sure—"

Rebel didn't let her finish the sentence. "You've got a lot on your mind. You need to figure things out before you rush into anything. Give it time."

"I love you," Sophie said.

"Love you right back," Rebel said and ended the call.

Sophie laid the phone to the side and peeked out the window above the sink. Emma was setting up the big easel for her and had laid the supplies out on the picnic table. Sophie had had friends, acquaintances, and fans, but she'd never had anyone like Em.

"Nothing and no one will ever keep us from seeing each other again, not even Victoria," Sophie declared. She went outside and glanced out over the land at the mesalike mountain out there in the distance. "I'm going to paint that mountain with that big tree in the foreground and a whole family of javelinas underneath it. They're as ugly as my mood has been, so it seems fitting."

"That might get some of this mood out of your system." Emma had set up a little tabletop easel and already had paint squirted out on a palette.

"I'm going to work on a bunny that Josh and I saw when we went on our adventure. When did you know that you were in love with Teddy?"

The question came out of the blue so fast that it took Sophie by surprise. "I'm not sure. It's been so long . . . ," she stammered and tried to put words to the feelings she had had when she first met Teddy. "I think I must've loved him from the day I first saw him, but I didn't admit it to him for a long time. Why are you asking?"

"I want to know what it feels like to fall in love," Emma said. "How do you know for sure that it's love, and not dependence on someone for your happiness? I have no money unless some of my paintings sell. I wouldn't ever want Josh to think I'm only interested in him for security. I want to be independent and make my own way."

"You won't be penniless for much longer. My lawyer is working with Victoria's lawyer, finally, and they're trying to reach an agreement about your money. She's being bitchy, but then, we expected that. And, honey, Josh would never think that of you."

"I hope not." Emma looked genuinely worried.

"But," Sophie added, "this is the first guy you've ever let into your life. Are you sure about your feelings?"

"Filly and I had a long talk, and she said that we're always hunting for something. That can be love, inspiration, or even the truth, or in my case, hunting for myself. I think I've found the truth, and I'm starting to find myself, but I'm not sure what it feels like to be in love. That's why I asked you," Emma said.

Sophie took a deep breath. "I'm a pretty poor excuse to ask about relationships right now. I just let my own pain and guilt get in the way of my relationship with Teddy, but my advice would be not to get in a rush, but yet not to go too slow. Never waste a minute of time. Do you think you're ready for the physical side of a relationship?"

"I don't know. Now that I've figured out what really happened, maybe I should get some more therapy and talk to a professional about that part of things." Emma blushed.

"What was it you read to me this morning?" Sophie asked. "Something about love putting you face-to-face with lots of obstacles. Well, this is a big one for you. But like that other part said, you've got to surrender to being loved. You are worthy of this, Em, whether it's with Josh or another guy."

"I trust you, Sophie. Please don't say that just because you know it's what I want to hear," Emma said.

"Honey, you should know me well enough to know that I would never lie to you," Sophie said. "Teddy's going to come home on Saturday, probably not long after we get there. Think you could stay with Filly a few days?"

"No problem." Emma nodded.

"You really have come a long way this past month," Sophie said.

"So have you, Sophie, and I'm going even further before my life is over. I'm ready to live, not just exist. I'm going to get in touch with Nancy. I liked her, and now that I'm away from Mother, maybe she can help me with the issues I have now," Emma said.

"That's a great idea." Sophie was so proud of Emma that she couldn't wipe the grin off her face.

Chapter Twenty-Two

When it was time to leave Big Bend, Emma lingered behind for a few minutes to say goodbye to the RV after Sophie had taken the last load out to the vehicle and was already behind the steering wheel. Emma really wanted to go back to the trailer park, but she still hated to leave her little vacation home.

"Goodbye, little house," she whispered as she closed the door behind her and left the key under the porch step. "I hope the next people enjoy staying with you as much as I have." She sighed as she crossed the short distance to the vehicle and slid into the passenger seat.

"Thank you for everything, Em," Sophie said as she started the engine and backed away from their parking area.

"Right back at you." Speaking past the lump in her throat wasn't easy for Emma. Until Sophie rescued her, she hadn't felt emotions in years— now everything either made her giggle or cry. Either emotion meant she was alive again—not just existing, but able to feel and to love again. Even the sadness was wonderful after living in a state of numbness for so long.

"How long until we are home?" Emma watched out the side window until the RV was completely out of sight. "I've got a FaceTime session with Nancy this evening at six. We're connecting so much better, even just in the two sessions so far, now that I have my memories back."

"An hour to Terlingua and then half an hour past that to the trailer park," Sophie answered. "Are you in a hurry to see Josh?"

"Of course I am, and speaking of the men in our lives, have you talked to Teddy?" Emma asked.

Sophie shook her head and stared out the side window. "A couple of times, but it's a little awkward, and I hate that."

They stopped at the Terlingua convenience store for a bathroom break and a cold drink, then did the last leg of the journey. Emma caught herself wringing her hands when Sophie turned off the highway onto the dirt road leading back to the trailer park. She tried to stop but she couldn't, so finally she tucked them under her legs.

"Nervous, are you?" Sophie asked.

"Little bit," Emma admitted.

"You've talked to Josh every night. Why are you edgy?" Sophie asked.

Emma raised an eyebrow. "How many boyfriends have you had?"

"Boyfriends as in a date or two, a kiss at the door, and then either he or I wasn't interested? Maybe a dozen. Relationships as in several dates that lead to sex, about four. But Teddy is the only one for many years," Sophie answered.

"Well, this is my first as in kiss at the door, and my first time to hope that it develops into something more," Emma said. "And I'm terrified that I'll mess it up. Nancy has told me to just let nature take its course, but that's tough to do when I feel the need to control everything. She says that's because I think if I'm in control, then no one can hurt me. She said I'm feeling this because I wasn't in control of my own life for so long."

Sophie patted her on the shoulder. "I'm glad you got in touch with her, and I don't mean to pry, but how are you paying for the sessions?"

"She said she would do them pro bono, but I told her that when I sold some paintings, I would pay her. Tell me that I'm strong," Emma said. "I need to hear you say those words."

"You are very strong. Look what you did for me. Just be yourself, and you'll be f—" She braked so hard that if Emma hadn't been wearing a seat belt, she would have hit the windshield.

Emma shifted her focus from Sophie to the trailers right ahead of them. "Josh, Teddy, and—oh my God!"

"Is that your father?" Sophie gasped. "When I saw three guys, I just figured the other one was Arty, but I see now that it's Wyatt. What's he doing here? He doesn't look much different than he did when we were kids. And what in the hell is Teddy doing here already?"

"I guess Mother sent Daddy as a last-ditch effort to make me leave this place. I hope he doesn't ruin my homecoming with Josh." Emma sighed.

Sophie took her foot off the brake and inched the SUV the rest of the way to the spot where she parked. "Teddy's walking toward us," she whispered.

"I guess he wants to talk. I'm getting out. He can sit right here and y'all can figure things out without all the rest of us hearing." Emma unfastened her seat belt. Suddenly, the door swung open on her side, and Josh held out a hand.

He helped her out of the vehicle and kissed her on the cheek. "I really, really missed you. Your dad is here, Em. He wants to talk to you."

She wrapped her arms around his neck and hugged him tightly. "Did he say about what? He came quite a ways."

Josh looped his arm into hers and walked with her across the yard. "No, he didn't. He's just been sitting on the porch waiting all this time."

"Daddy?" Emma pulled her arm free and held her hands tightly to keep from twisting them. "Did Mother send you?"

"Hello, Emma, and no, Victoria didn't send me," Wyatt answered.

"Why don't y'all go around to your back porch, Em, so you can talk in private," Josh said and then turned around and headed toward the picnic table.

Emma wanted to call out to him not to leave her, that she needed him to help her, but then she sucked it up and nodded toward Wyatt. "Follow me."

I am strong. I can stand up for myself. Nancy said I've made great strides, she thought.

Wyatt was one of those men who could easily get lost in a crowd. Nothing about him stood out except his light brown eyes that were so much like Emma's.

Awkward.

That's the only way that Emma could explain the situation. A morning breeze sent the aroma of fresh-brewed coffee right to her nose, and she wondered how her father took his coffee. Most of the time he was either off to work or about to leave by the time she made it to the kitchen.

She walked up onto the porch and found a pot of coffee, two mugs, and a plate full of cookies on the table between the two red chairs. Whoever did that had had the right idea, but she couldn't even think about eating cookies or sipping coffee right then.

"Help yourself," she said.

"Don't mind if I do." He poured a mugful and raised a dark eyebrow at her. "Want one?"

"No, thank you." She slumped down into the other chair.

"I wanted to see you before I leave the country," he said.

"Mother said you were getting a divorce." Emma's voice sounded strangely hollow even in her own ears. "Where are you going?"

"I know that she sent Jeffrey and that she was plenty mad when you called her that day." Wyatt smiled again. "She hates confrontation, even as mean as she is."

"I'm tired of the way she's made me feel, Daddy." The last word seemed a little strange in her ears when she said it this time, but he was her father, after all. "I'm not mentally ill. So, you are really getting a divorce?"

"Don't you think it's about time? Our marriage was a mistake from the beginning. We got married for the wrong reasons," Wyatt said.

"Did you stay together for my sake?" Emma asked. "If you did, neither of you did a very good job."

"I know that, too." Wyatt nodded. "I didn't know how to be a father, especially with Victoria griping about everything I did, so I gave up too easily and let her have her way. You know how she is."

"Oh, yeah, I do." She sighed and was beginning to feel comfortable enough to pick up a cookie and take a bite. "Think she'll ever change?"

"Not really. She'd have to want to change, and in her eyes, she's perfect the way she is. I wish her the best, but I can't spend the rest of my life with her, so Betsy and I are going to Belize to live. We've signed all the divorce papers, and an agreement has been reached. Your mother isn't happy with it, but I am." Wyatt laid a folder on Emma's lap.

Betsy? The name seemed to come out of thin air. Why hadn't she seen his dissatisfaction before now?

"These are your bank accounts with a pad of checks and a debit card. I set it all up in a bank in Dallas, but you can change it to one in this area if you want."

"How . . . what . . . ," Emma stammered. "Mother said . . ."

"I know what she told you, but the only way I would agree to let her have my part of the house was if she gave you back what was rightfully yours. She has been throwing a fit about Sophie hiring a lawyer, and this gives her a way out that makes her feel like it's not her fault. She's giving you the money to get me out of her life. She can blow the money from the sale of the company if she wants, but we've caused you enough pain without leaving you penniless, and for that I'm truly sorry. I should have been a better father," Wyatt said.

"Thank you." Emma ran a finger over the

folder. Now she was financially independent. That was one step in the right direction.

"Do you want to know about Betsy?" The smile on his face when he said her name spoke volumes.

"I would think that she's your new friend or girlfriend, right?"

Wyatt nodded. "She's a waitress at the café where I go for coffee every morning. That's where I met her, and we fell in love. I've invested my paycheck the past thirty years, and we are retiring to Belize because I don't want to live anywhere near Victoria. I'm sorry if that disappoints you. God knows that you deserve so much more than I've ever given you. Maybe someday you'll come and visit me, especially if you have children. I'd like to think maybe Betsy and I would be better grandparents than I was a father."

"She doesn't have children?" Emma asked.

"She had a miscarriage when she was just a teenager, and there were complications," Wyatt answered.

"Did Mother tell you about"—she stumbled over the words—"the rape?"

Wyatt's brow furrowed into deep wrinkles. "What rape?"

Emma took a deep breath. If she could tell Josh such a private thing about herself, then she could tell her father. "I buried the memory of it for a long time, but I'm getting better every day out here in this wilderness." She went on to tell him the story, ending with how Sophie had rescued her.

"My God!" Wyatt tucked his chin down to his chest. "I'm so, so sorry that I made things so hard that you couldn't trust me with this. When did you tell Victoria?"

"After I remembered what had happened and Sophie helped me sort through some of it. She asked me what I did to cause it," Emma answered. "But I'm past what Mother thinks, and to tell the truth, part of me knew she'd say exactly what she did. The only thing I regret right now is that I didn't face the whole situation sooner. I wanted her to love me like Rebel loves Sophie so badly that . . . well, you know." She shrugged.

Wyatt raised his head and wiped at his wet cheeks.

Emma left her chair and knelt in front of him. "Don't cry, Daddy. It happened. I'm learning to deal with the problems Mother caused right along with that. I've got a wonderful therapist who is helping me so much."

Wyatt wrapped her up in his arms. "You have to forgive her, Emma. Not for her sake. She doesn't deserve it. But for your sake, so that you don't become bitter like she is. I told her for years that she wasn't doing the right thing by you, but she wouldn't listen."

"Maybe someday." Emma moved out of his embrace and got to her feet. The happiness in her heart had nothing to do with the bank accounts and everything to do with the fact that at least one of her parents could be a part of her life.

"I should be going now. A word of advice, even though I don't have the right to give it." Wyatt stood up. "If you ever marry, make sure it's for love. If it's not, then you'll be miserable."

"I'll keep that in mind. Thanks for coming to see me, and for what you've done about my finances," Emma said. "I think I'm ready to manage my own life now."

"I can see that, and if you ever need anything— and I mean anything at all—will you call me?" Wyatt took a step off the porch.

Emma stood up. "I'll text you right now so you have my number. Will you keep in touch with me?"

"I'd love to do that," Wyatt said as he looked down at the text on his phone. "Are you never going back to Dallas?"

"Not right now, Daddy. My plans at this time are to live right here in this trailer park."

"Good for you. I haven't seen you this happy in years. Not since you were a little girl and Sophie used to come to the house."

"I'd love to hear that you and Betsy made it all right to Belize," Emma said.

Could it be that she and her father might build a father-daughter relationship in the future? She hoped so. Having a parent in her life, and maybe someday a grandfather for her children, would be nice.

"I'll do that. I think you've got a good life here with these people." He turned around, stepped back up on the porch, and gave her another hug. "Take care of yourself."

"I will," Emma promised.

Wyatt's smile was bittersweet, as if he wanted to say more, and the words wouldn't come. "This isn't goodbye."

"No, it's not," Emma agreed. "And thanks again for standing up for me where my money is concerned."

He just waved over his shoulder as he hurried away. In the blink of an eye, Josh was sitting beside her in the other chair. "Are you okay? We weren't sure what was going on. He said goodbye to everyone real proper like and then got in his car and left. Can I do something for you? Do you need anything? I'm here." His words tumbled out like a gush of water.

"I'm fine." Emma reached over and took his hand in hers. "And for the first time in my life, I really mean that I'm fine. I couldn't be better than I am right now. I'm home. You are right here beside me. Sophie has been rescued. The sun is shining, and my life is finally good."

"So, you had a good visit with your father?" Josh asked.

"I really did, and there's hope for something better between us in the future. Speaking of the immediate future, as in tonight. Are Teddy and Sophie making up?"

"I have no idea. They're both still in her SUV," Josh said, "and I haven't heard any screaming."

"Well, if they do make up, I might need a place to crash tonight," she said.

"My trailer door is open tonight or anytime you want to stay with me," Josh said.

"Thank you." Emma's heart skipped a beat and then raced with a full head of steam.

Chapter Twenty-Three

Josh had never thought he could be more nervous than he had been on the day he signed the papers to buy Hummingbird Trailer Park and all the acreage surrounding it, but he was wrong. That evening after supper, not even George Strait's songs calmed him. He paced the floor and reminded himself that he had slept with Emma two nights already, and this wouldn't be any different.

"If she isn't talking about us sharing a bed or a couch, and she just wants a place to sleep, I'm worrying over nothing." He tried to reassure himself as he checked everything one more time. Clean towels in the bathroom. Clean sheets on the bed. Pillow and blanket on the sofa for him, of course. Cookies on the bar, and plenty of milk and beer in the refrigerator if she wanted a nighttime snack.

Everything was ready, and yet he still nearly jumped out of his skin when she knocked on the back door, poked her head inside, and yelled, "Is it safe to come in?"

He met her at the door and took her tote bag out of her hands. "I'll just put this in the bedroom."

"I just need a place to crash. The sofa is fine. I shouldn't take your bed," she argued.

"I'm glad to sleep on the sofa." All the nerves were gone now that she was there with him.

"Well, then, thank you," she said. "Are those more of Filly's sugar cookies?"

"Yep, she made them while y'all were gone. She tends to cook even more when she's nervous, and she was worried about both of you. I'll put this in the bedroom, and we'll have a little bedtime snack if you want." He disappeared down the hall and set the tote bag on the bed, and then he realized that the picture he'd drawn of her was hanging on the wall where he could see it as he was falling asleep. He could take it down and shove it under the bed, but Emma didn't deserve to be hidden away. The artwork really should be in a gallery with a sign that said FOR EXHIBITION ONLY on it for the whole world to see just how beautiful she was.

"It's time for her to see it," he whispered.

"See what?" she asked.

She was standing so close to him that the warmth of her breath sent shivers down his spine. Without turning around, he pointed at the picture to his left. "I drew it when you first came here."

She stared at the drawing for what seemed like an eternity. If she hated it, he would take it down and burn the damned thing.

"You made me look beautiful," she finally said. "I still had so much raw pain in those days, but I see hope for a brighter future in the picture. I love it, Josh. Can I buy it from you?"

"Leo made me promise to give him first choice if I ever sell it, but I won't." Josh slipped his arms around her waist and sank his nose into her hair. "I just wish I could have captured the coconut aroma of your hair and the smoothness of your skin in the picture."

"Who says you are shy and socially backward? That was the most romantic line I've ever heard." She covered his hands with hers.

"Only around you, Em," he admitted. "When your father showed up, I had to make myself sit on the porch with him and Teddy. I can talk to Teddy some, but I was pretty nervous around your dad at first. He asked about my art, though, and before long we were talking like we'd always known each other. I liked him, Em, I really did."

She leaned back against his chest. "I was nervous with him at first, too, but I think we might find some common ground to be friends."

Time stood still for Josh. He and Emma were the only ones in the universe. The only thing that mattered was that they were together and would be forever. "Happy anniversary and welcome home."

She whipped around and wrapped her arms around his neck. "This *is* May first, isn't it? I've been here a whole month, and it *is* home. Thank you for remembering. Now are we going to take the next step and go to bed?"

"Are you ready for that?" Josh asked.

"I think I am." She went up on tiptoe just slightly, kissed him, and reached out and closed the bedroom door.

Emma awoke the next morning to the aroma of bacon and coffee. She reached for Josh, but all she got was a fistful of air. She realized that she was totally naked under the covers and sat up so fast that it made her dizzy. She pulled the sheet up under her arms as her thoughts and emotions swirled around like a hurricane approaching land.

"I'm all right," she whispered. "I liked making love with Josh."

Josh came through the door wearing nothing but a smile and carrying a tray in his hand. "Good morning. I thought we'd share breakfast in bed this morning."

"I feel like a princess," she said, "and I'm so glad that Sophie and Teddy got things worked out. If they hadn't, I would have been consoling her, not spending a wonderful night with you."

"You are not a princess. You are definitely the queen. Want me to draw you with a diamond crown to prove it?" He set the tray down on the bed, fluffed up the pillows behind her, and crawled into bed with her. "I have a confession to make. Last night was my first time. I was a thirty-two-year-old virgin," he said.

"Were you disappointed?" She felt a slow burn moving from her neck to her cheeks.

He leaned across the tray, cupped his hand under her chin, and kissed her. "Oh, Em, what we had was beyond words and went beyond even my wildest expectations. I was just wondering if it was good enough to set this tray on the floor and—"

"Oh, yes," she butted in before he could finish the sentence.

Sophie awoke the next morning with her cheek on Teddy's chest. How could she have ever doubted anything about him or their relationship? She lay there for several minutes listening to the steady beat of his heart that was so like the solid, kind man he was all the time. She eased away from him and slid off the side of the bed, grabbed his shirt, and pressed it against her nose for a second, breathing in the woodsy cologne that he wore. Then she slipped her arms into it and buttoned it up the front. She tiptoed to the kitchen and put on a pot of coffee, and when it had dripped, she poured herself a mugful and carried it to the porch. A steady breeze moved fluffy, white clouds across the sky. A cute little bunny dashed across the yard in front of her and headed off for the mesquite grove in the distance.

This must be what it would feel like to con-fess my sins, she thought. *The burden is lifted from my heart, and I'm ready to go forward with life.*

"Good morning, beautiful." Teddy came out of the trailer with a mug of coffee in his hands. He set it down on the rail of the porch, wrapped his arms around her from behind, and buried his face in her hair. "It's going to be a good day. How are you feeling this morning?"

"I'm fine," she said and smiled. "That's what Em said when I first found her, though she didn't mean it. I was so guilt ridden when I came back from Del Rio, I wouldn't have meant it, either, but now I'm fine and I mean that with my whole heart."

"Do you think Em feels the same way?" Teddy asked.

"I hope so, but why don't we ask her?" She nodded toward Josh and Emma heading toward them. "I'd say from the glow on both their faces that they're more than *just* fine."

"Good morning," Emma said.

"Mornin' to you," Sophie and Teddy said at the same time.

"Coffee?" Sophie asked.

"We've had breakfast." Emma grinned.

"Josh, I was wondering if I could get you to help me load up Sophie's things," Teddy said. "I thought we'd just grab a couple of bananas and some breakfast bars to eat on the way. We need to start taking care of business in Del Rio."

Josh let go of Emma's hand and brushed a kiss across her lips. "Sure thing. This shouldn't take long."

Emma slumped down in the chair beside Sophie. "So you got things all worked out, right?"

"We did," Sophie said. "We're going ahead with the house and the gallery, and even the commitment ceremony. We talked half the night and had makeup sex the rest of it."

"And you feel better, right? You're not going to let the past ruin the future?" Emma asked.

"I'm working on it, and Teddy has vowed to help me," Sophie said.

"You're going to be all right?" Emma asked.

"Are you?" Sophie fired back at her.

"I don't kiss and tell, but you don't have to worry about me being afraid anymore," Emma said. "And I'm home at this trailer park, no matter which trailer I sleep in at night."

"Even Arty's?" Sophie teased.

Emma air-slapped her on the arm. "Arty is like a favorite uncle, so yes, I'd feel right at home on his sofa if I needed a place to stay. Sophie . . ." Her voice cracked.

"I know." Sophie smiled. "Words aren't necessary between friends like us, and goodbyes will always be tough."

Neither of them could keep the waterworks at

bay any longer. They stood at the same time and wrapped each other up in a fierce hug, sobbing as if their hearts were broken.

"I'm getting tears on your shirt," Emma said, but she didn't take a step back. "Oh, Sophie, thank you is so little to offer."

"It's Teddy's shirt, and . . ." Sophie had to stop to catch her breath before she could go on. "And, God, this is hard."

"We're both happy, so why does it hurt so much?" Emma finally took a step back and wiped her eyes on the tail of her shirt.

"It's crazy, isn't it?" Sophie dried her wet cheeks on the sleeve of Teddy's shirt.

"I promised myself I wouldn't cry when you left," Emma said. "This is not the end of our friendship. It's the . . ."

With a new batch of tears streaming down her face, Sophie laid a hand on Emma's shoulder. "It's being friends forever."

"No, it's being family forever," Emma corrected her. "I'll see you on July Fourth, right?"

"No, I'll be back next week. Teddy and I don't want to wait until July Fourth to have our commitment ceremony. We're coming back next Saturday and having it on Sunday. That's Mother's Day, and Mama said she couldn't ask for a better present than a son-in-law. And before you ask, I don't feel like I'm rushing into anything at all."

"I'm so, so happy for you, Sophie, and for me since we get to be together for your ceremony in a week. Can I pretend that Rebel is my mother that day since it is Mother's Day?" Emma managed a weak grin.

"Of course you can. Rebel would have an adoption ceremony if there was such a thing to make you her daughter, too," Sophie answered. That brought on even more tears. "I'm so sorry that Victoria is . . . well . . . you know," Sophie said. "You deserve a mama like mine."

Emma stepped forward, and the two women wrapped their arms around each other again.

"Mother failed. She tried to make me weak and dependent, but I'm a strong woman who can make it on her own now," Emma said.

"Strong enough that you helped me, so . . ." Sophie wept. "We've got to stop this bawling like babies."

"We'll call them happy tears." Emma moved back a few steps. "Now, get dressed and go make a home and business with Teddy. Who all is coming to the commitment ceremony?"

"Teddy's father, Jonathan, and Rebel are the only ones coming from outside the park family, so don't go to too much trouble," Sophie answered.

Emma sat back down in her chair. "Tell Filly that. This is like her daughter getting married."

Chapter Twenty-Four

Josh slipped his arm around Emma's waist and pulled her close to his side that morning when Sophie and Teddy drove away in two separate vehicles. Arty and Filly came out of their trailers and waved from their front porches right along with Josh and Emma until the dust had settled back to the dirt road.

"Ready for a long inspiration walk?" Josh asked.

Emma leaned against his side. "Yes, but, Josh, I already miss her."

"She'll be back for the ceremony next weekend." Josh dropped his arm and took her hand in his. If someone had told him five weeks ago that a beautiful brunette would come into his life and he'd be so comfortable with her that he would have a relationship with her, he would have thought they were bat-crap crazy.

"I don't like change," Emma said. "I didn't realize it until right now. Maybe that's why I let my mother dominate me for so long."

"That's because the big changes in your life turned out to be disastrous. Think about it, Em. First your mother decided to have you tutored at home, and you didn't see Sophie anymore. You were isolated from all the people you knew at school. Even if they weren't your friends, you were used to seeing them." He kept her hand in his and stepped off the porch. "Then you went to college and the change you experienced there was really devastating. Don't be afraid of change now. Sometimes it's a good thing."

"I'm not afraid of anything anymore. If Sophie had decided to have a huge church wedding in Del Rio, I would have gone to that. But I am glad she's having her ceremony here. It's a special place."

"Yes, it is." Josh squeezed her hand gently and then stopped and pointed to a turtle hiding in a clump of grass. "Take a picture with your phone. I can see one of your paintings of this old boy with *hope* written on his back."

"Hope is the magic that heals hearts and souls," she whispered as she took several shots of the turtle.

The sun was straight up overhead when Emma and Josh returned to the trailer park. Arty and Filly motioned them over to the picnic table, where they had laid out sandwiches, chips, and Filly's homemade cookies for lunch.

"We were hoping you kids would be back in time to eat with us and talk about the wedding next week," Filly said.

"I was thinkin' maybe I'd make an arch for them to stand under when they say their vows," Arty said. "They'll pass through the arch to jump over the broom on the other side, and then we'll have a big reception for them. What do y'all think?"

"Sounds wonderful." Josh waited for Emma to sit down, and then he took his place beside her. He held her hand while Arty said grace, then passed the platter of sandwiches over to her.

"What do you want when you get married, Em?" Filly asked.

"The same thing as Sophie. My folks had the big wedding with the huge cake, big white dress, and a reception at the country club. That had to be the worst marriage in history, so I sure don't want anything like that," she answered.

"Smart choice," Arty said.

"I'll make a trip to town tomorrow for silk flowers. I'll need to make two bouquets plus a few corsages and boutonnieres for everyone. Plus, we'll need stuff to decorate the arch. Sophie left it up to me to pick the colors. I think red roses would be nice," Filly said.

"Why go to town? If you made an order now, they'd all be delivered to your doorstep in two days," Emma said.

"That's a great idea. After we get done eating, Josh can bring his laptop out here, and we'll get everything ordered," Filly agreed. "That will save the whole day that it takes to go to town, shop, and come home."

"What do we do if it rains?" Josh asked.

Filly glared at him. "It wouldn't dare. Not on Sophie's day. So, give me your opinion. Red roses?"

"Sophie loves this place so much," Emma said. "Maybe we should think about using cactus flowers, and what do you think about some little hummingbirds on the arch?"

"I could dig up some blooming cactus and desert grass, plant them in a couple of big pots, and put them beside the arch," Josh offered.

"I'm liking that idea." Filly nodded. "That sounds like we should use sage-green tulle instead of white?"

"I believe you're beginning to see the light." Arty grinned. "This will be the ceremony of the century."

Emma was already just a little jealous. This was exactly what she would want when she got married. This place and these people had saved her life. Maybe she could save all the decorations for the day when it was her turn to jump over the broom.

A rumble out in the distance took their attention away from the upcoming festivities. Emma shaded her eyes with her hand and stared at the dust boiling up behind a vehicle coming down the road. Sophie must have forgotten something, and Emma felt two ways about it. Part of her was excited that she could see Sophie again. The other part didn't think she could bear another goodbye.

"It's Leo," Arty said. "I wasn't expecting him just yet, but I do have a few things ready for him."

"We can tell him about the new gallery while he's here," Emma said.

The truck came to a stop, and Leo crawled out. "Howdy, folks."

"Come around and have some lunch with us," Filly said. "Want a beer or a glass of tea?"

"Tea is fine, and thank you." Leo crossed the yard in a few long strides and sat down beside Filly.

Leo hadn't shrunk in size one single bit. His looks hadn't changed at all, but Emma wasn't afraid of him anymore. *Another obstacle overcome,* she thought.

"What brings you out here at this time of the month?" Filly passed the sandwiches to him and poured iced tea into a red plastic cup.

"I was on my way up to Alpine to look at some big metal art like you used to do, Arty, and it's only five miles out of the way. Thought I'd swing by and deliver a check to Emma. Both of her paintings have sold, and they did very well." He put two sandwiches on his plate and removed a folded check from his shirt pocket. "This is right nice of y'all to ask me to have lunch with you. I heard through the grapevine that Sophie and Teddy are putting in a gallery in Del Rio. Is that going to cut into my business with you?"

Emma nodded. "After I deliver the first six paintings I promised you, I'm giving her an exclusive on my things."

"I understand and wish you well," Leo answered. "I'll still come by once a month and take whatever the other folks have for me, and if you ever change your mind, I'll take whatever you can produce."

Even with her newfound feelings of independence, Emma was relieved to hear him say that. As sweet as he had been, she wouldn't hurt his feelings for anything.

"I intend to do pieces for both places," Josh said.

"Me too," Arty and Filly said at the same time.

"Y'all got anything for me today?" Leo handed the check to Emma.

"You going to peek at that check or not?" Josh whispered.

"I'm afraid to," Emma said out the side of her mouth.

"I thought you weren't afraid of anything anymore," Josh teased.

Leo chuckled and took a long drink of his tea. "Don't be. I told you in the beginning you are a star. Just don't faint dead away. I'd hate to give you mouth-to-mouth resuscitation with chicken salad on my breath."

Emma opened it slowly and gasped. "Are you sure this is right?"

"Very sure." Leo nodded. "A big hotshot gallery owner from Seattle comes every three months to see what I've got. He took both of the pictures home with him. The bird with the storm went for a thousand dollars, which means he'll get three to five for it if he sells it. The other he took, he paid seven fifty for. From what he said, he'll be putting them on display as originals from a budding debut artist. He signed a deal with me that when they sell, and when he does reprints, that you will receive a percentage of all those sales, also, so this is just the beginning of your profits. He did that same thing with a couple of Josh's works, and now he's known all over the world. He offered two thousand for your eagle, but I held out until he gave me three, Josh. Same deal as always with the reprints and the sale of the original. I'll bring the rest of y'all's money when I come to collect what else you've got ready for me this month."

"That's pretty spectacular for your first work," Josh said.

Emma's hands shook as she stared at the check. This meant she could live right here at the park for a while without ever touching her trust fund money. She had proven that she could make it on her own with the money she earned.

"It's only about ten times what I was hoping for. Thank you so much, Leo." She smiled across the table at him.

"I wasn't shootin' a line of BS when I said you were good." Leo finished off his tea and filled his cup again. "This is just the beginning. A few folks have already seen what my buyer in Seattle took home and have called me for a peek at what else you produce. Between me and Sophie, we'll make you famous." He glanced over at Filly. "Mind if I take a couple of cookies and my tea with me? I should be going if I'm going to make it to Alpine at the right time."

"Not one bit. Want me to wrap up another sandwich for you to eat on the road?" Filly asked.

"They are delicious, but the cookies and tea will be fine, thank you," Leo said as he stood up. "I'll see y'all soon. Josh, don't you forget that I get first dibs on that picture of Emma if you ever want to get rid of it."

"Ain't goin' to happen," Josh said through a grin.

"Didn't think so, but I intend to keep you reminded." Leo waved over his shoulder as he went back to his truck.

"What picture?" Arty asked. "You been keeping things from us?"

"I'll be glad to show it to you," Josh said. "I

just didn't want to bring it out until Emma had passed judgment on it."

"I love it. Josh captures spirit and soul in his work." Emma tucked the check into her pocket and sent up a silent prayer of gratefulness for all the miracles that had happened in the past month.

"Well, go get it," Filly said. "You know how impatient I can be."

"Yes, ma'am." Josh flashed a smile and headed over toward his trailer.

In a few minutes, he brought the drawing back and stood it up at the end of the table. "What do you think?" he asked.

"I still say that's your best work ever. You could demand whatever price you wanted for that," Filly said.

"But some things aren't up for sale, are they, son?" Arty asked.

Emma nodded and thought that a person's heart wasn't for sale, but it could be given away.

"You got that right," Josh answered. "It will always be mine until I die, and then maybe I'll pass it down to whichever of my children appreciates good art."

"Does that mean we're going to get grandchildren someday?" Filly's eyes twinkled.

"One never knows what the future might hold," Emma answered. "Just a little over a month ago, I was stuck in a fancy institution with no hope in sight. Today I have money that I don't even have to touch because I've made enough with two of my paintings to pay rent and live right here for a few more weeks."

Suddenly she realized that she definitely wanted children, and she wanted Josh to be the father. Together, and with Filly's and Arty's help, they would figure out how to be good parents.

You are such a child. You didn't even think about protection when you were romping around on the bed last night with a guy that couldn't be worse suited to you. Victoria's voice was clear as a bell in her head. *You've never been able to think things through. You'll always pull stupid stunts if I'm not there to take care of you.*

"Go away," Emma whispered.

"What?" Josh asked.

"I was fighting with my mother," Emma confessed.

"Who won?" Arty asked.

"I guess I did, because I don't care what she thinks of me anymore," Emma admitted.

"Good girl," Filly said. "Now, Josh, take that gorgeous piece of art back to your trailer and bring out your laptop so me and Em can get busy buying what we need for the wedding. I've been putting aside money just in case Sophie would let us have her wedding here, and I can't wait to get things ordered."

Emma glanced down at her flat stomach. Was

426

there a baby in there? The idea excited her—
something that was a part of both her and Josh.
Someone that would be hers to raise, hopefully
to grow up healthy, both physically and mentally.
But how would Josh feel about that? Children
arriving all of a sudden when they'd only just
started a relationship?

She was still worrying with that idea when
supper was over that evening. Josh stayed on
her back porch with her for a while, but when it
got close to bedtime, he kissed her on the forehead and told her good night. She added a new
worry to the list—did he think they were moving
too fast or had all the wedding preparations that
afternoon spooked him?

After a long, warm shower, she got dressed in a
pair of pajama pants that Sophie had left behind
and a faded nightshirt and crawled into her twin
bed. She'd forgotten to turn the light off and had
to get up to do that. On her way to the switch, she
stopped and read the plaque again. "Face-to-face
with endless obstacles," she said out loud. "Well,
Josh, this is an obstacle that we need to face
and talk about, and the longer we put it off, the
bigger it will get." She crammed her feet down
into the pair of boots that Sophie had left for her,
took a deep breath, and marched from her back
porch to his. Evidently, Coco couldn't decide if
she wanted in or out, because the glass door was
open. As Emma entered, Coco raised her head

up from the sofa where she'd been curled up sleeping and meowed.

"Sorry, girl," Emma whispered. "I'll pet you in the morning. I'm on a mission right now." She took a deep breath and let it out slowly as she covered the distance down the short hallway.

Mercy! You've gotten brazen. She could hear Sophie giggling in her head.

I know what I want, and I'm not letting fear hold me back, she agreed with a nod of her head as she opened Josh's bedroom door.

The light was still on, and Josh was lying on his back staring at her picture. He didn't smile when he realized she was standing in the door.

"We need to talk." She sat down on the edge of the bed.

"I'm sorry about last night," Josh said.

"I'm not a bit sorry, so why are you?" she asked.

"I didn't think about protection. I was so wrapped up in the moment that"—he stumbled over the words—"you probably never want to see me again."

"Well, I wasn't thinking about protection, either. I haven't ever been on the pill or even thought about birth control," she told him, "and I wouldn't be here if I never wanted to see you again. If I got pregnant last night, then I'm happy about it. If I didn't, I hope there's a possibility that I will another time."

He pulled back the covers and smiled. "You never cease to amaze me, Em. I've fallen completely in love with you."

"I'm in love with you, too." She crawled under the covers and curled up next to him, sharing the same pillow. "I don't want to sleep alone ever again."

"Me neither." Josh started a string of kisses on her neck that ended with a steamy one on her lips. "Think maybe this place is big enough that you could move in with me?"

"I've always wanted a tiny house," Emma said, "and someone to love me just like I am."

"You've got both." Josh pulled the covers up over their heads.

Chapter Twenty-Five

Emma was busy braiding silk daisies into Sophie's hair when Filly popped into the trailer early that Saturday morning with a big pan of cinnamon rolls in her hands. "You've got to eat something or else you'll be too weak to get both feet off the ground. If you don't when you jump over the broom, then the marriage isn't valid."

"Thank you." Rebel yawned. "I'm starving. These two pesky girls had me up until after midnight. I can't believe how good Em looks with her tanned face. She was always such a pale little girl, but she looks so healthy now that I hardly recognized her."

"Fresh air, good food, and friends are magic," Emma said.

"Have you seen Teddy this morning?" Sophie asked. "Is he nervous?"

"Of course he is." Filly giggled. "He's afraid he'll stumble over his vows and embarrass you. I took the guys a pan of rolls and told him that if he ate two of them, he would sail through his vows."

"Then I'd better eat three," Sophie said,

"because I've been terrified of the same thing."

Emma patted her friend on the back. "Don't practice or write down anything. Just say what's in your heart. That's more important than all the rehearsed words in the whole world."

Sophie gave Emma a quick hug. "I'm so glad you're here to share this day with me."

Emma couldn't imagine being anywhere else that day, and someday she hoped that Sophie would be her matron of honor when she and Josh had a ceremony. "Not as glad as I am," she said. "Think about it. I could be a permanent resident of a mental institution."

Rebel shivered.

"Cold?" Emma asked. "I can turn up the thermostat if you are, but I didn't want Sophie's makeup to melt."

"No, honey, I was thinking about you being in a place like that for the rest of your life," Rebel said.

"Well, thank goodness, we don't have to worry about that these days. She and Josh are living together, and Josh is happier than I ever hoped to see him," Filly said. "Y'all enjoy those cinnamon rolls. I've got some last-minute touches to do on the cake. I'll see you at the arch at ten o'clock sharp. I'll be the one in the pink-and-orange hippie skirt, and I'll be handing you girls your bouquets. Rebel, is your corsage to your liking?"

"Filly, you've done an amazing job of everything," Rebel said. "Please, let me reimburse you for part or all of it."

"Posh!" Filly waved the idea away with the flick of a hand. "This is my pleasure. I won't be around when the granddaughters get old enough to get married, so you can handle that."

"Bull crap!" Emma said. "You'll still be making jewelry and feeding hummingbirds when you are a hundred and ten. You can't leave this earth until we say so, and that won't be for a long time."

Filly giggled. "It's good to be loved. See y'all in a little while."

Rebel cut out a roll and put it on a plate. "Today is the bride's day, so you get the first one. Milk or coffee?"

"Coffee," Sophie said.

"Milk for me, but help yourself first," Emma said.

"My heart is absolutely bursting with pride today to see you girls so happy." Rebel sighed. "That day when Sophie and I pulled away from your house, and both you girls were sobbing, I thought I'd never see a day like this. I only wish Victoria could see you this happy, Em."

"I don't think she cares if I'm happy. She needs to find peace in herself before she can care about others," Emma said.

"Amen, darlin' girl, amen!" Rebel nodded.

• • •

Josh and Teddy stepped out of the trailer at exactly ten o'clock and made their way to the arch. Arty had set up chairs so that Rebel and Jonathan, Teddy's father, who was the image of Teddy, only thirty years older with a little gray in his hair and maybe thirty pounds more on his frame, could have a place to sit during the ceremony. He and Filly took their places in the other two chairs. Josh hit a button on a remote control, and Shania Twain's voice filled the park with "From This Moment On."

Josh's pulse raced when Emma stepped out onto the porch and walked slowly down the stairs. She looked so beautiful in her flowing light-green skirt and matching tank top. She wore a necklace that Filly had designed with a hummingbird on a special stone that Josh had found that very week when he and Emma had been out walking. Her dark hair had been braided into a crown with yellow daisies that seemed to float in between the folds of hair.

Sophie came out next in her pretty off-white sundress that swept the ground. Teddy stepped to the bottom of the stairs and took Sophie's hand in his. Together, they walked up to the arch. Sophie handed her bouquet to Emma and took Teddy's hands in hers. She said her vows loudly and clearly. Rebel and Filly both sniffled when Teddy put the wedding band on her hand. Then he said his vows, and danged if Josh didn't have trouble keeping the tears at bay.

Josh pulled the remote from his pocket and hit another button. Naomi and Wynonna Judd sang "Mama He's Crazy" as the couple stepped through the arch, and together they jumped over the broom Emma had decorated with lace, ribbons, and flowers in light green and bright yellow.

Josh took a couple of steps forward and looped Emma's arm in his. "You are beautiful today."

"Thank you, but what I am mostly today is jealous," she whispered as they walked through the arch to be the first ones to congratulate the newly wedded couple.

"Well, the decorations are up, and I've got a pretty good idea of what I'd say to you," Josh whispered.

"This is Sophie's day," Emma said as she wrapped her arms around her best friend.

"What are you talking about?" Sophie asked.

"I was thinking that, since everything is already decorated . . ." Josh shrugged.

"I can't steal her thunder," Emma said.

"Honey, I can't think of anything I'd love more than making this a double, but only if you're ready," Sophie said. "Here, you take my bouquet and give me yours."

"But . . ."

"Hey, Filly, will you please go in my trailer and bring me the broom?" Sophie yelled.

"What for?" Filly asked.

"This ain't the time to ask questions, woman." Arty got up and brought out the broom.

Sophie picked up her broom and laid it to the side, then laid the undecorated one in its place. "Josh and Em have something they'd like to say to each other."

"Holy smoke!" Filly gasped.

Josh and Emma followed Sophie and Teddy back through the arch, then turned to face each other. Josh leaned forward and kissed Emma on the forehead. "Like the song says, from this moment, life has begun for us, Em. Fate brought you to me at a time when I thought I'd be lonely the rest of my life. I love you, and I give my hand to you right along with my whole heart. I never want to be apart from you."

Tears flowed down Emma's cheeks when she said, "My heart belongs to you, and I love you because you have helped me to find myself and to stand strong on my own. I look forward to our journey through this world together, and I never want to be apart from you, either."

She kept one of his hands in hers, and together they jumped over the plain old kitchen broom to the applause of everyone else in the park.

"And now you grooms may kiss the brides. Be sure you've got the one that belongs to you," Teddy's father called out.

Josh tipped up Emma's chin with his knuckles

and started to give her a sweet kiss when he noticed that Teddy had bent Sophie back in a true Hollywood kiss. That was way out of his comfort zone, but he wanted Emma to be happy, so he did the same. When the kiss ended, he groaned. "I didn't even have a ring."

"We can remedy that later," Emma said. "Today has been everything I ever wanted."

Rebel was the first one to reach them. She hugged first Sophie and Teddy, then Emma and Josh. "This is a dream come true for me. I'm so glad you made this a double wedding."

"Me too," Josh said. "I'm not sure I could have endured the stress poor old Teddy was under this morning."

Filly wiped tears from her eyes and then handed a hankie to Emma. "We'll keep this for the day your daughter gets married. Our tears are blended on it. It will bring her good luck. Let's cut the cake and have a party."

Josh slipped an arm around Emma. "They can have the cake. I have you."

"Oh, no," Sophie declared. "We'll cut one side. Y'all can do the other one."

"But there's only two champagne glasses," Emma whispered.

"I always liked beer out of a red plastic cup better anyway," Josh said. "Let's do this our way."

"Forever and always, let's do everything our way." Emma smiled up at him.

Epilogue

Five years later

Emma awoke that Thanksgiving morning to bright sunlight pouring into the bedroom, the aroma of bacon and coffee floating through the small trailer, and the sound of children giggling. Josh was such a good father, and despite her upbringing, Emma wasn't doing too bad at being a mother. Josh often accused her of being worse than a mother bear with the kids, but she couldn't help being a little overprotective.

"Good mornin', darlin'." Josh peeked into the room with Lia on his hip and Gracie hanging on to his leg. Four-year-old Jody made a flying leap right onto the bed with her. She hugged him tightly and then reached out her arms for the baby. Josh handed the blonde-haired little girl to her, and then helped three-year-old Gracie up on the bed. By the time he joined the family, there wasn't enough room to wiggle.

"I love mornings like this." He leaned across Lia and kissed Emma.

"Yuck," Jody said.

"You just keep thinking that until you're about thirty." Josh grinned.

"Or forty," Emma said and then pulled Josh over to her for another kiss. "I give thanks every day for what we have."

"One more kid and we're going to have to build another room onto the place," Josh whispered.

"Well, then, darlin', we'd better start building, because I took a test last night and number four is on the way," Emma told him.

"I'm the luckiest man in the world. Can I be the one to tell your father?" Josh shoved the kids to the foot of the bed and gathered Emma into his arms for a steamy kiss.

"Of course, but not until Sophie gets here. I want her to be the second to know," Emma answered. "If we can throw this passel of young foxes off our bed, I'd like to follow my nose to the kitchen."

"Bacon and pancakes are on the stove. I've already fed all the kids, even Lia." Josh kissed her one more time. "I love you, Mrs. Corlen."

"I love you, Josh." She caught the right moment and wiggled her way out of the maze of kids to the edge of the bed. "Let's just hope I'm not as sick with this one as I was with Lia."

"This is a boy," Josh said, "to even things out. Remember, you weren't sick a single day with Jody."

Emma crossed her fingers and held them up for him to see. "We can always hope."

• • •

Sophie was more excited about going home for Thanksgiving than the two kids in the back seat of the SUV. Two-year-old Anna Rebel didn't understand as much about the trip as four-year-old Johnny did, but she picked up on his excitement. When they turned off the road onto Hummingbird Lane, Johnny said, "Are we almost to the hum bird place? Is Jody still there?"

"Of course he is, and your auntie Em says he's waiting on the porch for you. He's got a brand-new puppy that he wants you to see," Sophie answered.

"Hurry, Daddy," Johnny said. "Go faster."

"Puppy. Go fast," Anna Rebel squealed.

"I can't wait to see Em. Seems like forever, and yet it's only been a month," Sophie said. "And your dad and my mama are already here. It's going to be a wonderful holiday. I'm so glad the sun is shining so the kids can play outside."

"Josh says Filly has been cooking for a week," Teddy said. "We kind of lucked out since the snowbirds aren't coming in for a few more days. We can stay in your old trailer. I understand Wyatt and Betsy are sharing one of the others. My dad is in the second one, and Rebel is staying with Filly. We've pretty well got a full house."

"Look, I see the trailers, and there's Em standing on the picnic bench waving at us," Sophie said.

"You and Em. You'd think you were blood sisters," Teddy chuckled.

"Honey, we're more than that. We are sisters of the heart," Sophie said and hopped out of the SUV the minute he parked.

She and Emma met in the middle of the yard and hugged each other just like they had when they were girls. "Guess what? I've got wonderful news. Number three is on the way. I'm about to catch up with you. I couldn't wait to tell you in person."

"Well, if you're going to catch up with me, you'd best have twins. I'm due in June with number four," Emma laughed.

"That's fantastic. For the first time, we get to have babies in the same month," Sophie said. "But twins or not, this is the last one for our family. How about yours?"

"We agreed in the beginning that four was our magic number." Emma looped her arm in Sophie's and led her toward Filly's house.

"Have you heard from Victoria?" Sophie asked.

"She called about a month ago. She said she might fit a short visit in next year. She really doesn't like this place or what I've done with my life," Emma answered.

"You are fast becoming the famous artist you always wanted to be," Sophie assured her.

"I'm happy, and that's what matters." Emma smiled.

Arty set Lia on the ground, and she toddled over to Filly and put up her arms to be held. Josh came around the end of the trailer with Gracie right behind him. Jody bailed off the porch, grabbed Johnny by the hand as soon as Teddy freed him from the car seat, and led him off to the porch, where two puppies tumbled around playfully. "Mine," Jody said seriously, pointing at one, then turned his finger toward the other one and said seriously, "Yours."

Teddy carried Anna Rebel across the yard and handed her off to her grandmother. "Here you go, Rebel. She's all yours for the next while." He turned to focus on Sophie. "I guess we just got a dog, Sophie."

"Looks that way," Sophie laughed. "Next Thanksgiving, we'll have a baby to add to this circus."

"That's fantastic news." Jonathan stepped off the porch of one of the extra trailers. "I always wanted a big family, but all I got was Teddy. I'm glad that I get lots of grandbabies."

"So am I." Rebel snuggled her face down into her granddaughter's wispy blonde hair. "We've all sure got a lot to be thankful for this year."

"Yes, we do," Filly said. "Me and Arty are about to bring out the food. Arty's turkey is perfect this year, and my pumpkin pies turned out great. I swear, it's always better when you kids all come home for Thanksgiving."

Sophie slipped an arm around Emma. "Yes, it is."

"Know what I'm most thankful for every day of every year?" Emma asked. "That you rescued me and brought me down here to this place. Heaven can't be any better than this."

"Amen," Josh agreed.

Dear Reader,

Friends come into our lives at different seasons for different reasons. That was the way with Emma and Sophie. They'd come into each other's lives as children and then were torn apart for several years, but when they needed their old friendship again, it returned at just the right time. While I was writing this story, I felt like Emma and Sophie were in the room with me, telling me all their heartaches and joys. I've laughed with them, cried with them, and gotten angry with them. When I finally wrote the last words, they were very real people to me, and I was glad to have had the privilege of telling their story.

As I've said before, it takes a village to produce a book. The writer starts with an idea, but it needs good editors to help the author give it polish and finesse. With that in mind, I have several people to thank for taking this from a rough idea to a finished product. First of all, my thanks to my agent, Erin Niumata, and my agency, Folio Literary Management, for all they do; to my editors at Amazon/Montlake, Alison Dasho and Anh Schluep, for continuing to believe in me; and to my team for everything from copyediting to cover designs; to my amazing developmental editor, Krista Stroever, who took a lump of coal and helped me turn it into a diamond; and to my readers for their support and love.

Special thanks for this book go to my son, Charles Lemar Brown, for the picture of the hummingbird on the cover, and to Vienna Pharaon for giving me permission to use her quote. As always, my love to Mr. B for everything he does to help me, from first edits to washing the dinner dishes so I can write one more chapter.

Until next time,
Carolyn Brown

About the Author

Carolyn Brown is a *New York Times*, *USA Today*, *Publishers Weekly*, and *Wall Street Journal* bestselling author and a RITA finalist with more than one hundred published books to her name. They include women's fiction and historical, contemporary, cowboy, and country music romances. She and her husband live in the small town of Davis, Oklahoma, where everyone knows everyone else, including what they are doing and when—and they read the local newspaper on Wednesdays to see who got caught. They have three grown children and enough grandchildren and great-grandchildren to keep them young. For more information, visit www.carolynbrownbooks.com.

Books are produced in the United States using U.S.-based materials	Books are printed using a revolutionary new process called THINKtech™ that lowers energy usage by 70% and increases overall quality	Books are durable and flexible because of Smyth-sewing	Paper is sourced using environmentally responsible foresting methods and the paper is acid-free

Center Point Large Print
600 Brooks Road / PO Box 1
Thorndike, ME 04986-0001 USA

(207) 568-3717

US & Canada:
1 800 929-9108
www.centerpointlargeprint.com